SEARCHING

for

MOORE

JULIE A. RICHMAN

C

CONTENTS

ℓ

f

h

BOOKS BY JULIE

i

To everyone who has been with me on the journey…

K

BOOK ONE

SCHOONER

CHAPTER 1

Schooner Moore did not like turning forty-three—not at all. It didn't sound as old as say fifty, but it wasn't as cool and sexy sounding as thirty-five or even thirty-seven had been. Forty-three—was that still even hot, he wondered. If he judged by the way women continued to come on to him, clamored to get his attention, overtly tried to pick him up—then yes, it was still hot. It just sounded so damn old and that was what was really pissing him off.

Leaning over the railing of a surprisingly empty deck at Newport Beach hot spot, The Dock, Schooner stood alone breathing in the humid sea air and listening to the boats clanking in the marina. Behind him, echoes of laughter pealed from inside the packed restaurant—a restaurant that his wife, CJ, had rented out in its entirety on a Saturday night for this little birthday soirée. He shuddered to think of what this had just cost him.

CJ meant well, but Schooner knew this shindig really had very little to do with him and everything to do with her coveted social standing aspirations. And a party for turning forty-three? Seriously, who does that? Forty, he could understand. Forty-five, he could understand. But forty-three? This party wasn't about him. And he knew it.

He heard the creaking of worn planks rather than footsteps and felt the familiar slap on his shoulder.

"Hiding, eh?" Beau Gordon leaned on the railing beside him. Beau was a dead ringer for Pee Wee Herman, and with a few drinks in him and the right audience, was significantly funnier.

Schooner laughed, "I can't get far enough away."

"Ahhh, it's not that bad." Beau breathed the dank harbor air in deeply.

"No, I guess it isn't," Schooner acquiesced, with an All-American boy smile, a smile that even at forty-three could stop women—from ages eight to eighty—dead in their tracks.

"There are some really hot babes in there."

Schooner let out a wry chuckle, "Watch out or you'll be picking up an extra mortgage by morning. Don't let those sweet, Botoxed looks fool you. That is a shark tank in there, my man, and you are shark chum," he ended, dramatically.

Beau leaned back on the railing and surveyed the crowd on the other side of the glass wall. "Yeah, I had a few store-bought racks, of the soon-to-be-divorced rubbed on me tonight. Not that I'm complaining. But those women were definitely not happy about having to be changing zip codes."

"Still have your wallet?" Schooner chided.

Beau patted his pockets, pulling something out and sauntered over into the shadows. Squinting over into the darkened corner of the deck to see where his old college roommate was going, Schooner smelled it before even hearing Beau's first loud exhale.

"You did *not* just light up a dube, bro." Schooner quickly scanned the deck, after a paranoid jolt to both his stomach and sphincter.

Beau sat down on a chair and put his feet up on the railing. Slowly inhaling a long drag of the joint, he held it before letting out a thin stream of white smoke that curled into the night air in paisley patterns. Schooner took the seat next to Beau, lifting his boat shoe clad feet to the rail and stretching his long, athletic legs. Beau silently handed his buddy the joint, and Schooner took it from him in a ritual that seemed nearly as old as they were. Gingerly dragging on the glowing joint, Schooner tried to remember the last time he had gotten high. A decade before, maybe—but he really wasn't quite sure.

Almost immediately, Schooner felt the relaxation spread through his body, feeling the tension roll away from his too tight neck and shoulders. *And there it goes. It's moving out with the tide,* he silently thought.

"Man, I need to hang out with you more often." Schooner coughed slightly.

Beau just smiled. They were in different worlds. Beau had never married, traveled extensively for work, and spent most of his free time vetting the world's great scuba spots, while unsuccessfully trying to pick up women. Schooner, on the other hand, had married CJ almost immediately upon graduation, after dating her for almost all four years of college. His photogenic, California-boy good looks, as well as his sharp business acumen, entrepreneurial spirit, and a hefty bankroll from a childhood modeling career had made Schooner a very rich man by the time he was twenty-eight. Everyone who was anyone, from Malibu to the OC, worked out in one of Schooner's clubs. State-of-the-Art equipment coupled with a concierge based staff and entertainment amenities catered to the elite under one roof.

Schooner and CJ. Like Ken and Barbie come to life. They were the epitome of every out-of-stater's fantasy of what the quintessential California boy and California girl looked like. Schooner and CJ. They were beautiful and they looked like they belonged together. Everyone said so, and they knew it the first time they had laid eyes on one another. They were like two sides of the same golden coin.

Beau handed Schooner back the joint and said, "Do you remember the first time we got high together?"

Schooner thought for a second and a slow smile spread across his handsome face, his clear sky blue eyes crinkling at the corners. He felt a warm glow in his chest, but oddly also felt the sting of tears behind his eyes. "Yeah, it was at that freshman retreat in the mountains."

"What was that chick's name, that friend of yours that we got high with?" Beau turned to Schooner, a questioning look on his face, trying hard to grab hold of a memory just out of his reach.

"Mia Silver." Her name tumbled out like a waterfall. Just verbalizing it, after all this time, put a smile in Schooner's heart.

"That was Mia Silver?" Beau broke Schooner's pleasant moment.

"Yeah, why?"

"The chick with the glasses? Seriously, Dude? That was Mia Silver?"

"Yeah, that was Mia." Schooner sat up straight in his chair, wondering what his buddy was about to tell him.

"I'll be damned," Beau shook his head. "I just got into one hell of a fight with her on Scott Morgan's Facebook page. She always was a freaking liberal bitch." He shook his head again, "She grew up nice though. She is smokin' hot now. I would not have recognized her, not in a million years."

I would have, something deep inside of Schooner screamed. Schooner felt like his heart was being mashed up in someone's hands—like dough being kneaded. The humid air was no longer making its way deep into his lungs. WTF? He shook his head. Not after all these years, to have such a visceral reaction. Must be the effects of getting stoned or maybe this turning forty-three bullshit.

He was trying to process what Beau had said… he'd had contact with Mia. *He'd had contact with Mia. Holy shit.* Schooner suddenly felt like he was ready to jump out of his own skin. He wanted to be anywhere but there. He wanted to be away from Beau. Away from the party. Away from all their supposed friends—a room filled with *Real Housewives of Orange County* clones. He knew he needed to take a deep breath and calm himself, because he wasn't going to be going anywhere anytime soon.

Chef Jonathan walked out onto the deck where Schooner and Beau sat. Beau silently went to hand him the joint, but Jonathan waved him off.

Looking out over the night harbor, he announced "Hey, it's cake time. You'd better go back in there, Birthday Boy".

"Lucky me," Schooner muttered.

He took a deep breath and silently said to himself, "Showtime," as he headed in to face the gaggle of his wife's friends, acquaintances and other assorted hangers on.

CHAPTER 2

Schooner politely made small talk, a plate of expensive, fondant-wrapped cake in hand. He could not remember if the woman he was talking to was on *The Real Housewives of Orange County* or wanted to be on it, or if she was from Beverly Hills. Maybe she was one of those Housewives. He couldn't remember her story and didn't care enough to ask. They all seemed to run together.

As he surveyed the crowd, he made an observation. All of these women wanted to look exactly like CJ and had spent a lot of money to try and achieve her look. He wondered why they didn't realize that what their doctors were doing to them stopped way short of the natural beauty his wife possessed. What was being done to them didn't look natural, not the long blonde hair, not the full lips, nor the perfect profiles. They all wanted to look like CJ, but they didn't. No one wanted to look different. No one wanted to be different. Typical Orange County, he thought.

The *Real Housewife* was touching him. Gently stroking his arm and standing too close as she spoke. Someone tried to push past in the crowd behind her and she had to step closer to Schooner. Her hand dropped and she let her fingers graze his crotch, her long manicured nails searching out his cock, which thankfully was uncharacteristically non-responsive. Schooner choked on the piece of cake he had just put in his mouth and politely excused himself, in search of a much needed single malt scotch. If I'm paying for it, he mused, I might as well drink what I like. And he needed a drink. Badly.

As he approached the bar, he spied Holly standing alone, surveying the crowd as if they were one big sociology experiment. Coming up behind her, he casually and gently slung an arm over his daughter's shoulder and kissed her temple as he pulled her close. Having her home from school for this abbreviated trip made enduring being the guest of honor slightly more palatable.

"How's my gorgeous girl?" Schooner asked his flaxen-haired beauty.

"Better now that I've got the most handsome man in the room all to myself."

He smiled at their banter. "Can we leave now?"

She laughed, "And endure the wrath of Mom? I think not."

Holly was so unlike her mother. She had CJ's cheerleader good looks, but they sat differently on Holly. A sophomore at Brown University in Providence, Rhode Island, Holly was not going to be a trophy, she was going to collect them. He missed her terribly and wished she'd stayed closer to home, hoping she'd choose a school in Southern California. But Holly wanted to go east and she wanted to go Ivy. A biological sciences major, his daughter was the antithesis of Orange County, and he was secretly thrilled that she'd escaped. He was also elated that she had flown in for the weekend for his party. Schooner missed his son Zac too, but Zac's prep school semester abroad landed him in Zaragoza, Spain—too far to journey home for a "forty-third" birthday party.

Holly's phone buzzed and she looked at the screen, laughed and started typing rapidly with both thumbs.

Schooner looked at her quizzically and she shrugged and offered "Facebook" as her explanation.

As if that explains it, he thought, peering look over her shoulder at what she was typing.

"Dad!"

"Okay, okay." Schooner held up his hands in surrender, smiled and continued on his journey for that single malt scotch.

Leaning up against the bar, he let the burn slide down his throat. *Damn, that's better than sex*, he thought.

As he let the amber liquid warm his insides and calm his rapidly fraying nerves, Schooner thought to himself, *I really need to join Facebook.*

CHAPTER 3

Schooner walked along The Quad, map in hand, trying to find Brewster Hall. The next part of orientation had the freshmen reuniting with their parents and he knew that is where his would be waiting for him.

The tree-lined Quad, a large rectangular park at the center of campus, was lined along its length with old Spanish Mission style buildings that were built in the early 1920's and capped with red barrel tile roofs. At the far end of The Quad, like a patriarch at the head of the table, was the University Chapel, with its bell tower standing out in relief against a mountain range partially obscured by Inland Empire smog.

He saw her standing on the sidewalk talking to her parents, white linen dress gently billowing in the breeze. He had noticed her in the last session. How could he not? She looked like an angel— long silky blonde hair flowing down her back, wide cornflower blue eyes and a pouty pink-glossed mouth. Tall, slim, and athletic, Schooner was betting she had been the prom queen at her high school. She was perfect. *We look like we belong together,* Schooner thought. She was the female version of him.

She smiled at him as he walked by.

Oh yeah, she had noticed him and from the look in her eyes, she liked what she saw. Schooner flashed his All-American boy smile, a smile that began gracing catalogue covers when he was only 4 years old. Her eyes widened and he knew she'd be finding a way to sit near him in the rest of the orientation sessions. He smiled to himself… oh yeah, college was going to be great.

He saw his parents talking with another couple outside a door to what he assumed was Brewster Hall. His mom waved him over. "Schooner. Over here."

Schooner had inherited the best from both of his parents. Had they had a checklist of physical attributes, he was the embodiment of all the checks in all the right places. From his mother, her fine bone structure and square jaw, high cheekbones, straight nose and full lips. From his dad, clear blue eyes and thick, fair hair with just a slight wave, making the ends flip out. Both parents were tall, and he was blessed with his mother's easy grace and his dad's wide shoulders and narrow hips.

Schooner approached his parents and the other couple.

His dad took over the introductions, "Schooner, meet Mr. and Mrs. Silver. Their daughter Mia is also a freshman."

Schooner shook Mr. Silver's hand. Mr. Silver had that east coast intellectual look about him, wavy gray, slightly long hair and gray-blue eyes. He turned to Mrs. Silver and offered his hand. Her forthright manner was immediately evident, as her warm brown eyes instantly captured him. He couldn't control his smile, a real smile.

"You are adorable," she said, exposing her strong New York accent.

Schooner felt himself blush and he never blushed. He was used to women—of all ages—fawning over him. But Mrs. Silver—there was something in her gaze that cut through all that external California bullshit. He felt that she was really seeing him, and she still thought he was adorable. In that moment, Schooner felt more special than he'd ever felt. Inexplicably, he wanted her approval and was so happy to have it.

"There's Mia," Mr. Silver's voice cut into Schooner's thoughts, jolting him, and he dropped Mrs. Silver's hand.

Schooner turned. Coming down the path to Brewster Hall was Mia Silver. Cocking his head to the side and taking her all in, he couldn't suppress the small smile on his face. Mia didn't look like any of the girls he knew.

Mia Silver bounded up the walk, quirky lopsided smile taking over her cute face, a mane of long dark curls bouncing behind her. She was wearing funky Lisa Loeb glasses, and as she got closer, he could see that the irises of her big eyes were an ombré green that grew lighter as they moved in toward her pupil. The pupil itself was surrounded by rich caramel colored flames. Not only was there sharp intelligence in her beautiful eyes, but Schooner thought they looked like a devilish invitation, like they were beckoning to him, "Let's be bad together. Let's have some fun." Schooner felt his chest tighten.

Mia could not have been more than 5'2", clad in faded Levis, a tee-shirt and clogs. He wondered if she realized she was probably the only girl in the entire freshman class not wearing a dress. He wondered if she even cared. What was she doing on this campus? She did not fit in.

"Hey." She smiled at him, confidently, her freckled nose scrunching up.

"Hey," he returned, captured by her energy. At 5 foot nothing, he was sure she made an entrance everywhere she went. This girl had presence. And she was different. She was clearly not a California girl and he wasn't quite sure what to make of her.

"Honey, meet Mr. and Mrs. Moore and Schooner," Mrs. Silver offered.

Mia beamed at the Moores, offering a firm handshake and immediately engaging Mr. and Mrs. Moore in conversation, while Schooner became acquainted with the Silvers.

As they entered Brewster Hall, he could see Mrs. Silver giving Mia a little nudge and instinctively he knew it was about him. Mothers loved him. Mia rolled her eyes at her mom. He loved that.

Over the next two days, the Moores and the Silvers spent the majority of their time together, while Schooner and Mia attended the different freshman sessions. As expected, the prom queen found a way to be seated near Schooner, separated by one of her friends who struck up a conversation with him, then quickly included the prom queen.

While Schooner started gravitating toward the prom queen, her equally pageant-girl-like friends and other jock guys from his dorm, Mia's growing entourage seemed to be a group from her dorm of Out-of-Staters, über-intellectual potheads and a few gays and lesbians. They were clearly migrating toward their comfort zones, which were as far apart as opposing football teams' goal lines.

On the last night of orientation, the Moores and the Silvers dined together off-campus. When they parted at the end of the evening, Mr. Moore pulled Schooner aside to where he and Mr. Silver were standing. "Keep an eye out for her, son," motioning toward Mia. "She's only sixteen. Make sure you're there for her."

Only sixteen? This little ball of fire who clearly already had her own following on campus was only sixteen. Wow—she had the confidence of a twenty-five-year-old, he thought. Only sixteen?

"I will, sir," promised Schooner, trying not to act stunned at the revelation.

He'd be turning nineteen in just a few months and little Mia was, well, in fact, little Mia. She certainly didn't seem to need any looking after. In fact, he felt pretty certain Mia Silver could take very good care of herself.

CHAPTER 4

Getting settled in the first few weeks of college turned out to be more of a juggling act than Schooner had anticipated. Classes. Studying. Tennis practice (he was determined to make first string his freshman year). Learning to live with a roommate (Beau Gordon was a trip, he could not sleep without the radio on all night and hated the way headphones felt). And CJ. Schooner had already started dating the prom queen, who had been, yes, in fact, the prom queen at her high school.

CJ MacAllister was well schooled in getting precisely what she wanted, and from that very first day of freshman orientation, Schooner Moore was everything she wanted. Incredibly handsome, smart, athletic, from a well-to-do California family. Schooner Moore was the bomb. And she was going to get him. And never let go. Their children would be magnificent. And CJ MacAllister was going to be the mother of Schooner Moore's children.

Showing up at the tennis courts to watch Schooner practice, she always brought a friend or two ("Bitches," Schooner thought, laughing to himself, "travel in packs."). He wasn't past putting on a show for the girls, taking his shirt off at the end of practice and letting them watch the sweat run down his impressive golden pecs toward his six-pack abs. Like clockwork, her friends would suddenly disappear when it was time for Schooner to get off the courts, leaving CJ waiting alone for him.

After a few days of walking CJ back to her dorm, she invited Schooner up to her room. Acting coy and coquettish (acting, being the operative word… and he was aware of that, but let her act), they had a hot make out session.

Schooner backed CJ up to her bed with its Victorian Rose pattern spread and gently pushed her down onto it. Propped up on her elbows, looking up at him innocently through long lashes, Schooner quickly recognized that CJ knew just how to get to him. This was clearly not her first rodeo, although she wanted him to believe that it was. He also knew, two could play this game and it would be so much fun to make sure he controlled it. Controlled a girl who always got what she wanted—no problem, he thought. Schooner was the master.

Schooner slid on top of her, kissing her deeply, her tongue meeting his perfectly in its dance. He slid his hands up the back of her thighs and wrapped them around his waist. The bulge in his tennis shorts was straining against his zipper and all he wanted to do was take it out and give it to her, hard. He pressed his hard package against her moist underwear and she moaned.

"Feels good?" he asked.

"Mmm-hmm," was all she could muster, as he relentlessly ground himself and rammed against her underwear.

He ran his thumb and forefinger over the front of her pink cotton blouse until he could feel her nipple harden to his touch. He kept running his thumb over it until her nipple felt like a stone, and then he dipped his head and sucked it through her shirt, biting it and pulling it with his front teeth.

Her sounds were telling him that she was coming undone fast. Grabbing her ass and pulling her into him, Schooner pressed shorts tighter against her. CJ strained against him, desperately trying to rub herself against the hardness in his shorts, trying to get herself off on the friction.

And without removing a single piece of her clothes or his, Schooner Moore gave CJ MacAllister one mind blowing orgasm. Dropping her back on the bed looking dazed, and still quaking, he adjusted the raging hard on in his now too tight, uncomfortable shorts.

"Thanks for coming to see me practice today." He leaned forward, gave her a rough kiss on her already bruised lips, grabbed his tennis racquets and left CJ's dorm room, stopping at the door long enough to turn to her, grace her with a full-blown killer smile and revel in how utterly stupefied she looked.

Carrying his racquets in front of him, to hide the sizable erection he was sporting, Schooner left the all-girls dorm with a smug smile on his face.

Tables turned, Prom Queen!

She'd be giving it all to him in no time flat, without having to wait for her to play the virgin game, deciding if she should "let him be the one." He'd met enough cock-teasing prom queens in his life. This was college now, and if CJ MacAllister wanted him, then she was going to play by his rules.

Four days later they became lovers.

CHAPTER 5

The following Saturday morning, The Quad was lined with buses for the entire freshman class to take them up into the mountains for Freshman Retreat. Freshman Retreat was mandatory. Schooner, Beau and assorted tennis, basketball and football players from their dorm headed to the buses together. He knew CJ would be looking for him and secretly hoped that she wouldn't find him (6'2" blonde god was hard to miss). He wanted to establish relationships with the other guys in his dorm, without being part of a couple and without the ribbing—which was already beginning.

The ride up to the retreat center in the San Bernardino National Forest seemed to take forever as the convoy of buses slowly meandered up the highway's steep incline and hairpin turns. One of the dorm RA's announced on the bus loudspeaker that a BBQ lunch was being served in the main lodge, class elections would take place immediately following lunch and the rest of the afternoon was free for hiking, swimming or the leisure activity of their choice.

Beau grabbed Schooner's arm as they got off the bus and motioned to a trailhead. "I brought a dube," he whispered.

"You are the man." Schooner acknowledged, heading down the trail.

Heading down the steep and narrow path for about a quarter of a mile, they began to look for some boulders to park on when Schooner saw Mia's telltale long dark curls in front of them. He called out to her and she turned and met him with a big grin.

She walked up to the guys and Schooner said, "How have you been doing?"

She just shrugged her shoulders, "I am so not into the group thing. I hate all this kumbayah shit."

Schooner laughed out loud, "You into smoking some shit?"

Mia's eyes lit up and that little devil, partner-in-crime look he had seen on the day they first met, reemerged.

The three found a path off the main trail and hiked a ways to an area where they wouldn't be easily found. It was hard for Mia to keep up with the two long-legged guys. Lounging on some large rocks, Beau pulled out the joint and lit it up. Schooner could tell that Beau was not comfortable with Mia. He doubted that his roommate had ever met anyone quite like her and he didn't know how to take her.

Schooner, on the other hand, thought she was a blast. He'd never had many girls who were just friends, not flirting their asses off to try and get his attention, and Mia was so comfortable to just hang out with—kind of like hanging out with the boys, but there was something so cute about her and damn, she had great tits. He had to remind himself that she was only sixteen.

Beau held up the joint to her, "I hope you're not a virgin."

Schooner saw the blush flare on her face and knew that while his little sixteen-year-old friend might not be a virgin to getting high, sexually she was really innocent. Her urbane New York exterior masked just how innocent she really was. Schooner felt this strong need bursting to protect her. Protect her like a little sister, he told himself.

They smoked the rest of the joint while Beau pointedly ignored Mia, just talking directly to Schooner, as if she were not even present. It was uncomfortable and Schooner wondered what the hell was Beau's problem. He thought maybe Beau was just used to pining over the California Barbies who shot him down, but whatever it was, Mia took off immediately upon finishing the joint.

"See you guys up at the lodge. Thanks for the smoke." And she quickly retreated up the trail.

Schooner wondered where her entourage was and why she seemed to be in loner mode today. But being stoned, that thought quickly evaporated and was replaced by something else, as was the fleeting thought that maybe he should not let her be wandering in the woods alone.

By the time Schooner and Beau made it up to the lodge, freshman class elections were well underway. They leaned against the wall near the door and Schooner surveyed the crowd. In the second row, paying rapt attention, were CJ and her soon-to-be group of sorority sisters. Continuing to scan the room, he finally saw Mia sitting on a chair in the back.

The look on her face was one of pure fright. Crouched down and clutching the back of her chair was Tim Vandergrift, freshman class President-elect and the class equivalent of douche bag Greg Marmalard from the movie *Animal House* (He looked like him, too!). From his bent over position, he appeared to be sniffing Mia.

Schooner and Mia made eye contact and he could see she was paranoid as all hell that Mr. Brownie Points was going to turn her in to some school authority for reeking of pot and that she was going to get sent home for getting high at the Freshman Retreat (which, of course, was held at a Christian retreat center).

Schooner could see Mia's eyes pleading with him for help as she mouthed the word, "Fuck!"

All he could hear was his father's words in his head to look out for her.

CJ noticed Schooner leaning against the wall and followed his line of sight back to Mia. She also noticed Mia locked in on her boyfriend.

The loud crash, as a pitcher of ice water smashed onto the Mexican tile floor, turned all heads to see the source of the shattering sound.

Schooner had "inadvertently" knocked a pitcher off the table and the crash brought Tim out of his crouched position to his full standing height of 6'4" and his attention to the left wall of the room.

Mia used the diversion to pop out of her chair and head out of the lodge's main room through a door on the right.

Schooner silently gave himself a pat on the back.

Mia was standing out at the driveway in front of the lodge waiting for one of the earlier buses back, when CJ noticed her there. CJ had been in search of Schooner, but thought, *let him have his boys' time. I've got something more important to take care of.* Grabbing her roommate and some girls from her dorm, she convinced them it was time to leave.

Sitting directly behind Mia on the bus, she went into full animation mode as she reveled her followers with tales of her prom court and of what a wonderful kisser her new boyfriend, Schooner, was (still playing the virgin act, she was not going to let any of her virginal friends/soon-to-be sorority sisters know that Schooner liked to pull her hair when she blew him or that he liked it rough… and that she was learning to like it that way, too). She even went so far as to make the prediction that he was *the one.* Her followers giggled with delight.

Mia sunk deeper into her seat, wishing she'd had her Walkman and some headphones with her, so she didn't have to listen to a show she somehow instinctively knew was being put on for her benefit. She couldn't understand why though. CJ was gorgeous and had clearly already captured Schooner's attention, and from the sounds of it, his heart. So why the big show? Why did she have to make sure Mia knew he was hers?

Silently wiping a tear that began to roll down her right cheek, Mia buried her face against the cold metal inside wall of the bus so that no one could see the wet trail beginning to stream down her face.

Mia had never felt so alone or so very far away from home.

CHAPTER 6

Schooner had been sitting with his mother in a coffee shop, eating a grilled cheese sandwich, when the man approached their booth.

Four-year-old Schooner was not very interested in what they were talking about, because the grilled cheese had bacon that tasted really good and the French fries had bumps (his mother had called them crinkle fries). His mother was also letting him drink Coke that day instead of milk with his lunch, which never happened at home. So everything on his plate and in his glass was much more interesting than anything this man had to say.

But Schooner knew, they were talking about him.

"Photograph so well...All-American Boy...Pay for his education..."

The man handed Mrs. Moore his card and two weeks later, Schooner was in a photographer's studio having his headshots and portfolio done. First, the photographer dressed him in a baseball uniform and posed him with a bat. Then, a bathing suit and had him stand next to a giant flowered surfboard, in front of a large mural of the beach. They finished up with school clothes and oversized glasses, pretending to be reading a book.

"A natural...The camera loves him...Big career in front of him..."

Schooner learned early the importance of his good looks and what those looks could do for him. From the age of four until fourteen, his photo graced the covers and pages of every major catalogue in the US (and internationally, too). All the while, a trust account in his name became sizable (a trust account that would one day help him to become a very successful businessman, at a very young age).

Schooner grew up looking in the mirror and worrying when his face started changing in adolescence, when his skin started to become prone to breakouts. Schooner worried that he wasn't perfect anymore and that would mean letting people down—especially his mother, who managed his career very tightly and whom he wanted to please more than anyone.

Sometimes during those extended sessions of studying his face in the mirror, Schooner would think about "the mask" he was looking at. The mask that had perfected the heart-stopping smile. And he would wonder, *what does my real smile look like* and *who am I really beneath the mask?* It frustrated him that he did not know the answers to those questions.

And so Schooner truly became the ultimate actor—acting out the role he thought would make his parents happy. He was the All-American Boy. Handsome, polite, top student, great athlete, buddy, boyfriend, son, soon-to-be frat brother. Schooner kept everyone happy.

Schooner Moore had no fucking idea who he really was.

CHAPTER 7

CJ and Schooner sat on the big stone steps outside her dorm studying for a Biology exam. It was a perfect fall day to be outdoors; the air was clear, free of smog, hosting puffy white cumulus clouds with towering tops that floated by on the breeze. The mountains appeared as if they were the campus' hand painted backdrop.

"But I'm still confused." CJ's pretty brows were knit together. "Which one is oxidation and which one is reduction?"

"Oxidation is the loss of electrons or increase in oxidation state, while reduction is the gain of electrons or a decrease in oxidation state," Schooner explained, again.

"But if it's a reduction, how is it gaining?" CJ was getting frustrated trying to grasp the concept.

"Okay, just remember OIL RIG for the test. Oil is the acronym for oxidation is loss and Rig is for reduction is gain. Write down Oil Rig when you sit down to take the test."

She sighed.

"The best thing you can do is to keep drawing the Citric Acid Cycle and the Electron Transport Chain over and over until you memorize it," he offered, pulling out a piece of paper from his notebook and handing it to her.

CJ stuck her tongue out at Schooner and snatched the paper from his hand. She dug into her backpack for colored pencils and started her drawing.

Lounging back on the steps, Schooner enjoyed the warm sun and the breeze on his face. He squinted in the bright sunlight under the visor of his tennis team cap as he checked out the people hanging out on The Quad. Frisbee players, people studying on blankets, a few footballs being tossed and a group of about six kids in a circle doing something weird.

He started watching the circle people trying to figure out what they were doing. At first it looked as if they were doing the wave, but then one popped up and jumped in place, spinning around. They each followed.

"Does this look right?" CJ asked, startling him.

He looked at her diagram. "Don't forget to show the loss of CO_2 and the $NADH+H_2$ reactions."

When she returned to her drawing, he started to watch the circle people again. They were all facing outward now, holding hands and doing an odd kick dance. He could tell they were laughing and having fun. They began a new formation, this time a line snaking around The Quad's famed California Live Oaks. It was then that he noticed the pack's leader was none other than Mia Silver.

Wearing a white flouncy gauze peasant shirt and jeans, Mia's wild hair was on a mission of its own, flying in all directions with each of the group's movements. He didn't even realize he was smiling watching her and her group until CJ asked him what was so amusing.

"I'm just watching that group, I have no idea what it is they're doing, but whatever it is, they're having a blast. It looks like some kind of improv thing."

Mia now had the group in a kick line and after a few attempted high kicks, they were soon all bent over in fits of laughter.

Schooner was laughing just watching them. Coordination was clearly not their strong suit.

"Ick, aren't they all from that stoner dorm?" CJ's lip was up in a sneer. "That place is like the *Island of Misfit Toys.*"

Schooner laughed, "Yeah, it really is an odd assortment of people there, isn't it?" He handed CJ another piece of paper. "Okay, give me the one you just drew, close your book and now draw it from memory."

Her eyes widened with panic.

"C'mon CJ, this is the one thing we know will be on the test for sure and it's the only way you're going to learn it. You have to know cellular respiration."

She grabbed the paper from him and gave him a dirty look.

He laughed. "You are a brat!"

As CJ attempted the diagram from memory, Schooner continued to watch Mia and her friends. They were now lying on their backs and pointing up at the clouds. They must be finding shapes in the clouds, he thought. He hadn't done that since he was a little boy. The memory of lying on his front lawn with the kids from his neighborhood made him smile.

He felt CJ's eyes on him. "You finished it?" he asked.

"Let's finish this upstairs." She stood and put out her hand to him.

Taking it, he followed her into her dorm.

"I'm going to give you a biology lesson now." She undid the button and zipper on his tennis shorts. "And I don't need a diagram for this."

Sinking to her knees, she took him deep in her mouth.

"Oh yeah," was all he could say, as he held her head in place, and drove deep into her mouth. It felt so damn good as he lost himself to the rhythm of pounding into her mouth. "Just like that."

He didn't want to come, it felt too good, he needed to make it last. Keeping one hand on the top of her head, he held her in place, as he continued to thrust. Eventually he opened his eyes, while still driving relentlessly into CJ's wanting mouth.

Outside the window, movement below on The Quad caught his eye. It was Mia and her friends and they were now doing a crazy, abandoned dance. Her arms were outstretched wide and her long hair was flinging with her head, her hips thrusting rhythmically. It was so much fun to watch her being so free. It was then that he realized he was thrusting into CJ's mouth to the rhythm of Mia's wild, abandoned dance. Feeling his balls tighten and the pressure begin to rise, he could no longer keep his control.

When he left CJ's dorm, Mia and her friends were still out on The Quad, sitting in the grass, hanging out talking. He caught Mia's eye as he walked past and did the head nod/smile acknowledgement. Mia did the same in return. Suddenly, he felt shy and hoped she didn't notice that he was actually blushing. Why did he feel like he had just taken advantage of her?

CHAPTER 8

The remainder of first semester flew by alarmingly fast. Schooner made first string on the tennis team, an unusual feat for a freshman, and represented the team in the fall regional tournaments with a string of wins. Come spring semester and the aggressive team schedule, he would be juggling studies and travel—including trips to many of the small Ivy's on the east coast. He looked forward to the travel matches and exploring campuses he had only seen in pictures.

The month of January was known as Interim. For four weeks, students took only one intensive class for four credits. Some classes were on campus, others were travel-oriented—European capitals, Theatre in NY, Outdoor Adventure: Australia/New Zealand, Spanish Immersion in Ecuador and dozens of other equally interesting classes.

For those who stayed on campus, the course catalogue offered intensive seminars on a wide array of subjects, including in-depth study on specific authors, film genres, American popular culture, music (from intensive instrument instruction to analysis of Beatles lyrics). While there would be papers to write and tests to take, Interim allowed students to actually enjoy studying and really delve into a topic of interest that wasn't a part of their normal core curriculum.

Schooner spent time between Christmas and New Year's with CJ's family. Parents loved him. Moms for the obvious reason, dads because he was an athlete and could be a man's man.

When CJ's mother, Barbara, had Schooner pose with the family on a staircase photo (they were each lined up on consecutive steps, leaning on the banister and all wearing red sweaters—CJ's Christmas gift to him), Schooner realized that CJ and her mother had this whole thing mapped out. Barbara MacAllister was clearly already naming her little blonde haired, blue eyed grandchildren and their last name would be Moore. It got worse when they took a few shots of just CJ and Schooner on the staircase, the banister decorated in garland and red bows, CJ and Schooner in matching red sweaters. This was clearly part one of a plan and railroaded was the word that kept crossing his mind.

As each piece snapped into place and CJ and her mom played out their hand, Schooner felt claustrophobic, used and manipulated. He was rapidly becoming less and less happy with the whole situation and what felt like a loss of control.

That night when everyone was asleep, an angry and frustrated Schooner snuck into CJ's room. Her pink satin robe hung over the back of a chair. Schooner silently pulled the sash tie from the loops of the robe and approached CJ's bed. He sat down on the edge and the movement from his weight woke her.

"Shhhh," he whispered, "keep quiet"

Taking her hands and pulling them above her head, he tied them tightly to the post of her canopy bed, using the satin sash

"Do *not* make a sound," his voice was gruff and commanding. CJ laid there wide-eyed, nodding her head.

"Your parents think you're a good girl, don't they?"

CJ nodded.

"They think you're a virgin." Schooner went on, "But we know better than that, don't we?"

CJ nodded again.

"We know what a hot little slut you are."

A moan escaped CJ's throat.

"I told you to be quiet," his tone was harsh. "You are such a slut that every day you suck my sweaty cock and balls when I get off the tennis courts. I don't even shower and I fuck you."

CJ started writhing, clearly turned on by Schooner's monologue.

"Stay still," he hissed and she stilled. "Tonight your mother lined us up on the stairs. Her sweet little virginal daughter and her hot boyfriend. Show me off to all of her friends. Brag to them. Well, if she only knew how much you love to suck my dick, do you think she'd still be bragging? And now I am going to fuck her little "virgin" in her pretty little girly bed." And with that, Schooner got between CJ's thighs and rammed his cock deep into her dripping wet pussy. "And you won't make a sound."

Schooner rode CJ hard, ramming into her, detached and deep in his own head. Angry at her manipulation. At her mother's manipulation. When he was done, he untied the sash, silently got up and left the room.

As had been previously planned for New Year's, CJ was a guest at the Moore's home and there was no way she was not going to be present at his family's annual New Year's Eve party, no matter how cold their son had been for the past few days. CJ had one chance to make a first impression and the Moores were going to love her.

By New Year's Eve, Schooner could not wait for winter break to be over. He wanted to be back on the courts, practicing like a motherfucker for a full month before the spring semester tennis schedule began. He was also secretly very happy that CJ would be off for the month exploring European capitals.

When she had first signed up for the class, he was not ecstatic about her being away for four weeks. But with intensive pre-season tennis practice, his own class and the feeling like a noose was being tightened around his neck, as his future was being decided for him, he was ready to tell CJ to "Have a great trip. See you in February."

Dee Moore was famous for her parties. She was the consummate hostess and had a natural knack for putting people together and launching conversations. She would get it started and quietly move on to the next group needing her help. Dee liked to think of herself as the sand in the oyster—she'd get it all started and then her job was done.

As she surveyed the room that night, she noticed Schooner's girlfriend, CJ, was part of her husband's conversation group, which was made up of all men. CJ hung onto Gavin Moore's every word and laughed brightly. While the girl had been nothing but pleasant and solicitous, Dee's motherly red flags were up. CJ was showing the Moores what she thought they wanted to see and Dee instinctively knew they had yet to see the real CJ.

Dee exited the great room wondering where her son might be. Gavin's home office was empty and Schooner was not with the crowd in the kitchen. Dee made her way to the family room and still there was no sign of Schooner. She saw a slight movement through the French doors and found her son out on the deck, alone.

Schooner was such a social young man, that finding him alone, instead of socializing with family friends he had known his whole life, told Dee that all was not right in her son's world.

"Getting some fresh air?" she asked, intruding on his silence.

"Hi Mom," he leaned down and kissed her on the cheek.

"CJ is very lovely, Schooner."

"Yes, she is. We look like we belong together, don't we." It was more of a statement than a question.

"No doubt about it, you two make a very striking couple. Whether you belong together is another story. While it's nice to see you in a committed relationship and caring for someone, you are both very young. First love can sometimes be overwhelming." Dee rubbed Schooner's back, reassuringly.

Schooner remained silent.

"Are you feeling overwhelmed?"

He closed his eyes and sighed, "Mom, I'm really glad she's going away for the month. Is that a bad thing? Is that telling me something I should be listening to?" Schooner turned to his mother, a pained look on his face.

Her heart ached at his confusion. "No Sweetheart, it's not a bad thing. It is what it is and those are your feelings. Whether it's telling you something or not—well, only time will tell—maybe it is, maybe it isn't. And the time you spend apart may give you a lot of answers. The two of you have just gone through several very intense months learning to live on your own, coming into your own. Take a breath and just give yourself credit for successfully embracing all the change in your life and doing a really great job with it."

Schooner hugged his mother tight. He just wanted to be the man she wanted him to be, yet he always had something gnawing, deep in his gut, that if she really knew what was going on hidden in his psyche, that he would disappoint her.

"Let's get inside." She led him toward the door. "It's almost the new year."

At the stroke of midnight, in a room filled with revelers, Schooner kissed CJ deeply. "I'm going to miss you," she said, lower lip out in a full pretty pink pout.

"I'm going to miss you, too," he whispered softly in her ear, not being able to voice it out loud. And in that moment, Schooner hated himself just a little bit more for telling her what she wanted to hear.

CHAPTER 9

January was historically a cold and rainy month and it looked like history was going to repeat itself. Half of the student population was abroad or doing domestic travel classes, leaving only about 1200 students on the entire campus. It kind of had a ghost town feel to it and Schooner thought it felt damn good.

No roommate. Beau was in Ecuador.

No girlfriend. CJ was going to be in London, Paris, Rome, Vienna and Prague.

Practice at the new indoor tennis center, which had just been completed over the holiday break, and an American Popular Culture class on the History of American music from blues to modern day, would be his life for one month. Sweet.

After a great two hours of returning serves from a relentless machine from 6:00 A.M.—8:00 A.M., Schooner headed to the dining hall for some breakfast. He thought this would be his January schedule. Early morning time on the court, breakfast, then class from 9:00 to 12:30, Monday through Thursday. Coach had practice from 2:00—4:00 daily and then the evening was his, open for studying, projects and hanging out. He liked this new plan and couldn't wait to get into the groove.

Refusing to carry an umbrella, Schooner pulled up the hood of his windbreaker and made his way across The Quad to Clawson Hall. The class was in one of the theatre-style lecture halls and Schooner did a quick scan of the crowd when he walked in, looking for people he knew and hopefully an empty seat.

She looked up just as he scanned the section in which she was seated and broke into a huge smile as their eyes met. A real smile, he thought. He smiled back (a real smile) and started up the stairs, two at a time to her row. She was at the center of the row and he had to climb over a few people to get to the empty seat next to her.

"Hey, how was your holiday?" He was really happy no one else had been sitting on her right.

"Great and yours?"

"It was good. My dad was asking about you. He said to say hello if I saw you."

"Please tell him and your mom hello from me." She gestured to her friends sitting on the other side of her. "Do you know Henry and Rosalie?" And she turned to them, "Guys, do you know Schooner?"

Schooner recognized Mia's two friends from her "entourage," but had never actually spoken to either of them before. He was pretty sure that both Henry and Rosalie were gay. He lived in the jock dorm and if anyone was gay, they were certainly not out. Mia, Henry and Rosalie lived in a dorm whose motto could have been, "Anything Goes."

"Do you know anything about this professor?" Schooner asked.

Mia's face lit up and she became very animated, "I had him last semester and he is the coolest prof on campus. He grades really tough though. He truly makes you think and expects a lot from your papers. I hate his freaking red pen."

"Oh crap. Writing is not my strongest skill," Schooner admitted.

"Rut roh," Mia did a Scooby Doo imitation, "It *is* my strongest skill and he still beat the crap out of me. But he's a great lecturer and he just makes everything really fun. He's also like the best guy to talk to."

Dr. Richard Stevens took the podium in the front of the room. He was dressed in faded jeans and a worn blue work shirt and looked every inch the "cool" professor. He was very articulate and there was just a hint of a British accent.

Schooner noticed that Mia was looking at him like he was hot. She definitely had a Prof Crush.

"Welcome to Interim," he began. "One class. Just one class. For those of you who are freshman and this is your first Interim, you are thinking that you just got an extra month of vacation. You're thinking you'll be keeping the ole' bong fired up." Chuckles and murmurs coursed throughout the room. "You're thinking marathons of Hearts and Spades. You're thinking you're going to be shitfaced for a month." He paused, "Well, you're wrong. For the next month, you will be learning about the American soundtrack. You will be learning how music is the universal connector from generation to generation, it is the mirror that reflects society and its mores. You will be sitting in your dorm rooms, quite possibly with a bong in hand," more chuckles from the lecture hall, "and will hear the music you are playing differently than you've ever heard it before. You'll want to write about it, dissect it, discuss it, argue about it and get lost in it. Listening to music will never be the same."

Mia smiled at Schooner, her eyes alight.

She was right, he thought, this guy is dynamic. This is going to be amazing.

"Four weeks. Three individual papers, the first one due this week." He paused and scanned his audience, "Yes, you heard me right. I said this week. There will be one group project. No tests." A small cheer from the lecture hall at the mention of no tests. Professor Stevens continued, "Your group project will make up 40% of your grade, each paper is worth 20%. So, as you can see, there is no room to screw up. There are twenty-eight of you in this class and you will break into seven groups of four for your group projects."

Mia looked left at Rosalie and Henry and right to Schooner, "Us four?" And they all agreed.

Professor Stevens turned to the board and began writing.

> Our culture finds its tension and its life within the borders of the glimmer and the dying away, in attempts to come to terms with the betrayal without giving up on the promise" ~ Greil Marcus[1]

He turned back to the class and pointed to the board, "If you haven't already begun to write down this quote, I would suggest you start immediately, because this is what we will be discussing for the next four weeks. This is what all of your papers will be about and this is what your final project will be about. Learn that quote, digest it, process it and start applying it to your thinking."

He turned back to the board and started to write again.

Harmonica Frank
Robert Johnson
Blind Lemon Jefferson
Muddy Waters
John Lee Hooker
The Band
Bob Dylan
Laura Nyro
The Grateful Dead
Creedence Clearwater Revival
Sly Stone
Allman Brothers
Elvis Presley
Bruce Springsteen
Chrissie Hynde
CSNY

Dr. John
Beach Boys

"This list goes on and on. It's dynamic and it's intertwined. Where does one influence end and another begin? Can they be separated?" Professor Stevens hit a button, static crackled through the room.

Schooner and Mia both looked at one another in the same moment, wide eyed and wide smiled, as the first strains of Robert Johnson's blues classic "*Come on in My Kitchen*" began to play.

Interim had officially begun.

---

[1] *Greil Marcus, Mystery Train: Images of America in Rock 'n Roll Music (New York: Penguin Group, 1975), 35.*

CHAPTER 10

Three and a half hours flew by as they listened to music and talked about its meaning, its cultural significance and the topics they would delve into daily—What is the American birthright? What are the promises? What are the betrayals? How, as a people, do we come to terms with the chasm between promise and betrayal, and how is that portrayed in music?

It was fascinating and being exposed to music they'd never heard before had the foursome pumped up. By the time they got out of class and walked across The Quad to the dining hall for lunch, their excitement was palpable, thoughts and theories beginning to formulate and flow out of them. As they walked through the food line, they tossed around topics for their project, which they didn't even have the guidelines for yet, but that's how psyched up they were.

Schooner found Henry and Rosalie to be down to earth, fun and really funny. He loved the way they busted on one another and the easy camaraderie in this group. They were just accepting him and taking him in. Making him one of their own. No questions asked. No judgments. No need for any particular status. He was okay with Mia, so he was okay with them. Ironic, he thought, absolutely the antithesis of how Beau had treated Mia.

When they all had their trays, they made their way to a table and the three had just assumed Schooner would say goodbye and head over to sit with some of his jock friends or tennis teammates, but he didn't do that. He followed them to their table and sat down next to Mia.

He could see the surprise register on Mia's face and he liked it. He'd had more fun with them in the past few hours than he'd had in his entire first semester with his dorm mates and the tennis team.

"So, 'Little Miss Writing is my Strong Point,' are you going to help me with my papers so I don't end up being totally annihilated by the famous red slash of death?" Schooner gave Mia his best megawatt smile.

Mia sneered back at him, "You're going to have to do better than that, Pretty Boy." And then she smiled, her freckle smattered nose, crinkling.

She made Schooner's heart smile—a feeling he didn't easily recognize, but was surely enjoying.

He just looked at her, loving that she had called him on his shit. "Seriously, can you at least look them over before I turn them in?"

Nodding her head, "Yeah, of course. No problem. I'm not going to let my team mate look like a stupid jock," she teased. "That would make us all look bad." She motioned to Henry and Rosie who joined in on the "Bust on Schooner" session.

Schooner knew in that instant that *this* is what he had been missing out on so far in his college experience. He thought back to his New Year's Eve conversation with his mom, where he was so out of sorts. He knew something wasn't quite right in his life (besides feeling railroaded into a predetermined future), something was missing. *This* was what was missing.

"Are you guys going to start reading and studying tonight? I've got tennis practice from 2-4 every afternoon, but I can meet after that."

Henry turned to Mia and Rosalie, "What time do you guys want to eat dinner?"

"5:30?" Rosalie offered.

Mia nodded her assent.

"Cool," smiled Schooner, "that gives me time to get back from the tennis center, shower, change and grab my books. I'll meet you guys for dinner and then we can go back to your dorm to work."

And that was how it began and a new group of friends formed. Schooner was amazed at his immediate comfort level with this group. They were funny, smart and not afraid to bust on him. They were fun. He didn't need to pretend with them. He could be Schooner and they actually liked him. It wasn't work to fit in with them.

When Schooner hit the courts that afternoon and Coach Boland started putting them through their paces, he felt a confidence that surpassed his usual bravado. This confidence was coming from a new place. Somewhere deep within which Schooner was not familiar with, but really liked.

CHAPTER 11

The nightly ritual had begun. Meet for dinner and then head over to one of the study rooms in Mia, Henry and Rosie's dorm. They would spend a few hours working in the study room: scanning the reference books, listening to tapes of the music, working on papers, batting around ideas. Their conversations were lively, punctuated by Rosie's sarcasm and Mia's quick wit. Often, they'd have to draw themselves back from off-topic tangents that would lead into fits of laughter. Schooner had never remembered laughing so hard in his life where his face would hurt and his gut muscles would ache. He and Henry often played the straight men (no pun intended) to the girls and their antics. It was a surprise to Schooner at how at ease he was with his burgeoning friendship with Henry. Henry was just another guy—and that really came as a revelation to Schooner. The issue of Henry's sexuality had become a moot point and Schooner was able to just enjoy his banter and discourse with his new friend. And if he were to really think about it, Schooner was more at ease with Henry than he was with any of his teammates.

After a few hours in the study room, they would leave the protected enclave and move the discussion to Mia's room. Mia's roommate, Caroline, was also on the European capitals trip. The three friends would break out the bong (which Professor Stevens had predicted) and Schooner would just stick to beer. With training four hours a day, he knew getting high would be detrimental to peak performance and he did not want to lose his hard earned, coveted first string spot.

The group would listen to music and the conversation would just flow. Sometimes it centered on what they were learning and how they applied it to themselves and their worlds. Sometimes they played marathon poker tournaments. Sometimes they just opened up and shared with each other.

Henry's first experience with another man happened when he was only nine. His mom's younger cousin from Ohio was living with them in exchange for babysitting Henry and his little sister when their mother was at work. One of the cousin's boyfriends had molested Henry and did so nightly under the pretense of helping him with his homework and putting him to sleep, while the cousin tended to Henry's little sister. The others sat horrified, listening to the details of what happened to the 4th grader.

Looking around the dorm room at the friends he had shocked into silence, Henry tried to put them at ease. "It's okay," he said. "I liked it."

"But you were just a child. He took advantage of you," Mia countered, horrified. "That was wrong."

Henry casually blew it off with a shrug of his shoulders. "If it wasn't him, it would've been someone else. At least he didn't hurt me."

Schooner wondered if the girls were thinking the same thing that he was—that this man had hurt Henry immeasurably. Henry actually thought he deserved it, deserved to be abused and violated. Feeling deep sorrow for his new friend, the brute jock in Schooner wanted to pull this guy's nuts off and hit them around the court with his racquet. It was then that Schooner realized how protective he felt of Henry and this crew. They were his people.

Rosie broke the tension with a snorting laugh. The other three just looked at her questioningly.

"I was just thinking about one of my *early* sexual experiences," she said, making quotation marks with her fingers at the word early.

She continued to laugh, shaking her head, before she was able to gain control of herself enough to share the memory.

"Okay, so when I was little, I used to defy my mother all the time. I know that's hard to imagine," she laughed and was met with a chorus of "Oh yeah, really hard to imagine." She continued, "So my mother used to put me up in my room to *think about what I had done* and told me that I could come out when I was *ready to apologize*." She stopped and laughed, "I'm actually surprised I'm out of the room now."

They all laughed.

"So, I would go up, sit on my bed and stew. I usually had no idea what I had done wrong or why my mother had put me up there. Maybe she needed a break. I don't know," she paused and loaded herself a bong hit, lit it and inhaled.

With the smoke still in her lungs, she continued, "So, I must've been about five years old." She blew out the smoke and started to laugh. "And my mother had put me up in my room one day and I got really bored and started checking out my toys. I had this magic wand. It was a wooden stick with a purple plastic star on one end filled with like water and glitter and a picture of a unicorn on it. I think it came with a My Little Pony."

Schooner sat up abruptly from the big overstuffed throw pillow he was lounging against and grabbed Mia's arm, practically spitting out his swig of beer, "Oh no, where is she going with this?"

They all started to laugh.

"You are a bright, bright boy." Rosie pointed at Schooner and continued, "So one day, I took off my frilly little pink and white panties. Do you believe she dressed *me* in frilly stuff? Lord knows why I'm so fucked up! Okay, back to the story. So, I took my panties off and started to masturbate with this magic wand. I remember masturbating with it and singing…La La La La La…"

Schooner, Henry and Mia were literally rolling on the floor laughing, all making hand motions and sing songing "LaLaLaLaLa."

Mia was pounding on the floor with her fists, her face planted in the carpeting and Schooner had his face buried in the back of her head, nuzzled into her hair, cracking up.

When they sat up, he turned to Mia and said, "When is her birthday?" Motioning to Rosalie—which set off another round of laughter. "You're going to be an easy one to shop for this year."

When they all regained control over their laughter, Rosie continued, "Okay, so picture this…"

"We are!" Henry interrupted and the laughter started again.

Through her laughter, Rosie continued, "So, I had no clue what I was doing, but I knew it felt good so I started getting in trouble on purpose, just so I could get sent to my room and do this thing that felt so great. I guess I had gotten away with it for a few weeks when my mother walked in during the middle of one of my sessions, saw the magic wand in me, freaked out and grabbed it." Rosie pouted out her lower lip, "She took my magic wand away," she sniffed.

"I got your magic wand right here for you, Baby." Henry motioned to his crotch.

Rosie scoffed, "You might have a magic wand for him." She motioned to Schooner, "but not for me."

"Ummm, I can have fun with my own wand," Schooner choked, blushing.

"I'll bet you can!" Rosie teased and they all broke into another fit of laughter.

CHAPTER 12

The general consensus on campus was that no new food had been delivered to the dining hall for Interim and that the staff there was just recycling old food and using leftovers. The already questionable food quality seemed to degrade by the day—making dining during the regular semester seem like a Wolfgang Puck inspired meal (which it clearly was not).

Everyone was pissed off and grumbling about how much their parents were paying for this high priced private college education and that they should at least get some decent food. How many days in a row were they going to be expected to eat 'Chicken Surprise'?

Sitting at the next table from Schooner, Mia, Rosie and Henry were some of the football jocks from Schooner's dorm. They were complaining loudly about the food and the one complaining the loudest was an offensive tackle known as Beast. Schooner realized he didn't even know Beast's real name, although he had lived in the same dorm with him since late August.

Fall semester, Beast had been rushing one of the jock fraternities. As part of his hazing, Beast spent one month, day and night, in a pink leotard and a pink lace tutu. He also was not allowed to shower for a month—or wash the leotard. Now while the leotard and tutu were a bit strange for Beast, not showering for extended periods of time was more the norm than the exception. A few days into the hazing, Beast was odiferous. By the end of the month, it was hard to walk past him without gagging. Tables in the dining hall cleared, classroom desks were rearranged to one side of the room and his roommate, Vince, took up residence on a couch in the dorm's lounge.

Beast was huge, 6'4" and 300 lbs. He had a head full of unkempt hair and a straggly beard. Not known for his eloquence or intellect, the joke around campus was that he would probably scare off small children and possibly farm animals.

"This food fucking sucks!" he proclaimed, loudly.

"Tell us something we don't know," Rosalie muttered, and the four chuckled.

"We don't have to take this!" his shouting continued.

Beast then stood suddenly, pushing back the bench he was sitting on and causing everyone down the entire length of the bench to be jostled.

"I'm revolting!" he yelled on the top of his lungs.

"Actually, you're disgusting." Mia countered in a loud voice and the whole dining hall broke into laughter.

Beasts eyes enlarged and his nostrils flared, creating the visage of an insane escapee. "Bitch!" he bellowed, as he dove toward Mia.

Schooner instinctively threw his body at Beast pushing him out of the way before he assaulted Mia full on. They both fell to the floor with a sickening thud. Rosie grabbed the food off of her tray and threw it at Beast and Henry followed. The rest of the jocks cleared off the benches to join in the mêlée and were met with hoards of flying food. Beast and Schooner were wrestling around on the food- slick floor.

Mia started to kick Beast, "Get the fuck off of him, you gross pig!" she wailed away on him, stabbing him hard in the lower back with her clogs.

The Campus Police arrived almost immediately and grabbed Beast off of Schooner, cuffing his hands behind his back. A second officer cuffed Schooner.

"Officer," Mia pleaded, "he was just coming to my defense when that guy tried to jump me."

The officer looked Mia up and down (stopping momentarily on her very attractive rack), all 5'2" of her, and then looked at Beast.

"He tried to jump you?" he asked, incredulously.

"Yes, he tried to attack me."

"Did you provoke him?"

"I told him he was disgusting." Mia's chin was stuck up high in the air.

"Maybe you should come with us, too."

Mia smiled sweetly at the Campus Police Officer and said, "Will you cuff me as well?"

He choked out a "no" and Mia pouted at him, causing the officer to stammer and blush.

Schooner watched her with amusement and remembered his first impression of her in front of Brewster Hall, that devilish look that said, "Let's be bad kids together." *Well, the devil is out in full force tonight,* he thought.

Smiling at Schooner, Mia put her lips close to his ear and whispered, "You look really hot in cuffs."

As the heat rose simultaneously in his face and in his jeans, he stared at her and leaned close to her ear, hissing, "Now is *not* the time to give me a raging hard on, Mia."

She backed away, an astonished smirk on her face and then she looked him square in the eyes, suddenly serious. Without saying a word, she silently leaned forward and kissed his cheek, softly. "Thank you for defending me tonight, Schooner."

He sighed, feeling his heart melt. *What was she doing to him?*

An entourage of about twenty-five students trekked to the Campus Police station following Schooner, Mia and Beast. The statements from everyone were consistent. Beast went to physically attack Mia and Schooner jumped in to thwart the attack. The Campus Police were alarmed that a student the size of Beast had a hair trigger temper that did not preclude violence toward women. The guy was bad press waiting to happen.

Beast was not seen again until spring semester.

CHAPTER 13

It was late by the time all of the paperwork had been filled out and Mia and Schooner walked back together toward their dorms.

Mia left the officer with a wink. "I'm still bummed you didn't have cuffs for me."

Kidding Mia, Schooner nudged her. "Your dorm is going to be seeing some extra patrol in the next few weeks. Let's go, Mia, before you start another riot," he ushered her out of the campus police building.

She smiled, his remark clearly pleasing her devil.

"Are you okay?" Mia asked, genuinely concerned. Schooner had a nasty cut on his cheek and some other scrapes.

"I'm fine." He made light of it.

"I would tell you that I'd come back to your dorm and help you clean out those cuts, but I have a feeling I'm persona non grata there."

"Yeah, probably not safe," he agreed. "Might not even be safe for me!"

"Oh fuck," her hand flew to her mouth. "I didn't even think of that. I am so sorry."

"It'll be fine. Everyone knows what an ass Beast is. These guys can be jerks, but I'd bet most of them have real issues seeing a girl being attacked. You notice no one came up to the Campus Police station in his defense."

"Hmm, that's true."

They walked along in the cool, dank late night air in silence. Schooner put his arm around Mia's shoulder and pulled her in to him as they continued to walk. She didn't fight him and seemed to find her place right under his arm.

She is so tiny, he thought and smiled. A tiny, uncontrollable fireball. "So, you like the way I look in cuffs, huh?" It was time to give her some of her own medicine.

"Mmm-hmm, you looked hot." She didn't miss a beat.

Schooner just laughed and pulled her tighter into him, this time her arm went around the back of his waist, and without thinking, he kissed her on the top of her head. She was really getting under his skin and he didn't know whether to be excited or scared.

They reached her dorm and Schooner stopped.

"You want to come in and I can take a look at your cuts?" Mia asked.

"I want to," Schooner whispered, "but it's after 1 A.M. and I've got to be on the courts at six. Not sure how good I'm going to be feeling in the morning or what flak I'll be taking from the coach when he gets a load of me."

Mia nodded her head. "Schooner," she paused, clearly grappling with word choice, "what you did tonight… well, it was amazing. That crazy son-of-a-bitch was going to tackle me. He could've really hurt me. And you went against one of the guys you live with. That's huge."

Schooner quickly closed the space between him and Mia and wrapped his arms around her tightly. He smiled as her arms circled his back. With his chin resting on the top of her head, softly he said, "I would never have let him hurt you, Baby Girl."

He was as surprised by the term of endearment as she was, and if he could have seen her face at that moment, she was smiling into his chest.

He gently pushed her away by the shoulders and kissed her forehead. "Get some sleep," he ordered and she giggled at his stern tone.

He quickly turned on his heel, heading in the direction of his dorm, leaving her standing there, as confused as he was, by the tremendous onslaught of feelings.

CHAPTER 14

On Saturday, the gang decided to take their studying someplace conducive to opening up their minds to understanding how American culture is reflected in music, and that meant being anywhere, other than stuck on campus. Schooner borrowed a teammate's car and pulled up in front of the dorm to pick up the gang.

"Nice wheels," Henry commented, easing his thin, lithe frame into the front passenger seat of the silver Camaro. The girls piled in the back, giddy with the prospect of getting off campus.

The weeklong rain had finally ended, and the low clouds lifted, revealing the raw beauty of the San Bernardino National Forest. The mountains appeared majestic against a pristine clear blue sky (that ironically matched Schooner's eyes) with their snow-capped peaks.

Down vests and hiking boots and gloves were broken out for the trip as well as cassette players, lots of cassette music, extra batteries and notebooks to work. In the backseat, Mia pulled a black knit cap out of her backpack and leaned forward and pulled it down over Schooner's head. "My gift to you from New York."

Schooner pulled down the visor to look in the mirror. "I like it." He smiled. "Can I keep it?"

"Sure, consider it a gift."

Schooner thought, she has no idea how much I will treasure this.

They headed up Hwy. 38 into the town of Mentone. "Hey, pull in here." Henry said to Schooner and jumped out of the car.

He ducked into a donut shop and the girls squealed in the back. The winter sun glinted off Henry's copper-tinged waves as he rushed back to the car.

"Get 'em while they're hot," he announced and flung open the heavenly smelling box of apple fritters.

Hands grabbed and sounds of "mmm" and "oh my god" filled the car.

"How'd you guys find this place?" Schooner asked.

"You forget we're stoners," Rosie offered, stuffing the last bite of an apple fritter into her mouth and slowly licking off her sticky fingers. Rosie had full-curvy deep pink lips that always looked like she was wearing lipstick, and later in life, people would wonder if she'd had "work done" on them. "We are not beyond traveling for munchies."

Once through Mentone, the highway started taking on sharp curves and a steep incline, as it became known as the Rim of the World Highway, sporting views of snowcapped saw backs and pine dotted ridges. The clear skies made the view seem as if it went on forever, creating the feeling that anything was possible.

Schooner looked back and laughingly said to Mia, "Hey, I remember the last time I was in the mountains with you."

She slapped him on the shoulder. "Oh crap, don't remind me!"

"Remind you of what?" Rosie asked and Henry turned to Mia to hear the story.

Mia and Schooner filled Rosie and Henry in on the event that took place during the freshman retreat and Mia's encounter of getting sniffed by Tim Vandergrift.

"He sniffed you?" Rosie appeared grossed out.

Before Mia could respond, a laughing Schooner chimed in, "Sniffed her is an understatement. He was nose raping her. The only thing that would've made him happier would've been if she'd handed him her panties to sniff."

"Eww! Stop that!" Mia started slapping Schooner on the shoulder, while the others hooted.

"Seriously, he sniffed you?" Henry asked through his laughing tears.

"He did," Mia laughed. "I thought he was narc'ing me out for stinking of weed. He was seriously hanging on my chair and sniffing me. It was freaky. I thought for sure I was going to get kicked out of school in my first two weeks and that my parents would kill me and give me the 'We knew you were too young to go away and be on your own' bullshit."

They were still laughing as Schooner pulled the car into a National Forest recreation area parking lot.

"But this guy saved the day." Mia patted Schooner's shoulder. "He caused a diversion and I escaped the evil sniffer."

"You know who that Tim guy reminds me of, that character Greg Marmalard from the movie *Animal House*. You know the straight-laced preppie guy who led the brigade against Otter, Boon, Bluto and the gang," Henry said.

"Exactly," Schooner chimed in. "Total dick. You should've seen the look on Mia's face," he laughed. "It was like get me the hell out of here. Now!"

They parked the car and grabbed their gear and began down the Big Falls Trailhead. About a half mile in, a clearing opened to a heart stopping, unobstructed view of Forest Falls. They all stood there silently enjoying the view of the unspoiled falls and listening to the rush of water as it flowed over ancient rock.

Crossing a creek bed, they cautiously stepping from boulder to slippery boulder until they reached the other side. There, they followed the trail alongside the creek bed until they came upon a huge sign, *These Falls Have Claimed Many Lives*. From there, they turned off on a trail through the woods, packing down snow as they hiked for about another twenty minutes, until they came to a large snow filled meadow that had yet to be disturbed by anything other than deer tracks.

As they walked onto the meadow, they were greeted by a different clear vista of the falls. Laying their backpacks on some large boulders, they walked toward the ridge to view the sublime waterfall. Overwhelmed by the perfection of nature, they all stood there silently for a few minutes.

Mia pulled out her Nikon SLR and started to take pictures of the falls. She used a low broken branch of a pine to set her camera on and act as a tripod as she pulled several lenses out of her bag. Schooner realized that he had seen her around campus shooting.

"That's a nice camera," he commented.

"Thanks. It was my birthday present to myself," she offered proudly.

"What do you most like to shoot?" Schooner was enjoying learning what made her tick.

"This." She gestured to the scenery around them. "I love landscape photography. If anything comes out good from today, I'll make you a print."

"You make your own prints?"

"Yeah, we've got a great dark room on campus. So, I roll my own—umm, film that is," she chuckled, "and then develop it and print it. Right now, I'm shooting black and white."

"Are you going to teach me how to shoot one of these days?" Henry nudged her.

"Any time you want," she responded, clearly too focused on the falls to continue the conversation.

"Just make sure she's behind the lens," Henry clued Schooner in. "She hates having her picture taken."

How odd, she's comfortable behind the lens and I've spent my life in front of it, Schooner thought. He wondered how she would see him through her lens, what she would see? Would she see him or just his brilliant disguise?

After a few minutes more of shooting scenery, Mia turned the camera to her compadres playing in the snow, rolling in the snow, making lewd snowmen with giant erections and pretending to throw one another off the mountain ridge.

Momentarily walking away from the group, Mia went off to put her camera back in her backpack, where it would be safe.

A few minutes later, Schooner heard her call his name and turned as a snowball whooshed past his head, missing him by mere inches.

"Oh, so that's how you want to play!" He gathered up snow in his hands and packed a snowball quickly and winged it at her.

"Ouch," she screamed, getting nabbed in the arm. "Son of a bitch!"

"You started it," he laughed.

Henry and Rosie joined in the fun with Henry chasing Rosie down and stuffing snow down the back of her jacket.

"I hate you." she screamed at him and smushed snow in his copper hair.

Schooner flung snowballs as if he were serving tennis balls and Mia was being bombarded. When he decided she'd been pelted enough, he walked over to her and smushed a handful of snow in her face.

"Oh man, you play dirty. I give up." She held her hands up in defeat and he beamed at his victory.

Putting his arms around her, he pulled her into his chest. "Body heat," he whispered in her ear.

She looked up at him and he pulled her cap down over her face playfully.

This was the first time either Henry or Rosie had seen him be physical with Mia. He wanted to kiss her in this light, perfect, fun-filled moment on a mountain alongside a waterfall, but they weren't alone and he didn't want to cause anyone any embarrassment. With feelings welling up deep inside, he wanted that moment to be just theirs alone, shared with no one, when the time was right.

They went back to the rocks where their backpacks were and sat down. Pulling out their cassette players and notebooks, they started listening to music and discussing how tracks would either fit in or not fit in with their group project.

After about thirty minutes, their butts and fingers and toes were so cold and so wet from their snowball fight, that they decided to bail on studying in the mountains and finish studying in a nice warm dorm room.

CHAPTER 15

The dorm room didn't feel much warmer than the mountaintop and the gang all changed into dry, warm oversized sweats and thick socks and lounged on throw pillows on the floor of Mia's dorm room.

"Okay, clearly we need to address Bob Dylan's work, Crosby Stills Nash, the Buffalo Springfield stuff," Henry said, as he made notes.

Schooner flipped through some books, "I don't want to ignore Woody Guthrie and Pete Seeger and we need to bring in the ties to Steinbeck's work. Honestly though, I feel like Phil Ochs gets totally overlooked and I really want to focus on him, but at the same time, I think we really have to be careful of it becoming too derivative."

"Yeah, that's my concern, too," Rosie chimed in, making a face. "Whoever thought we'd hear a jock use the term derivative."

Schooner tossed a pillow at her, which she arranged under her head, smiling at him.

"I think they all help build a linear foundation for groups like the Pretenders, for Leonard Cohen, for REM and for Springsteen," Mia said, without looking up from her notes.

"Oh no, here comes the New Yorker with Springsteen." Henry teased and Mia threw a pillow at him, still not looking up from her notes.

"Hey, if anyone's music focuses on the promise, the betrayal, coming to terms with everything on both a cultural level and a personal level—it's Bruce's. I've kind of been cataloguing it to look at what is more cultural than personal—if you can even separate it—and I think we can clearly make strong cases with: *Thunder Road*—the ultimate redemption song, *The Promised Land*—totally about coming to terms with the betrayal, *Badlands*—taking the power back, feeling the birthright, *Born to Run*." Mia continued, "Basically, a good portion of *The River* album can be tied back into Marcus' premise. Even some of the covers Bruce has chosen, Jimmy Cliff's *Trapped*." She looked around for her notes, "Oh, and trying to pull it down to the individual level—that of personal betrayal and questioning of the promise. Check this out, listen to this song."

She grabbed her cassette recorder and played with the forward and reverse for a few minutes to get the tape to the right point. The quiet guitar strains began to a bare, haunting tune.

Mia laid back on her throw pillow, eyes closed, quietly singing harmony as the others listened intently to the lyrics of the starkly beautiful song.

"Play that again." Henry asked and Mia rewound the tape and restarted the song, *One Step Up*.

Schooner listened closely again, slightly distracted by Mia's proximity on the next throw pillow. Hearing the lyrics a second time cut deeply. They were words of self-doubt and self-disappointment. And for Schooner, they hit too close to home.

Schooner Moore was concerned that maybe he wasn't turning out to be the man he hoped he would become.

Lively discussion ensued and after a few more hours, they'd worked out how they were going to divide the work amongst the group and how they were going to bridge it together into a seamless project. Putting together their opening statements, they began to plow through the exhaustive material for each of their sections.

It was past midnight when Rosie got to her feet, "I'm toast," she announced. "All that fresh air today knocked me out."

"Ditto," agreed Henry. "I need to peel these lenses out of my eyes."

Rosie pulled him to his feet.

"We got a lot done tonight, guys." Schooner was pleased.

"Yeah, I feel good about it." Rosie looked beat. "Have we lost you, Mia?"

Mia pulled the throw pillow off of her face and smiled. "Still here... barely," she giggled.

"Don't wake me for breakfast," Henry yelled back, as he and Rosie closed the door.

Mia rolled on her side and looked at Schooner. He reached out and took a long curl in between his fingers, playing with it.

Here it was, finally the moment they were alone. "C'mere," he said, pulling her head down on his chest as he continued to play with her curls.

Snuggling her face into his chest, she pulled off her glasses, placing them out of the way. Mia looked up at Schooner and he smiled at her beautiful ombre green eyes, eliciting a blush. Still smiling, he slowly rubbed her arm up and down, reassuringly.

This little devil, so outgoing and fearless, was actually so shy when it came to guys. *Wild and innocent,* Schooner thought. He wanted her to be his. And just the thought of that shot feelings of guilt through him. He was CJ's. Or so she thought. But what he was feeling toward Mia was something he'd never felt in his life. His heart felt like it was overflowing with emotion. He wanted to be with her every moment, yearned to know everything about her. Pervasive thoughts of wanting her in his arms all the time, by his side, looking up smiling at him, wanting him, were overrunning his consciousness. He didn't know he could feel these feelings for someone else.

Bringing both arms around her, he hugged her tightly, so overcome with feelings. He kissed the top of her head and she looked up at him, a combination of yearning and fear of the unknown in her eyes. Smiling down at her, he rubbed his nose against hers, which elicited a little giggle. This made him laugh and he kissed the tip of her nose.

"I think you've figured it out already." He couldn't stop smiling at her.

"Figured out what?" she asked.

"That I'm crazy about you."

She blushed and buried her face in his chest, too shy to look into his eyes.

God, she's adorable, he thought to himself.

"Mia, look at me."

She looked up, tentatively.

Smiling at her, he ran his thumb along her high cheekbone, then pushed a mass of curls away from her face. He brought his lips close to hers. "Really, really crazy about you, Mia. I want to be with you all the time. I never want to leave you at the end of the day."

"Then don't," she whispered.

He smiled, his lips up against hers and he could feel her returning the smile. Taking her face in his hands, he kissed her lips softly. She made a soft *mmmm* sound, which he felt immediately between his legs. When he kissed her lips harder, she opened her mouth, letting his tongue slip in to find hers.

Mia's tongue met his, cautiously at first and then a little bolder in its exploration. She let her fingers rake through his thick luxurious hair, pulling him deeper into her mouth. The urgency of their kisses increased until they were both breathless.

Schooner pulled away and reached up to Mia's bed and pulled down her blanket and draped it over them. Her head was back on his chest and he kissed the top of her head again.

"Oh, Baby Girl," he sighed, "you have no idea of what you do to me."

"It's smoochal."

They both laughed.

She snuggled deeper into his chest as he wrapped his arms around her tighter, and within minutes, they both drifted off to sleep.

CHAPTER 16

It was still dark out when Schooner woke up with stiff joints the next morning from sleeping on the throw pillows on the floor. He didn't want to wake Mia, but she was draped on him and he needed to get up for tennis practice. Maneuvering into a seated position with one arm behind Mia's shoulders and the other under her knees, he struggled to his feet and carried her to her bed. Gently laying her down, he tucked the blanket around her. Sitting on the edge of the bed and looking at her, Schooner gently moved her curls from her face.

She stirred, eyes opening a little, a smile overtaking her face.

He bent down and kissed her softly, "Hey you," he whispered.

"What time is it?"

"It's really early. Go back to sleep. I've got to head over to the tennis center."

"Mmmm." She sleepily stretched her body and just watching her made him hard.

If I don't leave now... he thought. "I'll bring you coffee and a bagel."

She smiled. "My keys are on the desk."

Kissing her softly, he headed for the door. "I'll see you soon, Baby Girl."

She was already curled up and back to sleep by the time he closed the door.

With her keys in hand (her keychain had a little silver camera charm hanging from it), he exited her dorm. First he needed to go back to his dorm, change clothes and grab his racquets.

He wasn't two steps out of Mia's dorm, when two of his teammates jogged by, racquets in hand, "Slumming, Moore?"

He heard their cackles and "Freaking crazy, son of a bitch. If he doesn't want his girlfriend anymore, I'll take her off his hands."

Reality was ramming its way into his bubble and he felt both sadness and anger start to surround him. He clenched Mia's keychain tighter in his hand.

CHAPTER 17

She was in the same position, had not moved an inch, when he returned several hours later and put the coffee and bagels down on her desk.

Sitting down on the desk chair across from her bed, he watched her for a few moments. Feeling his heart start to do that brim and overflow thing it had been doing lately, he said a silent, "thank you" to her for showing him who he really was, allowing that person to just be and exist. And amazingly, she seemed to really like that person.

Silently, he pulled off his tennis shoes and socks, then stood and pulled off his pale blue Izod shirt and white tennis shorts. Standing there in blue plaid boxers, he made his way over to her bed, lifted the covers and crawled in next to her. Spooning up against her tightly, he pulled her snugly against his chest.

"Mmm," she moaned, fitting herself against him securely.

He smiled into her hair thinking, *sorry about the morning surprise.* But he wasn't sorry at all—he'd had a raging hard on for days just at the thought of her.

Pressing his hard cock against the back of her sweatpants, he was surprised to feel her grinding back against him. He wasn't even sure if she was awake.

"You're killing me." He moved her curls back and whispered in her ear. Softly, he began running his lips down her neck before burying his face in the nook.

Slipping his hand underneath her sweatshirt, he quickly discovering she wasn't wearing a bra. He cupped her right breast. The skin was so soft and he pressed it in his hand.

She moaned into her pillow and he took that as an invitation to continue.

Slinging a leg over hers, he used his long limbs to pull her tighter against his hard cock and found her nipple with his thumb and forefinger. He gently rolled her nipple, which responded immediately, and added a little more pressure, until it was a hard peak.

He continued to nuzzle into her neck and she moaned, "That feels good."

He pinched her nipple tightly, "And this?"

"Mmm, really good."

He pressed his hips into her, "And this?"

"Really, really good." She ground her ass against his hard cock.

He grazed her neck with his teeth, gently biting her smooth, flawless skin, "And this?"

"Too good."

"Too good? Should I stop?" he teased.

"Nooooo," she protested, continuing her slow grind against his cock.

"You are trouble, Baby Girl."

She chuckled, "Certainly you're not just figuring that out now."

He pinched her nipple harder and she groaned. "I knew you were trouble the minute I laid eyes on you." He paused, "serious trouble."

Mia rolled over and turned to him, initiating a kiss. This was the first kiss that she had initiated and he smiled. Running her hands over his chest, which still had some of its golden tan from summer, she picked at the smattering of golden blonde hairs.

"What are you smiling at?" he asked.

"You're so big." She marveled at his chest and arm muscles, running her hands lightly over them.

He laughed and pulled her against his hard cock, "Mmm, yes, I am."

Her eyes widened and she blushed. "Schooner," she stuttered, "I, uh, don't know if I'm doing things right."

Her innocence and honesty were just adorable. He threw his head back and laughed.

She looked hurt.

"No, no, no, Baby Girl—don't look like that. Feel that," he ground himself against her.

Her eyes opened wide.

"That means you are doing everything very right." He kissed her softly. She was so sweet.

"Oh please," she rolled her eyes, "guys get hard at anything".

"Baby Girl," he raked her curls from her face, "you can't even imagine what I want to do to you."

"But you haven't," she whispered.

Schooner sighed, "No, I haven't." Inhaling deeply, he slowly exhaled. Her eyes were intent upon him and he spent a very long moment pushing his fingers through her curls. "There's a big Pink Elephant in this room. Pink being the operative word," he muttered, picturing CJ's pink robe, pink sweaters, pink frilly blouses. "No secret that I've got a girlfriend."

Two big tears popped from Mia's green eyes and started their journey down her freckled cheeks. Schooner brushed them away with his thumb. "Don't cry."

Mia looked at Schooner with a dubious glance, silently asking, "How can I not?"

"Mia, I don't feel for her what I feel for you." He let that sink in, but she just continued looking at him sad-eyed, not breathing. She was clearly waiting for the other shoe to drop. "I have never felt for anyone what I feel for you. This is the first time in my life that I can really be me in a relationship. And you still like me. And, honestly, that amazes me."

"Still like you? Of course I like you. Schooner, you are smart, funny, sweet, giving, so much fun to be with. You are a really good person. Why would I not like you?"

He leaned forward and kissed her lips lightly. She had just listed for him what she thought his greatest attributes were and not one of them had to do with his looks.

"I have spent my life acting, Mia. I'm good at playing a lot of roles. I'm just not really good at being me."

She cocked her head to the side, taking in what he was saying, but not really understanding it.

"And then you came along. And I could be me. I have never felt so connected to another person or so happy."

She smiled and more tears sprung from her eyes.

"You are so sweet and innocent and I want to make this really special for you. You mean that much to me, Mia." He reached out, running his fingers down her cheek. "I'm going to end it with CJ. But she's not here, so I can't do that and I'm not going to call her and ruin the rest of her trip. I owe it to her to do it in person." He closed his eyes and exhaled slowly, "I want your first time to be amazing, Mia. Your first time *is* going to be amazing."

She leaned forward and kissed him.

"It would be really wrong not to end it with CJ first though," he continued, "and then when we are together there is nothing hanging over our heads."

"And you wonder why I like you, Schooner?"

He felt a huge weight lift. Soon he'd be able to tell CJ and then he would be free to become Mia's first lover. Something very possessive inside of him knew that he wanted to be her first lover and her last lover. He pulled her to him, placing her body under his. With hands on either side of her head, he kissed her deeply. He let his hard cock grind into her so that she would absolutely have no doubt just how much he wanted her.

The next day he showed up in Mia's dorm room with a large travel duffle bag filled with clothes, toiletries, and other personal items. He also brought his racquets. With the exception of the time he had to spend on the courts, Schooner would be spending the rest of January with Mia. He didn't want to be away from her for a second. Searching his memory, he could not remember a time when he had felt so happy or so free.

Schooner Moore never imagined being himself could actually be so easy.

CHAPTER 18

The days leading up to the group presentation were the happiest days Schooner could remember. Their presentation was coming along and was going to be kick-ass, they just knew it. Professor Stevens had invited the whole class back to a party at his home after the presentations were over, and they were all really looking forward to that.

Schooner and Mia poured over the tennis schedule. Two to three weekends per month he'd be playing in matches and about half of them would require travel, taking him away for a few days.

"I miss you already," Mia told him, sitting in his lap at her desk.

He pulled her face in for a kiss. "I'm going to really miss this," he tightened his arms around her waist, "when Caroline gets back and I've got to move back into my dorm".

"Ugh, it's going to suck," she pouted. "I like waking up with you."

He leaned down and bit her pouty lower lip. "Grrrrr. I love waking up with you."

"I didn't know I could feel so addicted to someone," she admitted, a surprised look fleeting past her eyes. "I didn't know I'd ever want to," she paused, thinking. "It scares me. Yet, I don't want to lose this."

Schooner pulled her head against his chest and rested his chin on top of her head. "We won't lose this. I promise."

She looked up at him, searching his eyes, silently begging him to keep his promise, he thought. And for him, in that moment, the floodgates broke.

Taking her face in his hands, he kissed her eyes, her cheeks, the tip of her nose and then softly her lips. "Baby Girl," he sighed, "I love you."

Mia's eyes widened, registering her surprise.

He was nodding his head. "I love you. I really do. And I've never said that to anyone. I don't want to freak you out, Mia, and I'm sorry if I am, but I could see us together forever. Can't you?"

Breaking into a huge smile, fat tears coursed down her cheeks and she just nodded her head. Schooner took her face in his hands and started out softly kissing her lips, intensifying as she weaved her fingers into his hair, gently pulling. He heard a growl sound rumbling from the base of his throat and picked Mia up as he stood. Her legs were wrapped around his waist as he walked to the bed, their kiss never breaking.

He laid her down on her back and got beside her, facing her on his side. He pushed her irreverent mass of dark curls from her face and kissed her softly.

He leaned down next to her ear and whispered, "I want to make you happy."

Mia put her hand to his face, brushing her thumb across his cheek and smiling into his beautiful clear blue eyes. "You make me very happy."

Schooner reached down and unbuttoned the top button on her Levi's. Sliding the zipper down, he eased his hand into her underwear, his eyes never leaving hers. The smile on his face was real, as he dipped a finger into her, eliciting a moan.

"I love how wet you are." He pulled his wet finger out and rubbed it on her clit. Her eyes grew large with surprise and he laughed, "Did I get the right spot."

All she could do was nod, vigorously.

"Feels good, huh?"

She continued to nod, her smile matching his.

He pulled her jeans and underwear down together and she kicked them off her feet. "Much better," he acknowledged. Dipping two fingers into her, he moved them to a spot on the front wall that made her gasp. His smile took on a devilish lilt—he knew he had her now.

Pulling his fingers out of her, he slipped his forefinger into his mouth, sucking it slowly. "You taste good," he ran his middle finger, which had just been inside of her, along her lips.

She reached for his hand and sucked his middle finger into her mouth, tasting herself. Licking his finger from base to tip, she then sucked it back in her mouth.

"You are killing me," he growled.

She smiled. "Good."

And he laughed. Bending down, he nipped her playfully on her hipbone and kept nipping in a line to the top of her thighs. "Now we'll see who is going to kill who." And with that he buried his face in her, taking the tip of his tongue and licking slowly from back to front. When he reached her clit, he stopped and pulled his tongue away.

"Noooooo," she moaned.

He smiled and without lifting his head said, "No? As in no more? Okay, if that's what you want."

"Motherfucker," she growled and he smiled at her "Inner New Yorker" surfacing and the shy girl getting lost somewhere in the heat of the moment.

He felt her hands in his hair, pressing his face back toward her pussy. "Are you trying to tell me you want more?" He was most amused, "I'm not quite understanding what you are telling me, Mia."

"Son of a bitch!" She yelled, laughing at the same time.

"Umm, hate to break it to you, but those are not the magic words to get you what you want."

She sprang up in one move and knocked him on his back, surprising him. "Then, I'll just take what I want."

"What is it you want, Baby Girl?" He was breathless.

"You." She stared intently into his eyes. Suddenly very serious.

"Why is that?"

"Because," she searched his face, "because I love you."

And there they were, the words he had shared with her earlier. And she was now saying them back to him. He hadn't scared her away. He smiled at his sweet little freckle-faced Baby Girl, flipped her back over onto her back and made his way down between her thighs again. "Excuse me," he said, "but I was rudely interrupted."

CHAPTER 19

The four were all jumping with nervous energy as they got ready to give the oral part of their group presentation. They had a thirty-page supporting document that would also be a part of determining their grade, but the presentation was what would kick it off, and if they could nail it, they would be halfway home.

The "baby" of the group was taking the lead, because she was clearly the most fearless. She was also a great communicator, especially on subjects about which she was passionate. Schooner ran his hands up and down her arms as she took deep breaths.

"You okay?" he asked.

"Yeah, yeah. I'll be fine once I'm up there. This is the hardest part. It's like being a horse at the gate. Just let me run and I'm fine."

And that she was. They got up in front of the lecture hall and Mia kicked it off. Slides, music, analysis—they had it all. It flowed, it was logical, it was passionate, it was interesting and at points, even pushed the envelope.

Schooner watched Professor Stevens' composed face as they presented, thinking *I bet he's a great poker player*. But even great poker players have their tell and his was at the corners of his eyes. His pride in watching Mia was evident. She was clearly what made teaching at the collegiate level satisfying for him. Schooner was so proud of her and a tinge jealous at the same time of another man being entranced by her, even if it was just intellectually. They each took turns presenting and ended with a breathtaking and emotional slideshow to music portraying the dichotomy of the promise and the betrayal.

The class cheered when they finished and Professor Stevens joined the four at the front of the lecture hall, casually slinging an arm around Mia's shoulder.

"Wow!" he exclaimed. "I am actually speechless. What we all just witnessed was a master class in American Popular Culture. I am really proud of all of you. You took on some of the voices that others would have overlooked." He looked directly at Schooner, "Phil Ochs—what a joy to see him getting his due. Well done."

Schooner beamed.

"Okay, everyone, let's take a fifteen-minute break while the next group sets up."

The four gathered their materials and headed out into the hall for a group hug and high fives. It was an amazing culmination of a month long mission. Friendship, love, learning, success, growth—the four were flying over the moon.

Together they walked to the Stevens' house that evening. Rick's wife, Wendy, a former student fifteen years prior, was welcoming and clearly up to date on all that had happened throughout Interim. She was as excited for the groups as the participants were, already well-versed on the focus of each of the presentations.

Schooner stood behind Mia, his arms over her shoulders, as she leaned against him. They were "out" in public as a couple and he loved how it felt. He just wanted to say to everyone there, "You saw her today. That is *my* Baby Girl!"

Finding himself alone talking to Wendy, Schooner was surprised and impressed to find out she knew that he had made first string on the tennis team—the only freshman to do so. She clearly followed all of the university's sports teams and regaled him with stories of the team's past and some of his coach's minor indiscretions. Rosie joined them and Wendy had them laughing with stories of what the school had been like when she was a student.

Mia was engaged in a serious conversation with Rick, and Schooner consciously had to tell himself to chill out, that there was no reason to be jealous. Not used feeling jealous of other men, it was sitting oddly in his gut.

Wendy noticed Schooner's gaze. "Rick was so glad when she signed up for his Interim seminar," she began. "He came home after class one day last semester and said, 'I've got one that is really thinking" and so I asked him where she was from, figuring it couldn't be California," she laughed. "And Rick said, by the sound of her accent, I think she's a New Yorker. He wants her to TA for him next year. It's going to be a stretch getting approval on a sophomore—but he thinks if she's interested, he can get it done."

Schooner looked over at them and smiled. He was so damn proud of her.

"So, you think she'll be interested?" Wendy asked, hoping to get advance scoop.

"Well, I can't answer for her, but..." he paused, for effect, "I'd be really shocked if she wasn't interested." Wendy looked satisfied.

"So, Phil Ochs?" she said to him. "That's really freaking impressive. Rick's been teaching this seminar for five Interims and you are the first person to cover Phil Ochs. We've been waiting for someone to do it. He called me right after class today to tell me."

Schooner was beaming.

She looked at him slyly out of the corner of her eye, "So at the beginning of the month, Rick and I made bets on how many Springsteen songs Mia would incorporate over the month into her papers and the final project." Schooner nearly spit his beer on the floor, he started to laugh so hard. Wendy had a hand on his arm, steadying herself while she laughed, heartily. Mia looked over toward them with an inquisitive look on her face. He winked at her, turned back to Wendy and continued their laughing.

"That is freaking hysterical. You'll have to let me know who wins." He looked at his sweet Baby Girl talking to her prof, who clearly saw how special she was, and thought how much richer his college experience had become now that she was a part of it.

CHAPTER 20

They were still riding their high when they got back to Mia's dorm room. Entering the room was the first dampening of their moods.

Schooner's stuff was all over and he knew he was going to have to pack it all up and move back to his dorm. He didn't want to go. He didn't want to leave Mia's room. He didn't want to leave Mia's bed. He didn't want to leave Mia. He didn't want to leave Rosalie down the hall and Henry downstairs. He didn't want to leave the other people in the dorm who had been so accepting of him over the past few weeks. People who were so different than the people he typically knew. People who didn't fit in with the campus norm—and didn't try to fit in. They pursued what made them happy. They didn't fit in, so they expanded out. He had come to love and respect that about them and the thought of going back to an all-male jock dorm made him feel lonely and alone. *I am going to miss the quirky camaraderie of the "freak" dorm,* he thought. He had never felt more at home.

Schooner started to shove things into his duffle bag, while Mia sat cross-legged on her bed, watching him with a perplexed look on her face.

"Are you staying tonight?" she asked, tentatively.

"Do you want me to?"

Mia looked at Schooner as if he had two heads. "Are you kidding? Of course, I want you to stay. It's my last night without a roommate. I can't believe you are thinking about leaving."

The air in the room was starting to become tense.

Schooner stood in the middle of the room, belongings in hand, but didn't speak. He could see the sadness in Mia's eyes and he thought fear, also. Tomorrow they would all be back. Tomorrow, this idyllic little bubble they'd just spent the month in would cease to exist.

Cease to exist. The thought made his stomach start to ache and he felt a burning at the back of his throat.

Mia smiled at him and jumped off the bed. "Hey, I have something for you."

"You do?" He was glad she had saved the moment.

"Mmm-hmm." She nodded her head and her devil smile was back. "Sit," she ordered pointing to her bed.

He sat down.

From her desk, Mia pulled out a large manila envelope, then went and sat down next to Schooner on the bed. "This is for you." She beamed, her little freckled nose wrinkling.

"Should I open it?" He was intrigued.

She nodded, smile still bright on her face as he opened the envelope. He slid out a couple of thin pieces of cardboard that were taped together. Setting the envelope aside on the bed, he began to open the tape. She watched him intently, both smiling and biting her lower lip.

He smiled back at her, a real smile. What had she done for him?

Inside the cardboard was a stack of B&W prints. He looked up at her and smiled, "When did you do this? We're together all the time."

Smiling at him, "I've been logging in some darkroom time when you are on the courts."

He looked back at the stack. The first photo was of the falls. The landscape was perfect for a B&W rendition with white clouds in stark contrast with what appeared to be an almost black sky. "How did you do that?" he asked.

"Red filter." She seemed proud.

He went to the next photo in the stack. It was a picture of him and Henry pretending to throw Rosie off the edge of the mountain. They both laughed looking at it and he bent over to give Mia a soft kiss. She certainly knew how to make him feel better when he was starting to tank.

The third photo in the stack was of their lewd snowman with the giant erection. In this shot, he and Henry each had a hand on the snowman's penis and Rosie was kneeling before the snowman. They broke into hysterics seeing the picture.

"Oh my God, that is too good," Schooner hooted. "Holy crap."

Wiping tears from their eyes, they laughed at the funny memory, so perfectly (and lewdly) captured for all posterity.

Schooner moved to the next photo and wondered if his gasp was audible. Mia had shot a photo of him in a moment when he was not aware the camera was on him. It was an introspective photo as he was reveling in the pristine beauty of nature. He thought that he'd never seen such a perfect photo of himself. It was really him. "Would you mind if I gave this to my mother? I would really like her to have this."

Mia's smile was brilliant. "I love that idea." She clapped her hands.

There was one photo left and when he lifted the portrait off of it, he felt the stab in his chest. It was a photo Mia had shot of their feet. They were facing each other, his hands were on Mia's shoulders as she pointed the camera down and shot the photo of their sneaker clad feet, toes touching each other. Mia had hand painted the B&W photo, the bottom of her blue jeans, her red and white Converse sneakers, his white sneakers with blue laces and tennis socks with a navy blue border at the ankle.

It was the only picture of Schooner and Mia together that existed.

He stared at the last photo for a while—it wasn't lost on him that this photo was it, the only thing documenting their relationship. Mia had taken a simple B&W photo, painstakingly hand colored it, and brought to life their sweet, quirky love.

Schooner picked up the envelope and photos and put them on the desk so that they would not get ruined. Sitting back down on the bed at Mia's side, he took her face in his hands and kissed her roughly. Overcome by a myriad of emotions, her unexpected gift had been so personal that it touched him very deeply. He didn't think there was another soul on Earth who got him quite the way she did.

Mia reached over and started to unbutton his white Ralph Lauren shirt. He just watched her, smiling. A month ago she would have been way too shy to do this to him. When she had it unbuttoned, she pushed it off his shoulders and got up on her knees on the bed and leaned forward, gently kissing his shoulders and working her way to his neck, where she let her teeth graze his skin.

"Oh Baby Girl, the things I want to do to you."

"Can't wait," she whispered in his ear.

He woke her in the morning before he left for the tennis center. His duffle bag was packed and he held the oversized envelope of photos and his racquets. He was wearing the black knit cap she had given him. It was pulled down almost to his eyes.

Sitting on the edge of the bed, he brushed her curls from her face and looked at her intently. Not saying a word, he just leaned forward and placed a soft kiss on her lips.

Had he looked closer in the darkened room, he would've seen the two plump tears that had escaped the outer corners of her eyes and rolled into the curls he had just brushed off of her face.

But he was already out the door.

CHAPTER 21

He had put it off all day by spending time hanging with Beau, hearing all about his month abroad and the hot Ecuatoriana babes (not that he got any). He'd even spent an extra hour on the courts hitting balls. From the Psych class he had taken first semester, Schooner knew that this was classic "Escape-Avoidance" behavior. With something really unpleasant to do, and wanting to escape confrontation at all costs, he was working himself up to do it, but in the meantime, found every way he could to avoid it.

He began feeling bad for CJ, not wanting to embarrass her or make her feel like she'd been cheated on while she was away. But that is exactly what happened. He fell in love with someone else, and while technically he and Mia had not had sex (he was amazed at his own self-control and that Mia was still a virgin), they were lovers in every other sense of the word.

Schooner wondered how much CJ might have heard already about what his Interim had been like. Her roommate, her dorm mates had all seen him with Mia, Rosalie and Henry every day for a month, so this might not come as a huge shock to her. He'd missed every one of her phone calls, but one, and was thankful for the poor connection.

"Why does this all have to be so difficult?" he asked himself, "Why can't I just be with the girl I love?" Schooner's deep seated fear of disappointing people was raging in full throttle. He just wanted to get it over with and get back to Mia. Wearing the black knit cap pulled almost down to his eyes, he felt like he was taking a little piece of Mia with him that would give him strength.

Walking up the stone steps of the old dorm building, he entered the lobby, ignoring everyone who was sitting on the couches. Heading directly to the staircase, he bounded up two at a time. *Let's get this over with*, he thought.

Rapping on her door with his knuckles, he heard her turning the knob. CJ stood before him, looking perfect, wearing her pink satin robe. Before he could even utter a greeting, CJ had flung herself against him (her barely tied robe opening), arms around his neck, pulling him down to her lips. He stumbled through the threshold, not wanting this scene to play out in the hallway.

When she peeled herself off of him, she was leading him by his hand toward her bed which was covered with beautifully wrapped gifts and gift bags from Europe's finest shops. Although European Capitals had been a course offered through the Political Science Department, it appeared CJ had taken it through the Economics Department, supporting the economies of several European nations.

CJ went into monologue mode and Schooner feared that she knew he was coming to end it with her and was not going to let him speak. He wondered if she was operating under the premise, if he can't speak, he can't break up with me.

"I have missed you so much. Everywhere we went all I could think about was sharing the experience with you. Being away from you made me realize how much I love you and never want to be apart from you ever again. Wait until you see all the presents I bought you, you are just going to love the leather racquet covers I got for you in Italy and the silk boxers from France and the blue silk bow tie from England that matches your eyes perfectly ..." and she went on and on, not coming up for air.

"CJ," his voice came out harsher than intended, but he had to get her attention and he had to get her to stop talking, "we need to talk."

"Oh baby, we will." She got up off the bed and stood before him allowing her baby pink satin robe to puddle at her ankles.

"CJ, I'm serious." He stood up, not wanting to be on her bed.

"Schooner, I am too." One hand was on his crotch, rubbing his cock through his jeans. The other hand was unbuttoning and unzipping his jeans. She squeezed his cock. Squeezed it in a way he had taught her how to, because it immediately got him rock hard.

"CJ, please stop." He wasn't quite sure what to do. If she were a guy, he would have just shoved her away from him. But she wasn't a guy, and Schooner would never physically assault a female.

"Don't you like the gifts I bought you, baby?" Her hands were inside his pants and he was beginning to panic.

"We can't..." he sputtered, not finishing the sentence because in a heartbeat she had dropped to her knees and deep-throated him.

"CJ, no..." and he put his hands on her head to push her away. She reached around and grabbed him by the ass and pressed him deeper into her mouth. CJ was using the moves he had taught her against him.

He had never in his life not wanted to be somewhere more than he did not want to be in her room with his cock rammed down her throat. And as if a cruel joke of the universe, the guy who could control himself and make the pleasure last until he was ready, came in about 15 seconds flat. He was mortified and distraught that he had just come in her mouth, that he hadn't been able to get away from her in time.

CJ pulled away smiling, a dribble of Schooner's cum at the corner of her pink lips. She slowly cleaned it with a lick from the tip of her tongue.

"By how quickly you came, it's clear that you missed me, too," she purred.

Schooner didn't know how to decipher the onslaught of emotions flooding in and drowning him. Anger (at her or himself?), disgust (definitely at himself), disappointment (overwhelmingly at himself), confusion (how the hell did that just happen) and death of a dream.

The walls were closing in and sound was muffled, Schooner felt like he was tumbling down the rabbit hole. He would learn, much later in life, that this was a panic attack.

CJ picked up her robe and eased back into it, letting it hang open.

He looked at her blankly and said, "I've got to go." Practically running from the room. He could not escape fast enough.

As he closed the door, he heard her scream after him, "I hate that hat."

He made it to the stairwell and leaned his head against the cold stone wall. It felt good against his face. Taking a few deep breaths, he knew he had to get out of there fast as he rushed through the lobby, head down, ignoring the multiple greetings from all the girls who knew him as "CJ's boyfriend."

He made it outside, the night air a welcome caress to his hot cheeks, as he descended the stone stairs, less than a mere ten minutes after having ascended them.

He started to walk. There was no way he could go to Mia's dorm. Just the thought of his own dorm room, now with Beau in there, brought on an immediate feeling of claustrophobia. "Where to? Where to? I need to think," he muttered aloud.

He walked over to the track and began to run.

What the fuck did I just let happen? I didn't break up with her. She fucking sucked my cock and I freaking came in her mouth. What do I tell Mia? She grabbed me and before I knew it my cock was in her mouth and I didn't want to come, but I did—really fucking fast. I love you, Baby Girl, and I was just in someone else's mouth, but I didn't fuck her (great consolation).

Holy crap, I can't go to Mia's room now. How can I tell her the truth? And if I did, she would probably throw me out. She's going to hate me. Fuck, I hate me. Could I disappoint more people? Could I be a bigger fucking disappointment? How the hell did I fuck this up so royally? What the fuck am

I going to do? How do I make this better? How do I fix this? Fuck. Fuck. Fuck.

Over an hour later, Schooner stepped off the track. He had no answers. He couldn't go to Mia tonight and tell her what had happened. He couldn't bear to see the hurt, the disappointment. But if he no showed her tonight, she'd think they were over, that he'd gone back to CJ. And although they probably were over, because of what he had let happen, he couldn't even consider being back with CJ.

Finally, he went back to his dorm, where thankfully a jetlagged Beau was crashed out. Schooner went to his desk and took the oversized envelope out of the drawer. He pulled out the picture Mia had shot of their feet and just stared at it.

"I am so sorry, Baby Girl," he whispered to the picture. "I love you so much and I know I don't deserve you. I don't know how to fix this." He slid the picture back into its envelope and placed it back in the desk drawer.

Lying in bed, staring at the darkened ceiling for what felt like hours, Schooner knew that he had just ruined everything. He ached, realizing the pain it was going to cause Mia. The pain was overwhelming, knowing that five minutes of his life had robbed him of everything he ever wanted and dreamed of. Lying on top of his blankets, fully clothed, he pulled his black cap over his eyes, and at that moment, felt close to the character in Springsteen's *The River* whose loss of dreams felt like lies. How ironic, he thought as he finally drifted off into an uneasy sleep, even he was now thinking about Springsteen songs and he'd never know if Rick or Wendy won the bet.

CHAPTER 22

Schooner went into a deep funk, avoiding everyone and everything, with the exception of the tennis courts. He'd never experienced anything like it before. Getting out of bed every day took everything he had, his concentration was shit, he had to force food down his throat to keep his strength up to make it through tennis practice.

Every night after he finished his reading and homework assignments, he went to the track and ran. Running was the only time he could get into his head and process his misery. It helped ease the pain which felt like it was oozing out of him in waves.

His weight was dropping and his boyish face becoming more angular. With his black cap (a new permanent feature, except on the courts where it was against regulations) pulled down to his eyes, it became a part of his dark, haunted look. Now, instead of looking like a gorgeous All-American boy, he had the look of a handsome bad boy model.

Knowing Mia's class schedule, Schooner made sure to avoid all the routes he knew she would be on. He stayed away from the dining hall when he thought that either she or CJ might be there. When he wasn't in class, he was on the courts or in his room studying.

His first travel weekend came and he was glad to get off campus and away from everything that added to his misery and, unfortunately, there was very little that did not exacerbate it—he couldn't look anywhere on campus without something reminding him of their time together. He loathed himself for destroying the best thing he'd ever had and for hurting the only girl he'd ever loved.

On Valentine's Day, CJ showed up at his dorm room. Beau happily let her in, she flirted with him a little and then he quickly cleared the room to give Schooner and CJ some privacy.

She handed Schooner a package wrapped in red.

"I don't have anything for you," he said.

She nodded and said, "Please open it."

He carefully tore the paper from package and opened the box. Inside was a black photo frame holding an 8 x 10 of Schooner and CJ in their matching red sweaters on the stairs in her parent's home.

Can this get any worse? he thought, but smiled politely and thanked her. He even told her she looked very beautiful in the photo.

"Schooner," she began, "I'm offering an olive branch here and I hope you'll take it. I want you to know that I forgive you."

"You forgive me?" he tried to keep his tone even, but was thinking *what the hell are you talking about?*

"Yes, Schooner," she said through very tight teeth. "I forgive you." She paused, "This is a small school. Not a lot happens that people don't find out about."

He just looked at her. Feeling positively dead inside, he thought if he'd had a pair of sunglasses sitting on his desk, he would've slipped them on, even though it was nighttime and he was indoors.

When he didn't answer, she continued. "I want to put Interim behind us. I want you back, Schooner."

"Why?" he asked, totally stupefied.

"Because I love you."

Sighing, he sat down on his bed. "CJ, you love the idea of me. You do not love me, because frankly, you have no clue who I am."

"How can you even say that?" she protested, her beautiful alabaster skin starting to turn red, as the tension increased.

"Because it's true. You love that we look great together, and I'm not going to lie to you, that was part of the initial attraction for me, too. We look like we belong together. But I'm not me around you, CJ. I'm someone you want me to be. And I don't want to be that person anymore."

She sat down on his bed next to him and took his hands in hers. "Please don't give up on us. I know I can make you happy."

He was shaking his head no. Only one person in the world could make him happy and he'd never have the chance to show her just how happy she made him. He didn't deserve her.

"I can. I can," she insisted. "Please let me."

And so he let her. This time he didn't come so quickly (another tragic joke from the universe, he thought, wryly) and decided that maybe this was what he deserved.

After she left that night, Schooner picked up the picture frame and looked at the toothpaste commercial photograph inside the frame. Turning the frame over, he opened it up and slipped out the picture of him and CJ. Opening the desk drawer, he pulled out the oversized envelope and extracted the feet picture, inserted it into the frame and closed the back. Turning the frame over, he studied the hand painted B&W photo.

Setting the frame down on the desk next to his bed, he faced the feet image so that he could view it.

"I am so sorry, Mia. I am so sorry."

It was a few days later, when he was walking on The Quad, that Mia and Rosie were walking toward him. It was the first time he had seen her since he'd left her in her bed that last morning. He felt his heart stop at just the sight of her. As they approached, he said, "Hi," searching her face for something, anything. She stuck her chin up in the air and did not make eye contact with him. As he passed them, he heard Rosie say, "You should get your fucking hat back from him." Schooner turned around and Rosie was turned around sneering at him. Mia never turned around.

He closed his eyes and exhaled, the force squeezing his heart not letting up. Consciously, he breathed in deeply through his nose and blew it out slowly through his mouth until the pain in his chest subsided. Telepathically, he tried to send her a message, "I'm wearing your hat, Baby Girl—doesn't that tell you something?"

The next two times he passed them on The Quad, the exact same thing happened. He said, "Hi" to them and Mia's chin went up in the air. The first time Rosie muttered, "Douche" and the second time he thought he heard her say, "God, he really looks gaunt."

He looked in the mirror that afternoon, doing an examination like he had not done in a long time and realized Rosie was right. The tennis, the running, the appetite loss—he did look gaunt. He thought, "I look like shit."

And for the first time in his life, he felt his inner vision matched his outer visage.

A week later, he saw them again walking toward him on The Quad. Maybe someday I'll get a hello back, he hoped. As they approached, he said, "Hi." There was still no verbal response, but Mia looked at him for the first time. Her eyes seemed flat and he hoped his eyes said to her, "I am so, so sorry, Baby Girl."

It was an evening in early March when he saw Mia, Rosie and Henry in the dining hall for the first time and he ached to go sit with his old friends. He knew that wasn't possible and went and sat with his dorm mates at the next table. Sitting on the bench facing the opposite direction of Mia, so that he could look at her, all he wanted was to steal a few glances, even though every one shot a stabbing pain through his chest.

Schooner pretended to listen to the guys and made a few attempts to laugh at some of their jokes. Catching her looking at him, he tried to smile at her, but a cold veil dropped back down over her face and she looked away. He knew he had made it worse by never going to talk to her. Hours had stretched into days, which slowly became weeks, and now over a month had gone by. It was too late to try and rectify the damage.

Over a glass of milk, he was willing her, Mia look at me, just look at me and she did. He put the glass of milk down and was just beginning to mouth to her, "I ....." when he saw her eyes, first questioning, and then widening, as CJ and her roommate sat down next to him, and momentarily blocked his view, before he finished what he was trying to say to Mia. He felt the panic rise. He didn't finish telling her. She saw CJ sit down next to him. Shit. Shit. Shit.

CJ was talking to him, but he couldn't hear her, he was trying to look past her to make eye contact with Mia again, but her seat was empty. Looking toward the exit, he was just in time to see her mane of curls pass through the door. His first thought was, "I need to stop her."

CJ put a hand on his forearm, dragging him back into reality. He looked at her, not focused and she asked sweetly, "Will you please pass the salt?"

He passed it to her and then sat silently while she chatted with her roommate.

I cannot catch a break, he thought.

CHAPTER 23

Schooner was passing by the Coach's office at the end of practice when he heard the coach call to him.

"How are you doing, Schooner?" he asked.

"Great, Coach. I think having the indoor tennis center and extra practice time has made a huge difference in my game. I feel good."

Coach's glance was intense. "I'm concerned about you, son. Why don't you have a seat."

Oh shit, thought Schooner. *This is not just a casual conversation.*

"Sir?"

"The intensity you have brought to the court these last few months, well—it can be good and bad. The good is, we've been clocking your serves at 144 MPH and you're only a freshman. If I have you on the team for a few more years, we'll be kicking everyone in the division's butts and you'll be at the top of the NCAA rankings. But after watching you these last few weeks, I'm not so sure this intensity is borne out of a good thing. You are angry, Schooner."

Schooner sat silently for a moment and then took a deep breath. "Yes, Coach. I am angry."

"Who or what has made you so very angry?" pressed the coach.

Schooner looked Coach directly in the eyes. "I'm mad at myself, sir."

Coach nodded and didn't say anything for a while. "Son, I see you as leading this team. I think with another year under your belt, you will make a fine team captain."

Schooner was shocked by the coach's statement and sure that the surprise was registering all over his face. "Wow. Thank you, sir. That is a tremendous compliment. I really appreciate your faith in me."

"I'd like to see you have that same faith in yourself, son. I don't know what the circumstances are that you are continuing to punish yourself for, but what I see is a young man filled with remorse. Whatever it is, you need to let it go. You can't keep up this penance, Schooner. It's not healthy and you need to work on getting healthy."

It was a few moments before Schooner looked up at the coach. "I didn't realize it was that obvious."

"You need to look in a mirror more often, son. Your weight loss has been pretty dramatic and you look haunted."

"I've been running." Schooner offered.

The coach made a "Hmm" sound. "You certainly have been running. It's time to stop. You need to figure out a healthier way to work through your issues."

Schooner sat silently for a few moments, then looked Coach in the eyes. "Thank you. I appreciate this talk."

Coach nodded. He was done talking.

Schooner left his office. The talk had been like a splash of cold water on Schooner's face. It was time to take control again. He'd been spiraling downward for so long, it was hard to figure out how to put the brakes on, but the coach was right and he needed to figure out how to pull himself out of this.

Some habits die hard, he mused, for the only thing he really wanted to do that day was to tell Mia that the coach felt he could be the team captain. Team captain of one of the top ranked tennis collegiate programs in the country.

He still wanted her to be proud of him.

CHAPTER 24

CJ showed up at Schooner's room with another package in hand. "What's this?" he asked.

"It's part one," she responded. The box was from Hugo Boss. "I bought this for you in London."

Inside was a blue raw silk bow tie. "It's really nice," he looked up at her, questioningly.

"Well, when I was in Hugo Boss, I bought something for myself, too," she smiled and shrugged.

"I'm thinking there's a dress in this color, somewhere in this story."

CJ laughed, "You know me well." She then took a deep breath. "Will you take me to the Spring Fling?"

The Spring Fling was the annual spring formal dance and the tradition was that the girls invited the guys and then took them to dinner before the dance. The dance was usually held in the ballroom of a hotel facility and this year's was at The Huntington Sheraton in Pasadena.

CJ immediately picked up on Schooner's hesitation and forged right on. "I have not asked much of you and this really means a lot to me, Schooner." CJ had made a ritual of showing up at Schooner's room several times a week. Sexual activity was limited to CJ blowing Schooner. He knew that her hope was if she waited it out, all would go back to *normal*.

"Okay, sure."

"Really!" she squealed and threw her arms around his neck, planting kisses all over his face. "We are going to have the best time."

"Sounds great," he offered, trying to sound a little more enthusiastic. He had taken the coach's talk to heart and knew it was time to start living again. His misery had been spiraling down for so long that he knew taking little steps, like saying yes to CJ for this dance she wanted to go to, would help stop the descending momentum.

Baby steps, he thought, but at the same time wondered if Mia was going to be there. Maybe she'd take Henry or maybe there was someone special in one of her classes this semester. He didn't know. He didn't know anything about her world anymore.

He came up with a fantasy about the Spring Fling. He would see Mia there, come up behind her and her date as they danced, and cut in. Mia would be in his arms before she had the time to protest and somehow he would find the words to make it all right. She'd see how much he loved her. And this time, he would not let her go.

He knew chances were, Miss I'm-Not-Into-the-Group-Kumbayah-Thing, would probably not be there... but if she was. There would be at least one dance in his arms. He would not take no for an answer.

CHAPTER 25

The Huntington Sheraton had been built just after the turn of the century and was one of the architectural gems of Pasadena. The hotel harkened back to a time past of refinement and luxury. CJ, her roommate and another friend had rented a limo to take them all to the hotel, where they had arranged dinner for the guys before the dance.

CJ looked breathtaking that evening in her Hugo Boss dress of sky blue raw silk that matched Schooner's eyes. Her long blonde hair was styled in an elaborate updo with soft tendrils falling around her face. In his black suit with the matching bow tie that CJ had given him, Schooner and CJ were red carpet worthy. A photographer could have come along and shot a Vogue spread of them that evening.

CJ tucked her hand inside of Schooner's in the limo and smiled at him. Giving her hand a squeeze, he did not pull away. He had vowed he would make the best of the evening and be on his best behavior, which meant no sulking.

There were photographers set up at the entrance to the hotel, capturing photos for the arriving couples that would later be available for purchase. Schooner and CJ posed in the grand entranceway and Schooner, no stranger to the camera, was able to give CJ the photo he knew she so very much wanted.

Heads turned as Schooner and CJ walked through the lobby of the hotel. And it wasn't just a few people—every head turned. People staying at the hotel assumed they were some young Hollywood stars. A leading man and his beautiful starlet lady. They had people that they did not know literally walk up to them to tell them how beautiful they looked. CJ was in her glory. Schooner was mildly distracted, but mostly embarrassed. And it dawned on him, he really had changed. Somewhere along the way, the superficial California boy had been left behind.

The girls had arranged for dinner to be set-up in a small wine cellar, affording them a lot of privacy, without a million sets of eyes watching as they ate. Dining with them was one of his dorm mates, Dane. Schooner knew Dane only casually, and was pleasantly surprised when Dane turned out to be an amusing conversationalist, keeping the dinner talk going and regaling them all with stories of growing up abroad. As a State Department brat, he'd lived throughout Southeast Asia from the time he was six, until he came back to the states for college. Fluent in multiple languages, his plans were to join the Foreign Service upon graduation.

From dinner they headed upstairs to the Georgian Ballroom, one of two ballrooms retained throughout many remodelings of the grand hotel. An arched ceiling, dotted with crystal chandeliers and intricate gilt work, canopied the ballroom and transported its occupants more to a Baroque era than a Georgian one, Schooner thought.

The ballroom was crowded, dark and smoky. Tables were set up along the perimeter of the room with the dance floor located center. It was very loud and impossible to hear what anyone was saying. Schooner found himself smiling and nodding at people, not having a clue as to what they were saying to him. Nod every so often and laugh at intervals and you'll be good, he decided.

He danced much of the evening with CJ, her roommate and several of her friends, hung out with some of his tennis teammates and dorm mates and spent a lot of time people watching. CJ was truly in her glory and he could envision her in the future throwing lavish events and holding court—clearly the most beautiful woman in the room.

The evening was not nearly as painful as he had anticipated. It was actually good to be amongst the living again, even though his fantasy dance with Mia did not come to pass. Although he'd hoped, he hadn't really expected her to be there.

As they were descending the hotel steps toward their limo, CJ noted, "Wasn't so bad, was it?"

"I had a really good time tonight. Thank you." And he meant it.

The limo dropped them off and he walked her up to her room, secretly thrilled that her roommate was right there. He stayed in the hall to say goodnight to her.

She put her hands on both of his arms and looked up at him. "Tonight meant a lot to me, Schooner."

He smiled at her, "I know."

"Thank you," she mouthed the words. Then asked, "Can you promise me something?"

"Depends."

"Promise me you'll try."

"CJ, why do you want to settle for this?"

She looked at him wide-eyed, "Because I know how good we can be together. Please try," she pleaded, "please."

"I'm not trying to be difficult, CJ, but neither of us should have to be trying. It should just be natural. This shouldn't be work."

A hurt look eclipsed her beautiful face, "I'm work?"

"I didn't mean it that way. Look, I had a great time tonight. I really did. Thank you for asking me. Thank you for a great dinner. And thank you for this." He fingered the beautiful, classic silk bow tie which was now hanging untied around his collar.

"Can we call tonight a start?" she asked.

He smiled and nodded his head, "I can live with that."

"Okay, me too." She smiled.

He gave her a hug and a quick kiss on the lips. "You looked beautiful tonight." And with that, he was off down the hall, bounding down the steps of the dorm and turned onto the sidewalk of The Quad.

Hands in his suit pockets and head down, he started toward his dorm. He was glad he'd made it through the night, and fairly painlessly, until the end, and he wondered if tonight was actually one step forward and two steps back. As much as he'd had to push himself, he realized the socializing was good for him and that he'd actually enjoyed it, after his months of self-imposed exile. It was time to rejoin the world. Tonight was a start at trying to have a life again—but was it also a step backwards, he wondered, thinking about his conversation with CJ. Was it a start or merely a restart?

Schooner knew he needed to learn from his mistakes and that falling back into old patterns would be anything but a new start. He also realized that he was no longer the same person he had been when school first started in the fall. And now, he so desperately wanted to be happy again. It was as that thought crossed his consciousness that he saw her walking up ahead on the empty quad. The telltale mane of dark curls bouncing behind her.

"Mia," he yelled. He hadn't planned to. It was a gut reaction, as was taking off in a fast jog to catch up to her. "Mia. Mia stop."

She kept walking, quickening her pace (which was a moot point based on the difference in their leg lengths).

"Mia." Schooner caught up to her and was walking beside her. "Mia, talk to me,"

She remained silent, walking as fast as she could, head down.

"C'mon Mia," he pleaded.

"Schooner. Leave. Me. Alone."

"Sorry, but you are not getting that lucky tonight." He was now a foot in front of her walking backwards and talking to the top of her head, because she wouldn't look up at him. "Mia, I know I fucked up. I fucked up because I didn't come and talk to you. What you assumed happened, didn't happen. Actually, it's never happened. But something did happen and I felt so awful and I just didn't know how to come to you because I thought you'd just tell me to go fuck myself and I didn't know what to do and clearly doing nothing was the worst thing I could've done. I am so, so sorry, Mia."

"Schooner, go fuck yourself. Okay, you happy now? Self-fulfilling prophecy. Now leave me the fuck alone," her voice was rising dangerously loud and high.

He stopped walking backwards and she either had to stop or bump into him. She stopped and he immediately put his hands on her shoulders.

Mia stepped back to get away from him, recoiling from his touch, which landed like a sharp blow to Schooner's gut. She had actually cringed when he touched her and the devastation rushed over him in a wave, dragging him under. As she stepped back to avoid his touch, the light from the streetlamp captured her in its glow. It took Schooner a moment to process that something did not look quite right. Mia's shirt was ripped open, exposing part of her right breast and it looked like there was blood on her shirt.

"Oh my God, Mia, what happened to you? Who did this to you?" Alarms were going off inside of him like a string of Roman candles on July 4th.

She tried to sidestep him. "Schooner, get the fuck out of my way. *Now.*"

"Not a chance." He blocked her with his body. "Mia, look at me."

"Schooner, please let me go," her voice cracked.

He felt his own throat close up. The irony of those words were not lost on him.

Reaching out, he gently lifted her chin so that he could see her face. She winced and he realized that he was hurting her. He felt the bile rising in his throat as the streetlamp revealed her bruised jaw and bloody lip—which from the looks of it, was still bleeding, as fresh, wet blood glistened in the light, over the already caked, dried blood.

Enveloping her in his arms, crushing her against him, she immediately stiffened like a steel rod.

"Oh my God, Baby Girl."

"You have *no* right to call me that," she hissed and it felt as if her body were shrinking in his arms, as if she were imploding upon herself, trying to become smaller and smaller, so that she could actually disconnect totally from his touch, and disappear.

In that moment, he was glad she was as stiff as steel, because his knees were starting to buckle and although she didn't realize it, she was holding him up. He could feel the pain and fear radiating off of her and intuitively he knew, beyond a shadow of a doubt, that this was not just a mugging.

His Baby Girl had been raped.

CHAPTER 26

Schooner stood there with his arms around Mia, swaying back and forth, for what seemed to be a long while, but he guessed that maybe it was only a few short moments. She let him hold her. And he needed to hold her. He needed to give her his strength, his protection and he tried so hard to transfer that energy to her by just holding her tight.

I'm going to kill the motherfucker who did this to her. Kill with my fucking bare hands. Calm down, need to protect, don't scare her, keep a level head, I'm going to kill whoever did this, we need to go to the police, I need to get her to the ER, I should've been with her tonight. His thoughts were all over the place, as he fought to streamline them into a coherent plan of action. He needed to take care of her and he needed to do it now. He needed to take control. She needed him to think for them both.

He held her and kissed the top of her head, gently. "Mia, we need to go to the police."

She panicked and began to thrash in his arms. "No. I can't go to the police. I'll get sent home. They'll make me go home." She was in full panic mode, her eyes wide with fear.

"Okay. Okay. Okay." He held her tight, still rocking back and forth, gently stroking her hair in an attempt to calm her, or maybe to calm himself—he wasn't really sure. "No police," he understood what she was thinking.

Mia was a minor. Her parents would come and pull her out of college. But it made him sick to think this animal would be out there and get away with this. This scum could do this to someone else. He consciously pushed his rising anger away. We'll deal with that later, he thought. *Take care of Mia now.*

He slipped out of his suit jacket and draped it over her. Putting his arm around her shoulders, he turned her around and started walking her toward the entrance of campus. She went along willingly. Sobs racking her body every few minutes.

"Shhh, it's going to be okay, Baby Girl." But he wasn't really sure that it would ever be okay again.

They walked for several blocks in silence before she seemed to realize that they were no longer on campus. "Where are we going?" she asked, through her tears.

"To the ER," he said softly. Then added, "Is that okay?"

She nodded and he pulled her closer into him and kissed the top of her head. *I am never going to let her out of my sight again,* he thought. *Ever.*

As they walked through the silent streets of the city, he felt closer to the animal kingdom than he'd ever felt before (he would feel this way a few more times in his life, when each of his children were born). Animals protect and kill. He got it.

There was so much he wanted to say to her, to promise her. But it all was going to have to wait. What he wanted didn't matter right now. The only thing that mattered was getting Mia immediate medical attention and then helping get her through the aftermath. If she'd let him.

The hospital was finally in view, just a few blocks more to go. "You doing okay?" he asked.

She nodded her head.

"Good girl." He rubbed her arm.

They entered the bright, unfriendly glare of the emergency room, eyes adjusting to coming in from the dark. There were only a few people in the waiting room. A Hispanic couple with a small infant, a guy who had his arm in ice and his friend who was with him and a middle aged couple. The large waiting room was nearly empty and there was plenty of room, so that they would not have to sit near anyone else.

"Sit here." Schooner led her to a bank of chairs in a section where no one was seated. "I'll go see about getting you checked in, okay."

As Schooner approached the reception desk, the nurse looked up and smiled, appreciatively. It was then he realized he was still in his white dress shirt and suit pants with his sky blue bow tie hanging open.

"Hi," he began. "I'm here with a friend of mine and she's been attacked tonight and I think she's probably been raped."

"You're not sure if she's been raped?"

Schooner shook his head. "No. But I think it's highly likely."

She handed him a clipboard to fill out some basic information and he went back to where Mia was sitting.

"You hanging in there?" he asked. She looked like a little kid playing in her parent's closet in his suit jacket. He was glad that she was wrapped up in it and the telltale evidence of her ripped shirt out of view.

"Barely."

"You're doing great." He smiled at her, "Help me with this, okay." He wanted to distract her and motioned to the clipboard.

"Birthday?" He realized he didn't even know when her birthday was.

"July 12th."

"Ahhh, a summer baby. You never had to be in school for your birthday," he commented, as he wrote down her birth day, pausing at the year, before writing down the year of his birth, instead of hers. She was right, the fact that she was still a minor would cause a whole host of issues. He wanted to spare her anything she didn't think she could deal with or need to deal with.

Mia saw what Schooner wrote and whispered, "Thank you."

He looked at her and winked, conspiratorially. She smiled for the first time and he could see how much it hurt her lip to smile.

"Insurance?" he asked.

"I'm covered under my parent's plan, but I don't want…"

He could see the tears welling up and the panic grabbing her like a riptide, and immediately, he cut her off. "No worries." He pulled out his wallet and filled in his credit card information on the form.

She started to cry.

"Hey," he said to her, pointedly.

"Sorry." She sniffed and he smiled at her.

Schooner brought the completed form back to reception and waited with Mia until they called her in to Triage.

He walked her to the door. "I'll be waiting out here. If you want me with you at any point, send someone out to get me, okay?"

She nodded, a sob escaping.

He hugged her tightly once more and kissed the top of her head. "I'll be right here."

And she disappeared behind the door.

Schooner went and sat back down. He wanted to be there on the other side of the door with her. *This has got to be so scary for her*, he thought. Or was it? Compared to what she'd already endured that evening. He was on overload, just muddling through and could not even begin to imagine what Mia was going through.

"Mr. Moore?" A hand on his shoulder drew him out of his reverie. How long had he been sitting there?

"Is she okay? Is everything alright?" he asked the young emergency room doctor. He was glad for Mia's sake that the doctor was a woman.

"She's doing okay, considering the circumstances." She paused, "Do you know much of what happened to her tonight?"

"No." He shook his head. "I saw her walking. It didn't take long to realize there was a problem and I got her to come here."

The doctor smiled and put a hand on Schooner's forearm. "You're a good friend."

Not quite, he thought.

The doctor continued, "She told me that it was alright to fill you in on some of the details. Sometimes it's easier to have a third party deliver the information." She paused again, "Mia was raped by two men tonight."

Sound began to fade away; he could see the doctor's lips were still moving for a brief moment before he felt the room start spinning. Schooner hurtled head first, tumbling down a tunnel. He heard his voice say, from somewhere, "bathroom" and the doctor lead him by the arm to a bathroom luckily only a few feet away. He made it as far as the sink before vomiting. He couldn't stop. Waves and waves wrenched his gut muscles. Two men, oh my God. One must've held her, while the other... and the retching began again.

When the dry heaves finally ended, the doctor was waiting with a cup of water. She led him out to the chairs again and they sat down.

"Are you okay?" she asked and he nodded.

"Mia doesn't want to bring in the authorities."

"I know. I wanted her to go to the police, but she refused."

"Do you think you can change her mind? I wouldn't pressure her about it tonight, but maybe over the next few days. These animals need to be off the street."

"I agree, Doctor." He felt his anger rising again and consciously told himself to check it.

"She's got some pretty significant bruising, but x-rays didn't show any fractures. I'm going to be giving her some high dosage hormones that we typically use in rape cases. They basically make the uterus an inhospitable environment for egg implantation and we can help mitigate the odds of pregnancy."

Schooner felt the warm rush of tears coursing down his cheeks. This was a fucking nightmare.

The doctor continued, "The biggest side effect we see with this type of treatment is nausea and vomiting, so don't be alarmed if that happens. If it appears she's dehydrating, I want you to call me. I'm also going to prescribe pain killers and some anti-anxiety medication that will help her sleep." She handed Schooner her card. "I'm going to sew up her lip now and she asked if you'd come back and be with her while I do it."

He followed the doctor back into the authorized area passed small curtain partitioned rooms, until they got to Mia's.

"Hey you..." He smiled at her. He knew he had to keep it together for her and had collected himself quickly walking through the ER to her room. "So, you want me back here for the gory stuff, huh."

"Stitches seemed like a guy thing,"

He was so happy to see her bantering.

The doctor was loading a syringe of Lidocaine to numb the area. "I think I can do this in about four stitches, Mia, and I'm going to make them as small as I can so that you won't have any significant scarring."

Maybe not of her lip, Schooner thought and was hoping Mia was not thinking the same thing.

"Okay, I'm going to numb the area and we'll let it sit for a few minutes to take full effect."

Mia grabbed Schooner's hand tightly as the doctor injected the numbing agent around her mouth.

He rubbed her knuckles with his thumb to calm her down. "You're doing great, Baby Girl," he encouraged, squeezing her hand.

"I'll be back in a few minutes." The doctor left Mia's room to attend to one of the other patients.

Schooner sat on the side of the bed facing Mia, still holding her hand. "You are so brave," he whispered. "I have always been in awe of you."

Two fat tears rolled slowly down her cheeks. "I wanted you to be my first," her voice was choked.

He felt hot tears splashing down his face and leaned his forehead against hers. "I will be, Baby Girl. When you are ready, I will be the first guy to make love to you. I'll be your first." Schooner didn't know if his face was wet from his tears or hers, but cheek to cheek they sat and cried together. Cried for the loss of a dream that had been savagely ripped from them.

Your first and your last, Baby Girl, Schooner vowed to himself. *Your first and your last.*

CHAPTER 27

Mia fell asleep lying in the back seat of the cab with her head in Schooner's lap.

"Baby Girl, we're here." Gently waking her as they pulled up in front of the dorm, he paid the cab driver and they walked up the front steps. Schooner took Mia's keys from her and opened the door. He felt the little dangling silver camera and smiled. It was past 4 A.M. and the lobby was dark and empty. They walked down the hall and up the staircase, Schooner with his arm around Mia who was still wearing his suit jacket.

He unlocked the door to her room and flipped the light on. Thankfully her roommate Caroline was staying at the Sheraton in Pasadena with her boyfriend, Dennis. He tossed the keys onto Mia's desk and turned to her.

She looked up at him and sighed. "What a fucking night."

He cocked his head to the side and with a sad look just held out his open arms to her. She went to him, wrapping her arms around his waist and he held her tight.

"You got really skinny," she observed, looking up at him with a wry smile.

He wanted to tell her that it was called "The Misery Diet," but he didn't want to say anything that would make her feel bad or upset her.

"Let's get you in bed, Mia. You need to rest." He opened their mini-fridge and pulled out a bottle of water and poured her a cup. Taking the prescription bottles out of his suit pants pocket, he got Mia the pills she needed.

She had changed into an oversized tee-shirt while his back was turned and he suspected there were probably some bruises she didn't want him to see. She sat down cross-legged in the center of her bed and he sat on the edge and handed her the water and medication.

"You'll tell Rosie and Henry?" she asked, eyes filling with tears again.

Schooner nodded and reached out to stroke her cheek.

She leaned her face into his hand, closing her eyes.

"Okay, under the covers, Baby Girl." She slid underneath her bedspread and he tucked her in, smiling down at her.

Mia reached for Schooner's hand and brought it up to her lips, kissing his palm and then held his hand in both of hers. "Thank you for everything tonight."

"Shhhh." He stroked her hair gently.

After a few minutes, she drifted off to sleep, a combination of exhaustion, pain meds and anti-anxiety pills taking effect.

He waited several minutes to make sure she was in a deep sleep, leaned down and softly kissed her forehead.

Grabbing her keys, Schooner headed down the hall to Rosie's room. Aware that it was now after 4:30, he knew this was not going to be a pleasant greeting when he knocked on her door.

Rosie opened the door, looked at Schooner and sneered, "What the fuck?"

"Good morning to you, too. Throw on a robe Rosie, we need to go grab Henry and talk."

"What are you, high?"

"I wish I was. Get your robe on." And he leveled her a "do what I say now" glance. He was beyond taking her shit tonight.

Schooner was three steps in front of Rosie when she started following him down the hall, into the stairwell and downstairs to Henry's room.

He began the process again. Although Henry was a little more civil. "Hey, sorry to wake you. Throw on your robe. We need to talk."

Henry emerged from his room and Rosie just shrugged her shoulders at him as Schooner started walking toward the study lounge, the room where they had spent many hours together laughing and creating their masterpiece. They just followed him silently.

Flipping on the lights, they entered the room and Schooner motioned for them to sit, before closing the door.

"Nice outfit," Rosie snarked. His blue bow tie was still hanging open around his neck, but now the top few buttons of his shirt were open.

"Yeah, well it's been a long night." He ignored the snark. "Mia is upstairs in her room and she's asleep. She's okay, safe in bed, but she wanted me to talk to you guys." He could see the immediate alarm on Henry's face. Rosie was too pissed off to register any emotion other than, well, pissed off.

"I ran into Mia a few hours ago walking on The Quad and she had been attacked."

They both screamed, "What?" and "Oh my God!"

"What do you mean attacked?" Rosie was yelling and Henry put a hand on her shoulder to calm her.

Schooner sighed, "She was roughed up pretty bad. And she was raped."

Rosie burst into tears, her tough resolve evaporating at the mention of the word rape, "No. No. No," she moaned.

Henry put his arms around her and Schooner could see the anguish in his eyes and the pulsing tension in his strong jaw.

"I took her to the hospital and she received medical attention. She needed a few stitches because they busted her lip."

"They?" Henry's eyes flew open wide.

Schooner just nodded, the sick feeling rising up again, tears springing from his eyes. He took the heels of his palms and wiped away his tears. When he could get control of his voice, he continued. "There were two," his voice cracked, despite his best efforts to hold it together. "The doctor gave her some hormones to help mitigate the chances of pregnancy," his voice broke on the word pregnancy, "and pain killers and anti-anxiety medicine." He sat down and put his head in his hands.

"She doesn't want to bring in the authorities, because she's afraid she'll get sent home. She was adamant about it. And I understand her not wanting to go through all that shit, but those fucking animals are out there." His anger was flaring, "and I just want to kill them."

"What can we do to help her?" Henry asked, softly.

"She doesn't want anyone to know about this," they nodded and agreed. "If you can bring her meals to the dorm and get class assignments and stuff. I don't think she's going to want anyone to see her just yet."

"Are you going to stay with her?" Henry asked.

Schooner nodded, yes.

Rosie flashed him a look filled with venom. "And what are you? The fucking white knight? You blow in playing big man savior and then you break her heart to pieces again. Don't you fuck with my girl." She was out of her chair and wagging a finger in Schooner's face.

He surprised her by taking her finger and kissing it. Her big brown eyes were wide and confused.

He began softly, "I know I'm not your favorite person, Rosie. As a matter of fact, I haven't been my favorite person either. Something happened, and it's not what you think happened, but I didn't want to hurt Mia and I didn't want her to tell me goodbye, and I fucked everything up. I just fucked up." He looked up at the ceiling, as if to stop a torrent of tears and then he looked Rosie straight in the eyes, "But I never stopped loving her for a single second. I don't think I'll ever stop loving her." And the tears he tried so hard to stop fell freely from his beautiful eyes.

"We're going to need to tell Caroline when she gets back."

"Caroline can stay with me, if she wants to, so that you can stay with Mia," Rosie offered and Schooner nodded.

"Schooner," Rosie began, "you look like shit."

He knew she was referring to his new "haunted" look.

"I think he looks hot!" Henry countered, putting his arms around Schooner and giving him a much needed hug, which Schooner gladly accepted.

They walked Schooner up to Mia's room. "We'll bring you guys breakfast."

Schooner quietly opened the door and he knew they wanted to come in and see their friend and make sure she was really okay. Mia was on her back snoring loudly and that gave them all a relaxing chuckle. Seeing her pretty little face bruised up was heartbreaking.

Rosie took Schooner's hand on the way out of the room and gave it a squeeze. No words were needed.

He sat down in the desk chair across from her bed and stretched out his long legs and tried to start processing everything, but his mind was just too jumbled. Schooner knew he needed sleep and maybe things would be clearer after a few hours of rest, but he just wanted to look at her for a few minutes more. Watch her sleep. Know that she was safe.

He finally took off his dress shoes and socks, they had been on his feet way too long. Hanging his shirt (with the bow tie still dangling from the collar) and suit pants over the back of the chair, Schooner crawled into Caroline's bed in his boxers. He hoped she didn't mind.

Lying there, listening to Mia breathe for a while, he drifted into a fitful sleep, dreaming of the hospital and the Sheraton, searching hallways for Mia where hotel rooms had hospital beds with green curtains on tracks. He felt her climb into bed next to him, but wasn't sure if it was a dream, until she rested her head on his chest and he pulled her close into him.

"You okay?" he asked, nuzzling his face into her curls.

"Mmm-hmm." Her arm tightened around him.

"It's going to be okay, Baby Girl." He kissed her forehead. He just had to believe it would be all right. There was no other option. They would get through this together. He would help her. He'd be her strength, her guide back from Hell. Her love. And when she was ready, her lover.

"Don't let me go, Schooner."

"I won't, Mia."

She nuzzled into his chest. "Promise?"

"I promise." He tightened his hug around her and the irony did not elude him as to how easy this promise was to make.

"They really hurt me tonight. I wanted to die."

His heart ached. It ached for her, it ached for him and it ached for everything he'd never be able to change.

"I'm so sorry, Baby Girl. I am so sorry this happened to you. I wish I could change it for you."

"Me too. It was horrible."

"I'm here for you, Mia." He threaded his fingers through hers and brought her hand to his lips. She was silent, so he went on. "I never stopped loving you, Baby Girl. Not for a minute."

"Don't make me smile, Schooner, it hurts."

He laughed. "Okay. Sleep." And she nuzzled back into his chest and fell back to sleep, while he gently stroked her hair.

As he held her tight, he knew that he would get her through this. He would get them both through this—together. This was the start. And this time, he was ready for it. She was his and he would do whatever he needed to protect her and to help her heal. He would always take care of what was his and that would start now.

He wondered if maybe he had been wrong earlier that evening. Maybe a restart could be a good thing after all.

CHAPTER 28

He felt her stirring in his arms and looked at his watch. 8:45 A.M. His head ached from lack of sleep and tension. Closing his eyes, he tightened his muscular arms around her.

"Schooner?"

"Yeah, Baby Girl?" He looked down at her on his chest, looking so sweet and so young.

"Nothing. I just felt like saying your name."

Schooner smiled and kissed her forehead. "How are you feeling?"

As she looked up at him, he pushed her hair from her face, and his heart brimmed at the sight of her ombre green eyes.

"I feel like I got hit by a Mack truck." Mia moved off of his chest and up to the pillow, looking into his eyes, which were now a mere few inches away. "I dreamed you told me that you never stopped loving me. Not even for a minute."

He gently ran a finger down her swollen, bruised cheek. "It wasn't a dream, Baby Girl."

A tear squeezed from her eye, "I thought you'd stopped. Then, I just thought that maybe you never really did."

He wiped her tear away with his thumb. Shaking his head, he whispered, "Never stopped. Never will."

"Me neither." She tried to smile, but the pain and the swelling stopped her.

"Awww, poor baby." Kissing the tip of her nose, he could see the smile forming in her eyes.

"Mia, I want to talk to you about something," he paused to stare into her beautiful eyes for a moment. "I don't want to upset you, but I also don't want to fuck up. And more than anything, I don't want to lose you. Ever." He sighed and looked up at the ceiling. "I will do this any way you want to, my only concern is you, keeping you safe and making sure that you don't have to deal with any shit."

Schooner could tell by the confusion on her face that she wasn't following. "I'm not leaving your side, Mia, from now, until the end of the semester. And maybe not even then." He smiled and ran his thumb down her cheek. "So, I know I am going to get some flak and I want to make sure I handle it in a way that there isn't fallout for you."

"You're talking about CJ," she whispered and he nodded.

"I don't want her or any of her bitchy little friends bothering you. She still wants a relationship and..."

"... and you were at the Spring Fling with her last night," Mia interrupted, her eyes starting to fill up.

"Yes, I was."

She thought for a moment. "So, it will be a shock to her for everything to just be different."

"I could tell her I love you and she just needs to deal with it. I just want to do what's best for you. And I want to protect you from any nastiness that you don't need to deal with."

"You could tell her we're friends and you're helping me deal with something. That's not a lie." His brows furrowed and she continued, "And then maybe that way she'll feel less threatened and won't act out. I'm okay with that. As long as she doesn't know what happened to me."

"She'll never know. It's not her or anyone else's business."

There was a knock on the door and Schooner got up to answer it. Rosie and Henry had trays of food.

"Nice outfit." Rosie reprised her remark of the night before, gesturing at Schooner's plaid boxers.

"Very nice outfit." Henry concurred, taking in Schooner's bare broad chest and tennis player arm muscles.

Henry bit his lower lip and made a hand motion fanning himself to Mia, who attempted to smile. "Don't make me laugh, it hurts," she scolded.

"Oh Girlfriend, you are rocking some poufy lips." Henry kissed her cheek, softly.

"You just watch, they're going to come into vogue. You know what a trendsetter I am," Mia countered. "It's a New York thing."

Schooner looked through the food offerings. "Good job, guys. Mia, there's a bunch of things that are soft. Scrambled eggs, grits, oatmeal, applesauce."

"Okay."

"Okay to all?" Schooner was surprised and thrilled as Mia nodded, yes. Her resilience and spirit were just a marvel to him. A good appetite was a good sign, he thought, and as soon as he got food into her, he would make sure she took her meds.

Schooner was sitting in the middle of Caroline's bed with his back up against the wall, and after eating her entire breakfast, and taking her meds (at Schooner's insistence), Mia came and sat down between his legs, leaning back against him. His arms were around her and she was holding onto his hands. It was then, in the safety of Schooner's arms, that Mia began to open up about some of the details of what had happened to her. Schooner was learning along with Rosie and Henry of her ordeal.

They sat silently listening, not a breath taken between them.

She had been working late in the darkroom, which had been virtually empty all evening with many people off-campus for the Spring Fling. As the last person to leave, she locked up the darkroom for the night and left to come back to the dorm. Shortly after exiting the Fine Arts Building, she was jumped by two guys and dragged to the park across from campus. When they were done, they left her there on the ground, casually walking out of the park as if nothing had happened.

Mia was choking on her tears as she finished recounting the details.

All Schooner could do was hold her tighter to him. She felt very small and defeated in his arms.

Feeling his intense anger building, Schooner knew that Rosie and Henry were seeing it on his face and in his eyes. He was glad Mia's back was to him and that she could not see his rage. It scared him to realize of what he might be capable.

He felt very close to the Animal Kingdom.

CHAPTER 29

This is really not going well, Schooner thought. He hoped she would be cool about it, but there was nothing cool in her demeanor at the moment. CJ MacAllister was spitting mad.

"I don't understand why you are going to be spending time with her and not with me."

He tried to stay calm and appeal to reason. "CJ, if there was some shit going down in your life, wouldn't you want the people you consider your friends to be there to support you? Mia is my friend. I know you don't get that, but she is a really sweet kid and she needs my friendship right now."

"And you're not going to tell me why?" Her hands were now firmly planted on her hips.

"Would you want me sharing your shit with other people?" He just shook his head.

She didn't answer, so he continued, "No, you wouldn't. And I wouldn't share your personal business with other people."

Then he had a stroke of brilliance. "This is really important to my dad, CJ."

"Your dad? What does your dad have to do with this?"

He had her listening now. CJ labored overtime at Christmas working her magic in an attempt to ensure Gavin Moore liked her. She wanted Gavin as her father-in-law and now her curiosity was piqued.

"My dad and Mia's dad became friendly. And my dad asked me to take care of this. I don't want to let him down, CJ." Okay, it was a stretch on the truth, but it was based in reality and it seemed to be doing the trick.

She sighed. "Oh, I didn't realize that."

"Look, there's only a few weeks left of school here, just let me do the right thing."

She nodded her head okay, but it looked to Schooner as if her wheels were still spinning.

"And I'm telling you now, CJ—Mia gets no shit from you or any of your friends. Is that clear?"

"We would never," she began her protest, and he cut her off.

"I am dead serious, if anyone fucks with Mia in any way, shape or form, I will be so fucking pissed. Clear?"

"Clear." Her wide-eyed, tight-lipped response contradicted her words. CJ was not happy.

What he really wanted to tell CJ was that there was not a shot in Hell that they were ever getting back together again. He wanted to tell her that Mia was the love of his life and that all he cared about was Mia's happiness and well-being.

But he knew if he did that, CJ and her evil minion would do something heinous to hurt Mia and all he really wanted to do was keep them all away from her through the end of the semester.

As he left CJ's dorm, he thought, crisis averted for now and by the time fall semester comes, he and Mia would be old news and CJ would be moving on.

Protecting Mia was his utmost concern.

CHAPTER 30

Schooner was lying in bed holding Mia in his arms. "So, tell me about New York beaches."

"They are wonderful." Mia's smile was back to its adorable state now that she had finally healed and her stitches were out.

Schooner made a face at her. "I'm from Newport Beach, California—it's going to take a lot to impress me."

"Okay, well we have different kinds of beaches." He loved seeing how excited she would get talking about home. "Up on the North Shore, we have rocky beaches. That's on the Long Island Sound and there are great harbors and little 300-year-old whaling towns and the sailing is great up there. And on the South Shore, we have ocean beaches, so it's just miles of dunes and sand and good waves. The east end is really nice with Montauk and the Hamptons."

"That's where the Hamptons are?" Schooner asked and Mia nodded. "I've heard my dad talk about ancestors that were in Southampton, Long Island in the 1600's. Does that sound right? 1600's? Could that be possible?"

"Yes, absolutely. That is when those towns were first settled. We could research your family. Maybe find some old family graves. And maybe some living relatives, too. Wouldn't that be amazing? I can't believe your family was in America in the 1600's. That is so cool."

"That would be a fun thing to do." He kissed her lips, softly. With her stitches now removed, he was loving being able to finally kiss her lips again, a pleasure he had patiently waited for as she healed, and was treating them as if they were made of porcelain. "What are you thinking?" He was looking at her dreamy face.

"I was thinking about after a day on the beach, when the sun goes down and it gets chilly and you're even colder because you're all sunburned, so you throw on a sweatshirt with your shorts. And I was thinking about us doing that and going to one of the lobster places on the water and picking out our lobsters from the tank and getting steamers and corn-on-the-cob and just sitting out at a picnic table by the water, having the perfect night, after having the perfect day."

Schooner just smiled at Mia who was painting a picture for him of memories with her that they were yet to create, but that he could see vividly. He could see the late afternoon sun on her sunburned, freckled cheeks, smell the salt on the breeze, hear the tide lapping against the shore, feel the salt water dried in her curls.

"I love you, Mia, and I really don't want to be away from you this summer. I will find a job there. I can teach tennis, lifeguard, bus tables—I don't care. If your parents are cool with me staying, I really want to spend the summer with you in New York."

"My parents loved you, Schooner—and they have plenty of room, so I don't think it's going to be a problem."

He pulled her close to kiss her some more.

"Mmmm, I feel that." She was referring to his hard-on that he was trying desperately not to press into her. He inched the lower half of his body away from her, hoping he wasn't making her fearful or uncomfortable.

"Mmm-mmm." She shook her head "no" while continuing to kiss him and slung a leg over him and used it to pull him closer to her, his cock now pressed up hard against her.

He pulled away from their kiss to search her face. She smiled and touched his cheek. "It feels good," she whispered, and he moaned just hearing her say that.

"Tell me what you want, Baby Girl. You have to call the shots here."

She gave him a shy smile and cast her eyes down for a moment before returning his intense gaze. "I'm ready, Schooner. I really am. I don't think I can wait another day. I don't want to wait another day."

"You sure?"

And she nodded.

His deep kiss was soft as he said against her lips, "I love you so much, Baby Girl, but I'm so afraid I'm going to hurt you."

Mia pulled back to look at Schooner, pushing fallen blonde locks from his forehead and smiled. "Hurt me? Schooner, you have been my protector, you watch out for me, take care of me. You keep me safe. I know you're not going to hurt me."

"You know we're the real deal, Mia." He watched the smile from her lips reach her eyes.

She nodded.

Pulling her underneath him, with arms on both sides of her head, he kissed her lips softly, exploring her mouth, pulling back to look at her and smile and then kiss her some more. He was used to being turned on and feeling the heady rush of sex, but he wasn't used to feeling his heart brim and overflow. He wasn't used to caring or wanting the experience to be amazing for his partner. Never had he really thought about what it was like for the other person.

In the past, it had been about his own physical release and need for control. It had been about the hunt and the victor, but as he looked down at Mia's sweet face, he realized the only thing he cared about was that this was wonderful for her, that she knew how much he loved her, that this was the ultimate expression of his love for her, and that his love could erase any ugliness that came before it, replacing that with a warm, loving experience and beautiful memories.

Pulling his shirt off over his head, her hands immediately went to his shoulders, gently moving down his arms, reverently. He watched her face as she explored him, loving that she was enjoying his body. Schooner tugged her tee-shirt and pulled it over her head, swinging it like a lasso before tossing it off into the room. They both laughed. His eyes were smoldering like pale sapphires. He had never felt so turned on. Pushing the shoulder straps from her bra down, he lifted her gorgeous tits out of her bra. He rimmed one nipple with his tongue and she moaned. He grazed it in his teeth, before saying, "You absolutely have the most gorgeous tits on campus."

"Oh, do I?"

"Without a doubt." And between sucks, "The day we met, I noticed your gorgeous eyes and smile and this damn fine rack."

She giggled and he bit down on her nipple, causing a yelp.

"My damn fine rack. Mine." He staked ownership.

Her fingers threaded through his thick blonde locks as his sucking and pinching drove her wild. She wrapped her legs around him, moaning.

"You have such sensitive nipples. I love that," he marveled, as he moved back up to her mouth, kissing her deeply.

She pulled at his hair and he ravaged her mouth without restraint. Feeling her hand reach for him, he curled into her so that she could grasp him, gasping into her mouth, when her little hand encircled his throbbing cock.

Gently, she ran her fingernails over his balls and he shivered. "Feel good?" she asked.

"Oh yeah," he breathed into her neck.

"And this?" She gently kneaded his balls in her hand. He knew his cock felt like steel. It was so hard, it hurt.

"Feels damn good." He looked at her face to see her satisfied little smile.

"I love getting you hard." She smiled at him.

"You have quite the knack for it," he was gasping. He gave her a hard kiss and her arms went around his neck. "Are you ready for this?"

She nodded and he got off the bed, rustled through his duffle bag and came up with a condom packet. As he sat down on the edge of the bed, Mia looked at him wide-eyed. "

I don't want you to feel like we have to do this."

She was shaking her head. "I want to do this. I want to do this with you."

The look in her eyes was pleading and he realized that she needed this to wipe away the nightmare and replace it with something wonderful. He leaned forward and kissed her. Schooner was honored to help make wonderful memories with her.

"Want to help me with his?" he asked, opening the condom packet. Starting the condom, he took her hands in his and hand over hand had her roll it down over him. He wanted to make it "their" experience. And what she didn't realize was that everything that was happening was new ground, with new emotions for him, too. He loved the touch of her rolling the condom onto him and smoothing it out, with such care.

She looked pleased at her *handiwork*.

He pulled her beneath him and kissed her as the head of his cock starting to sink into her. "You ready?" He searched her eyes.

She nodded her assent and with his eyes locked onto hers, he mouthed, "I love you".

She mouthed "I love you" back and with a quick thrust he was inside of her.

She gasped, but was still smiling. He realized he was smiling too and just took a moment to enjoy how tight she was around him before he began driving into her. He bent down to kiss her, thrusting into her deeper, quicker, harder. She returned his kiss passionately and he lost himself in the sensation... she was so tight around his cock, she felt so damn good. He pulled his face back to look at her. Her eyes were closed and he could tell she was coming undone.

"Mia," his voice was hoarse, "look at me."

Mia opened her eyes.

He wanted to watch her as she came, but he also wanted to make sure she was okay and didn't go anyplace dark. "You are so beautiful."

She smiled at him and he rammed into her hard. "So, so beautiful." Harder. "You. Are. My. Baby Girl." Harder and faster. "Come. For. Me. Baby Girl." And those were the magic words.

Her eyes widened and her muscles clamped down and spasmed around him, milking his cock.

He could hear both their moans in his ears and "Oh God, Schooner," which totally pushed him over the edge.

He collapsed on top of her, forehead to forehead, both panting. Pushing her curls from her face, he smiled down at her. She smiled back at him and his heart relaxed. She was okay.

"Wow," she was rendered speechless.

"Wow is right," Schooner laughed.

"Is that what it is always like?"

He shook his head no. "I have never experienced anything like that before," and he wasn't lying.

There was a self-satisfied smirk on Mia's face. Schooner kissed her softly. He had still not pulled out of her and started to gently grind into her.

Her eyes grew wide and he laughed. "Figured that would wipe that self-satisfied smirk off your face."

"Oh, did you now?" She squeezed his cock hard with her muscles and his eyes flew open. "Two can play that game."

"Yes, two can… and two is going to need to help me with another condom if she keeps this up." He ground into her clockwise.

They kissed and laughed and made love again and all of Schooner's protective instincts were satisfied for one night.

He had made good on his promise. He promised her that he would be the first person to make love to her. And he was. Seeing the way she responded to their lovemaking and her happiness in the aftermath was a heady, powerful feeling for him. He had given this to her. And she had given herself to him. She was his.

CHAPTER 31

Finals and packing and goodbyes and the last tennis matches, the days were winding down quickly and if Schooner had an extra second to just stand still and feel, he would have recognized his mounting ambivalence. Although he was ready for the semester to end and for finals to be over, this last month with Mia was a moment in time that he forever wanted to hold onto.

Schooner shoved the last of his belongings into his duffle bag as Mia and Caroline continued to pack and tape their boxes.

Their dorm RA, Dawn, poked her head into to the room to remind the girls that all cartons being shipped needed to be packed, sealed and addressed and out in the hall by 9 P.M.

"I'll walk you out." Mia grabbed her keys.

"Have a great summer, Caroline." Schooner gave Mia's very accommodating roommate a hug goodbye.

They stopped by Rosie's room. She was just about finished packing. "Eight A.M. final and I am outta here!"

One more stop for Schooner to say goodbye to Henry, but he was nowhere to be found.

Mia and Schooner walked out of the dorm and stood on the front steps.

"Stop pouting," he said to her. "You're killing me."

"I'm not used to spending the night without you. I miss you already."

"C'mere, Baby Girl." He sat down on the stone balustrade railing and pulled her between his legs. Her arms immediately went around his neck and they got lost in a kiss. "I'll be by right after my final. We'll have at least an hour before the limo comes for you."

She continued to pout.

"You'd better put that lip away or I'm going to bite it," he threatened.

They stayed that way for a long while, with Mia standing between Schooner's legs, arms wrapped around his neck, foreheads together.

"Tell me again, what's the place we have to get to by boat?"

"That's Fire Island. We'll take the ferry over and there's no cars. Just little red wagons to cart groceries with and bicycles. No streets, just boardwalks. Ocean on one side, the Great South Bay on the other side."

He smiled and kissed her. "And that's where you want to spend your birthday?"

She nodded, smiling.

"Okay, your birthday on Fire Island. I just can't wait to see these places you talk about. They just sound so idyllic."

"That, they are!"

"Do you want me to bring you anything from here when I come?"

"Certainly not pizza and bagels," she laughed. "Just bring you, that's all I need."

He took her face in his hands and kissed her deeply. "I'd better go study. Flunking out of school will not go over well with my parents. I'm thinking I should probably finish my test between 11:30 and 12:00 and I'll come right over, okay."

He squeezed her hand and they held hands until he was down the steps and their fingers finally broke contact.

Schooner turned around, "Hey," he yelled, "those pizzas and bagels better be as good as you've been bragging about."

Mia just stood on the steps smiling at him, watching him go.

It was dusk when he reached his dorm on the other side of campus. As he crossed the lobby, he got a lot of ribbing from the guys hanging out.

"Hey, do we know this guy?"

"I remember him... vaguely."

"Ah, the Prodigal Son returns."

Beau was in their room studying for a Chemistry final. He looked up when Schooner walked in, "Oh hey, did you see CJ?"

"No, why?" Schooner pulled his books out of his duffle bag to study.

"She just left a few minutes ago. She was looking for you." He punched some numbers into his calculator.

"Did she say what she wanted?"

Beau just shook his head. "No. I just assumed it was to say goodbye. She hung out for a little bit waiting for you and then finally left."

CHAPTER 32

Schooner filled in the last of his answers and took a run back through the test to see if he'd missed anything. There were four questions that he'd put checks near to flag that he needed to go back and relook at them. He looked at his watch. 11:25 A.M. He was still in good shape to finish up and have some time to spend alone with Mia before she left. He went back to concentrating on his final. At 11:38, Schooner handed his test booklet into the professor and wished him a good summer.

Crossing The Quad, heading toward Mia's dorm, Schooner felt that joy of freedom experience that hits once every spring when school is over and summer officially begins. What a year! So much had happened. As he walked past Brewster Hall, he smiled thinking about the first time he'd laid eyes on her. His first impression was that she didn't belong here. He also thought that he fit in perfectly. He was wrong on both accounts.

Walking into Mia's dorm, it was already starting to resemble a ghost town. Doors to dorm rooms were open and the rooms were bare, just institutional mattresses on frames, dressers, desks and chairs still in the rooms. All the posters were off the walls, books were gone, green plants taken home for the summer, all cartons for shipping had been removed from the hall. Schooner headed up the stairwell and down the hall toward Mia's room.

The door was ajar, so he walked in. He didn't immediately process that the room was completely empty. Nothing was in the room. No one was in the room. No Mia. No luggage. He looked at his watch. It was 11:55 A.M. Mia wasn't supposed to be picked up until 1 P.M.

"Mia," he called out. He ran down the hall to Rosie's room. It was empty, too.

Maybe she's waiting in Henry's room, he thought and ran down the stairwell. He could feel panic beginning to rise. Something was not right. What the hell was going on? He knocked on Henry's door. His roommate answered. Henry had left hours ago. And no, he hadn't seen Mia.

He ran down the hall checking rooms, maybe someone knew where she was. He checked the lobby again. She wasn't anywhere. He went back up to her room. That's where she would look for him. She knew approximately what time he was going to be there. She'd meet him at the room. Maybe she was just saying goodbye to someone.

He got back up to her room. Still no Mia. No luggage. Nothing. He paced around her room. 12:15. 12:20. 12:25. What the fuck happened? Maybe the limo came early. Maybe she left a note. He searched her desk. Nothing. All the drawers. Nothing. Her dresser. Nothing. Under her pillow. Nothing. He got on his knees and looked under the bed, under the desk, under the dresser. Nothing. Nothing. Nothing. He checked her closet. Nothing.

He heard a key in a door down the hall and went running from the room. It was Dawn, the RA.

"Dawn"

"Hey Schooner." She looked surprised to see him.

"Have you seen Mia?" He searched her face.

She looked confused. "Schooner, Mia left hours ago."

"Hours ago?" he repeated, emptily. "Mia left hours ago?"

She nodded. A look on her face saying "sorry"—like she was sorry to deliver bad news and he also saw something more on her face, something that said sorry this is happening to you. And then she locked her door and headed down the hall to leave for the summer.

He turned and started to walk down the hall. What the fuck? Why had she left like this? Was she okay? Was everything okay? Surely she would have left him a note or had someone get a message to him. And that's when it dawned on him that he didn't even have her number. He was going to get all that info before she left and give her his. And now she was gone. Just gone. And he had no way to find her. No way to find out what had happened. No way to find out why she had left him. When they said goodbye last night, everything was fine. They were going to spend her birthday on Fire Island... together. And now she was gone, without a trace.

He felt like his brimming heart was rapidly deflating and the pain from it was like being knifed with a shredding blade. His handsome face was contorted with anguish as he yelled out in the empty hallway, "Why Mia? Why did you leave me?" and took the side of his closed fist and slammed it into the institutional green cinder-block cement wall. The sound of bones breaking was deafening, but he neither heard the sound nor felt the pain radiating up his arm because the pain in his heart eclipsed anything he felt physically.

One week earlier, after the last match of the season, Coach Boland had predicted to his staff that Schooner Moore would lead their highly regarded tennis program to a National Championship and be the top ranked NCAA player in the United States within two years.

Three surgeries. Six months in a cast.

Schooner Moore's promising tennis career came to a shattering conclusion in a dormitory hallway on the last day of his freshman year.

CHAPTER 33

Dr. Malcolm Faulkes was a golf buddy of Gavin Moore. He was also an orthopedic surgeon who specialized in Sports Medicine and had a client roster that was a Who's Who of LA sports teams. He had seen Schooner play tennis many times over the years and had been following his impressive first college season.

When Gavin called to say that Schooner's right hand suffered an injury, Dr. Faulkes met them at his office after hours. The x-rays showed multiple fractures and he immediately admitted Schooner to the hospital where, that very evening, Faulkes performed the first of what would be three surgeries. Schooner stayed in the hospital heavily drugged, with his hand immobilized, for the next three days.

A week later, Schooner was back at Dr. Faulkes office. Malcolm asked Dee to stay out in the waiting room while he spoke to Schooner alone.

His office was dark cherry wood and his love of golf was evident everywhere. Schooner sat down in one of the Hunter Green leather and wood chairs across from the doctor's desk.

"On a scale of 1-10 where is your pain level?"

"About a six," a subdued Schooner replied.

"The surgery I performed was a first, Schooner. From what I can tell, you're going to probably need at least two more within the next three months."

Schooner winced at his words and nodded as the doctor continued, "I'm not going to kid you, that hand is held together by pins right now. You did extensive damage to the bones."

"Guess I won't be Team Captain this year." Schooner looked up at the ceiling.

"Son, I'd like to be optimistic, but after your surgeries, there is going to be an extensive rehab period. The good news is, you're young and you're strong. Will you ever regain the strength in that hand to grip a racquet tight enough to knock out those 140 plus MPH serves again?" He paused, "Schooner, I don't know if that is going to be in your future."

Schooner continued to look at the ceiling, trying his hardest not to let the tears burning at the back of his eyes have their way.

"The reason I wanted your mother to wait outside today was so that you and I could talk. I've known you most of your life, Schooner. You're a good kid. You've always been a happy, level-headed kid. Clearly, there's something going on here." Malcolm's voice showed honest concern and Schooner could feel that.

"Dr. F., I just got dumped. And it came as a shock and I just wasn't thinking and slammed my fist into a wall. Not the brightest thing I've ever done. I wasn't thinking. I just reacted."

"Heartbreak will do that to you." Malcolm sat back in his chair.

"I got blindsided," Schooner began. "She left without a word. I was supposed to spend the summer with her in New York. I don't even have a number to find her. Everything was fine the night before and then she was gone. I don't even know why she left me." Schooner's eyes told the doctor everything he needed to know.

"Can't you get her number from Directory Assistance?"

"Her last name is Silver and she lives in New York."

Dr. Faulkes actually laughed out loud and Schooner laughed with him at the absurdity of it. "That would be like finding a Smith in most areas of the country, I suppose." He sat back in his big leather chair, tapping his finger against his lip. He looked at Schooner and smiled, "So, let me see if I've got this right—you're heartbroken and now you have no plans for the summer—except for a few dates with me for surgeries."

"Pretty much sums it up, Doc."

Faulkes smiled at Schooner, a gleam in his eye. "So, that pretty much frees you up for an adventure."

Schooner cocked his head, narrowing his eyes at the doctor, wondering what he was getting at.

"You know Schooner, in my experience, two things can help you get over a broken heart. The first is—fall in love with someone else, the second is a change of scenery. Since my daughter is only nine, I can't offer you the first, but I can help you with the second. I'm going to be spending four weeks in Zambia this summer, helping to set up a hospital in a rural area of their Southern Province. There's a lot of work to be done and we can always use an extra set of hands. Or in your case, hand." He smiled at his own joke.

Zambia? I don't even know where the fuck Zambia is, Schooner thought. Somewhere in Africa. Zambia. Helping people. Getting a hospital set up. Zambia.

And in that moment, Schooner felt alive again. He had a purpose. He was going to Zambia.

And with the quintessential Schooner Moore smile on his face, he asked Dr. Malcolm Faulkes, "Where do I sign up?"

After a day and a half of travel, they arrived in the capital of Lusaka, a vibrant modern city with wide avenues lined with Jacaranda trees. The friendly natives predominantly spoke English, and Schooner made quite the splash with children at the Lumumba Market, who wanted to follow around the tall, blonde haired, blue eyed young man. Before heading out on their five hour Jeep ride to Macha, they visited the Moore Pottery Factory and Schooner bought his Mom a tea set decorated with a local native motif from this namesake gallery/factory.

They drove over rough, rutted dirt roads through the savannah, not coming upon villages for hours at a time. Schooner documented the journey with his new Nikon camera from the vast plains to the small grass roofed huts in the villages. As they passed through, the children would wave and run after them until they reached the edge of the village.

They arrived in Macha late in the day and Schooner was captivated by its stark beauty and simplicity. They began to unload the supplies and equipment that had been shipped in containers from the U.S. Local children looked on, smiles covering their faces. The news of the American specialty doctor's arrival had spread quickly. Soon villagers were welcoming them, bringing local specialties such as Chikanda, a vegetarian sausage made from orchids, Samp, a dish of cooked hominy and dried beans and other assorted delicacies made from boiled leaves. The offering took on the feel of a street festival and Schooner felt proud to be a part of the doctor's important work.

Their accommodations were simple; cots had been set up for them in the schoolhouse. Schooner was struck by how little the people had and how little they needed. There wasn't much in the way of industry, one coffee house/gathering spot in town (mostly for ex-pats) and a general-type store, several places of worship, a school and the new hospital, which would serve a large area in the southern region of the country. That was all they had and they didn't appear to need more. The people seemed content and happy. It struck him that their happiness was not contingent upon having a lot. It was just about being.

Schooner spent the first few days unpacking supplies and helping the medical staff set up. The word was out of their arrival and natives from near and far began to arrive. There were so many orthopedic issues ranging from small crippled children to the arthritic elderly. The doctors saw as many patients as they physically could in a day. The ophthalmologists, dentists and prosthetic specialists with them were equally stretched with their caseloads.

After a few days, Schooner approached Malcolm. "Dr. F., I've been thinking about how I could be of most help here and what I've noticed is that people are coming long distances for care and they are bringing their children with them, who then have to wait for hours with their parents. Maybe I could take the kids and do a sports camp with them to keep them busy while their parents are getting medical attention. I could teach them how to play soccer—I don't need my hands for that." Schooner held up his casted hand.

Malcolm clapped Schooner on the back, "That is brilliant and will make things so much easier for the families. I love it. Do it!"

The first day, Schooner had four kids in his Sports Camp. He started the kids in the morning with stretching, mat exercises and running. Then they started working on the basics of soccer. Within a few days, Schooner's camp not only encompassed kids whose families were seeking medical treatment, but local village children were waiting every morning for the big blonde instructor they called "Coach." There were nine local children, six boys and three girls, who became the core of Schooner's camp. They were there before everyone arrived in the morning, setting up the exercise mats and the makeshift soccer goals and the last to leave at night, after they broke down camp.

This core group would go to the hospital every day and find the children that were waiting with their parents and escort them to camp. They also became expert recruiters within their village and soon Schooner had enough participants to form teams. With the help of hospital staff, he also taught the children about lifesaving techniques such as oral-rehydration therapy and CPR.

At night he would fall onto his cot, exhausted, but his mind would race a million miles an hour. He wondered where she was, what she was doing, was she thinking about him, did she miss him, did she hurt as much as he did, was her heart missing a huge chunk too, did she still love him? And the same question always plagued him—why? Why did she leave without a word? What had happened? What changed everything?

He wanted to remember every detail of this trip so that he could share it with her. She would have loved the village and the people, especially the children. He imagined her finding photographic images in all that surrounded her.

And every night before sleep finally saved him from the demons that haunted his heart, he would try and send her a message, "Come back to me. Just be there in August. We'll make it right. Baby Girl, come back to me."

On their last night in the village, Schooner held the "Macha Grand Soccer Tournament" and all the local families were on the sidelines cheering their children. Families brought food to share with the doctors and staff to thank them for their work. It was Macha's first sports event/tailgate party.

One of the village elders, Levi Mambwe, sat down next to Schooner. "You seem to have found your calling."

"Maybe so," Schooner agreed.

"You have a passion for this. You are a born leader, Coach Schooner. You have made a lasting impact on the children of Macha. You have taught them the importance of exercise on health and have made learning fun for them. It is a gift. Follow your passion and share your gift."

The next morning, they left Macha for the last time. The children followed them to the edge of the village waving after them. Schooner was surprised at how sad he was to leave the simple village. He thought about Levi's words from the night before and thought that they had given him as much, if not more, than he had given to them.

The last leg of the journey was to Livingstone to see Victoria Falls—the largest waterfall in the world. They drove to the Zimbabwe border and followed the Zambezi River to the falls. Hiking down paths through the rainforest, every so often they captured glimpses of the magnificent falls whose roar filled the air with its growling magic. When they came to the Knife Edge Bridge, they were afforded a full view of nature's majesty and force.

Schooner stood there in awe trying to mentally etch the image into his mind and then parked his Nikon on the railing, using it as a makeshift tripod, a trick he had learned at another waterfall. White clouds stood in relief against an azure blue sky. Schooner screwed a red filter to the end of his lens so that the clouds would pop out against the dark sky. He shot short exposures and long exposures knowing that the effects would be very different. *I did listen, Baby Girl, when you tried to teach me this stuff,* he thought.

Before they hiked back to the Jeep, he had Malcolm shoot a picture of him with the falls in the background.

He thought that shot might make a great gift.

CHAPTER 34

Schooner dropped his bags off in his dorm room and headed out to The Quad. He was amazed at how many people he knew as he walked toward Mia's dorm. Everyone wanted to stop and say hello, ask about his summer and ask about his casted hand. All he wanted to do was get across campus. He had waited for this day since May. Today he would get his answers.

He got to her dorm and took a deep breath as he walked through the front door. In the lobby were several people he knew (since he had basically been a resident there Spring Semester). Everyone wanted to know about his hand. The new freshman girls were checking him out, trying to catch his eye.

He finally made it through the lobby and up the stairwell. And there he was standing outside her door. He reminded himself to breathe. His hands were shaking as he knocked on the door with his good hand.

The door opened and Caroline stood there, "Schooner!" She gave him a big hug.

"Hey Caroline! How was your summer?"

It was then he noticed the girl with the short blonde hair putting her stuff out on Mia's desk.

She stopped when she saw Schooner and gave him a bright smile, "Hi, I'm Alison."

"Hi. Schooner."

He turned to Caroline, "Where's Mia?"

"I don't know. I was hoping you would tell me. We were supposed to room together." She looked concerned.

"Did you hear from her at all this summer?" Please say yes, a voice inside him begged.

"Not a word. Didn't you spend the summer with her?" Her confusion was apparent.

He shook his head, "She bailed before I had a chance to say goodbye to her that last day."

"No fucking way." She ran her hands through her hair as if she were thinking something and then just shook her head. "What did you do to your hand?"

"These walls are made of cement."

Her hand flew to her mouth, "You didn't."

He nodded his head, "Yeah, I did."

He could see the pain on her face as she realized something went very wrong for two people who seemed hopelessly in love with one another. He gave her shoulder a squeeze and left the room.

He checked both Rosie and Henry's rooms, but neither of them were there.

Beau was still not in their room when he got back and he was glad. He was not up for answering any more questions about his hand.

Opening his backpack, he grabbed an oversized envelope. Inside were photos of his soccer team, village huts, Victoria Falls and the photo Dr. F. had taken of him in front of the falls. He'd had them made for Mia. He wanted to tell her of his journey and show her his photography, a now common passion that he looked forward to sharing with her.

With the envelope in hand, he headed for the dining hall. Maybe there he'd finally get the answers he wanted.

He stood at the entrance surveying the crowd. Where were they? And then he saw Henry waving to get his attention, a huge smile on his face and Schooner felt relief. He maneuvered through the crowd to get to Henry's table.

"Hey man!" They hugged.

Rosie stood and her arms went around Schooner, surprising him, "Schooner." He gave her a tight hug.

Before they could ask about his hand, he blurted out, "Where's Mia?"

"She's not back." Henry shrugged.

"What do you mean she's not back? What is going on?" He didn't know it was going to hurt so much again this time, as his heart started to crumble just as it had done the last day of spring semester.

"When she wasn't in her room and Caroline didn't know where she was, we asked the dorm director and he said she wasn't on the list of returning students." Rosie was as clearly in the dark as he was.

"What the fuck? What the fuck happened to her?" Schooner spit out angrily, shaking his head. This was the nightmare that he prayed every night would not come to pass. *What the fuck, Baby Girl,* he thought.

"Didn't you guys spend the summer together in New York?"

"No." Schooner sat down on the bench, because he knew his knees would buckle if he kept standing. "I never even said goodbye to her. I got out of my last final, went to her room to go hang out with her and she was gone. She didn't even leave me a note."

Rosie put her forehead into her hands and shook her head. "That doesn't even make sense."

"Why'd she leave me?"

His friends had no answers.

CHAPTER 35

It was the night before Christmas Break that a candle ceremony took place in an all-girls dorm across campus. All the dorm's residents, as well as selected friends from other dorms, were invited to participate.

The girls gathered in a circle as the dorm director lit a candle and handed it to one of the girls. The girls would pass the candle around the circle from one girl to the next. When the candle stopped, everyone in the circle would know that the girl holding the candle was the one who had just become engaged.

That night, the candle stopped on a beaming CJ MacAllister.

CJ and Schooner were engaged.

NOW ...

CHAPTER 36

"Don't poke the bear!" Yolanda Perez came into Schooner Moore's office carrying very tall lattes.

Schooner laughed and motioned her in.

"So, rumor has it you've ripped a few new assholes this morning." She made a face at him saying, *is that true?*

He loved Yoli. She was the only person in his world who always told it like it was. No bullshit. No pretense. And that was why he could trust her. They'd been together for twenty years— she'd been with him since the beginning. Earlier in the year, on her twentieth anniversary with the company, he gave her a percentage ownership of the business. CJ went ballistic when she learned about it. She totally did not get Schooner's relationship with Yoli.

He laughed. "None that didn't deserve to be ripped."

"So how was the big party?"

"If you miss another one of my birthday parties, I am firing your ass." He pointed his finger at her.

"You're going to have to buy me out, buddy." They laughed.

"The big party was a *Real Housewives* Reunion Bash masquerading as my birthday party." Schooner rolled his eyes and shook his head.

"I would've so fit in."

Schooner almost spit out his coffee laughing at Yoli's snark. Yoli was a cargo pants and tee shirt lesbian with short, awful colored red hair.

"Bet you could've gotten some action," he teased and this time she almost spit out her coffee.

"Oh yeah, Real Housewives in search of a taste of the other side. Think I'll pass! How's my sweet girl Holly doing?" Holly and Yoli had a kindred spirits relationship from the time Holly was a toddler.

"Awesome and she said to send you and Debbie her love. She was bummed you two weren't there. At one point, I looked over at her and the look on her face was classic, like she was taking in data on a roomful of aliens."

"With the amount of chemicals those women have had injected into themselves, they might not be classified as human anymore."

Yoli was the one person who could instantly put him in a great mood. He knew why—he could be himself with her. And that reminded him of someone else, the person responsible for teaching him to be himself.

"So, are you on Facebook?" Schooner abruptly changed the subject.

"Umm, yes. Why do you ask?" Yoli looked at Schooner with a 'where did that come from?' look.

"I guess everyone is on it, but me. How does it work? Can everyone see what you say on there or can you talk to someone privately?" It was time to get schooled.

"Okay, well you set up your profile and your own page, known as your wall and then you friend people. If you write something as your "status," it goes on your wall and all the people you friend can see it. Same thing if you write on their wall. But if you just want one person to see your conversation, you can private message them and then the conversation is only between the two of you."

"Okay, good." He nodded.

"So, you want to go on Facebook?" Yoli was surprised.

"I'm thinking about it." Schooner tried to keep pokerfaced.

"No. No. No. No. No. Don't you play that game with me, Schooner. All of a sudden you want to go on Facebook and you want to know about sending private messages. Spill it!"

He sat back in his chair and tapped his forefingers against his lips, wondering how to start this conversation. Or if he even should. But it was the only thing he could think about since Beau had brought her up on Saturday night. He couldn't get her out of his head—not even for a second. And Yoli was truly the only person he could trust enough to confide in.

"When I was in college, there was this girl. Her name was Mia." He smiled, "You guys would have been best friends. Oh my God, you would have loved each other. Anyway, I was crazy in love with her and I thought she was in love with me, too. We were supposed to spend the summer together and then she just disappeared. I mean. literally, disappeared. I went back to her room after my last final. We were supposed to hang out together that day until she left for the airport and when I got there, she was gone. No note. Nothing. And we had been like living together up until that point. And she just freaking disappeared and never came back to school. Gone. Without a trace."

"I thought you were with CJ all through college?" Yoli looked puzzled.

"Well, except when I was with Mia. I left CJ for Mia. Oh man, did CJ hate Mia."

"Maybe CJ killed her." Yoli's eyebrows shot up in mock horror.

Schooner laughed. "Don't think that hadn't crossed my mind." He took a sip of his latte and shook his head. "So anyway, at the party Saturday night, my old college roommate Beau Gordon …"

"Pee Wee Herman?" Yoli interrupted.

"Yes, Pee Wee Herman." Schooner laughed, "Beau and I start talking about this thing that happened freshman year and he asks me who the girl was that was with us, and I tell him it was Mia, and then he tells me that he just had a fight with Mia on Scott Morgan's Facebook page."

"Scott Morgan, the advertising guy?"

"Yeah, he went to our school. I didn't even know Mia knew him. I mean he's really kind of a random person to be in touch with."

Yoli's palms were up in the air. "So have you looked her up on Facebook yet?"

"No, I don't even know how."

She got up to come around to his side of the desk. "You are so useless. What would you do without me?"

Schooner leaned his head into her arm. "I'd be lost."

"That's for shit sure! Okay, let's see if we can look at Scott Morgan's page and his friend list without you being on Facebook yet. It's going to depend on what he's got his privacy settings on. Let's Google him first because there are probably a lot of Scott Morgans." She continued to punch away on his keyboard. "Okay, bingo, here he is. Let's hope he doesn't have his info set to private."

Schooner could feel his stomach knot. He was so close to finding Mia—after all this time. Yoli might just be a few keystrokes away. He could feel his hands shaking. Just knowing he was so close to finding her still had such a profound physical effect on him.

"Thank you, Scott! Okay, here is his Facebook page. He's got 319 friends and we are looking for Mia who?"

"Mia Silver."

"Okay, let's put that in search. Bingo. Is that your Mia?" She turned to him.

He sat back in his chair and let out a long, slow exhale. He nodded his head, because he couldn't speak, and when his voice finally came out, it was choked and cracking, "Yeah. That's my Mia."

Yoli punched him in the arm, "Shit, she's cute. I'd do her."

He laughed.

Mia, all grown up. She looked the same, just older, more mature. Still so pretty. No glasses now and the wild curls were now soft shoulder-length waves with long dark bangs hanging in her eyes. He wanted to reach into the picture and push them from her eyes. He realized he was sitting there smiling at her picture and Yoli was standing there smiling at him.

"Talk about the antithesis of OC women," Yoli observed. "So are you going to just sit there and stare at her picture all day long?"

"Yeah, I just might"

"Okay, shove over. Let's get you on Facebook." She began tapping away again. "We need a picture of you." She went around to the other side of the desk and picked up her cell phone. "Smile. No. No. No. Don't give me that bullshit male model smile. Think of Holly looking at the Housewives like they were aliens." And she snapped the picture. "Perfection! If I do say so myself. Okay, I am emailing this to you and then we are going to attach it to your profile. Done." She came back around the desk. Tap. Tap. Tap. "You are now officially on Facebook. Ready to send her a friend invite?"

"What if she doesn't answer or doesn't accept it?" Yoli was shocked to see the ancient serpent of rejection rearing its ugly head in a man she knew to be in control and extremely confident in all he did, especially in his dealings with women.

"Well she definitely won't answer if you don't send it." Yoli's hands were on her hips.

Schooner just stared at the screen. What if she didn't want him to find her? He was looking at her. He was looking at Mia. There she was. *There she was.* He couldn't pull his eyes away from the beautiful ombre green eyes on his computer screen.

"You really loved her." Yoli said, softly.

Schooner nodded his head. "I really loved her."

And with that admission spoken aloud, he pushed the Send Friend Request button.

BOOK TWO

MIA

CHAPTER 1

"Could today get any freaking worse?" Mia rhetorically asked her assistant, Seth Shapiro. She raked her hand through her hair, while staring at her computer screen. "I can understand losing a client because we didn't do a good job, because we didn't deliver. But because his daughter got engaged to some guy who works for a competitor? Do we need to start pimping out our staff? Because I am not above pimping out our staff." Mia was on a tear. "Fuck!"

"Kami thinks you're going to fire her." Seth looked a little scared of Mia at the moment.

"That's ridiculous. She's done everything to keep these assholes happy. This is not the way she deserves to lose this account." Mia pulled up a spreadsheet on her computer. "This really hurts our cash flow."

Seth had been Mia's right hand since before she started the agency—there was no aspect of the business that she didn't confide details with him, which is why they made such a great team.

"Do not make me give up my massages." Seth glared at Mia in the way only an over the top queen can.

"Don't worry, Princess, we won't be eating cat food for another few months yet." She sneered back at him. "Do you have the latest weekly sales pipeline?"

Seth handed Mia the report, she tapped the page a few times with her index finger and then dialed an extension, putting the call on speakerphone.

"Hey Boss," the voice came through the phone.

"Hey Dave, so how far away are we from automating that new work from American Express? Give me worst case scenario." She and Seth looked at each other, holding their breath.

"Well, you know what they're like with the endless conference calls and doing everything by committee, but their IT guy and I have been kind of doing our own thing. So I'd say worst case is live traffic in six weeks." Mia fist pumped the air and mouthed a silent "YES" to Seth. "Excellent, Dave. You made my day!"

He laughed on the other end, "I thought that might make you happy and I'll step it up even more to see if we can be live in four to five weeks. I know what a hole we've now got after today's bullshit."

"Yeah, bullshit is right," Mia agreed. "I'm going to start pimping out the staff. It's the only answer," she kidded.

"Count me in, Boss. Pimp me anytime."

Mia laughed, "That's why I love this staff, Seth."

"Ho!" Seth yelled at Dave.

"Damn right, I get the job done," he kidded back.

They disconnected the call and Mia looked at Seth, "Okay, let's plan on two months of it being tight. I don't want to stop the sales team from selling, but expenses need to be kept down until we have the additional cash flow from AmEx."

"Memo or staff meeting?" Seth asked.

"Staff meeting—let's do this face-to-face and get Kami in here first. I need to talk to her before she slits her wrists and bleeds out all over her office." Mia smiled at Seth, "Mondays suck!"

Two hours later, a drained Mia and Seth sat in her office alone again.

"I'm glad we did the meeting, Mia. They were all freaking about losing their jobs."

"The last thing I want to do is lay off people. We have never had to lay off anyone. I will give up my salary if we need to make payroll."

Seth loved working with Mia. She had built a small ad agency that was more like a wonderful dysfunctional family than a place of business, and Mia saying she would give up her salary not to lay off people was not just empty words and he knew it. That was the ethos of the organization and precisely why Mia's staff would run through walls for her.

She looked at her watch and smiled. "I bet the turkeys are out of the oven at the deli." She went to get her purse out of her drawer and Seth stopped her.

"Sit down. Let me run down and get you a sandwich. I'm sure this morning put you way behind schedule. Turkey on rye with Russian dressing and an Iced Tea?"

"Yes, thank you. Put your lunch on my card, too." She handed him her Gold Card.

"Shall I close your door?" Mia nodded, as he headed out.

Thank God for Seth, she thought. If anyone could keep her life in order and keep her on track, it was Seth. Anal, persnickety, bitchy as all hell, incredibly loyal and very competent. He was her rock as well as her personal fashion police, making sure that her somewhat BoHo style was always trendy and chic.

Mia took a swig from a bottle of water on her desk and thought, *today has sucked and it's only lunchtime on Monday. Please don't get any worse, I've had enough already.*

She woke up her sleeping computer screen, clicked her email icon and started to scan her email. Geez—in just a few hours fifty-seven unread new emails—Junk, junk, junk, deal with later, delete, delete, delete, Business Journal, NY Times alert, junk, Advertising Age, Facebook friend request from Schooner Moore …

Facebook friend request from Schooner Moore.

She just stared at the email subject line, her heart racing, the air in the room disappearing. *Breathe, Mia, breathe*, she consciously told herself. Facebook friend request from Schooner Moore. Ho-ly Shit!

She opened the email.

Mia stared at the little block with the confirm button. Schooner had sent this. This day was getting stranger by the minute. Schooner had sent this. He had sent this to her. Ho-ly shit!

Mia closed her eyes and took a deep breath. She tried to still her thoughts, but every cell in her body was in overdrive and each and every one of those cells, including the ones in both her head and her heart (which rarely agreed), were in perfect harmony.

Mia hit confirm.

CHAPTER 2

oly shit. Schooner just friended me. Mia was astounded.

She quickly logged onto Facebook and went to her friends list. There he was, she clicked his name and went to his page. He had one friend. She was his first and only friend. Holy shit.

She clicked on the picture and it came up full sized and she heard herself gasp. She was looking at Schooner. He was smiling at her. His real smile. He was a grown man now. Still so handsome. She could see the crinkles in the corners of his eyes. Those beautiful clear eyes. She realized she was smiling at her computer screen. She also realized there were tears in her eyes and her throat had tightened. In her mind, he had always been nineteen. Not this man she was looking at. But this was Schooner. This stranger, who was not quite a stranger, was Schooner.

She heard the ding and the message screen popped up.

> Schooner: Mia, are you there?
>
> Mia: Yes
>
> Schooner: What's your phone #?

She just stared at the screen. Her hands were shaking. Literally shaking.

> Schooner: Mia, what is your phone #?

Wow. He was forceful.

She typed in her cell number, with badly trembling hands and hit send. A nanosecond later, her cell phone rang, the display portraying a number with a 949 area code. Mia realized she was somehow expecting a 714 area code. Their old area code. Times had changed.

"Hi," she tried to keep her voice even, but it came out breathy.

"Hi," it was his voice. A little more mature sounding. But it was Schooner.

She knew it was her turn to speak next, social grace's would dictate a "How are you?" but she had paused for a moment and he jumped right in, this time his voice hoarse and tight, "Why did you leave me?"

Wham to the solar plexus. She literally was thrown back in her chair. The air momentarily knocked out of her.

"You told her what happened to me." They both knew to whom she was referring.

"No. I never told her. Mia, I never told her anything," his voice was adamant. "Did she tell you I told her?"

She could hear the tension crackling off his voice.

"Schooner, it was a long time ago." Mia could feel the pain, as if it were yesterday, and she didn't want to revisit it.

"Mia, I didn't tell her. I never would have betrayed you that way. All I ever wanted to do was protect you. And I didn't know why you left me. I never knew why you left me. But I swear, I never, ever told her."

They were both silent, clearly equally reeling from one another's revelations.

He was the first to speak again, "If she told you that she knew, then she was bluffing and she played you." Mia let out an involuntary sob and he paused and then sighed, "Holy Fuck," as if he'd come to some huge realization.

Mia thought she was going to be sick.

"Please believe me, Mia. You know all I wanted to do was protect you."

And with those words, it all came flooding back. Now with twenty-four years of hindsight, Mia finally realized that she had been played, and CJ had gotten the knee jerk reaction out of her that she had intended. Mia had played right into her hands and the enormity of the ramifications of how it had changed her life and how she had hurt Schooner came down on her with a weight so heavy she thought her chest was going to cave in.

She started to cry, "Oh my God, Schooner, I am so sorry. I am so, so sorry. Oh my God."

"Do you believe me?" his voice was soft.

"Yes," she managed between sobs. "I do."

She heard him sigh.

"Schooner, how do I begin to apologize for being an immature sixteen-year-old, for not trusting you, for believing what she said? I am so, so sorry I hurt you."

"Shhh, don't, Baby Girl. You were a victim in this, too. What she did was malicious with the intent to hurt you and to put an end to us. And my whole freaking life has been based on a lie."

She could hear the anger in his voice and it was then Mia realized that Schooner had married CJ and her tears began anew. She won. She fucking won. She played a dirty game and won.

There was a soft knock on her door and Seth peeked in. She motioned for him to come in and he put the bag with her lunch on her desk. His eyes telegraphing alarm at coming in and seeing her so distraught.

"Schooner, my assistant just came in and I've got to prep for a 2 o'clock meeting."

"Schooner?" Seth mouthed, "Schooner?" and muttered "Are you talking to a boat?"

"What time are you up until at night?"

"I'm kind of a night owl, usually between midnight and one."

"Mia, are you going to answer the phone when you see my number come up?" his voice was very soft.

"Yeah."

"Say it, Mia," his voice more forceful.

"I will answer your calls, Schooner."

Seth was looking at her, brows knit in a "what's going on here" look.

"You promise?"

She smiled, "Yes. I promise."

"Okay, I will call you later."

"Okay."

"Mia. It's really good to hear your voice."

And that caused another sob to escape. "It's really good to hear your voice too, Schooner," she replied, softly.

"I'll talk to you later, Baby Girl."

A torrent of tears flowed from her eyes at his final two words. "Okay. Bye." And she hung up her phone.

Seth sat there looking at her, completely speechless.

"Am sure I look lovely," she smiled at Seth, wiping her running nose on the sleeve of her sweater.

"Schooner?"

"Schooner."

"First off, who names their kid Schooner? Is this some WASP thing?"

"Might be," Mia laughed, tears still running down her face.

"Was he totally teased for being named Schooner?" Seth was obsessing over Schooner's name.

"No. Not at all. It totally fit him. I'm sure there's a generation of little Schooners out there born to women who were crushing on him."

"So who is he and why were you crying hysterically?" He unwrapped her turkey sandwich for her and put the straw in her Iced Tea and slid them across the desk to her.

"Schooner was my college boyfriend freshman year. He was my first love."

"Go on."

She clearly was not going to get away with the abridged version with Seth.

"Do you remember I told you about being raped in college?"

Seth nodded.

"Well, Schooner was the one who found me that night and took me to the hospital. And then he didn't leave my side the rest of the semester. The last night of school he went back to his dorm to study for his last final and his ex, this bitch CJ—who I think he probably married, showed up and said a bunch of stuff that led me to believe he told her what had happened to me and I freaked. I thought he betrayed me and I cut out early the next morning and got an earlier flight home. I just left and never said goodbye or spoke to him ever again, until, well, you just heard it."

"Oh my God." Seth's hand flew to his mouth. "What did he say?"

"He asked, 'Why did you leave me?'." A small sob escaped, accompanied by a fresh gush of tears. "And I told him that he betrayed my confidence with her. He was adamant that he never told her and that she was probably bluffing and that she had played me and that I fell for it."

"Holy shit, Mia. Do you believe him?"

She nodded, "I do. He was clearly very angry. That fucking bitch played me."

"And so he never knew why you left him. Until now. Oh God, this is so tragic. You loved him?"

Mia nodded, "I loved him so much, Seth. No one has ever come close, not even remotely."

"Mia, he came and found you."

More tears.

Seth flipped open his iPad case. "What's his last name."

"Moore"

He began typing. "Schooner James Moore of Newport Beach, California. Is that him?"

Mia nodded.

"Ok, there's a Wiki here on him. Schooner James Moore, American Entrepreneur, age 43, his birthday was just two days ago, wow, it was Saturday. Holy crap, Mia, he owns Level 9. Totally famous health clubs in LA. The Real Housewives work out there. Oh yeah, he married her, Colleen Janice (CJ) Moore, two kids, Holly, 19 and Zac, 17. Let's Google Image him."

He looked up at Mia, mouth hanging wide open. "YOU are the Queen BBC!" He yelled. "The Queen. The Ultimate!" His mouth hung open and he was pointing a finger at her.

BBC was their acronym for "Bitch Be Crazy"—women who acted crazy or did wacko things or were just plain loopy, were known as BBCs.

"Why?" laughed Mia.

"You walked out on this man? Bitch, you *are* crazy." He looked up from his iPad, "I love him."

"Let me see." Mia grabbed at Seth's iPad.

He pulled it out of her reach. "No. No. No. You are not taking Schooner away from me, Bitch."

Mia laughed and got up and walked around to the other side of the desk. She looked over Seth's shoulder. "It's so weird to see him as an adult. He was so gorgeous when he was young."

Seth shot her a BBC look, "He's still gorgeous. Robert Redford wished he looked like this in his best days. Mia, this is your Schooner?" He flipped through the pictures.

She nodded and more tears sprung from her eyes, "That's my Schooner."

CHAPTER 3

Mia paced around her apartment. Her cell phone had not rung and it was 12:10 A.M. *I'm waiting for his call like a teenager,* she sighed. Maybe he'd reconsidered after their brief talk earlier in the day. He now had the answer to his question and after all, CJ was his wife. They had kids together. They had built a family. They were a family. Mia looked around her beautiful apartment, a place that usually provided her solace, but tonight she felt both alone and lonely. No kids, no family, no current significant other.

Thanks, Schooner, she thought, *you really needed to find me so that I can dwell on being forty and alone.*

Finally, at 12:30, Mia crawled into bed and turned off the lights. *Today has been so emotionally draining,* she thought. *Lost and found. Today was lost and found. How crazy is that,* she thought.

She was in that quasi-sleep state having odd dreams of Schooner, when her cell phone rang. She reached for it and it displayed that 949 area code. It also said it was 2:47 A.M.

"Hi," she tried not to sound sleepy.

"Hi," his voice sounded like silk and she curled up deeper into her blanket. "I'm sorry it's so late. No, go ahead and put those bags over there," he said to someone else. "Sorry, I'm just getting settled," he sighed. "I moved out tonight. I'm at the Ritz in Laguna Niguel."

"Oh my God. I'm so sorry, Schooner."

"This was a long time coming. I just didn't know how long until today. What she did to you. What she did to us. There's just no coming back from that." He sounded absolute.

"Are you okay?" her voice was sweet and soft. She wanted to comfort him.

"There's a yes and no to that, Mia. Today has been a lot to process."

Mia was nodding her head on her side of the call, as if he could see her. "If I could change things, Schooner," she let out a long sigh. "I should've come to you. I'm so sorry."

"I know. I wish you had. Everything would have been different," he sighed. "Mia, I went to pieces when you left. I was so blindsided. I really thought we were going to spend our whole lives together."

She was silent and he asked, "You still there?"

"Yeah, I'm just lost in thought and I'm listening to your voice. I never thought I'd hear your voice again."

"Well, talk to me so that I can hear your voice, too." She could hear him settling in on the other end of the phone. "After I left California, I just sort of crawled inside myself for a long, long time. I don't think I've ever been really great at relationships."

"I don't agree with that," he whispered and she smiled. "I didn't even ask, are you married?"

"No, never married, no kids. I own a small boutique advertising agency here in Manhattan. Been involved in a couple of semi-long term relationships, but never got married."

"Well I guess that you figured out that I married CJ."

There was a silence.

"Why Schooner? Did you always love her?" Mia tried to keep the hurt out of her voice, but she could hear it creeping in. She realized that she was nervously twisting her blanket in her hands.

"Oh Mia. No, I didn't love her. This is just so fucked up. I loved you, but I didn't want to ever again hurt the way I did when I lost you. Best way to avoid hurt, don't put yourself in a situation that can hurt you. That's what I thought I was doing. I was in a situation I could control. What we had was out of control. I knew I would never be emotionally over my head like that with her."

How sad, Mia thought. She was sad for him. The thought of him hurting was gut wrenching, but on some level she was so happy to hear him say he was with CJ because he didn't love her deeply. There was something very satisfying in that knowledge, especially after today's revelations.

"Are your kids wonderful?" she asked, needing to change the subject and get away from all the hurt they'd inflicted upon one another.

She could hear the smile in his voice when he spoke of them and she listened intently, hearing the pride and love in his words and tone.

"Schooner, things played out the way they were supposed to so that you would have your kids."

"Maybe so. I definitely don't have any regrets there. Did you ever want children?"

"I kind of tried not to go there," she began. "The relationships I've been involved in weren't right to bring a child into, so it just never really worked out."

"But did you want them?" he persisted.

His personality was so much more forceful and no nonsense as an adult. *He's really tenacious,* Mia thought. "If the situation had been different, I might've let myself go there, but it wasn't, so I put it out of my reality."

"I'm sorry," he whispered.

"Don't be," she sighed, smushing deeper into her covers. "It is what it is."

They were silent for a few minutes and he asked, "Did you miss me?"

She was silent, trying to pull her thoughts and composure together so that she wouldn't cry.

"I guess that's my answer," he sadly assumed.

She could hear the fresh hurt in his voice. "No. That is not your answer. I was just trying to make sure that I didn't start crying again." She took a deep breath. "Schooner, it felt like part of me died when I left. It was years before I was even semi-ok again. I just hid inside myself. I was angry and hurt and immature and losing the guy I loved felt like I'd had my heart cut out."

"You never lost me."

"I was a freaking emotional mess," she went on. The floodgates were now open. "So yes, the answer to your question was yes, I missed you. I was just empty. Broken. How do you even start with someone else after us? Nothing felt like that and it was my only point of reference—the way that we were together. It took me a long time to figure out that every relationship was different and that no two were alike. I wanted to feel again what I felt with us."

"Did you ever find it?"

She could hear the concern for her in his voice.

"I think at times I tried to convince myself that I did. But eventually I'd figure out that I was lying to myself. So, the answer to that question would be no."

They were silent for a while, but it wasn't uncomfortable. She could feel the intense emotion and energy across the telephone line. This was so much for each of them to process. Years of preconceived notions, dispelled. Truths that they had convinced themselves of, crumbled, turning out to be a House of Cards, a House of Lies.

"I'm really glad I found you again, Baby Girl."

She smiled. "You know what?"

"What?"

She could hear his smile.

"I'm really glad you found me, too."

CHAPTER 4

I t was 4:45 A.M. when Mia texted Seth.

Mia: Are you awake?

Seth: I am now.

Mia: He moved out tonight. He's staying at The Ritz.

Seth: Holy shit, he didn't!

Mia: Holy shit, he did!

Seth: I love him.

Mia: LOL

Seth: So when's he coming to NYC?

Mia: Not soon enough!!!

Seth: There's hope for you yet, BBC. There's hope for you yet.

CHAPTER 5

I t was Thursday morning at 6:45 A.M. and Mia's cell phone was ringing. It no longer displayed the 949 number. It now said "Schooner—mobile".

"Hey," she answered. She'd already been up for about half an hour, too wired to sleep. She had woken up and looked at the time on her phone's clock every hour throughout the night.

"We're on the tarmac."

She could hear the PA announcements in the background. "Welcome to New York!" Mia was beaming, ear-to-ear. Oh my God, he is here.

She had so much nervous energy that she felt like she was vibrating on another frequency. Holy smokes—in less than an hour he'll be at my apartment, she realized. He had flown in on the Wednesday night red-eye. What a crazy few days.

She had arranged for her favorite limo service to be there to meet him.

"I'll see you in a few."

She could hear the smile in his voice. "Oh my God, Schooner." Mia was already shaking with nerves.

"I know, Baby Girl. I'll see you soon."

Mia texted Seth.

Mia: He's landed and he's on his way!!!!

Seth: OMG

Mia: I'm a freaking wreck!

Seth: What are you wearing?

Mia: Since it's only 6 A.M., I don't want to overdo it. Jeans, black v-neck cashmere sweater.

Seth: V-neck is good. Show him that great boobage. Cashmere is touchable. Shoes?

Mia: Right now barefoot.

Seth: Stay that way. I know you just had a pedicure. Make-up?

Mia: Just a little blush.

Seth: Do a little brown liner at the outer corner of your eyes. Hair?

Mia: It's down and I'm having a good hair day.

Seth: Bangs in your eyes?

Mia: Yes.

Seth: Sexy. Love it. I am so nervous 4 u!

Mia: Ditto. I feel sick. Too bad it is 2 early in the morn to eat a Xanax!! Ok, will call you later. Wish me luck!

Seth: All will be great. He found out about u on Sat. night and Thurs morning he is here. I love this. So romantic. Don't fuck it up BBC!

Mia: LOL. Pray 4 me!

Mia tried staying busy to keep her nerves in check. She made a pot of coffee. Sliced bagels. Unloaded her dishwasher. Turned on the TV. Tried to watch CNN. Brushed her teeth for a second time. Dabbed her lips with just the slightest bit of gloss. Tried to do deep breathing exercises to stop from shaking. But she just could not stop trembling, no matter what she did.

The call came from the doorman in the lobby and she had them send him up. He was in her building. Getting into her elevator. It was all so surreal. In just moments, she would be face to face with Schooner again. She remembered the last time she saw him as he walked down the steps from her dorm, not letting go of her hand until their fingertips no longer touched.

And there it was, the knock on the door. She whispered, "Showtime" as she went to open the door (not knowing that he whispered the very same word to himself on the other side of the door).

Holding her breath as she opened the door, she prayed that she didn't do something embarrassing like hyperventilate and pass out.

There he was.

She looked up into his handsome face and was sure her smile was as wide as his. She didn't think about it, her arms just went around his waist immediately and she felt his arms tighten around her, crushing her to him. She felt his lips in her hair and heard an "mmm" come out of her.

She looked up at him and his beautiful smile eased away a good portion of her nerves (not all).

"Come on in," she finally said.

"I was so nervous on the ride here," he admitted.

She held out a hand to show him how she was shaking and they both laughed.

"I want another hug," she whispered and he complied, wrapping his arms around her again. She buried her face in his chest, deeply breathing in his clean scent, feeling the hardness of his stomach muscles and nuzzling her face into them. She looked up at him again and he gave her a small soft kiss on her forehead. She knew she could not wipe the silly smile off of her face.

She led him over to the breakfast bar in her open kitchen. "Coffee?" she offered. "You hungry? Can I make you some breakfast?"

He sat on the bar stool, his long legs stretched out, just smiling at her.

"What?" she asked, smiling back at him.

No one should look that good in faded jeans, she thought. Faded jeans and a blue Henley sweatshirt—the man was a living Brooks Brothers ad. And there he was in her kitchen. Smiling at her. Schooner Moore was sitting at her breakfast bar, in her apartment, in Manhattan. Surreal didn't even begin to describe the situation.

He just shook his head. "Saturday night I was at my own birthday party in Newport Beach and I was miserable. Truly miserable. I was out on a deck alone, away from everyone at my party. Away from my party. And Beau Gordon shows up out on the deck with a joint—I haven't gotten high in like ten years—and we smoke this joint and start talking about that time we got high at the freshman retreat and he asks me who was the girl that was with us? I tell him it was you and he tells me that he had a fight with you on Facebook. That was Saturday night. It's 8 A.M. on Thursday morning. And I'm here with you. In your apartment. In New York."

Mia could not wipe the smile off of her face. "Pretty fucking surreal, huh?"

He laughed, "Very fucking surreal."

Mia poured two glasses of orange juice and handed one to Schooner. She held hers up in a toast, "To Beau Gordon, you AK-47 toting son of a bitch. Thank you!"

"Here! Here!" Schooner clinked glasses with her and they laughed.

It's still easy, Mia thought. It's still so easy with him.

She grabbed the bagels that she'd cut apart earlier to help calm her nerves. "Hungry?"

He shook his head, yes. "Do you have whole wheat?"

Mia gave him a 'what are you crazy' look. "Whole wheat? Did you just ask me for a whole wheat bagel? What's next, are you going to want to spread avocado on this?"

He laughed, "Bite me."

"So tempted," she volleyed back. "Okay, your choices are onion, everything and pumpernickel."

God, he was gorgeous and he was sitting at her breakfast bar. This man, whom she had loved more deeply than any other man in her life. This total stranger.

"Please tell me you know what pumpernickel is," she teased.

"Well by process of elimination, it's that one." He pointed to the pumpernickel bagel.

She knew she'd been smiling ear to ear since he'd gotten there. "Did you sleep on the plane?"

"I can't sleep on planes." He shook his head.

"Oh no, not good. Well, after this adrenaline rush wears off, you're going to crash." Mia began, "I need to do a conference call, which I'll take from here, at 9 A.M. It should last about an hour and a half. You should nap. Go crash out in the bedroom."

"Can I crash on the couch, so I can hang out with you? If that doesn't bother you."

"Whatever is comfortable for you," Mia offered.

"I'm a guy, just put me on a couch".

Mia laughed, "Okay, I'll stick the remote in your hand, that should put you right to sleep."

Schooner reached out and took Mia's hand in his and gave it a squeeze. "I need to get gloves later. It's really cold here and I didn't think about bringing any."

"We can go do that after my call."

Schooner had arrived with a blast of arctic air. The day's high was only going to be twenty-three degrees and down into the teens at night with below zero wind chills. But the day was bright and sunny and the sky was the color of his eyes.

After breakfast, Schooner got on the couch and Mia brought him a pillow from the bedroom. Within minutes, he was fast asleep. She brought a quilt in and covered him, then just sat there staring at him. *Un-fucking-believable*, she thought as she watched him sleep in her living room.

She took a picture with her cell phone of him sleeping peacefully on her couch. She couldn't take her eyes off of him. This wasn't real. This just could not be real.

She texted the photo to Seth.

> Seth: OMG, he's adorable.
>
> Mia: I know. Can I keep him?
>
> Seth: LOL
>
> Mia: Please please please. Please let me keep him!
>
> Seth: Are you ok?
>
> Mia: Yeah, a little nervous. Not quite sure—Do I touch him? Not touch him?
>
> Seth: Stop over thinking it, BBC.
>
> Mia: Ok.... got to get ready for conf. call
>
> Seth: Update me later.
>
> Mia: Will do

Schooner didn't stir the entire time Mia was on her call. He looked so beautiful sleeping. There was a hint of the young Schooner that she used to watch across her pillow as he slept. She was having a hard time processing it all. What were they doing? What was this? They were two people who had once loved each other deeply and had it ripped away. But who were they now?

Their marathon phone calls over the past few days had been deep, cathartic, brutally honest and surprisingly easy. But what about being together? She was attracted to him, how could she not be... but was it mutual, she wondered. He had a room reserved uptown at The Stanhope—he didn't want her to feel pressured about staying in her apartment and now that was hanging over her—where would he stay? Would he even want to stay with her?

At the end of the weekend, what would it be? Nice to see you again?

Seth's words starting ringing in her brain, "Don't over think it" and clearly she was.

She didn't have the heart to wake him, so she wrote him a note—this time she wouldn't leave without a note. Not making that mistake twice, she mused.

S—Ran out to the store. Will be back soon. Make yourself at home. Extra towels are out in the bathroom, if you need. See you in a few. —
M

An hour later, Mia reentered her apartment, to find Schooner no longer on her couch.

"Hey, I'm back," she yelled out.

"I'll be right out," he called back from the bathroom. She put the bags down on the couch and took off her coat, scarf and hat. Her teeth were chattering; she was still so cold. Today was the kind of cold that just got deep into your bones and hung on tight.

The bathroom door opened, a cloud of steamy air escaped and Schooner emerged behind it, a towel wrapped around his waist, as he dried his thick fair hair with another towel. He smiled at her, clearly enjoying her reaction to his near-nakedness.

"I own health clubs," he offered, a very self-satisfied smirk on his face.

"And I eat bagels. This is so not good." Mia shook her head and walked over to the kitchen, needing water for her suddenly very dry mouth.

Schooner emerged a few minutes later, hair still damp, in his faded jeans and a button down Ralph Lauren, sleeves rolled at the cuffs—barefoot. Faded jeans and barefoot and 6' 2, Mia took another sip of water for that very dry mouth of hers.

"C'mere," Mia said, sitting down on the couch and grabbing the bags from Barney's New York/Co-op. "I went and got some stuff for you while you were sleeping."

A real smile took over his face and she handed him the first box. Inside were black leather cashmere lined gloves. "I hope they fit. I knew you needed them."

He took them out of the box and put them on. "Perfect," he declared and leaned forward and kissed her cheek.

Okay, cheek kiss, *not good*, she thought.

Mia planted a smile on her face and pulled another box out of the bag for him. She handed him the box. "What did you do?" he asked.

She just shrugged.

Inside the box was a Scottish cashmere scarf—a blue plaid in navy and sky blue—a perfect match for his eyes. He brought it up to his face to feel the soft, plush cashmere. "This is really gorgeous, Mia."

Mia took the scarf from Schooner's hands and wrapped it around his neck, holding a side in each hand. She wanted to pull him forward and kiss him, but instead just smiled at him. "It's very you," she said. "It matches your eyes."

His arms went around her and he hugged her tight.

"You ready to go out and brave the cold, California Boy?"

"Show me your New York." He stood and grabbed his coat. "Hey Mia," he turned to her and smiled and out of the pocket of his black and royal blue Columbia ski jacket he pulled out a black knit cap and pulled it onto his head, down to his eyes.

Mia's heart melted and stung at the same time. *Do I smile or cry*, she asked herself? He had the hat. He still had the hat. "Well, look at that, I'm good for gloves, scarf and a hat," she joked.

When in doubt, make a joke.

The tears burned at the back of her throat.

CHAPTER 6

They hit the streets and headed south from Mia's apartment in Chelsea to the West Village.

"Okay, so you had New York bagels this morning, it's now time for part two of your Big Apple culinary tour." Mia bounced down the streets of New York City. She always tapped into the city's rhythm and never quite walked when she was in her hometown.

Within the first few blocks, Schooner was bouncing beside her as she played tour guide.

"Please tell me part two is pizza." He raised his brows questioningly and she enthusiastically nodded back. "You weren't kidding about the bagels." He smiled down at her.

"We'll have to send you home with a bag," she offered and then immediately saw a shadow cross his face. She grabbed his hand, her other hand going to his forearm, "I'm not looking to get rid of you."

Squeezing her hand, he smiled at her. "You'd better not be."

He didn't take his hand away and they walked down Sixth Avenue holding hands.

I'm walking down Sixth Avenue with Schooner—holding hands, like a couple. This is truly mind numbing, she thought, and if it weren't for the cold, biting wind stinging her cheeks, she would've thought she was dreaming. Stealing a glance at his handsome profile, just the sight of him, with the black knit cap she'd placed on his head nearly a quarter of a century before, overwhelmed her. *Is this what truly happy feels like,* she wondered.

They stopped for lunch at John's Pizza on Bleecker Street and Schooner had his first taste of New York coal oven pizza, thin crust almost slightly burned, fresh mozzarella gracing the top.

"I'm not allowing you to put pineapple on this," she teased. "That's considered heresy in these parts."

Their day was the perfect mix of sightseeing, fresh air, stopping into little places for something quintessentially New York, or just to warm up. They walked across the Brooklyn Bridge and back through lower Manhattan along Battery City Park, and ended the evening at one of Mia's favorite little hole in the wall restaurants on Cornelia Street in the West Village. From there they began walking back up to her apartment building in Chelsea.

The last few blocks before her apartment they began to run, laughing along the way, as they tried to escape the below zero wind chill gusts and reach the warmth of Mia's lobby quickly. Mia was shivering by the time they got into the elevator.

"Are you sure you want to go out to the beach tomorrow?" she questioned Schooner.

"Yeah, it'll be fun in this cold," he nodded and looked at his watch. It was almost midnight. "What time is the ferry we have to catch?" he asked.

"There's a 10:10 A.M. out of Bay Shore. We'll be going against traffic, but I still think we should leave ourselves plenty of time. There's supposed to be snow flurries overnight and in the morning, but if we're on the road by 8:30, I think we'll be ok."

"So, should I be back here by about eight?" he asked.

Mia nodded, her heart sinking. He was going to his hotel. Keep smiling, she reminded herself. Don't tank out now. Don't ruin a perfect day. Perfect until now.

Schooner grabbed his soft black Tumi bag and slung it over his shoulder. He smiled down at Mia, "This was a great day. Really, really great."

Then why the fuck are you leaving, Mia wondered.

"It was," she concurred, smiling back at him.

He gently grasped her upper arm, bent down and kissed her cheek. "I'll see you in the morning."

She couldn't speak. The salt from the tears rising toward their release was already burning the back of her throat. *Is he just not into me*, Mia questioned herself?

She stood in the doorway as he walked down the hall toward the elevator.

There was no way she was going to spend the night wondering and torturing herself. "Schooner…" she called, as he pressed the elevator call button.

He looked at her.

"Schooner. I don't want you to leave." There. She had put it out there. It was all on the line. She had to know.

He stood looking at her, his face inscrutable. The elevator door opened.

"Don't get in," she silently begged. "Don't. Get. In."

He stood there for a second, not moving, and then started down the hall toward her.

She couldn't read his expression. His eyes looked kind, but he wasn't smiling.

He reached where she was standing in the threshold of her apartment's doorway and stood before her. Taking her face in both of his hands, his eyes locked on hers.

Here it comes, she thought, *the friend speech*. Her eyes filled with tears, the hope of the feelings she'd felt resurrected the last few days quickly being extinguished. Her heart burned. Why did I allow myself to go there, she chastised? Another dream dies. Please don't cry, she begged herself, don't cry. Don't make him feel even more uncomfortable.

He held her face, looking directly into her eyes, his face expressionless.

She wanted to look away, to cry, but he held her face and her gaze. If her eyes could speak, the words she was silently trying to tell him were, "I just want you to love me again and I don't think I can take this rejection from you."

He pushed her bangs out of her eyes and a smile slowly overtook his handsome face. He ran his thumb over her bottom lip and bent down and softly kissed her lips. Parting her lips for him, his tongue explored in a way that felt both familiar and new. Mia wrapped her arms around his neck and did not hold back, kissing him passionately, she let him know how much she wanted him, how much she wanted them again. She felt her tears finally release from where she was holding them at bay and run from her eyes to her temples. This time she didn't try to stop them.

He pulled back and looked at her, still holding her face and gave her a rough kiss on her lips. "I was hoping you'd ask."

She could feel her brows knit together in a questioning look.

"This had to come from you. It's been really hard to be hands off with you—but it had to come from you."

"I was thinking you didn't want me," just put it out there Mia, she told herself. This time you need to be totally honest with him—all the time.

He caressed her cheek, "Crazy girl." He laughed.

She thought Seth would be screaming BBC at her at that moment.

"Don't you know how I feel about you?"

She shook her head no. "I think you should show me." She smiled at him.

He pulled her tight against him and she could feel his erection through his jeans pressing against her stomach. He gave her the Schooner smile.

She smiled up at him, tears still streaming from her eyes.

He wiped her tears with his thumb. Leaning down, he whispered in her ear, "It *is* real, Baby Girl," answering her unasked question.

Taking her by the hand, he led her back into her apartment.

CHAPTER 7

Mia was curled up in Schooner's lap on her couch, arms around his neck, as they made out like teenagers. She felt sixteen again. All the anxiety from the day was gone. They were totally on the same page—they still wanted one another after all this time. His hotel reservations had been canceled and he was staying where he belonged, with her.

He brushed her bangs from her eyes, "I have something for you."

Wriggling in his lap, "I know, I feel it." She raised her eyebrows and smiled at him.

Laughing, "That too. But you're just going to have to wait on that."

Her eyes were wide and she faux pouted. Taking her bottom lip in his teeth, he growled at her.

How can it just be so easy with *someone*, she wondered? *So damn easy.*

Moving her off of his lap and onto the couch, he stood and stretched then walked across the room over to where his luggage sat by the door. She watched as he gracefully bent down and unzipped the outer compartment of his bag, removing a flat package. As he walked back toward the couch, she could not help but admire his athletic grace, there was a fluidity to the way he moved and she could almost see him back on the courts covering the space with lithe ease.

Sitting down next to her, he smiled and silently handed her the package. She cocked her head to the side, looking at him and took it.

"Open it," he demanded and she did, pulling opened a tabbed end of the cardboard.

Inside was a large envelope and she carefully slid it out from the cardboard sleeve. Mia looked up at him and he nodded, urging her to go on. She opened the envelope and inside was a stack of 8x10 B&W prints.

Carefully, she removed the photos. The first image in the stack was of a small African boy holding a soccer ball that was half his size. His beautiful smile revealed a wide gap between his two front teeth. The boy was standing on a rutted dirt road with thatched roof cottage-sized dwellings in the background.

Mia looked up at Schooner, quizzically. "Did you shoot this?"

He nodded, smiling.

"Where? When? This is really good, Schooner." She was looking at him for answers.

"That was shot in the village of Macha in Zambia. I went there the summer after freshman year."

Mia started looking through the stack of starkly beautiful landscapes Schooner had captured, impressed with his natural ability for strong composition that led the eye around the frame. His portraits of the children were raw, journalistic and pure.

She looked up at him. "You are so talented."

Smiling at her response to the images, "I've wanted to share these with you for a very long time. When I shot them, you were in my head the whole time reminding me about all the things I listened to you say about composition and lighting. When I got back, I had these made for you."

"What were you doing in Africa?"

"Well, I was kind of heartbroken that summer and my plans to come to New York kind of blew up. A family friend, an orthopedic surgeon, my orthopedic surgeon, suggested I come to Zambia with him and a group of other specialists and help them in establishing a hospital. He thought the change of scenery would be good for me. And it was. I definitely found my calling over there. I helped the doctors get set up and after a few days I realized that there were all these families traveling long distances to the hospital and the kids had to wait all day for their parents, so I started a sports camp for them."

Mia's eyes widened and a smile lit her face as she listened to Schooner. "Your first health club venture!"

He laughed, "Essentially, yes." And then, "Okay, look through the rest," he ordered.

She went back to the stack of photos, understanding the joy Schooner had brought to these beautiful children and then she came upon a picture of a waterfall that made her gasp.

"You gave me a picture of Forest Falls as a gift and I wanted to return the favor with a picture of Victoria Falls," he whispered into her ear.

Mia was in awe of his romantic heart, he'd saved these pictures, he'd saved the black wool cap. She just stared at him.

"What?" he asked.

"You. You just blow my mind, Schooner. There is so much to you. Do people know who you are?"

"A few." He took her hand and kissed it, "There's one more photo."

She looked back at the stack and lifted the photo of Victoria Falls. Underneath his beautiful B&W of the falls was the only color photo in the stack. Standing in front of Victoria Falls was a devastatingly handsome nineteen-year-old Schooner Moore, smiling at the camera, a real smile, and squinting in the bright sunlight.

Mia caught her breath staring at the photo she now held in both hands. Smiling back at her was her Schooner, the Schooner she had carried in her heart, buried, for twenty-four years. She looked up at the man sitting next to her on the couch, smiling. Her Schooner. He was just watching her intently. She looked back at the photo and that's when she saw his casted right hand.

"Your hand? What happened?" There was alarm in her eyes as she searched his handsome face.

"I got into a little fight with a wall in a dorm hallway."

It took her a moment to process that. "You punched a wall?"

He nodded. "Not the brightest thing I've ever done."

Mia took Schooner's right hand in both of hers. Gently running her fingers over his knuckles. She brought his hand to her lips, tenderly peppering it with kisses, as she took in the enormity of what had happened. His casted hand meant that he couldn't play tennis and if this happened in a dorm before summer break, it happened the day she left him. He punched a cement wall. Lost in thought, she rubbed his hand against her cheek.

He just watched her.

So much more had been lost than she had even initially thought. The heaviness in her heart felt unbearable as she processed the casted hand, the orthopedic surgeon, what he must've felt that day not finding her after their sweet goodnight the previous evening, the damage to both his hand and his tennis career.

Mia stood, with Schooner's right hand in hers, placing it against her heart. "We are done hurting each other," she declared, and holding his hand in both of hers, led him into her bedroom.

CHAPTER 8

"**D**amn, it's cold in here!" Schooner grabbed Mia and pulled her close.

"Will be much better under the down blanket—naked," Mia said into his chest.

The now gale force winds were slamming her bedroom windows, chilling them with each rattle, a fine snow had begun to fall and sounded like a shovel full of sand hitting the window with each gust.

Mia started to unbutton Schooner's shirt and he took her hands. "Baby Girl, I'm getting naked under the blanket. It's freaking freezing in here."

Pulling her toward the bed, he lifted the down comforter.

"Afraid of shrinkage?" she teased, getting under the blanket next to him and pulling off her clothes.

He pulled her underneath his now naked body. "This feel like shrinkage to you?" He pressed his hard cock against her.

She threaded her fingers through his hair and pulled his lips to hers. "It feels like Heaven to me."

"Feels like home to me," he smiled into her mouth, before kissing her deeply.

Mia wrapped her legs around Schooner, his warm body covering hers completely. With each kiss she could feel herself becoming wetter and wetter, wanting him inside of her desperately. She ran her hands down his back, feeling the definition of his muscles, kneading them, trying to memorize what he felt like to her touch.

His teeth were at her neck, softly grazing one of her most sensitive areas. Moaning, she tilted her head, giving him access, wanting to feel his teeth. Pressing his head into her neck, she could feel the pressure of his teeth biting harder and she wrapped her legs around him tighter and pulled his hair.

He moaned and his lips went back to her mouth, his kiss savage and rough.

She could feel the head of his cock pressing against her, maybe an inch away from where she wanted him, needed him. Pulling her mouth away, they were both panting, blood rushing. "Schooner, did you bring condoms?" Even in the dark, she could see the shocked look on his face.

"Fuck. No. You're not on anything?" He was searching her face, trying to get his bearings.

"Forty and not dating anyone." She shook her head. Schooner gave Mia an incredulous look saying how could you not be seeing anyone.

She loved him for the way he saw her.

"Okay, ummm." He looked at her wide-eyed. "What do you want to do?"

"Well, there's a 24-hour Korean grocer about two blocks from here." They both looked toward the window. A heavier snow had begun to fall, swirling and dancing in the street lamps below, then being whipped in sheets by the relentless wind gusts. "Okay, not a good idea."

Schooner went to move off of Mia and she held him tightly in place on top of her with her arms and legs. "You are not making this easier." He gave her a soft kiss on the lips.

"That's because it's my job to make it harder." She pulled his head back down to her for another kiss.

He brushed her bangs from her eyes. "What do you want to do here, Baby Girl?"

She took his face in her hands and kissed him deeply. "I know what I want, Schooner. To me, there's no downside to this." She searched his beautiful eyes.

He sighed and smiled, "Are you sure?"

She nodded, "Are you?"

"You don't even have to ask," his voice was rough. She smiled and nodded.

He pushed her bangs from her face and the love in his eyes was more intense than she'd ever seen. It made her breath hitch and he smiled at her reaction. "It's everything I ever wanted," he whispered in her ear.

Mia looked at the beautiful man staring down into her eyes. *How was this even possible*, she wondered.

"Schooner."

His gaze was riveting.

She nodded her assent and he was inside of her. She heard a sound coming from her, a mewling.

"Oh God, Baby Girl," he growled into her ear, "you feel so fucking good. I've waited a lifetime. A lifetime." He drove into her hard. Harder. "You are mine. No one is ever going to take you from me again. No one is ever going to touch you again. No one. Ever."

"Come in me," she whispered in his ear.

He stopped moving and looked down at her.

"It's mine," she whispered. "All mine."

And he rammed into her hard.

She watched his face as he was coming undone and seeing his pleasure threw her over the edge and she squeezed his cock tight. His eyes flew open and she was smiling up at him. "Give it to me, Schooner. Give me what I want."

And that was all he needed to hear to unleash his seed deep into her.

When they were done, they lay side by side facing each other. "Are you ready for us? For the future?" he asked, stroking her cheek with his thumb.

She smiled, taking his hand and kissing his thumb. "It's everything I ever wanted," she repeated his words from earlier, making him smile.

He brushed her bangs from her eyes with his fingertips and kissed the tip of her nose. "Your first and your last," he whispered.

She smiled at the realization and nodded. "My first and my last," she repeated. As it sunk in, her smile grew wider. "My first and my last. I love that."

"Is that all you love?"

"I love bagels," she teased, smiling at him.

"Yeah, with avocado slices."

"Ewwww!"

He laughed at her. "You're not going to tell me what else you love, are you?" He tightened his arms around her.

"You just want to hear me say it, don't you?"

He nodded at her.

Mia looked into Schooner's eyes and smiled. She traced his cheek with her fingers. "Schooner James Moore," she began, "five days ago, I was having the worst morning imaginable. We had just lost a big account and I knew it could potentially have devastating effects on my company. I was wrung out just from the events of the morning. And then I saw an email. And your name was on it. And I stared at it in disbelief. Schooner Moore sent me a friend request. *Schooner Moore* sent me a friend request? And I didn't even have to think for a second before I hit confirm. I went with my gut, my heart. I just reacted. Five minutes later, I was listening to a voice I thought I would never hear again in my lifetime and just the sound of your voice touched me in a way I didn't even know I missed. It made me yearn for more, made me want more. More of you. All week, every conversation, I just kept saying to myself, how can it be this easy? This right? How can I just click... fit with someone so easily? And then today, today was perfect and I felt right for the first time in... forever. I felt right because you were with me and you get me and I can be me and it's fun to be me with you and I love everything about you... your heart... your sweetness... the way you are with me, the way you make me feel."

She took his hand and placed it over her heart. "Do you feel that? Because it feels like it's going to beat out of my chest. Over the past five days, I swear, it has gotten five times bigger. I feel like it's going to explode, it's so full. I look in your eyes and, well the first thing I think is, I can't believe I'm looking into your sweet, beautiful eyes. Your eyes." She smiled and pushed the hair from his forehead. "It's every dream I ever wanted, come true. Dreams I would never even dare to let myself consider, places I wouldn't allow myself to go, are now not only possibilities, but may actually be my reality. My reality with you. With you, Schooner. And to say I am mind blown is the ultimate understatement. So, if you want me to tell you that I love you, I will do that—but I don't think those words even begin to describe what I feel for you and I don't know what the right words are."

"You just said them."

CHAPTER 9

Mia stretched out in her bed. She could feel how cold the air was on her face, but her body under the down comforter was toasty warm. Outside the window, the snow still fell from a gray sky, making it difficult to tell what time it was. Mia grabbed her phone off her nightstand. It was 8:20 A.M. Wow, she had slept late. Schooner was nowhere in sight. She reached over to his side of the bed. The sheets were cool, so he must've been gone for a while.

Mia saw Schooner's shirt on the floor, laying in the heap it had fallen, when she peeled it off of him. She grabbed the cold shirt and put it on under the covers and stayed there until the icy cold cotton warmed up. Finally getting the nerve to brave it, she got out of bed and went to her closet for a pair of Mukluk boot slippers. Mia knew the secret—when feet were warm, all else was bearable.

Schooner was sitting at the breakfast bar, cell phone in one hand, coffee mug in the other. *He looks so damn good in my kitchen*, Mia thought. The man looked so at home and so natural—like he was in his own space.

His face broke into a wide smile when he saw her approaching in his shirt. Putting the coffee mug down, he drew her to him, planting a big kiss on her lips. Holding her tightly to him, he continued his phone conversation.

"Yeah, well I'm not too worried about that because Yoli will always vote with me and maybe we can just buy her out. As far as the rest of it, let's just give her what she wants. She's going to get 50% of everything. I'm not going to contest it. Just give it to her, I want this to happen fast... and smooth." He was listening. "No, I haven't talked to them yet. I'm going to do that as soon as possible." Listening. "Aaron, I don't really care. None of that matters. So, when can we serve?" Listening. Big sigh. "Okay, do it." He hung up without saying goodbye.

Schooner pulled Mia against his chest and wrapped both arms around her tightly. He kissed the top of her head. A gesture that always made her smile. A gesture that was always theirs.

She pulled back to look at him. "You okay?" Her concern for him was evident.

He nodded, smiling at her. "Yeah. Not easy stuff. Just want it done, yesterday."

She reached up to his cheek and he laid his face in her hand, smiling.

"We said a lot of things to each other last night, Mia. By the light of day…" his voice trailed off.

"I can only speak for myself, Schooner. By the light of day, nothing changes. I meant everything I said to you last night. I don't ever think I've ever laid my heart on the line so openly." She smiled, "it's pretty scary."

"C'mere." He pulled her tightly into his arms and held her against him. "The next few months may get a little funky. I'd be naive to think CJ will just give me this divorce without a fight— especially with you in the picture. That's going to go over like a lead balloon. I'm basically going to give her everything she wants, with exception of control of the business. Everything else she can have. It doesn't mean anything to me. I just want out."

Mia pulled back to look at him, his face was so sincere. "The kids?"

Concern clouded his beautiful eyes. "I'm going to fly up to Providence in a few days and talk to Holly. I'm sure she'll be upset, but something tells me she'll get it. Holly and CJ are not close. She's Daddy's girl." He smiled and Mia could feel his love for his daughter radiating from him. "And I know she'll want me to be happy. I also think you two will end up having a very good relationship. She will get us, Mia—I know she will."

"And Zac?"

"That's going to be a tougher nut to crack. He looks like me, but he's CJ through and through".

"Oh shit." Mia had a look of mock horror on her face.

"Oh shit is right," Schooner laughed. "That boy is deadly. He's doing a semester abroad in Spain right now and honestly, I hope this is a done deal by the time he steps foot on U.S. soil again." He sighed, "Be prepared. He's going to be a shit to both of us, but I will not put up with him disrespecting you, so he and I will get that clear right from the start."

Mia just looked at him, her mind racing a million miles per hour. It seemed so much less complicated under the warmth of her down blanket and now by the light of day, reality had a lot of details.

Schooner stood and poured Mia a cup of coffee. "What do you take in your coffee? So much to learn," he smiled.

"Just milk." She watched him pull the carton from the refrigerator and pour it into her coffee.

He handed her the coffee. I can get used to this, she thought. "So, let me run something by you...," he began.

She cocked her head, listening.

"I'm supposed to leave at the end of the weekend. I don't think in 48 hours I'm going to be ready to leave you."

She could feel the smile growing on her face. "Then don't. Schooner, you can stay here for as long as you'd like. Use the apartment as an east coast base."

He smiled at her across the breakfast bar and she reached out for his hand.

"I know it's not a lot of space. Us New Yorker's get used to living in small spaces, but I would love for you to be able to think of this as your home. Our home," she corrected.

He squeezed her hand. "Let me cancel my flight."

Mia stood over by the living room windows looking out at the snow piling up. A real New York snowstorm, the kind that brought the city to a standstill. It looked so beautiful while it was falling, smooth drifts blowing into high peaks. Schooner came up behind Mia and wrapped his arms around her.

"Well, the weathermen got this one wrong. Not a beach day," she observed.

He laughed, "I've never had a snow day."

She turned to him and smiled, "We'll get out and play in it later. I've been thinking about where I want to take you in a snow storm."

"Where is that?" He nuzzled her neck.

"Well, the place I would love to hang out with you and watch the snow fall is The Oak Room in the Plaza Hotel, but it's closed for renovations. So, I'm thinking maybe The Champagne Bar at The Plaza instead. Sort of an old New York way to weather a snowstorm."

He tightened his arms around her. "I'm smiling into your neck right now."

She laughed, "In the meantime, we can play indoors." And she led him back into the bedroom.

"Damn woman, this room is freezing!" He griped, snuggling immediately under the covers.

"Western exposure. Winds out of the west." Mia climbed on top of Schooner, "I'll warm you up."

"I love New York," he smiled up at her.

"That's good, because you're about to become bi-coastal." She kissed him softly and then looked at him, her expression serious, "Have you ever thought about expanding to New York?" She rolled off of him and they tangled arms and legs, holding one another tight.

"Actually a few months ago, Yoli and I had a serious conversation about putting a "Flagship" facility in Manhattan. A lot of our clientele have places here too and we would launch with a big built in celebrity clientele who are already members."

Mia's brain started spinning and Schooner broke into a huge smile.

"What?" she asked.

"I can see that brain of yours spinning, you're already marketing the property in your head."

She threw her head back laughing, "You know me! That is exactly what I'm doing. What an amazing opening event you could do. I'm also thinking about location. You're known for your celebrity clientele, so a location downtown, here in Chelsea, The Village, SoHo, TriBeCa, I would think that would be where your "stars" are."

"That's where I'm definitely going to need your help. We'll really need to do some feasibility studies because I don't know the city at all. I don't know the personalities and demographics of each of the neighborhoods. And I really want to see what my new agency thinks about expansion to the east coast."

"Oh, who are you working with? Are you one of Scott Morgan's clients?"

How fun was this, Mia thought, to be all tangled up with Schooner, feeling his hard cock pressing against her and brainstorming business. Mia was excited on so many levels.

"No. He's a dirt bag."

Mia laughed at Schooner's accurate assessment of Scott.

"No, we're going to be joining the client roster of a little boutique agency here in Manhattan. I have a personal relationship with the owner and I know we'll get the personal attention that I demand." He pressed against her, watching her eyes widen.

"Are you a demanding client?" she asked, throwing her leg over Schooner and pressing his ass with her foot, his cock sliding deep into her. She gasped, biting her lower lip, but maintained eye contact with him.

"I'm a very demanding client." He thrust into her hard and deep. "I expect 100% attention on me at all times. Can you accommodate that?" He grabbed her ass and rammed into her. "Do you think you can keep me satisfied?"

"Absolutely, because unlike the large conglomerate agencies, who will sell you a bill of goods and stick you with underlings, you will always get attention from the very top with us." She pushed him on his back, straddling him and smiling down at him.

He thrust up into her. "Will you commit to personally handling my business?"

She reached back and fondled his balls. "I think I can commit to that. I'm very hands on with my clients." She squeezed his cock and balls at the same time, "I will commit all my resources to you."

"How do I know you're not just selling me a bill of goods?" He pressed up into her, causing her to gasp.

"What can I do to convince you?"

"I'll require a contract."

She looked into his clear eyes, silently asking with her eyes, *Are you asking me what I think you're asking me?* "I'd be very happy to solidify this relationship with a contract." She squeezed his cock tight.

"Good." He grabbed her hips and thrust up into her. "Consider it a done deal."

"I like the way you do business." She smiled down at him.

"I like giving you the business." He held her hips tight, grinding his cock into her.

"That's good, because I want all of your business."

"I'm willing to give you every last inch of it."

"I can handle it."

She laughed... Seth was going to tease her relentlessly about pimping herself out for business, but this new business was truly going to be a labor of love.

CHAPTER 10

"**G**ood morning, sunshine," Mia sing-songed, as she breezed by Seth's desk, depositing his favorite Starbuck's latte in front of him.

Putting her own latte on her desk, she hung up her coat behind her door and proceeded to unpack her laptop from her vintage leather Ghurka bag.

Seth appeared in her doorway, latte in hand, watching her every move. She pretended to ignore him as she plugged in and booted up her laptop, took her phone out and got settled at her desk.

Then, she looked up at him, smiled and said sweetly, "Is there something I can help you with?"

"Don't you hold out on me, BBC!" She laughed and he continued, eyes narrowing, as he looked at her. "You seem to be a happy BBC this morning. One might even say a glowing BBC. Frankly, I was expecting a sad, pining BBC today."

She shook her head, "Nope. Happy BBC."

"Aren't you sad that he left?" Seth made a sad face.

"Who said anything about leaving?" Mia looked like a Cheshire cat.

Seth gasped, "He's still here?"

Mia smiled and nodded.

"Oh my God!" Seth clapped his hands together. "Why aren't you home in bed, fucking his brains out?"

Mia laughed, "Because I don't want you eating cat food, Princess." Seth looked at her with a "tell me more" look and Mia continued, "He's working out of the apartment this morning and he'll be here this afternoon. We'll be using the conference room. Is Kami in yet?"

"Yeah, she's in her office dialing for dollars trying to find new clients. He's going to be here today? How do I look?" Seth immediately began primping, pulling at his collar, straightening the neckline on his argyle cashmere sweater.

"Please let her know I'd like to see her."

Seth stood. "You are holding out on me."

"All in due time, my little princess. Now go get Kami."

"Wicked Witch BBC," he called over his shoulder. Mia laughed.

Kami Townes knocked on Mia's open door and Mia signaled her in.

"Good morning. How were your days off last week?" Kami asked, all soft southern drawl.

Mia smiled, "Exceptional."

"I'll bet they were!" They heard Seth yell from the outer office.

Both women shook their heads and laughed.

Like Seth, Kami had been with Mia since before the agency. She was Mia's go-to person and the staff member to which Mia entrusted the most important business. Kami was brilliant, driven and approached business with both left and right brain sensibilities. She was also very loyal. Kami and Mia had seen each other through personal hardships and some very wild, very hazy memory times, including an impromptu trip to New Orleans that was never, ever discussed.

The two women balanced one another out well. While Mia was a what you see is what you get, balls to the wall New Yorker, Kami was the epitome of Southern Belle.

Raised in Birmingham, Alabama, Kami was the daughter of a prominent cardiologist and a member of local society. She was a southern debutante whose pearls never came off—ever. Like any accomplished, good southern girl, Kami could insult you right to your face with such smooth grace and finesse that you never really knew what hit you... until later.

"We've got a really exciting opportunity," Mia began, "and I want you to be the primary on it. I'm going to be totally hands on, beside you on this baby—but you are going to be breathing, sleeping and eating this."

"I'm excited, what is it? Can you talk about it yet?"

"Have you ever heard of a California outfit Level 9 Health Clubs?"

Kami's face lit up and Seth came running into the office, parking in the chair next to Kami.

"No you didn't!" he screamed.

Mia laughed, "Oh, yes I did."

"My friend Shelby Lee, the lawyer for Universal, is a member at their Studio City property. I went there with her last time I was in LA. Amazing facility. We have nothing like it here." Kami was intrigued.

"The first thing we're going to work with them on is finding the space for their first New York City location and we will handle everything—the launch, marketing, advertising, PR. Everything—this baby is ours."

Kami sat there with her mouth open and Seth started to squeal. Mia sat back and smiled at them. It was so nice to deliver good news.

"Your main contact is going to be their CMO, Yolanda Perez. She goes by Yoli. We have a conference call with her this afternoon.

Their owner, Schooner Moore, will be here with us on-site for the meeting."

"Oh my God, I'm so excited he's coming here." Seth swooned.

Mia nodded, "He's coming here. And we have lots to do this morning to get ready for that meeting. We need to start pulling competitive data, look at where competitors are located. Let's make a list for Yoli of things we'll need from her. I want to see what their West Coast agencies have been doing." Mia pulled up their website on her laptop. "Slick site. This is beautiful."

"How did this happen? If you don't mind my asking," Kami inquired.

Mia smiled and she could see that Seth was bursting at the seams. "You want to tell the story? I'm sure you'll tell it so much better than I will."

Seth turned to Kami. Mia knew this was going to be dramatic and sat back in her chair, smirking. He looked down at his iPad and typed something in, then sighed and turned his iPad toward Kami.

Her pretty blue eyes shot open wide, "Hottie Toddy!"

And Seth continued, "That is Schooner Moore. Schooner James Moore, our new client and owner of Level 9 Health Clubs. Isn't he beautiful?"

Kami nodded, vigorously.

"Well, it appears our little Miss Mia has been holding out on us all these years. This gorgeous man, who let me state for the record, I am in love with, was Mia's first love. And the bitch broke his heart. Left him. Heartbroken." He turned to give Mia a mock glare. "Last week, Mr. Moore tracked down the evil tart who broke his heart and flew here to see her, hence, her time off from work last week. Clearly their reunion was a happy one because he is still here in New York and did not leave at the end of the weekend as was planned and is now opening a New York facility and we are their new agency. And there you have it."

Mia clapped, "Very good. You did it justice. And succinct too, I might add."

Kami put both hands up to her forehead with her thumbs on her cheeks, a common gesture she made when thinking or processing information, then she looked up at Mia. "Did he just make that sound incredibly romantic or is this incredibly romantic?"

"Look at that shit-eating grin on her face." Seth hit Kami in the arm playfully.

"So, what happened, Mia? C'mon don't leave us with just Seth's synopsis," urged Kami.

"I don't even know where to begin." Mia put her palms up, "The man was the love of my life and turns out he is still the love of my life." She looked at Seth, "and you will love this... he's serving CJ with divorce papers today."

"Noooooooooooo"

Mia nodded, "Yes!"

"Oh karma is such a bitch." Seth was preening. He turned to Kami to fill her in, "CJ is like this Real Housewife of Orange County and she purposely sabotaged Mia and Schooner when they were in college and that is why BBC over here left this beautiful man. She's evil, pure evil. Tall, blonde and evil." He turned back to Mia, "I can't believe he's divorcing her!"

"He's flying up to Providence tomorrow to talk to his daughter."

Mia reached inside her Ghurka bag and pulled out an envelope. "I have something to show you." She was smiling as she handed them the photo of Schooner at Victoria Falls.

"He was so beautiful, Mia." Kami actually gasped taking in the image of nineteen-year-old Schooner smiling his real smile for Mia.

Mia just nodded, feeling suddenly overwhelmed and emotional.

Seth was staring at the picture and then looked up at Mia, serious for the first time. "You deserve this, you know that."

Mia nodded, her eyes filled with tears.

"It's your time, Mia." He stood, picture still in hand, "I'm going to go get a frame for this." He smiled at Mia and left.

CHAPTER 11

Mia was brimming with pride as she gave Schooner a tour of the agency. This was her baby, and the look on his face and in his eyes when he saw what she had built and met her staff, made her beam. The sleek, trendy space screamed New York cool with its warehouse look and exposed brick walls.

"Get that off of your computer right now!" Mia hissed in a whispered tone into Seth's ear. His new screensaver was the picture of Schooner sleeping on Mia's couch. She backhanded him on the side of his head.

After a very productive hour and a half phone session with Yoli, where she and Kami seemed like they had worked together for years, Mia brought Schooner back into her office and closed the door.

He sat on the edge of her desk smiling. "Come over here." He held out his hand to her.

She took his hand and he pulled her to him, between his long legs. Her hands were in his hair and she just looked into his beautiful eyes, smiling. She kissed him, softly.

Taking her face in his hands, "Do you know how much I love you?" he asked, searching her eyes.

She smiled and nodded. There was stress in his eyes. She could see it, feel it.

"I talked to CJ this morning," he began, "it didn't go well. She's not going to make it easy, Mia."

"Does it matter?"

He thought for a second, as if that question had not yet occurred to him. "No, actually it really doesn't. I was concerned that it might matter to you."

"Me? How so?" Mia played with the locks of hair falling on his forehead, making him look nineteen again.

"That I'm still going to be legally married to another woman. She's going to drag this out."

Mia smiled and leaned forward, kissing the tip of his nose. "So, let her. The only grief she is going to cause is to herself. I don't want you stressing over that, Schooner." Mia stopped and thought for a second and then looked at Schooner with her devilish grin. "I'm a concubine!" she announced and they both broke into much needed laughter.

"My concubine," he staked claim, kissing her.

"Damn right," she hugged him and then pulled back to look at him, "Seriously, as long as we are together and things are good between us—that's all I need. I'm good, really."

"Yeah, but I want to give you more." His eyes were serious again.

She took his face in her hands and shook her head. "I have everything I want, Schooner. Everything. The rest doesn't mean anything without this. And I have this. So seriously, I don't want you stressing over it. The rest will be great when it happens. Trust me, if she sees she can stress you out, she'll step up her game even more. If you don't give a shit, then it's no fun fighting with you and she'll stop."

"Yeah, but in the meantime, I want to protect you. I want to make sure you are protected, Mia. I spoke to my lawyer today about ways in which I can do that."

"Schooner, look around," her hand swept around her office. "I'm fine."

He shook his head no. "No Baby Girl, I need to do a better job protecting you and I need to make sure all the legal aspects are in place." He put his hand on her stomach and she looked down at his hand and then he looked into her eyes, "I need to protect what is mine. Do you understand what I am saying?"

She nodded.

"You're mine now," he whispered in her ear in a gruff, emotion-filled voice. She smiled and laid her head on his shoulder.

CHAPTER 12

Mia reached for her buzzing phone to read the incoming text.

Schooner: Damn I am missing you!

Mia: How's Rhode Island?

Schooner: Even colder than NY.

Mia: How is it going with Holly?

Schooner: She's taking it really well. I told her everything.

Mia: Everything?

Schooner: Yes

Mia: Holy crap. That's pretty heavy.

Schooner: She needed to understand

Mia: Does she?

Schooner: Yes, she told me that growing up she knew that CJ and I didn't act like parents of her friends. I feel terrible that she wasn't shown a more loving relationship

Mia: :-(

Schooner: I know. I'm taking her and her boyfriend out to dinner

Mia: Have you met him before?

Schooner: No

Mia: Don't scare him!

Schooner: LOL. Call you from the hotel later

Mia: Have fun.

Schooner: Love u

Mia: It's smoochal

Schooner: :-) ear 2 ear

Mia: smoochal 2 :-)

Mia was sitting in bed working when Schooner called, "Did I wake you?"

"Nah, I've got this new client. Lots of work to do to onboard them. How's Holly?"

Schooner's voice sounded relaxed, "Today went surprisingly well. I laid a lot on her and I kind of feel bad. She wasn't surprised about me and CJ, she was very surprised to learn about you."

Mia sighed, "I'll bet she was. That can't be easy."

"After she told me about how she grew up knowing that CJ and I didn't have the same kind of relationship that she saw in other families around her, I just had to have a really honest conversation with her. It was a good chance for me to talk to her about mistakes and doing things for the wrong reasons and hopefully impart good advice about being true to herself and not settling." He paused, "She wants to meet you."

Mia scooched under the covers, "That really makes me happy to hear that. I know it won't be easy, her loyalty is to her mother."

"I don't think she sees it that way. She wants me to be happy. She said the difference in me from ten days ago, at the party, to now was... how did she put it... a transmutational shift."

Mia laughed, "Wow! Transmutational shift, huh?" They both laughed. "What's her boyfriend like?"

"Really nice kid. His name is Jared Goldman. He's pre-med. Totally smitten with Holly and from what I can tell treats her really well. I'd say they are in love."

"Oh Schooner..." Mia was smiling.

"It's weird to see. But I'm glad I had a chance to meet him. That's who she was Facebooking and texting all last weekend. Hey, how do you feel about the two of them coming to spend the weekend with us?"

"I'd love it. When do they want to come?"

"Friday."

Mia laughed, "Sounds like we're going to have a fun weekend." Mia heard an odd sound, "What is that?"

"I'm punching my pillows, trying to fluff them. Crappy pillows here in this hotel. Not like we have at home."

Mia smiled at his home reference.

"Are you in bed?" he asked.

"I am."

"Remind me not to sleep without you in the future," he sounded lost.

"It's so weird that you say that. How many years did I sleep in this bed without you and tonight it just feels empty and lonely and cold. And I hate it." She paused, "remind me not to sleep without you in the future."

CHAPTER 13

Schooner paced the apartment like a caged animal on Friday afternoon awaiting Holly and Jared's arrival. He was wound tight when Mia came home from work, and the apartment felt smaller than usual, as he stalked around with long-legged strides. She could feel the tension radiating off of him and see the stress in his eyes.

"Hey." She wrapped her arms around his waist, trying to get him to stop moving. "I know this makes it real."

"Yeah," his voice sounded choked.

"Don't worry. We're going to have the best time. I have a couple of big surprises planned for you guys." She looked up at Schooner, her devil smile at full luminosity, immediately brightening his mood and allaying his fears.

"What do you have up your sleeve, Baby Girl?" He took her face by the chin and kissed her.

"I'm only going to tell you part one, because you are going to be soooo excited. I'm so excited."

He searched her face and she went on.

"Okay, so, I was talking to a dear old friend of mine today. We've been good friends and business associates since the 90's. He owns an event security firm and is very familiar with a lot of spaces around the city—really, really cool properties, the kind that lend themselves to photo shoots and events. I told him that we were looking for a Level 9 Flagship location in New York and he told me about a space that just became vacant that sounds like the perfect amount of square footage, great neighborhood and has mass amounts of charm, history and quirkiness to it. He got the keys from the owners and is going to meet us this evening, after the kids get in, to show it to us." Mia's excitement was contagious, "Schooner, if Charles says it's good, it's going to be good. He and I have done enough events together over the years that I totally trust his opinion and he is really, really high on this space."

Schooner pulled Mia in for a tight hug. "You're amazing."

"Here's what I was thinking," she began. "After they get here, let's go meet Charles and view the property first, before we even go out to dinner. I think it will be an amazing ice breaker, give us all a lot to talk about. And if it's amazing and you love it, then we'll all be pumped up out of our minds and there will be no awkwardness in the conversation."

As Schooner ran his thumb down Mia's cheek and bent down to kiss her, the doorman call button rang. Mia told the doorman to send Holly and Jared up.

Mia and Schooner walked to the apartment door and turned to one another and simultaneously said, 'Showtime'. When they opened the door they were both laughing, evoking immediate smiles from both Holly and Jared.

"Hey there, beautiful," a happy and now relaxed Schooner wrapped his arms around his daughter.

Mia couldn't help but smile looking at the two of them, though in the very first moment, she had to consciously remind herself that this was Holly and not CJ. The resemblance was staggering.

Schooner let Holly go and she looked at Mia. Mia immediately embraced her warmly and enthusiastically greeted, "Hi Holly, I'm Mia," and then embraced Jared with the same warmth.

Any fear that had gripped Schooner, immediately dissipated as Mia set the tone with her warmth, openness and positive energy.

"Come on in, guys, and drop your stuff. Oh, it is so good to meet you." Mia's smile could've melted an icecap.

"What a great apartment. Wow, you can see the river," Jared commented. "I love Manhattan. My dream is to do my internship and residency here after med school and live here." Holly joined Jared at the window, admiring the view of the Hudson River.

Mia looked up at Schooner and smiled; he held his arms out to her and enveloped her in a hug. Holly turned to her Dad who met her gaze, the happiness in his eyes vastly evident at the immediate harmony between the two women he loved.

"Would you guys like a glass of wine?" Mia offered, grabbing a bottle and a corkscrew. "We're going to head out in a little bit to do something that should be really fun."

"A friend of Mia's found a space that sounds amazing for L9 and we're going to go check it out."

The love in Holly's eyes was evident as she looked at her Dad.

Mia thought she saw something else there and wondered if this was the first time she had seen her father this happy and connected to someone.

Charles Sloan stood very tall and still in his dark wool overcoat and navy scarf, observing everything and everyone with barely a movement of his eyes. He always reminded Mia of Jason Statham in The Transporter movies. While he appeared detached, he was anything but.

Charles broke into a wide grin as Mia and her group came into view.

"Meezie!" He enveloped her in a big hug.

"Chazicle!" she returned affectionately, kissing his cheek.

"Only you can call me that and not get killed." They smiled at one another with the genuine affection of old friends.

"Charles Sloan, I'd like you to meet Schooner Moore, Holly Moore and Jared Goldman."

Ever the gentleman, Charles shook Holly's hand first, then Jared's and then turned to Schooner, and much to Mia's surprise, said, "Nice to see you again, we've met before."

Schooner smiled, taking his hand. "Yes, we have. It was the Studio City event, wasn't it?"

"Yes, it was," Charles concurred.

A surprised Mia looked at Schooner and said, "One degree of separation this whole time. Who knew?"

Charles began to work on a series of door locks and opened a massive door. They followed him in as he began to flip a bank of light switches that elicited a collective gasp from the group.

The entranceway they stood in opened to a massive rotunda whose ceiling was lit with cove lighting spotlighting immense frescos of mythological creatures, gods and beasts. On one end was a sweeping marble staircase with an elaborate wrought iron railing that led to a mezzanine level and a third level mezzanine above that.

"This building has housed churches, private clubs, theatres and is a space most New Yorker's don't even know exists," Charles explained. "Meezie, do you remember that gang that had the club in the church? They even owned it for a while. They were supposed to fully renovate it, but never completed it."

Mia started to wander around the space. She felt Schooner's arm drape protectively over her shoulder. "Meezie?" he whispered in her ear.

"Stop that. We go back a long way." She backhanded him in the stomach.

"I know. It just reminds me that I missed a big portion of your life."

"Excuse me? Your daughter is here. Talk about feeling the gap."

He smiled down at her, a sad look in his eyes and bent down to kiss her.

Mia put her arm around Schooner's waist. "C'mon let's check this place out. It's gorgeous and so interesting. Funky vibe, right?"

Holly and Jared caught up to them. "Dad, this place is amazing. That third floor could be a track. Imagine running under those frescos."

"Schooner, let me show you the offices," Charles offered and Schooner left with Charles.

"So what is it that you call him?" Holly asked.

Mia laughed, "Chazicle?" and Holly nodded. "Oh, that nickname goes way back. Charles hates to be called anything but Charles, and when he's working, he's like an ice man, he's so focused and unflappable. So, the Chaz was me just being obnoxious with him because he hates being called that and putting Chaz and icicle together and calling him Chazicle."

"Was he Secret Service?" Jared asked. "He looks like he was a Covert Ops guy."

Mia laughed, "If I told you, he'd probably have to kill me." She smiled at them, "Let's go check out upstairs."

The three wandered around upstairs, finding a variety of rooms off the second floor mezzanine. The place was massive and many of the original details from intricate wainscoting to wood and stone carvings still existed.

Schooner and Charles caught up with them and they continued to explore the space, looking for practical things like plumbing for bathrooms and showers.

"Do you think the renovation will make it cost prohibitive?" Mia asked Schooner.

"Hard to tell, but it actually appears to be in pretty good shape because previous owners have done a lot of renovations on it already."

"I can help hook you up with some inspectors to take a look at this, if you're interested." Charles offered.

Schooner nodded.

The two appeared to Mia to have bonded during their time alone.

"I am definitely interested. It's worth at least an initial discussion with the principals. And if that progresses, I'd want to get Yoli in here and an architect. It's a really interesting space." He was looking around, taking it all in.

Mia turned to Charles, "Imagine an opening here. Could be spectacular."

"There would be nothing else like it in New York. Really would be an amazing extension of what's already a unique concept in California, and housed in a peerless space."

"So exciting."

Schooner, Holly and Jared had wandered off. Mia watched Schooner looking around with a critical eye. She knew he was envisioning his unique concept.

"Oh, before I forget." Charles took an envelope out of his pocket and handed it to Mia. "All instructions are inside."

Mia gave Charles a hug. "You are the absolute best. Thank you so much. I cannot tell you how much I appreciate this." She kissed his cheek.

She felt Schooner's hand on her shoulder as he addressed Charles, "I'm definitely interested."

"Great. Would you like me to see if I can set something up for next week?"

"That would be great." Schooner pulled Mia into him.

"Oh Meezie, before I forget, Gaby wants to know if you two will be available for dinner one night next week."

Mia smiled up at Schooner and looked back at Charles, "We'd love to. Tell her to give me a ring."

As they parted at the entranceway, Mia gave Charles a big hug, "I can't thank you enough… for everything."

He smiled, "My pleasure, we'll see you next week. Schooner, I'll call you on Monday after I talk to these guys. Holly, Jared, great meeting you. Have a good weekend everyone."

He winked at Mia and was off.

CHAPTER 14

"**I** love that space, Dad."

They sat in a corner table of an intimate, hole in the wall Italian restaurant with possibly the best Caesar salad in Manhattan.

"I like it, too," Schooner admitted.

"The location is good," Mia added. "It's central to a lot of the neighborhoods where celebrities keep their New York homes, it's easy to get to, multiple subway lines close by, plus it's a very safe neighborhood with a great demographic for the concept." She smiled at Schooner, "This is really exciting."

"What's that look you're giving me?" Schooner asked Mia, "You've kind of got a shit-eating grin on your face."

She giggled, "You know me well." Mia looked at all of them and said, "I've got a really fun surprise," then dug around in her purse. She pulled out the envelope that Charles had given her, opened it and pulled out keys. "Charles and Gaby have been nice enough to let us use their beach house on Fire Island for the rest of the weekend."

"So, that's what you were off talking to him about?" Schooner was all smiles.

"Yes, that's what I was talking to him about! And what was with you getting all possessive tonight? What was that shit all about?" She called him out on his behavior, giving him a playful little whack in the arm.

He smiled and leaned down and whispered in her ear, "Mine."

Mia snorted at him, shaking her head. "His wife is one of my best friends in the world."

Holly and Jared just watched them and Mia looked at Holly and rolled her eyes as if to say, "Men!"

Holly had that same look in her eyes that Mia had seen earlier, and Mia wondered if she was seeing her father for the first time the way Mia had always seen him.

"After dinner, we should stop into Trader Joe's and pick up groceries to bring out to the beach. If we're lucky, one of the bars in town out there will be open, but I'm not really sure. Basically, the island is pretty much deserted in winter."

Schooner explained to them that they would have to take the ferry out and that there were no cars allowed out on the island. "Just miles of endless deserted beaches to walk."

Holly and Jared were in awe of the evening they had already had and now they were going out to a beach house on an island in the middle of the winter.

As they walked back to the apartment later in the evening, Holly and Mia were a few feet behind the guys, when Holly said, "Mia, thanks for making us feel really comfortable."

Mia put an arm around Holly and gave her a little hug, "I know this isn't easy for you."

"It's different," Holly admitted. "But he's so happy and I just love seeing him this way. It makes it a lot easier. Clearly Mia, you make my dad very happy."

Mia smiled, "He and I have always had a knack for being able to truly be ourselves with one another, if that makes sense." She looked at Holly and Holly was nodding, "So, I think because of that, we really bring out the best in one another."

"I'm glad you guys found each other again."

Mia gazed into the face of this beautiful young woman, who looked unnervingly like her mother, but possessed her father's sweet soul. "You are very special."

"Well, I love him and I want him to be happy." Holly's eyes radiated the depth of emotion she felt for her father.

"We have that in common." Mia smiled at her.

Schooner and Jared had already reached the building and were waiting for them. Mia could see how happy Schooner was watching them together and her heart soared.

As the ferry crossed the choppy waters of the Great South Bay that Saturday morning, they stood on the top deck, windblown and shivering, in the freezing cold sunshine. By the time they reached the ferry terminal at the town of Ocean Beach, they departed with runny noses and dripping eyes and red wind burned cheeks. Walking through town, they noticed that one pub, The Castaway, was indeed open. Following Charles' directions, they headed down windswept boardwalks to their friend's home on Ocean Breeze Walk.

Weathered shingles on the outside, the inside of the house was light and airy in pale blues and whites with driftwood furniture. There was a large stone fireplace downstairs and three bedrooms upstairs, two of them with decks overlooking the ocean and miles of unspoiled beach.

Holly and Jared immediately took off for the beach, leaving Mia and Schooner to unpack groceries, get the heat in the house going and start a fire in the fireplace.

Mia poured glasses of icy cold white wine (it had been on the ferry with them) and handed one to Schooner. She took him by the hand and led him to the couch in front of the fire, where she snuggled into him. *This just might be Heaven*, she thought.

Schooner kissed the top of Mia's head and played with her hair. "Today is really special, Baby Girl." She looked up at him and he kissed the tip of her nose, "Being here with you on Fire Island was a fantasy I played over and over in my mind for so many years, you can't even imagine."

Mia took his hand in hers and looked into the fire. "Well, now that fantasy is your reality."

"No, it's not," he countered.

Mia looked up at him, surprised.

"It's our reality."

She smiled, "Holy shit, you're right. It is."

And they both laughed.

Later that afternoon, Schooner and Mia walked the beach hand in hand, another fantasy that they'd waited a lifetime to fulfill.

"Do you remember how I once told you that since I was a Newport Beach guy, that it was going to be hard to impress me with your New York beaches?" He bent down and picked up a smooth piece of cobalt colored sea glass and turned it over a few times in his hand.

"I do remember that." She smiled up at him and body bumped him.

He bumped her back. "Well, this is really amazing and you know what?"

"What?" She bumped him.

"It's almost exactly as I imagined it would be. Actually, it's even better."

Mia threaded her arm through his and sighed, "I'm trying so hard to stay in the now and think about our future, but sometimes Schooner, I just start mourning the lost moments. Which is crazy because how can you mourn something that never was? Pull me back to now when you see me going there, okay."

He put his arm around her, pulling her close and kissing the top of her head, "I can do that, I'll pull you back and no it's not crazy. But Baby Girl, the now is so good. So, so good. We've got a lot of memories to make, Mia. So, let's try and keep each other right here." He stopped walking and faced her, putting his hands on her shoulders, "And this is just the start. You know that, don't you?"

Her arms went around his waist and she held him tight, reveling in the feeling of her face against his chest. And there they stood on a beach they had dreamed of so long ago, finally making the memories they had dreamed of making, so long ago.

Later in the afternoon, while having drinks and laughing with Holly and Jared at The Castaway, Schooner flipped through a local newspaper. He ripped out a page, folded it and put it in his jean's pocket.

Mia looked at him curiously.

"Do you remember your birthday wish?" he whispered in her ear. "Because I do." He pushed her bangs out of her eyes and kissed her lips softly, then kissed the tip of her nose.

"We could rent a place for the week of my birthday."

Schooner shook his head, no.

"No?" Mia was surprised and a little disappointed, especially since he had just taken a page from the paper.

"We need our own place here." He pulled the folded paper out of his pocket and unfolded it, revealing an ad for a beautiful house for sale with a deck off the main living area and one off of the master bedroom that went directly out to the beach. "This is going to be our family getaway. This is where we are going to spend summers or just come to chill out, hang out, dig our toes in the sand, build sandcastles and eat lobsters and steamers in our sweatshirts after a long day on the beach."

Holly's mouth was hanging open. "Dad, you're going to buy a house here?" Her excitement and surprise was evident.

"Mia and I are going to buy a house here." Schooner squeezed Mia's hand. He leaned forward and whispered in her ear, "Happy early birthday, Baby Girl," letting his lips graze her cheek.

Mia was stunned into uncharacteristic silence. The look in his eyes told her everything. This was part of Schooner's grand plan to protect her, to take care of her and to build their future together. He wasn't kidding when he said he took care of what was his. Mia had never felt so loved or so in love in her life. And it was with her Schooner.

CHAPTER 15

Seth rapped lightly on Mia's door and stuck his head in.

"I've got CJ Moore on line one," he announced, his eyebrows standing at full attention.

"Oh really..." Mia gave Seth a WTF look, took a deep breath and hit the speaker button on her desk phone.

"Mia Silver," she answered, professionally. Seth sat down in one of the desk chairs facing Mia, his eyes wide.

"Mia, this is CJ Moore, Schooner Moore's wife," her voice was cool.

Almost Ex- ... Bitch Mia scribbled on the yellow legal pad in front of her.

"What can I do for you, CJ?" Mia's voice was even, professional.

"What can you do for me?" Her voice was tense and started to rise, "For starters, you can stay away from my husband."

Do not rise to the bait!!!

"CJ, why are you calling me?" Mia had a mildly annoyed attitude.

Seth nodded, smiling, proud Mia was staying cool.

"I told you, I want you to stay away from my husband," her voice was now icy and tight.

255

"That's what you want?" Mia paused. "CJ, what would ever possess you to think that I would care what you want?"

Do not rise to the bait!!! Mia again reminded herself.

"He's my husband, Mia, and just like he's done to you before, he's going to come back to me. You are just a little mid-life fling. We've built a family together."

Mia sat back and chuckled, "CJ, tell yourself whatever you need to get by, but this is a conversation you should either be having with your lawyer or with Schooner. I still do not understand why you are calling me."

"I'm not just going to sit back and let you steal my husband."

Mia typed something into Google.

Shaking her head, Mia sighed, "Do not mistake your husband leaving you for someone stealing him." She paused, "CJ, I just want to inform you, that starting right now, I am taping this conversation. Although here in New York, I legally do not have to advise you of that, it appears that under California law, I do."

Seth was doing a happy dance in his chair at Mia's bluff.

Bitch played me once ... won't get fooled again!

"I thought we could have a civil conversation," CJ began, "but I can see that you are very defensive and hostile, when I am the victim here."

"Oh, *that* is rich!" Mia's voice dripped of sarcasm. "CJ, you have never been a victim in your life. But as someone who was once a victim of your selfish manipulation, you have to understand, it is impossible for me to feel any empathy for you. The collateral damage you have caused people you *supposedly* love has been extreme."

"I'm not letting him go," CJ snarled.

"He's already gone," Mia's voice was a little more than a whisper.

"Don't count on it," CJ threatened.

Mia was done, her face masked in disgust. "Okay, at this point you are just embarrassing yourself, so I'm really not going to let you go on here. As I recommended at the beginning of this conversation, you probably want to broach these things with either your lawyer or Schooner."

"Well, I'm not done …"

Mia cut her off, "Actually you are. Goodbye, CJ." And Mia hit the speaker button on her phone and ended the call.

"Bitch!" Mia screamed at the phone on her desk.

"Oh my God, you were fabulous!" Seth was clapping his hands together.

Mia picked up the phone receiver and slammed in back in its cradle, "Cunt!"

And again, "Whore!"

She looked up at Seth and did a primal scream, laughing at the same time.

"BBC, I have known you for a million years and you cuss like a sailor. I know it's part of your charm, but I have never, ever heard you use the "C" word!"

"Cunt," Mia screamed again.

This time Kami poked her head into the office. A surprised and amused look on her face.

"I bet that felt great." Seth was clearly enjoying Mia's tirade after the tension of the call.

Mia held her hand out, it was still shaking. "Was my voice shaking on the call?"

"No. You sounded so in control. I think that is what totally unnerved her." He was clearly pleased.

Kami sat in the extra chair, "Is anyone going to tell me what I missed?"

Mia looked at Seth, giving him the go-ahead to start, "Schooner's wife just called Mia."

"Nooooo…" Kami's eyes were like saucers. Her mouth hanging open.

"Yesssss…" Was the stereo response she got in return.

"What did she want?"

"She wants Mia to stay away from Schooner," Seth hissed.

"What is this? High School?" Kami was clearly astounded.

"Guess she still thinks it's freshman year in college and that she can intimidate me. The M.O. worked for her back then. Fucking deluded bitch."

"So, what did you say?"

Seth continued for Mia, "She was brilliant. Totally in control."

Mia handed Kami her legal pad so that she could see what she the notes she was writing herself during the call.

"She accused Mia of stealing Schooner and Mia told her not to mistake her husband leaving her for him being stolen away," Seth and Mia screamed and laughed.

"You didn't?"

Mia laughed, "If Seth says I did, then I did. I honestly don't even know what I said to her. I just went into auto-pilot. I was trying really hard not to get baited and at one point," Mia stopped to laugh, "I informed her that I was recording the call."

Kami clapped her hands together, "Brilliant and evil. I love it!"

"Oh, oh, oh…" Seth went on with a point he remembered, "She said she wasn't letting him go and Mia told her he was already gone."

"How did it end?" Kami asked.

"Mia told her she couldn't let her go on embarrassing herself and click, pressed the speakerphone button and the evil witch was gone."

"Holy crap. What possessed her? I can't imagine her lawyer would have advised it." Kami just shook her head, "Yoli hates her.

She is so thrilled Schooner left her. From what I can gather, CJ doesn't give Yoli the time of day and looks down her nose at her."

"Sounds like typical CJ," Mia concurred. "She and her pageant-girl friends hated me and my friends at school because we were different."

"Are you going to tell Schooner about the call?" Seth's eyes were suddenly very serious again.

"No." Mia shook her head.

"Why not?" Kami was clearly surprised.

"Schooner is very protective. I think he'll have a kneejerk reaction and call her and go ape shit and that is just what she wants. She wants to get to him. She wants to get to us."

"BBC, do not keep things from him. Seriously, the last time you didn't tell him about a little visit from her, look what it cost the two of you. Please tell me you learned from that mistake."

Mia sat back and listened to Seth's words. He was right. She could not let CJ come between them again. "Okay, I'll tell him."

Kami chimed in, "Mia, seriously. If Schooner finds out from CJ that you two spoke and that you didn't tell him about it, it will be a huge breach of trust for the two of you. You can't give her that power."

Mia had not even considered that, "Thanks, guys. You are right. I'll tell Schooner about it tonight. I don't want to ruin his day and I don't want him going off on her." She laughed, "So I'll tell him in bed or something... when he's, err, compromised." Mia smiled her devilish grin.

CHAPTER 16

As they walked in the cold, brisk air down Sixth Avenue, taking in the sounds and smells and movement of Manhattan on a winter's night, Schooner commented to Mia how refreshing it was to be able to walk everywhere.

"I think we don't even realize how much fresh air and exercise we get here because we don't get in a car to go everywhere. It just becomes the norm and you don't think about it." Mia had her arm around Schooner's waist and was smushing into him for warmth.

"I really like just being able to walk outside and get everything I want." He laughed, "I can't believe I'm turning into a city boy."

"You've always had a city boy's soul," Mia commented and he pulled her closer to him. "So, I think you are going to love Charles and Gaby's place. They have the bottom two floors of a brownstone, so they have a little backyard. It's amazing to have outdoor space in the city."

"Am I going to want to buy one of these, too?" Schooner laughed.

"I don't know, Mr. Real Estate Mogul—opening a health club in New York City and buying a beach house on Fire Island, while going through a divorce would be pretty financially strapping, I would think." Mia looked up at Schooner. She could see he was doing some sort of inventory in his mind.

"What do brownstones sell for?"

"It depends on neighborhood, condition, size. Here in the West Village, where these guys are, I'd say anywhere from $5 million on the low end to probably about $25 million."

He laughed, "That's quite a range. Having a little outdoor space sounds amazing though. A hot tub and a grill—what else do you need?"

"Schooner?" They heard a woman calling and turned toward the voice.

A very recognizable Katie Chisholm, looking even more radiant and beautiful than she did on the big screen, and her daughter Sari, were rapidly approaching. Katie was wearing a surprised smile.

"What are you doing in New York?" she asked, kissing him on both cheeks.

"Katie, how are you? I'm living here now, actually I'm kind of bi-coastal these days." He pulled Mia close, "Katie, I'd like to introduce my fiancée, Mia Silver."

"So nice to meet you, Mia. Congratulations, to you both. Any chance we'll get an L9 here in the city now that you've become one of us?" Katie was looking for the scoop.

Schooner gave her the All-American boy smile, "Well, I'm planning on spending the lion's share of my time here now, so..." his voice trailed off.

The pops and bright strobes of camera flashes ended their moment as the paparazzi descended on Katie and Sari, taking photos of the four of them.

Katie rolled her eyes and sighed, "It's a school night, we'd better get going." She gave Schooner a kiss on the cheek and Mia a hug. "I hope to see a lot more of you both now that you're here in New York! And congratulations," she called as they headed down the street.

Mia smiled up at Schooner with her devil grin and raised eyebrows. "Fiancée?"

He pulled her close to him, "Mmm-hmm."

"Did I miss the memo?" she laughed as they turned onto West 11th Street.

"Wow, I love this block!" Schooner's eyes started searching the brownstone lined street. "I really love this."

"Well, maybe if Katie Chisholm invites all her New York friends to join L9 we can afford to live here. And... you changed the subject on me."

He laughed and hugged her into him, "I actually wanted to tell her what I really feel."

"Oh, and what is that, Mr. Moore?"

"That you're my wife." He leaned down kissed the top of her head, "but I unfortunately can't say that just yet."

Mia didn't look up at him, she looked straight ahead and kept walking. The morning's phone conversation with CJ was weighing heavily on her, as she knew that was a conversation they had to have... later.

"We're here," she said brightly, as they climbed the stone steps to the brownstone's main entrance and rang the bell.

Charles answered the door, holding in his arms a beautiful doe-eyed little girl with long silky dark brown hair and a cloud-chasing smile. She was already dressed for bed, wearing Little Mermaid footie pajamas.

"Auntie Meezie," she flew out of Charles' arms into Mia's.

Mia covered her face in kisses, as she giggled. "What are you doing still awake, my little angel-pie?"

"Papa said you could put me to bed."

"Oh, did he now?" Mia continued to kiss her, "You smell so good, I'm going to eat you."

Schooner and Charles shook hands and exchanged greetings as they entered the front hall vestibule, "Paola, I want you to meet someone very special. This is Schooner."

She gave him a shy smile and Mia whispered in her ear, "Isn't he cute?" Eliciting a round of giggles.

Gaby appeared in the hallway behind them, flowing in gracefully, as only Gaby could.

Charles had met Gabriella Rossetti on a photo shoot in Positano, Italy when she was modeling for the Elite Modeling Agency out of her hometown of Milan. He was providing security for Gaby and four other models and was totally entranced the moment he laid eyes on her. Tall and willowy with a sheath of shiny dark hair, expressive luminous dark eyes and olive skin, Charles knew that he was not leaving Italy without her.

After the shoot had wrapped up, he didn't go back to the States with the rest of the security detail, but instead followed her back to Milan where she was still living in the family's ancestral home.

Her father was leery of the tall, quiet American who was coming around to see his daughter. Until one Friday night, when Charles was welcomed to join the older man for Friday night services at the local synagogue. As Charles recited all the prayers in Hebrew, Giancarlo Rossetti warmed to the young man, who was about to become a fixture in their home.

Three months later Charles and Gaby were married.

"Mia," she embraced Mia warmly, kissing her on both cheeks. "I have missed you."

"Gaby, this is Schooner."

Gaby smiled up at him and greeted him with a kiss to each cheek. "I am very pleased to meet you, Schooner. Charles has told me much about you." She turned to Mia and Paola, "I think it's bed time. Auntie Meezie and I will put you to bed now."

Charles held up a bottle of Johnny Walker Blue, "Schooner, will you join me?"

"I knew I liked you, man." Schooner laughed, as he took in the charm of the brick walls and working fireplace and original ceiling medallions.

Mia could see the real estate lust in his eyes.

"We're going to need this," Charles informed. "We're on grill duty out back." They clinked glasses and then shared the look men have on their faces when that first stream of single malt scotch begins its satisfying burn southward.

Gaby and Mia headed down the wide mahogany staircase with Paola. Her room was Classic Winnie the Pooh and stuffed animals lined the floor. They tucked her, and a very bedraggled yellow stuffed rabbit, into her youth bed, with its white eyelet comforter. Then both sat down on her tiny bed.

"Your Schooner, he is so handsome, Mia."

Mia smiled and nodded, "Yes, he is."

"Charles tells me that you know him since you were young." She tossed her long sheath of hair over her shoulders.

"I was sixteen when we met."

Gaby's eyes widened, "He was your first love, Mia?"

Mia nodded at her friend.

"He looks at you with such love, this Schooner." Gaby was smiling at her friend.

"We ran into Katie Chisholm and her daughter, Sari, on our way over here. Katie knows Schooner from his health clubs in LA. He introduced me as his fiancé. I almost fell over."

Gaby grabbed Mia's hand and squeezed it. "He is the one, I know this."

"Gab, he's been the one since I was sixteen."

"This is so romantic."

Mia rolled her eyes, "More like tragic. We missed twenty-four years of each other's lives."

Shrugging as she stroked her daughter's hair, the little girl was fighting to keep her eyes open and listen to the conversation. "That is the past. Now you have forever. This Schooner is very much in love with you, Mia. I can see that. And you, this is your love?"

Mia smiled at Gaby, "Yes, this is my love."

Mia and Schooner walked back up Sixth Avenue, arms around one another talking about their evening.

"I belong here," Schooner ventured. "People are real. It's not about the bullshit or show. This city and the people," he gave Mia a hug into him, "this is me."

She looked up at him. "You feel at home here, don't you?"

He nodded, "Just the way I have always felt right with you, I feel that way in this environment. I was more comfortable tonight hanging out with Charles and Gaby than I have been hanging with anyone I know in Newport Beach. Tonight felt like I'd been a part of everything my whole life. I didn't feel like the 'new guy' in the bunch."

Mia smiled, "That makes me happy."

"Me too, Baby Girl." He kissed the top of her head.

They were holding hands and swinging arms, like kids, when they walked into the building. The doorman and the guard at the front desk smiled widely at them.

Mia leaned up against Schooner as they waited for the elevator, snuggling into his side.

As they got in and the doors closed, he backed her to the corner and tilted her chin up, "I could not wait to get you home tonight." He put a hand on her lower back and pulled her up against him, his erection pressing hard into her stomach.

Mia's arms went around Schooner's neck pulling his mouth down to hers, threading her fingers through his hair. The elevator doors opened and he grabbed her hand, pulling her down the hall, breathless, stumbling and laughing.

Schooner fumbled with his keys, trying to get them into the lock.

"Sticky fingers?" Mia teased.

He turned to her, hooded eyes and a sexy smile, "We'll see who's got sticky fingers soon."

They made it through the door, peeled off their jackets and gloves. Schooner had Mia backed up against the inside of the door. He pulled her hands above her head, his palms flat on her palms, pressing the back of her hands against the hard, cold wood of the door. He ground his hips into hers and kept his lips hovering near hers.

Mia lunged for his mouth and he pulled his head back, taunting her, just out of reach. She tried to pull her hands away so that she could grab his head, but he held them immobile above her head. She was panting, out of breath, wanting to kiss him, trying to kiss him, feeling his rock hard cock grinding into her and pinning her up against the door.

"I loved watching you with Paola tonight," he whispered, kissing her neck.

She moaned as his teeth gently grazed her skin. He knew the spots to get her out of control, fast.

He ground his cock into her harder, "I want you to have my baby." Letting go of her hands, he pulled her legs around his waist and carried her into the bedroom.

Schooner fell onto the bed on top of her and she wrapped her legs around him. "I'm not kidding, Mia. I want you to have my baby."

She stroked his cheek and smiled, "Aren't I supposed to be the one worrying about the biological clock?"

He sat up straddling her and unbuttoned his shirt, slowly, letting her enjoy his gorgeous muscles. His eyes were blazing as he stared down at her.

"What?" she asked.

He smiled. A slow, sexy smile. "I want to get you pregnant."

"We haven't been using anything."

"Would you consider IVF if we don't get pregnant on our own?" he asked.

Mia hesitated, "Honestly Schooner, I've never even thought about it." She saw the disappointment cross his face and grabbed his hand. "I'm not saying, no."

"Do you want a baby?"

In that moment, she knew she would do anything to make him happy because it would bring her equal happiness to do so. "I want your baby. Yes." And she reached for the button on his jeans, unbuttoned it and unzipped his fly.

He rolled off of her and kicked off his jeans and boxers and helped her peel off her jeans and panties.

They lie facing one another, softly kissing. She turned over so that her back was toward him and pulled his leg over her as she slid down his body until she could feel the head of his cock ready to press into her from behind. He pulled her tight against him, face buried into her neck, teeth grazing her shoulder, as he rammed deep into her.

"Oh yeah," he whispered in her ear and she squeezed his cock tight, "oh yeah, just like that," and she squeezed harder. "I'm going to fuck you so hard," he growled.

"Then do it," she taunted and he rammed into her hard. "That's what I need, Schooner. Give it to me. Give. Me. What. I. Need." He slammed into her harder. "Just like that. Just like that." And she clenched her muscles tight around his cock.

"Yessssssssssss," he hissed in her ear, "that's it, Baby Girl. Milk it out of me." He put his hand on her stomach and pressed her back into him as he buried himself in her as deeply as he could. "Come for me. I want you to come for me"

She took his hand from her stomach and moved it down to her clit. With his forefinger in hers, she pressed her clit hard and started moving in circles until their fingers found just the right spot that sent electric volts scattering through her.

She started to quake under his finger, muscles convulsing around him, squeezing him hard.

"Oh fuck yeah," he hissed pulling her over the edge with him as he drove up into her, deep and rough.

She collapsed back against him, panting and quaking with aftershocks.

He kissed her shoulder, "I love you, Baby Girl."

She rolled over and placed a hand on his cheek and kissed him softly, "I love you too, Schooner," she said, breathlessly.

She stroked his cheek and looked directly into his beautiful clear eyes, "I have something I need to tell you."

He looked at her, "Okay…"

"I didn't tell you earlier, because I didn't want to ruin your day and because I didn't want you to get pissed off and go ape shit."

"What's going on?" Concern shadowed his eyes.

"CJ called me this morning."

He pushed back from her and screamed, "What? And you are just telling me this now? Why didn't you call me this morning? Immediately." His face hardened in anger, a total transformation from the man who had been lying next to her mere seconds before.

"I didn't tell you because I knew you'd be pissed off and call her and I didn't want to give her the satisfaction that she was even important enough for me to go running to you about."

"What exactly happened?" He ran his hand through his hair, clearly exasperated.

Mia recounted the details of the phone call and Schooner listened silently. After she finished, it was a moment before he spoke.

"On one hand, I want to kiss you for handling her so brilliantly," he leveled Mia an angry glance, "but on the other hand, I cannot even begin to verbalize to you how pissed off I am that you did not call me about this immediately."

"I think you should just kiss me for being brilliant," Mia said, softly.

He shook his head no, "I'm really pissed at you, Mia."

"Schooner, she wanted a reaction and I didn't want to give it to her."

"That's all good and well, but that was a decision we should've made together. First, you need to tell me these things, so that I can contact my lawyer immediately, who will contact her lawyer, and have her stop her harassing you. More importantly, however, is you not keeping things from me—especially where CJ is concerned. Last time you did that it cost us twenty-four years of our lives, Mia."

She felt sick. To hear Schooner verbalize that her actions, or inactions, had cost them twenty-four years felt like a huge wet slap in the face. She rolled away from him and went to get out of bed.

"Where are you going?"

She didn't answer, but instead continued to walk into the kitchen to get a glass of cold water. She leaned against the breakfast bar and sipped the water.

Schooner joined her in the kitchen and stood in front of her. "Are we going to finish this conversation?"

"I'm listening." She looked up at him, full blown New York attitude on her face.

"You can't hide stuff from me, Mia. Why is it that you feel you can't come to me?"

She shrugged. "Look, I once told you, I'm not very good at relationships.

"Bullshit," he screamed, startling her.

She put her glass down on the breakfast bar and crossed her arms over her chest. "Well, I've never had a successful one," she scoffed, maintaining her defensive pose.

He shook his head and rubbed his forehead, "Listen, I'm sorry I screamed at you, but here's the deal. I need you to be totally honest with me all the time, not hide *anything* from me—especially where CJ's concerned—and have enough faith in me that I will handle situations appropriately and always do what is best for us. Us, Mia."

"I'm sorry, Schooner. I understand why you are so upset, I really do. Especially with a situation where CJ pulls something and I don't tell you. I get it—it will always be a big gaping wound for us. My poor handling of it in the past fucked up both of our lives. I get that. I just didn't want her to win this time and by treating her like her call meant nothing, helped me marginalize her. Does that make sense?"

"Yes, Baby Girl, it does." He walked toward her and she stood still, arms still crossed in front of her, "but you have to promise me that you will always come to me immediately with everything. Give us a chance to work it out together, Mia. You always want to take on everything alone. You are not in this alone anymore." He put his hands on her shoulders, "Look at me, Mia. I'm not going to always get it right. I'm going to fuck up. Sometimes royally. I'm going to react with anger or I'm going to want to protect you. And that is exactly why we need to do it together. No secrets. Let's learn from our past and then leave it there."

He was right. Seth and Kami were right. Holding back anything from Schooner had been and would continue to be their undoing if she didn't start thinking of them as a team in every aspect. This man, who willingly was giving up half his world, starting a new life 3,000 miles from the only home he had ever known, and told Katie Chisholm that she was his fiancé, was asking for a little faith and she would be the biggest fool in the world not to give him all that he was asking of her. Losing him again was not an acceptable option.

She uncrossed her arms and wrapped them around his waist. "No more secrets." She looked up into his eyes, "I promise." And then whispered into his chest, "Ever."

He smiled and whispered into her hair, "You really told her you were recording her?" She nodded and he tightened his hold. He laughed, "You are so freaking awesome."

CHAPTER 17

Mia sat at her desk, reviewing Excel spreadsheets of operating expenses when the text alert on her cell phone sounded. She looked at the display. Schooner, texting from LA. She smiled.

Schooner: Sitting across from her now.

Mia: You're at the lawyer's office?

Schooner: Yes

Mia: And you're sitting at the table texting?

Schooner: LOL—that I am!

Mia: You're so bad!!

Schooner: That I am!

Mia: It's part of your charm.

Schooner: So you tell me.

Mia: So ... how is it going?

Schooner: She's going to drag her feet. Nothing we didn't anticipate.

Mia: :-(

Schooner: Don't be sad, Baby Girl

Mia: Sad for you. Hate anyone making you unhappy.

Schooner: LOL she's clearly pissed I'm texting

Mia: LOL... tell her I say hi.

Schooner: Not!

Mia: Still seeing your parents tonight?

Schooner: Yup

Mia: Please send my love.

Schooner: I want your love.

Mia: You have my love.

Schooner: I hate being out here. Can't wait to come home.

Mia: :-) love having you home.

It was close to 10 minutes before her cell text beeped again, surprising her as she was absorbing the spreadsheet's numbers.

Schooner: This whole thing is starting to piss me off.

Mia: Oh no :-(

Schooner: Tell me something good.

Mia: Ummm... I love you

Schooner: That is very good. And it's smoochal, Baby Girl.

Mia: :-) yes, it is.

Schooner: God, she's such a huge bitch.

Mia: No comment! Do you need me to come out there and scratch her eyeballs out (or just hang the phone up on her again)? LOL

Schooner: Lol. Oh, that embarrassed her good when she was told to stop harassing you (I think I was smiling).

Mia: God, I love you.

Schooner: Oh God, she is laying it on really thick now.

Mia: And you're texting.

Schooner: Yeah :-)

Mia: So you know how you always want me to share things with you?

Schooner: Yeah...

Mia: It may be nothing, but...

Mia: I barfed my guts up this morning.

Schooner: Holy shit! Have you taken a test?

Mia: No, will wait until you get home to do that. Want to do it together.

Schooner: I have to leave this meeting now and come home

Mia: You'll be home in two days.

Schooner: I want to be home NOW!

Mia: Soon and forever...

Schooner: Soon and forever (never going to be able to concentrate now! If she ends up with the business it is your fault, Baby Girl)

Mia: Lol... go concentrate. Call my ass when you get out of there.

Schooner: Call your ass hot.

Mia: :-) Bye! Concentrate.

Schooner: Bye :-(Never going to be able to concentrate after the barfing bombshell.

Mia: Hmmm ... Barfing Bombshell ... I think you called me that after too much tequila in college.

Schooner: LOL... ok about to stick it to her and not in the way she wants. Bye.

Mia woke to his arms wrapping around her and his long leg slung over her, pulling her into him, kissing her beneath the ear.

"Mmmmm." And through her cobwebs, "you're back?" It was a question more than a statement.

"I couldn't stay away." He nuzzled into her neck, his fingers finding her nipples and pinching them.

She moaned and ground her ass into his hard cock.

Pulling her beneath him, he positioned his hands on either side of her face. Half asleep, she couldn't keep her eyes open and started dozing off. He spread her legs with his thighs, and without any foreplay, rammed into her hard. She gasped, her eyes opening and a smile overtaking her lips.

"Morning, Baby Girl," he growled and kissed her hard while fucking her at a punishing rate. He rammed into her relentlessly, taking what he wanted. This was going to be quick. When he was through, he curled up behind her and pulled her close. They were both asleep in a matter of seconds.

When Mia woke, she found a surprise on the bathroom counter. Inside a Duane Reade Drugstore bag was a package containing not one, but two pregnancy tests. She smiled and thought, how very Schooner. Unwrapping one of the sticks, she realized that this was the first time in her life that she was hoping for a positive result.

As she watched, the pink line started to form, and within a minute, it turned into a cross. Clicking the cover back onto the test stick, Mia crawled back into bed next to a sleeping Schooner. She bit him on the shoulder. *As good a way as any to wake him*, she thought.

He rolled over to look at her and with a shit-eating grin she waved the test stick in his face. His eyes shot wide open as he realized what she was doing and he grabbed her hand mid-wave.

"Very good hand-eye coordination, I'm impressed," she laughed.

He focused in on the stick and saw the plus sign and looked up at Mia, who was nodding her head and smiling.

The look in his eyes melted every inch of her. "Baby Girl," he whispered hoarsely, as she smiled at him. He pulled her head down to his chest and kissed her hair. She peeked up at him and could see his mega-watt gorgeous smile, but he was lost somewhere.

"Where are you, Schooner?"

He smiled at her, "Thinking. I want this divorce NOW."

"Don't worry about that," Mia reassured.

"But we have a baby coming," he was verbalizing it for the first time and she could see the enormity bursting in his every thought.

"I promise I'll put your name on the birth certificate." Mia gave him her devil grin.

"Bitch!" he laughed, grabbing her and tickling her until she yelped. He then smiled at her and took her face in his hands, becoming serious again. "Mia Alyse Silver, you are having my baby."

"Schooner James Moore, yes I am."

His smile was so beautiful that Mia thought if there is one moment she wanted to take with her into the next life, this was it right now. The feeling in her heart and the look in his eyes and his smile, made her think, this is all I want from this lifetime. It doesn't get better than this.

"Hand me my pants. They're on the floor by your side of the bed," he pointed. Mia rolled away from him, grabbed his jeans and flung them at him, whipping them into his face, "Ouch."

He pulled his jeans off of his face and smiled at her. "You know," he began, "sometimes parents are very smart. Take my parents, for example, they are very smart people. They loved you the minute they met you. Me, well, I was not quite as smart. I was totally intrigued from the moment I met you, but I was also more than a little intimidated by you. You were different and cool and you totally embraced it and you clearly didn't give a shit. Me, I was afraid to be different, even though deep down, I knew I was. So I did everything I possibly could to fit in. I didn't quite know what to make of you, Mia, and frankly, I didn't know how to act around you because I thought you'd see right through me and my bullshit. I was afraid you would know what a fraud I was and that you wouldn't like me. You were this total enigma, this cool New York girl and I already knew you were so much fun to be with, just from the time we'd spent together and from watching you around campus." He nodded his head with the admission, "Yes, I watched you—in the dining hall, on The Quad. And I envied the fun you and everyone around you were always having. But you, you were always at the center of it. So, on that first day of Interim, I was thrilled when I saw you sitting there, because I knew I was going to have a chance to get to know you and that was something I really wanted. And later that day, you called me out on my shit and I went back to my dorm that night and lied in my bed thinking about you and how you made me feel. It was like the fairytale where the wooden boy comes to life." He laughed, "Except I was a plastic boy and you made me feel real. That magic that I had watched all first semester, well now I had a front row seat in that magic circle. And I just wanted to be with you all the time. You were my high, Mia. You taught me how to let me be myself and to like that guy and that is probably the greatest gift anyone has ever given me. Ever. And you liked that guy, too, and that made my heart soar. I wanted you to like me, not Mr. Hotshot Tennis God. I wanted you to like me. And it was when we were on that mountaintop together, that I was actually able to put it all together. I was in love and it hit me like a brick or maybe a snowball. I had fallen in love with you."

Mia stroked his face and smiled at him, her eyes filled with tears.

"So, yesterday afternoon I sat down with my parents and told them everything for the first time. And they are thrilled that you are joining our family." He reached out and brushed away Mia's tears with his thumb. He stuck his hand in the pocket of his jeans, "Mia Alyse Silver, the minute, and I mean the minute, that my divorce is final, I want you to be my wife, forever." Out of the pocket he pulled a ring box. "This was my grandmother's. My mother wants you to have it and I want you to have it." He opened the box and removed a platinum and diamond art deco ring. "Marry me, Baby

Girl." He slipped the ring on her finger and then held her hand tightly in his.

Mia was momentarily lost in his eyes, swimming through the turquoise blue waters that she had spent most of her lifetime dreaming about. It was finally their turn.

She smiled and nodded, "Schooner James Moore, aka Baby Daddy," they laughed through their tears as Mia found her voice, "I guess we can just face the fact that I am smarter than you because I was totally smitten from the moment I first laid eyes on you. You were so damn pretty, your eyes and a smile that should be outlawed. And I was so shy meeting you, but I remember thinking that we could be really good friends and have the best time together, like crazy adventures good times. And although I was seriously crushing on you, I knew you were looking for a prom queen type, which yes, we can both admit, I was not," they laughed. "And I didn't quite know how to deal with you, so aloof was a very safe and easy way for me to relate to you. And interestingly enough, I have been told by more than one man in my life that I am aloof. But I digress... so when I looked up in that lecture hall that first day of Interim and saw you, my heart skipped a beat. Then you came and sat down next to me and my heart was pounding in my chest. I was afraid you could hear it and I was also afraid you could read my mind. So cool girl came in and took over, to protect me. I needed someplace to hide and she always provided the perfect ruse. And then Rick said that we had to break into groups and at that moment, I just took control because it meant I'd get to spend time with you and I might really get to know you. And what surprised me most of all was how you just fit in with us right away, you just came and took your place. And it was easy and I didn't need cool girl there, because I could be me with you and we were totally on the same wavelength. And that night after the mountains, you kissed me for the first time," she smiled at him, his eyes bright with tears, "and I slept in your arms and from that moment on, my life was never, ever the same. I remember thinking, *the realization of a secret dream,* which was this horoscope that came packed in some lip gloss I got when I was a really little girl, like 5 or 6 years old, and I hid it and held onto it for years and years. And that is what I was thinking that night as I dozed off with my head on your chest. The realization of a secret dream." They both had tears streaming down their cheeks. "I can't wait to be your wife, Schooner."

She held out her hand to look at the stunning ring, "Now this is the smartest thing you've ever done." They both laughed. "Are you sure this shouldn't go to Holly though?

He shook his head, "This one is yours. I think my mother may have put it in safekeeping for you right after freshman orientation."

Mia laughed, "You were not kidding. She is a very smart woman. I knew I liked her."

Mia picked up her phone and took a photo of the ring on her finger. She looked at Schooner, devil smile at full tilt.

"Oh no, who are you texting that to?"

She just smiled, enigmatically.

"Your Mom?" he guessed.

"Nope."

"My Mom?"

"Nope."

"Seth."

"Nope, he'll be second."

"Kami."

"Nope."

"Gaby."

"Nope."

"CJ," he teased

"Ugh, nope," laughing, "I don't want to be responsible for an earthquake in LA."

He shrugged his shoulders, palms up. "I'm out of guesses."

"Katie Chisholm," smiled Mia and they both laughed.

CHAPTER 18

Schooner's right leg bounced up and down at a frantic pace as he and Mia sat in Dr. Gary Cohen's waiting room. Dr. Cohen, one of the top-rated physician's in Manhattan for high-risk pregnancies, was known for his laid back caring manner and was universally adored by his patients.

Mia had been one of Gary's first patients when he joined a prestigious gynecology and obstetrics practice—long before he was known as "The Man" for high risk pregnancies. A friend of Mia's, a nurse at Columbia Presbyterian Hospital, had recommended a doctor when Mia was suffering from irregular cycles and prolonged periods of bleeding. The senior doctor in the practice was no longer accepting new patients, so Mia was assigned to the new guy, who was just starting out and trying to build a patient roster. Nearly twenty years had passed since.

"You're making me nervous. Stop that." Mia placed a hand above his knee and gave him a pointed look.

"Sorry." He took her hand and squeezed it.

"So when is Yoli flying in?" She needed to distract him or his nerves were going to start making her even more nervous than she already was.

"I think she lands about 11 P.M. tomorrow night." His eyes were darting everywhere.

"Schooner…"

He looked at her.

"Stop."

"Sorry. I can't believe I'm this nervous." His eyes were wide and he looked like a lost boy to Mia.

Smiling at him, she thought, *God, he is sweet.*

She leaned over and kissed him, "This is going to be a long freaking nine months. Keep it up and I'm sending you back to LA."

He smiled against her lips. "Bitch," and they both laughed.

"Mia Silver," a nurse was at the door.

Mia and Schooner stood and in sync looked at one another and said, "Showtime." They laughed as they headed back toward the exam room, hand in hand.

Dr. Gary Cohen entered the exam room, arms outstretched for a hug, "I hear my favorite patient is here."

Mia gave Gary a warm hug, "I'll bet you say that to all of your patients."

"You and I were babies when we started." They both laughed.

"Gary, I'd like you to meet my fiancé, Schooner Moore."

Gary extended a hand and a warm smile to Schooner, "So, you're the guy responsible for knocking her up, huh?"

Schooner beamed, "That would be me."

"Good job, man." Gary clapped Schooner on the shoulder.

"Alright, Miss Mia, I'm going to do a sonogram in a few minutes. We'll take a look and make sure this is a viable pregnancy, and then discuss some of the risks of being forty and pregnant, things we need to look out for, regimen, etc.

"Okay, let's get you up on this table, feet in the dreaded stirrups. I'm going to do a vaginal ultrasound on you. What we're looking for is a fetal pole, or possibly even, a fetal heartbeat, depending on how far along you are." He squeezed gel onto the head of the ultrasound wand. "Are your periods still so irregular?"

"Yup." Mia nodded, bracing herself for what she knew was going to be a cold, goopy wand.

He laughed, "You've always been a mess. Ready?"

She nodded, holding her breath and biting her bottom lip. Schooner grabbed her hand and squeezed it. He smiled down at her, his eyes saying all she needed to hear. He was surprisingly calm after his mini-meltdown in the waiting room.

"Ahhhh!" Mia stiffened from the cold, wet feeling probe.

"Relax," Gary smiled up at her. He manipulated the wand, eyes intent on the screen.

She squeezed Schooner's hand tighter. Please, please, please, she said a silent prayer. Gary kept making adjustments to the wand, moving it left, center, right.

And finally a whoosh, whoosh, whoosh sound and Schooner let out a, "Yes!"

Mia looked from Schooner's smile to Gary. He was nodding his head, "Good job, Mia," he was smiling. "We have a heartbeat."

She felt the familiar sting of tears in her eyes and turned to look at the monitor. The tech pointed out the baby's heartbeat and Gary told her to print it.

She looked up at Schooner who was watching the fetal heartbeat and mouthed the words, "Our baby." He brought her hand to his lips and kissed it. She knew he couldn't speak.

"Okay, let's get some measurements and we'll calculate a due date." They moved markers around on the screen and pressed buttons that sounded like snapshots to Mia. "Okay, we've got it." Gary informed his tech. "Mia you can get dressed now and why don't you and Schooner come meet me in my office." He handed her a wad of tissues with a smile and she wondered if it was for her tears or to clean off the nasty goop.

Schooner and Mia entered Gary's ultra-modern office, hand-in-hand, and he motioned for them to have a seat.

"First, let me congratulate you. This is a very exciting day and I'm really thrilled for both of you. Schooner, I've known Mia for a long time and she is absolutely one of my very favorite people, so this pregnancy and her health are personally even more important to me than it typically is with a patient. I consider Mia a friend."

Schooner smiled at Mia, "She does have that effect on people, doesn't she?" He rubbed her hand in both of his, smiling ear-to-ear.

"Have you known one another long?" Gary asked.

"Twenty-four years," Mia offered.

Gary's eyes widened in surprise.

"We went out freshman year in college."

Gary was smiling. "How'd you guys get back together?

"Facebook," Schooner responded with a smile, as if that explained everything.

"Good for you." Gary looked at them, shaking his head. "Okay, let's get to the serious stuff. Here's the good news, Mia you conceived right away, with no problems. Considering your age, irregular periods and irregular ovulation pattern, that is great. The fact that the embryo implanted normally and we now have a heartbeat is also really good. The embryo has a CRL measurement of slightly over 5MM. Again, perfectly within the norm and very good news."

"What is a CRL measurement, Gary?"

"Crown to rump length."

"Cool." Mia was smiling, picturing a little head and bottom all curled up sleeping.

"Based on that measurement, we're looking at a fetal age of about 5 weeks and a gestational age of 6 1/2—7 weeks. If you go full-term, Mia, we're looking at a birth date right before Christmas."

She backhanded Schooner in the arm, smiling at him, "How's that for a gift from a Jewish girl!"

He grabbed her hand and brought it to his lips. Schooner was exhilarated.

"Now, let's talk about the elephant in the room," Gary began, "Mia, you're forty. So what does that really mean? It means we need to test for certain things, look for certain things, keep our eyes open and be prepared to make some decisions, should we need to."

Mia held her breath as she looked at Schooner. He rubbed her hand in his and the look in his eyes said, "No worries, Baby Girl."

Gary continued, "At age forty, the biggest risk is for Down's Syndrome. The statistics are 1 in 90 births, which is considerably higher than 1 in 1300 for a woman who is twenty-five."

Mia realized she truly wasn't breathing. She could feel the strength emanating from Schooner's hand to hers, like radio waves. It was that same strength he infused in her the night that she was raped.

"In about a month, we'll do some blood tests looking for some normal first trimester proteins, a few weeks after that we'll do Alpha-fetoprotein testing and at the same time we'll do an early Quad Marker Screen testing for four substances that come from the baby's blood, brain, spinal fluid and amniotic fluid. At that point, we'll also do an amniocentesis. We have a Geneticist here on staff and I'm going to have the two of you meet with him."

He stopped and looked from Mia to Schooner then back to Mia. "You are in good health, Mia, and we're going to watch you closely. If there are any issues, we're going to detect it early and act accordingly."

"Meaning?" Mia asked.

"Meaning a lot of different things—if we need to put you on bed rest, we'll put you on bed rest." He turned to Schooner and smiled, "Good luck with that one," and the two men laughed. "Like I said, you're in good health and your chances for a normal pregnancy are good. But you are high-risk and we'll watch you. For now, enjoy your life, eat healthy, don't drink, moderate exercise, take your prenatal vitamins and enjoy being pregnant."

As he saw them out, he gave Mia a huge hug, "I am so thrilled for you both." And to Schooner, "Take care of our girl."

CHAPTER 19

Yoli stood in the middle of the rotunda looking up at the frescos. "Holy shit, Schooner, the pictures did not do this place justice. I cannot believe this. This space is not for real."

Schooner just smiled, looking up at the cove lit murals. "Pretty amazing, huh. We're coming along on the build out faster than I thought."

"I can see. They really do things in a New York minute here, huh." They were ascending the main marble staircase. "Amazing." Yoli was blown away looking at all the architectural details.

"Come, let me show you the offices." He ushered her into an area away from the rotunda. They entered a space with floor to ceiling windows. "Like my new office?" He flashed his catalogue smile, as he stood next to one of the windows.

"Are you ever coming home again?" she asked.

"I am home, Yoli." He gave her a real smile.

"I was afraid you were going to say that." She leaned up on the window frame facing him. "We need to talk about California."

"I want you to run it—all of it. It's about time I made you COO and let's backfill you in the CMO role. You've got some good people working under you, I don't think you'll need to go outside, unless there's someone you want to bring in."

"Did you just promote me?" She had a look on her face saying, "You didn't really just do that?"

He nodded and laughed, "*You* are the only thing I've missed about California." Opening his arms, she went to him for an embrace.

"Yeah well, I've missed your cranky ass, too." She gazed out the window, "What am I looking at?"

"Downtown. The financial district. That's the Freedom Tower."

She nodded and continued to look out the window before finally turning back to Schooner who was casually leaning against the opposite side of the carved window frame watching her. "You're happy, Schooner." It was a statement. "I've never seen you so full of life as you are here. Mia is clearly really good for you."

He nodded. "She is really good for me. I did not think I'd ever be this happy again in my life, Yoli. It's a gift and I know it and trust me, I am treating it accordingly," Schooner admitted.

He put an arm around her shoulder and they started back toward the rotunda. "Let's head over to Mia's office, I know she and Kami were bringing lunch into the conference room and we're going to make it a working lunch." He shrugged, "Working lunch. Totally a New York thing. I'm really excited to have you finally meet Mia, but I also have to admit that I'm more than a little scared."

"Why is that?" The first hints of early spring were in the air when they stepped through the massive front entrance of the soon-to-be L9/NYC into the bright sunshine. Schooner stepped to the curb and hailed a cab, making Yoli think, he's really got this down.

"I really want you two to like each other."

"Well, I really like Kami a lot and she says wonderful things about Mia. And…" She looked at him out of the corner of her eye.

"…And what?" He shifted to face her, the black leather seat of the yellow cab creaking.

"I spoke to Holly." Yoli looked almost contrite. Almost, being the operative word.

"…And?" Schooner urged, surprised by Yoli's admission.

"She had great things to say about Mia, but more importantly, the thing that struck her the most, Schooner, was the change in you. You're happy."

Schooner nodded and looked out the window as the streets passed by.

They were laughing so hard; it didn't feel like they were working. Yoli was immediately blown away by the casual chic atmosphere of the agency that clearly came top down from their Levi's clad owner. *Levi's*, Yoli thought refreshingly, *not 7 For All Mankind or Dolce & Gabana, but a well-worn, broken in pair of Levi's.* And they weren't even camel-toe tight, they were more like boyfriend jeans.

"I think you'll be soft-opening in summer," Mia was saying, "which is good, because a lot of people are out of town and it's just a great time to work out the kinks." They all agreed. "My recommendation is that we don't do the big event until after Labor Day when everyone is back in town. Here's what I'm thinking, Fashion Week is the week after Labor Day, make it part of the Fashion Week festivities. Means a lot of stars in town. Everyone is party hopping, throw a big opening gala in conjunction. It will give everyone something to look forward to in the fall social season."

"Do we run the risk of getting lost in the shuffle?" Kami threw out on the table.

"We do if we don't do it right. If we do it right, we can garner a lot of press out of it. If we launch prior, it's pre-Labor Day and no one is in town and if we wait until later in September, we lose a lot of the star power that will be in town for Fashion Week—many of whom are already L9 members. I think we're locked into a box and we just need to manage it to our advantage."

Yoli made some notes on her laptop. "I'll pull a member roster so that we can start taking a look at who we think will be in town for Fashion Week. We have a lot of models."

"We have enough time," Mia began, "to pull this together and really work on the details and make it a huge event. My concern is that it runs smoothly and the fact that we're brand new, transparent to the attendees."

Grabbing a Black & White cookie from a tray at the center of the conference room table and looking at it like "I can't believe I'm going to eat this," Schooner turned to Yoli and said, "Do we have our list together of staff that we want here for the opening and transition period?" Yoli pulled a sheet from a manila folder and slid it over to Schooner.

He looked over the list. "I wonder how they're going to feel about sleeping bags?" Schooner muttered. All eyes turned to him. He looked up stone-faced and looked around at all the sets of eyes on him, then broke into a huge smile, a real smile, "Scared you all, huh?"

"Asshole," muttered Yoli.

"Love her," Mia informed Schooner, pointing to Yoli.

"A woman to abuse me on each coast. Some guys just have it all," he quipped.

Mia looked at Yoli with her devil grin and lifted her hand for a high five, which Yoli was right there to meet.

Later in the afternoon in a small dark pub around the corner from the office, drink in hand, Yoli sat with Schooner watching Mia talk and laugh with Seth, Kami and other members of her staff.

"So, what do you think?" he asked.

"I think you got it right this time. She's so real. And you, you're a different person."

"I'm me." Schooner countered, lifting his Johnnie Walker Blue to his smiling lips.

"How bad is CJ going to make this?"

"She's going to drag her feet for as long as she can, but it's inevitable," Schooner shrugged.

"And how is Mia with all of that?"

"Surprisingly unfazed." He turned to Yoli smiling and shaking his head, "She could care less. She's just worried about the aggravation it causes me."

Yoli tossed back the rest of her drink and motioned to the waitress for another, "Well excellent, that is one less thing you have to worry about."

Schooner turned to Yoli, a huge grin on his face, "Did you hear that CJ called Mia?"

Yoli's mouth momentarily hung open, "Are you serious?"

Schooner nodded, still laughing. "She accused Mia of stealing me."

"She didn't," Yoli laughed.

"And Mia told her," he was still laughing, "not to confuse me leaving her with being stolen away."

Yoli began to choke on her drink and Schooner patted her back, "And then she told her she was recording the call." They were both hysterical laughing.

"I knew I liked her!" Yoli confirmed.

Schooner went on, "I guess Mia said something to her about that she was just embarrassing herself and that she wasn't going to let her go on and CJ told her that she wasn't done yet and Mia said, 'Actually, you are,' and hit the click off on her speaker button and hung up on her ass."

They were both roaring with laughter. Mia smiled across the dark bar at them, clearly happy to see Schooner so at ease and laughing.

When Yoli could speak again, "That's it, it's official, I love her."

"Ditto. She is pretty damn adorable." Schooner beamed looking at his love across the room.

CHAPTER 20

Heading home in a cab, Schooner sat staring blankly out the window.

"Hey, where are you?" Mia asked as they stopped at a red light.

"I'm here." He brought her hand to his mouth and kissed her knuckles.

Mia had noticed his preoccupation growing over the past few weeks. He had a lot on his plate; the divorce, building L9/NYC, still living two lives on two coasts while he transitioned California operations to Yoli.

"Let's not go right home." Mia suggested, "Let's go get some frozen yogurt and take a walk on The High Line and watch sunset."

As they walked The High Line, a linear elevated park built on an old railway spur on the West Side of Manhattan, Mia could feel the tension radiating off of Schooner, even though they were in this peaceful environment of people leisurely strolling and enjoying the beautiful balmy evening air, an early precursor of the spring that was waiting right around the corner.

"What is bothering you, Schooner? Please talk to me." Mia looked up at his handsome profile, wondering how she could pull him back to her.

Mia spied an unoccupied bench and started steering them toward it. Sitting down, tugging on Schooner's hand to sit with her.

"I'm lost," she looked at him, "please talk to me. I've watched you going off into a space that doesn't seem like a happy space for a few weeks now and I don't know what's going on."

A couple with a baby in a stroller and a toddler holding mom's hand passed by and they watched them silently.

"I'm just concerned about the tests coming up," he finally admitted.

Mia took his face in her hands, so that she could look into his eyes. "Me too."

"I'm afraid you and I will have different answers if things don't turn out as well as we're hoping." His eyes looked sad.

Mia understood what he was saying and looked down for a moment to get her bearings. She sighed, "Schooner, can we cross that bridge when we come to it?"

"I've already been crossing it, Mia."

Mia nodded her head. She knew what he wanted to hear. He wanted to hear that whatever the news was that she would continue with the pregnancy.

She took his hand and rubbed it between hers and brought it to her face, rubbed her cheek on it and kissed it. "Okay, here's where you and I differ."

His beautiful eyes looked grave.

"I can't go there right now." Mia continued, "I can't go where you are going. I just can't do it. Just thinking that things are not going to be perfect upsets me, I can physically feel the anxiety and my blood pressure gets all crazy. So, I just can't go there. If I need to go there, because it's reality, then I will. But I refuse to go there when it's still speculative. I can't do that to myself or to the baby."

He nodded, "I just worry, Mia."

"Well stop, Schooner. Right now you are worrying about a problem that doesn't exist and may never exist. If we find out differently, we're two intelligent people, we'll figure it out. Please just enjoy this time. It's my bliss time, Schooner. Please share it with me."

They sat in silence watching people stroll by, skateboarders, dog walkers, and the sky turn from a blue the color of Schooner's eyes to opalescent pinks and oranges into rubies and then dusk.

As they walked back to the apartment, Schooner finally started to vocalize. "I just have this overwhelming need to protect you, Mia. I feel like I have failed to do a good job of it so many times in my life."

Mia sighed, "Schooner, Schooner, Schooner. There are some things we can't control."

"You'd be surprised," he was now smiling.

Mia laughed, "How do I get you to chill out?"

"Maybe sometime in late December, when we have a nice healthy baby." He hugged her to him as they waved hello to the doormen.

"Oh puhleeeze." She tightened her arm around him, "I think that's when your crazy neurosis is going to be in full bloom." They entered the elevator.

He laughed, "I swear I was much calmer about this in my twenties."

"Great, so what you're telling me is CJ got the good end of things here?" They both laughed, "That's just not fair."

"I promise to try to chill." He kissed her as they entered the apartment.

"C'mon Baby Daddy, make it up to me." She pulled him into the bedroom.

CHAPTER 21

"You called Gary?" Mia was shocked.

"Mmm-hmm." Schooner nodded, long legs stretched out from where he sat at the breakfast bar, coffee in hand.

"I had questions. I want to understand the whole procedure, the risks to you and the baby, when to expect results."

"And to make sure you could be in there with me?"

He nodded.

Mia stood in front of him, between his legs. "Did you buy a lab to get immediate, priority results?"

"It occurred to me." He stared straight into her eyes.

"When did you become such a control freak, Schooner?" Mia cocked her head, looking into his calm blue eyes.

"You are seriously asking me that?" he asked, with a bemused look, putting his hands on Mia's shoulders.

She nodded.

"Mia, I always control everything. I always have. With the exception of you. You have always been the one out of control thing in my life. You. Everything that happens to you. What you do. How you react. Out of control."

Mia stood there thinking, while Schooner took one hand off of her shoulder and grabbed his coffee cup. "People. Situations. Business. Emotions. I've always controlled them or was in control of them."

Mia's brows were knit, clearly doing a mental inventory of their past and their time together.

"But you, my Baby Girl, are like a vortex. I get sucked in and spun around and nothing is ever in control. And it's always certainly out of my control."

Mia smiled at him and pushed his hair from his forehead. "And does it surprise you how happy you are in my little out of control world?"

He nodded and she leaned forward and kissed him. "Exciting, huh?"

"To some extent," he admitted, taking a sip of his coffee. "But also very disconcerting. You've always controlled everything, Mia. Whether you realize it or not. I gave up control when I fell in love with you. You know why?"

She shook her head.

"Because I stopped putting me first."

"And this clearly gives you heartburn, Schooner?"

He nodded. "Mia, you have the power to pull the rug out from under me. I'm helpless. I'm just along for the ride."

She took his face in her hands. "Schooner, I probably shouldn't tell you this, but we are standing on the precipice together. You have a lot more power here than you give yourself credit for."

"I do what I can in little ways to try and gain some semblance of control over things." He stood to rinse his cup in the sink before putting it in the dishwasher.

"Like call Gary?" Mia realized she had her arms crossed in front of her and dropped them, consciously not trying to take on a defensive pose.

He nodded. Schooner's eyes were fixed on Mia's and very serious.

Mia gestured, palms up. "And? Do you feel better?"

"I do."

She rolled her eyes. "Don't make me drag this out of you."

"Gary and I both think that it's best that you don't do the tests as an outpatient. He's going to keep you overnight, in case there are any issues," Mia nodded and he continued, "and we can do something called FISH results and have answers the next day that Gary says are usually pretty accurate."

Mia nodded, turned on her heel and walked into the bedroom. Schooner walked in a few minutes later and Mia was sitting on the bed in running shorts and a sweatshirt, tying the laces on her sneakers.

He leaned in the doorway arms crossed, taking up most of the doorframe watching her. "Going for a run?"

"No. Probably more like a fast walk." She didn't look up at him.

"Are you angry?"

"No."

"Then why are you going out?"

She looked up at him for the first time. "I need space and I need to think."

"You need space from me?" he sounded annoyed.

She nodded. "I do. I need to think, Schooner. I'm really trying not to react."

"And you don't think walking out of here to think is not a reaction?"

Mia stood. "Yeah, it's a reaction, but it will give me time to process everything."

"Fine." And he turned and walked back into the living room.

Mia found him standing in front of the living room windows looking outside. Instead of grabbing her keys, she approached Schooner from behind and wrapped her arms around his waist, laying her cheek on his back.

"You overwhelm me, Schooner. I think when it comes to me you sometimes don't understand boundaries. I have to keep reminding myself it's because you love me and always want to protect me." She could feel his muscles begin to relax. His hands went to her hands, covering them. "Why didn't you talk to me before calling Gary?"

"Well, I knew he could answer my questions directly."

"I shouldn't be learning about it as an afterthought." She kissed his back.

"You would've stopped me." He turned in her arms to face her.

"Mmm-hmm," she acknowledged. "Or I at least would've been part of the decision-making process, Schooner."

He nodded. "You're right."

"I'm not porcelain," she whispered.

"When you were sixteen, my dad told me to watch out for you." He looked up at the ceiling, slowly letting out a lungful of air. "Do you know that I always felt that I let him down, that I let your dad down and most of all, that I let you down."

She grabbed him tighter, cheek against his chest. "Will I always wonder what our lives would've been like had I not left you. Yes, a little bit maybe. Okay, maybe more than a little, but Schooner, I've had a good life—so many of my dreams have come true. You've had an amazing life. And now, we have this chance. This chance to do it right. And we both have the life experience and the maturity to really appreciate and value it all. And we're having a baby. And the only thing either one of us should worry about controlling is our happiness. You have to lighten up."

He lifted her hand to his lips. "Not likely, Baby Girl."

Mia looked up with sad eyes into his beautiful clear blue eyes, turned and grabbed her keys off the breakfast bar and walked out of the apartment.

CHAPTER 22

Mia had been walking for a while, zigzagging through the streets, not really paying attention to her surroundings, the dialogue in her head drowning out all else. Schooner was usually the calming factor to her over the top reactions, tethering her back to Earth, but now his desire to control and protect was oppressive. Mia wondered if it was just driven by his fear that their baby wouldn't be okay or if this was really just Schooner.

Really, who was he? Some guy she had known for a short while, a long time ago, who just came back into her life. A guy who had just left his wife for her (okay, the wife who stole him away with lies in the first place). And now she was pregnant with his baby. And at forty, this baby might not be healthy and could she deal with that? Did she want to deal with that? Could she even consider not dealing with it? She told him that she would cross that bridge when they came to it.

She reached the corner of Greenwich and Gansevoort before she stopped. What to do? What to do? *Okay, one more block and I'll be at Christian Louboutin,* she thought. *I'll look at Louboutin shoes, that'll be a feel good.*

As Mia stood in front of what was considered the mother ship to many women, she realized that she didn't have her wallet or her cell phone with her. She couldn't buy shoes and she couldn't call Schooner and the thought upset her greatly.

And as she stood there looking at the beautiful red-soled skyscrapers, she realized that she couldn't buy Louboutin's anyway because every woman she knew that had a child said their feet grew as a result of their pregnancy, and just the thought of that, was enough to push Mia Silver over the edge.

Mia stood in front of Louboutin's window and sobbed. She cried for all the beautiful size 7 1/2's in her closet that she would never wear again, she bawled for all the shoes she couldn't buy until her feet morphed into their new size, she wept for her favorite Old Gringo cowboy boots that she was not going to fit into as a cool new mother. Tears streamed down her cheeks because her feet were soon going to be huge swollen platters that would only fit into Birkenstocks, and that alone, the thought of having to wear Birkenstocks, was reason enough to sob uncontrollably.

A gay man walking his Yorkie handed Mia a tissue. She thanked him and decided it was time to head home before the staff at Louboutin alerted the psych ward at Bellevue.

On the way home, she tried making a mental list. Schooner was so good to her and so sweet to her and he was right, he always put her before himself. She thought back to what he was like even as a teen. He put his life on hold when she was attacked, taking over so that she could heal. He took over then, too. Why hadn't she seen that this was his way?

She wondered if maybe she was the only thing he couldn't control because they were both alphas. Could two alphas live together and complement one another without smothering or killing the other?

It was dusk by the time she reached her building, she knew that whatever their issues were, they needed to figure them out because she was not going to live without him again.

She entered the apartment and Schooner was sitting on the couch with blueprints spread out on the coffee table. He looked up at Mia, his expression unreadable.

"Sorry I didn't call. I left my phone here," she began.

"I know. I was worried," his voice was terse.

Mia sat down next to him on the couch. "I should not have walked out. I'm sorry."

He sighed. Head cocked to the side. "We haven't really changed that much, have we. Our M.O.'s are pretty much the same."

Mia was shaking her head, no.

"How can you say no, Mia? You just walked out."

"I went out to think. You know that."

"And?" his voice was clipped.

"And I thought a lot. I thought about how little we know one another. I thought about how we knew one another for a short time, a long time ago. I thought about here we are involved in this big way and we're having a baby together. I thought about the fact that I can't buy Louboutin's because I don't know what size my feet will be after I have the baby. I cried in front of Christian Louboutin, Schooner!"

His eyes were wide and a little scared looking, as if he were pondering how to respond, knowing the slightest miscalculation could mean his head.

"That's right, you should be looking at me like I'm a crazy pregnant woman, because I am a crazy pregnant woman. And you are making me crazier. I think we're both alphas, Schooner, and we need to figure out a way to live with that, because I refuse to lose you again."

The impassive mask on his face cracked and the smile led all the way to his eyes. He opened his arms and Mia fell into them. He pulled her in tight, kissing the top of her head.

"You need to learn to let me take care of you, Baby Girl. You don't have to be so tough all the time." He tightened his arms around her, lips in her hair.

CHAPTER 23

"Are you ready to take a look at your baby?" Gary asked an anxious Schooner and Mia.

They both nodded, smiling. Schooner held tightly onto Mia's hand.

"They need to come up with a warming version on that jelly," Mia complained.

Gary started moving the wand over Mia's now rounded belly. "I'm going to do a full ultrasound first, we're going to take a lot of measurements today, then we'll do the amnio and quad markers and then I'll do another ultrasound after the amnio. You ready?"

Mia nodded.

"Okay, here we go."

Within seconds, a 3-D image of a little head appeared on the screen. Mia heard a mewling sound come from her throat and felt the burning tears welling in her eyes. Schooner squeezed her hand tighter and she looked over at him. He was beaming at the screen. As Gary moved the wand down, they watched the heart beat. Slowly, he moved down the length of the fetus, down long legs to the feet.

"The baby is looking good. We've got ten fingers and ten toes. Size and development look on target for this age." He smiled at Mia, "I'm going to do some measurements of the head and the brain, take multiple view shots of the heart, take full body measurements and long bone measurements. This is going to take a few minutes, so just enjoy your first home movie."

"Look at that little nose and mouth." Mia was bursting with joy. She felt Schooner's lips on the back of her hand and turned toward him.

His eyes were crinkled in the corners and tears streaked his face.

"I love you," Mia mouthed.

"Love you too, Baby Girl," he whispered in her ear and kissed her temple.

"Looks like you've got a little thumb sucker." Gary laughed as the baby moved its thumb to its mouth.

As the baby moved positions, Mia asked, "Ummm Gary, am I looking at some family jewels?"

He laughed, "You most certainly are."

Mia looked up at Schooner, "We have a little show off! I can already see my little lady killer preening on the courts."

Schooner just stared at the screen, too moved to speak.

"The measurements all look good. Everything is developing right on schedule. Okay, let's get ourselves ready here for the amnio. I'm going to put a little topical numbing cream on your stomach. What you're going to feel is basically the pinch of a shot and then some pressure. The whole thing won't take too long."

Schooner sat down so that his head was next to Mia's. "Look at me, Mia."

She looked at him, her head now turned away from the screen and from her stomach.

He squeezed her hand. "You are doing so great, Baby Girl. I'm so proud of you."

She winced as the needle inserted and he kept talking, "Just a few days and we close on the beach house." He brushed her bangs from her eyes. "I can't wait to wake up to the view off of that deck. It's going to be so relaxing just to be out there. Walk miles of beaches." He leaned in and kissed her softly. "Barbeque at night. Get you to take it easy a little."

"You did great, Mia." Gary gave her other hand a squeeze.

"All done?" she asked.

"All done," Gary nodded. "I want to take a few more pictures of the baby and give you guys a gift for your refrigerator," they all laughed. "We're going to get you back to your room. I want you to relax tonight, let Schooner and the nurses pamper you. You might have some cramping and discomfort, and if that happens, I want you to let the nurses know immediately. We'll have the FISH results before you leave tomorrow and then full results in about 10 days."

Seth and Kami were waiting in the room for Mia and Schooner.

"BBC, I was so worried about you. How did it go?" Mia handed him the strip of photos.

"Oh my God, it's a baby," he exclaimed. "Well, it looks like it's got your big head, BBC. Oh, and what is this, Schooner's big head?" They laughed.

"Yes, meet our exhibitionist son. Handsome and well-endowed! Just the way I like my men." Mia laughed.

"Was it scary?" Kami asked, as Seth plumped up Mia's pillows.

"No, Schooner distracted me, so I was just looking at him when they did it. It felt like a shot and some pressure, but I didn't see any of it, which is good."

"Did you look?" Seth asked Schooner.

He shook his head no. "I was too focused on my beautiful Baby Girl."

Seth bent down and whispered into Mia's ear, "I love him."

"You have good taste, Princess." She squeezed Seth's hand.

Seth grabbed a bag off of the couch and perched on the side of Mia's bed. "I have a treat for you, BBC." And slowly out of the bag he pulled a small Styrofoam container and a plastic fork. "Junior's Cheesecake."

Mia gasped in delight and Seth proceeded to feed her the creamy delicacy.

"Mmm mmm mmm." Mia finished the last bite. "A girl could get used to this spoiling."

Schooner stood next to the bed, smiling down at her and brushed the bangs from her eyes. He leaned down and kissed her softly. "Get used to it, Baby Girl."

The next morning Dr. Gary Cohen delivered the news Mia and Schooner had been waiting for with bated breath, preliminary results showed a healthy baby boy.

They could now share this time of bliss fully, without the specter of additional issues hanging over them. It was finally time to enjoy the start of their new family.

CHAPTER 24

"Call me or text me. I'm going to be worrying about you." Mia held onto Schooner's hand as she walked him to the front door.

"No worries from you, Baby Girl. It's all going to be fine." he bent down and placed a soft kiss on her lips. "I'll call you later."

And he was gone. Off to Kennedy Airport to meet up with CJ and Holly and await Zac's flight from Spain. They were meeting as a family to break the news to Zac.

The apartment felt empty without Schooner, and if Mia were to admit it, she felt empty without Schooner there. She didn't like being left out of his life, but she certainly did not belong with him or his family today. His family. A family she was not a part of. It was still hard for her to process that.

She was his family. She and their baby. And Holly. Mia loved her growing relationship with Holly. It was healthy and honest and this young woman, CJ and Schooner's daughter, had accepted her into her life as her father's partner and soon to be wife. It was so hard for Mia to conceive of the fact that there was another family, another life. Yet, she had lived an entire lifetime without Schooner.

Mia picked up her phone and texted Seth.

> Mia: He's off to JFK to meet with CJ, Holly & Zac
>
> Seth: Are you freaking?
>
> Mia: Yes!
>
> Seth: Why?

Mia: I'm just afraid it's going to be really ugly and I hate that for him.

Seth: If anyone can control the situation, it's Schooner.

Mia: Understatement! LOL

Seth: Want me to come over and help you pack for the beach house?

Mia: Thought you'd never ask!

Seth and Mia had suitcases, shopping bags and beach bags packed and lined up waiting by the door when Schooner and Holly arrived.

"Holly!" Mia greeted her with a hug. She had not been sure who, if anyone, would be accompanying Schooner.

"Mia, you look adorable. Wow, you really are pregnant!" Holly had not seen Mia for a while, and today Schooner broke the news to the family. Holly put her hand on Mia's belly and smiled, "I hear I'm going to have a baby brother."

Mia nodded, "So, how did it go with your other baby brother today?" She bit her bottom lip waiting for either Holly or Schooner to respond.

Schooner made his way to the refrigerator and took out the orange juice and was chugging it straight from the carton.

"Want some vodka with that?" Mia asked.

He shook his head, "I don't think that would've even helped. I am so glad that is over."

"That good, huh?" Seth interjected.

Holly and Schooner just looked at one another. "Let's just say, I don't think we're all going to be one big, happy blended family anytime soon."

Mia went to Schooner and put her arms around his waist. "I am so sorry." She could see the sadness and disappointment in his eyes.

He hugged her to him, kissing the top of her head.

"The good news is, they are on their way back to LA and we're on our way out to the beach. Seth, are you joining us this weekend?" Schooner asked.

"Well, it's your first weekend out there..."

"Please," Mia begged. "I could really use your help in setting up the house."

"Well, then let me run home and pack a bag. I can be back in an hour."

Mia sat down in the living room with Schooner and Holly. She looked from one to the other.

Schooner began, "Zac is very angry with me. He doesn't understand why we're getting divorced. He feels like I've betrayed everyone. He said some pretty ugly things. All I could do was let him know that I love him, that this wasn't about him and that I want him in my life. In our life."

Mia took Schooner's hand in hers. "It's a lot to process."

"And he's a shit," Holly piped in.

Schooner gave her a pointed look.

"Don't give me that look, Dad. He is, and you know it. He's a cocky, arrogant shit that only cares about himself. This was all about him today, not you, not Mom. Him."

"It wasn't the homecoming he expected, Holly."

She rolled her eyes. "I know that, Dad. But there's this little thing known as empathy, and he clearly was out partying with his friends the day that was handed out."

"I can't argue with you there." Schooner looked sad and resigned.

Mia rubbed Schooner's arm. "Give him a few days, call him and try talking again. Maybe he'll join us out on the beach at some point this summer."

"Don't ruin your summer, Mia." Holly got up and stalked off to the bathroom.

Mia turned to Schooner with a surprised look, this was so unlike Holly.

"Today got very ugly. She's very protective of me."

"I'm sorry." She laid her head on his chest and he began to play with her hair. "The beach will be good. For all of us."

As they walked through their small beach town later, little red wagons in tow, Schooner spied tennis courts. "We're joining whatever club this is, I'm ready to be out on the courts again."

"I'm going to sit in a beach chair and just grow bigger before everyone's eyes," Mia added.

"Maybe I can get a babysitting job and spend the whole summer out here," was Holly's contribution.

"And I'm just going to freeload off of you people for as much and as long as you'll let me," Seth chimed in as they walked the boardwalk toward their house.

They reached the end of the boardwalk and in front of them was sandy beach and the Atlantic Ocean, side lit by the late afternoon sun. They all just stood there for a moment, breathing in the salty, sea air and taking in the tranquility of the moment. The breeze off the ocean was still cold and Schooner reached down and scooped up a surprised Mia into his arms, hugging her to him. He tossed Holly the house keys and she walked the short path through the scrub pines and unlocked the front door.

"You're carrying me over the threshold?" Mia smiled at Schooner.

His eyes were locked on hers, crinkled at the edges. "Mmm-hmm," he nodded.

"I love you. I love you. I love you. I love you," she said against his mouth, kissing him.

Schooner carried Mia to the couch in the great room and put her down. "Now you sit there and relax and we'll put everything away and set things up."

Mia began to protest and Schooner silenced her with a "Don't-Mess-With-Me" glare and she just sat there grumbling, while the others unpacked and set up the kitchen.

After dinner, Schooner joined Mia on the couch, a single-malt scotch in hand. "Rocky start to the day, but a perfect ending. We get to begin that summer we never had."

Mia curled up and put her head in his lap. "Do you think he'll come around?"

Schooner shook his head. "No. Or at least not for a long time."

Mia could see the tension in his strong jaw. He took a long sip of his scotch.

"Well, we'll just keep trying."

Schooner smiled down at Mia, brushing her bangs from her eyes, his look portraying his deep appreciation of everything she was doing to make his life happy. "Maybe he'll come spend some time at the beach with us. The beach is like an elixir, cures a lot of ills," Mia tried to sound hopeful.

Seth and Holly came in from the deck. "Definitely need sweatshirts out there now," Seth informed Mia and Schooner. "Come on out, the stars are amazing."

The four grabbed sweatshirts and headed out onto the lower deck, sitting 100 feet away from the water lapping onto the sand. A jagged, iridescent strip of moon glow lit a path along the gentle surf. Mia went and stood at the wooden railing on the deck's edge, looking up at constellations hovering high above. Schooner came up behind her, wrapping his arms around her and she leaned back into him.

"This is my fantasy come true," she informed him.

"Mine too." He kissed the top of her head.

And finally, almost exactly twenty-four years after the fantasy had been conceived, the moment they dreamed of sharing together was at hand, and it was richer than they had envisioned so long ago, for now they shared it with two people they deeply loved and the baby that would soon join them.

CHAPTER 25

Mia woke to an empty bed and staggered out to the deck off of their bedroom. No Schooner, but she was immediately distracted by the ocean, the light on the waves and the smell of the sea breeze. Sitting down in one of the white Adirondack chairs, she closed her eyes, enjoying the song of the gulls and the soft breeze lightly tickling her skin.

She heard the sliding glass door and felt his kiss before even opening her eyes.

Sitting down in the Adirondack chair next to her, when she finally opened her eyes, it was to the surprise of Schooner dressed in tennis whites, a racquet casually laying across his lap. Mia's smile was automatic.

"First time I've held one of these in twenty-four years," he said quietly, fingering the racquet's grip.

Mia held out her hand and Schooner took it. They sat silently for a long time.

"I want you to spend the summer out here with Holly and Seth," Schooner began, breaking the silence. Mia was glad, as his voice pulled her back from a "what-if" darkness remembering a bright tennis career, one with the words *potential top ranked NCAA player* attached to it, that she felt fully responsible for snuffing.

She nodded. "I'll miss you."

He squeezed her hand. "I'll be back every Thursday evening. I'll try to schedule things so that I don't have to leave here until early on Monday mornings."

She looked at him and nodded.

He smiled. "What did you do with my Mia, you are clearly an alien imposter."

She laughed.

"What? No fight over this?" Schooner's face registered mock shock.

She shook her head no. "No fight. Just a little sad that you'll have to be in the city part of the time, but you need to be there, especially now. And I can do everything I need to do via phone and laptop. And frankly, pregnant in the summer heat in Manhattan or pregnant in a beautiful beach house? I'm no dummy!"

They both laughed.

Mia looked at Schooner and shook her head, "I'm assuming you've already talked to both Seth and Holly about this."

He just smiled at her and she shook her head.

"You are going to get your way with me, aren't you?" she laughed.

He nodded. "I'm just glad you are taking this so well. This could have gone either way."

Mia squeezed Schooner's hand. "You are absolutely right, it could have. But you know what?" she paused. "I love that you've thought through all the details and are doing everything you can to make sure I have an easy summer—especially with the opening coming up."

Schooner moved his racquet to the floor and pulled Mia by her hand to him. She curled up on his lap. "Kami, Yoli and I can run point on everything in the city, you and Seth can Skype with your team from right here on the deck. Jared's going to come spend some time, so that makes me feel good that he'll be here with you, too. Gaby and Paola are two blocks over. I'll try and get Kami and Yoli, when she's in town, to come out with me on weekends." He laughed, "Charles and I are already figuring out our carpool schedule."

Mia buried her face in Schooner's neck. "You make me so happy."

He kissed the top of her head. "It's smoochal, Baby Girl."

"So, tell me about this new racquet." She looked up at him.

"I saw those courts when we were coming in yesterday and I just thought, 'It's time'."

Mia nodded. "Was today the first time since…"

"It was," Schooner confirmed. "The last time I held a racquet was my last match freshman year, which I won." He smiled at the memory.

Mia buried her face back in his neck, she couldn't look at him. Couldn't let him see the guilt in her eyes.

"I know what you're doing," he said. "Mia, you did not make me punch a wall."

"What I did made you punch a wall, Schooner."

He gently stroked her hair, sighing. "It's not that simple, Mia. It was a whole cascade of circumstances, you know that. Stop taking that on and please let it go."

"You were really great…"

He laughed. "Yes I was. But that wasn't the way my life was supposed to go." He felt her tears on his neck and pulled her head away so that he could look at her face. "We're here together. Now. We're having a baby. We're on Fire Island and we're going to spend the whole summer with the people we love. *Our* family. And by the end of the summer, I'm going to be kicking some butt on those courts, you watch." He wiped her tears away with his thumb and kissed her roughly on the lips.

CHAPTER 26

"**H**e is just beautiful to watch." Seth stopped just short of drooling.

Holly looked at Mia. "He must've been amazing when you two were in school."

"He was the rising superstar," Mia confirmed. "In his freshman year, the coaching staff was already talking to him about being team captain. He's just a natural athlete."

They watched him bouncing the ball with his racquet, getting ready for a serve. Just a few weeks of playing and Schooner was already formidable again on the courts.

"They used to clock his serves at over 140 MPH." Mia looked at him, still in awe.

"Holly, Holly!" Paola came running up to them and Holly scooped up her new little friend.

Gaby and Charles were several yards behind.

"Damn, you're getting bigger by the week," Charles greeted Mia.

"I'd say something nasty to you, except it's true," Mia laughed, hugging him and Gaby.

They all stood watching Schooner for a few minutes. "I am never getting on a court with him," Charles mumbled.

"He moves so gracefully," Gaby commented. "He is so tall, but he almost floats out there."

"Where did you tell Schooner to meet us?" Charles asked Mia.

She pointed. "Just right across the street at The Tross."

They started toward The Albatross, but Mia hung back for a minute watching Schooner cover the courts with his lithe grace. His agility was truly a sight to behold as he slammed a return at his opponent.

She wondered if she'd ever get over the rush she felt at just the sight of him. It was the same heart stopping flash today as it was walking up the path to Brewster Hall when he turned around and smiled at her coming toward him. He had looked at her, head slightly cocked to the side, with a look on his face of both bewilderment and excitement. Her heart had skipped a beat at just a glimpse of his oxygen-stealing smile. He was so beautiful, but it wasn't just that, there was something in his eyes that said he had the spirit to run with her.

Mia caught up to them on the small outside deck at the front of The Albatross, or the Tross, as it was known on the island.

"We ordered some Cajun Calamari," Seth informed he., "And I got you water."

"Not Iced Tea?" Mia pouted.

"No BBC, you should not be having caffeine." Mia made a face at Seth.

"You two are very funny," Gaby laughed.

"I'm surrounded by men who want to control me," Mia complained. "Including this little devil." She tickled her stomach, causing the baby to move and her stomach to do the wave.

They all laughed.

"Do that again," Charles requested.

Mia got Paola's attention, "Paola, do you want to see the baby dance?"

Paola nodded vigorously, pigtails bouncing. Mia tickled her belly and the baby scurried to the other side. They all laughed and Paola came over and started to tickle Mia's belly.

Joining them, Schooner came up to the table and stood there watching with a huge smile on his face as Paola tickled Mia. Mia looked up at his handsome smiling face with a beaming smile of her own.

He bent down and gave her a big sweaty kiss and put his racquet down.

"Kick butt out there?" Charles asked.

"Oh yeah, annihilated him." They high fived. "I just signed up for a tournament." Schooner was back in his element and the happiness beamed off of him like a solar flare.

Mia turned to Holly and winked. She knew his daughter was wondering who this man was.

The waiter delivered the drinks to the table and Schooner immediately downed his water, "What time is everyone getting in today?" He grabbed a menu from the center of the table.

"Jared's going to be on the 2:30 Ferry." Holly was all smiles and anticipation.

Seth pulled out his iPad, "Yoli and Kami are hoping to make the 4:10, if not, they said they'd definitely be on the 5:10."

"Perfect timing for cocktails," Charles concurred.

This was it, finally the big beach bash for Mia's 41st birthday. Lobsters and steamers and corn on the cob on the beach. She looked for Schooner's hand under the table and squeezed it.

He looked at her with an *are you okay* look and she just nodded and smiled.

She was more than okay. She was experiencing the brimming heart syndrome that Schooner knew well from falling in love with Mia.

Stuffed with buttery lobster as the sun was setting, Yoli sat down next to Mia on the deck.

"You know our boy sold me a bill of goods," she confided in Mia.

"Rut-roh…" Mia was not quite sure with what Yoli was going to hit her.

Yoli smiled, running a hand through her bright red hair that was now standing straight up from the humid beach air. "The guy gives me all of California to run and this is how you people are living."

Mia laughed. "I know people think California is La-La Land! They clearly have not spent a summer here."

"This is amazing. It is like no place I have ever been before. I'm really glad you are getting to take care of yourself and the baby and spend the summer out here, Mia."

Mia looked into Yoli's big brown eyes and reached for her hand and squeezed it.

"As crazy as he makes me sometimes, that man is the most amazing gem in the world. I have never met anyone with such a deep sense of responsibility for those he loves." And Yoli clearly loved her best friend.

They were both looking at Schooner across the deck talking to Jared and Charles.

"He's the best friend I've ever had, Mia. And it's really refreshing that you don't have an issue with that." Mia knew she was referring to CJ's disdain for their relationship. Mia gave her hand a squeeze and Yoli reciprocated.

"And what's so wonderful is, I finally see him as one whole person. The way he's always been with me is the way he is 100% of the time now. He's not so conflicted anymore."

Schooner looked at them across the deck holding hands and talking and his heart was soaring in seeing the harmony amongst the people he loved the most in his life,

"I'm in so much trouble," he said to Charles and Jared, indicating the two women.

They laughed.

Across the deck, Yoli and Mia laughed.

"You've got that right," Mia yelled at him. "He's freaking out right now."

Evil laughter came from the two women, who just looked at each other smiling.

"So, tell me about Zac," Mia asked Yoli.

Yoli leveled a glance at Mia.

"That bad, huh?"

Yoli shook her head and exhaled. "You're going to want to like him because it's like looking at a young Schooner. So for you, I can imagine it might be even more intense—because you have memories of Schooner at that age. But make no mistake, Zac is not a young Schooner."

Mia cocked her head, taking it in, as Yoli continued. "Schooner is intense, but if he loves you, he loves you. That's the way he's made. If you cross him, watch out, because he can be deadly."

Mia's eyes were wide, not blinking, as she listened to Yoli.

"I've seen people cross him in business, Mia, and I would not want to be on the other end of that wrath. But with Schooner, it has to be provoked for him to go there. He goes into protect mode. It's reactive, not proactive."

Mia nodded. "Schooner is very protective of what or who he feels is his."

Yoli agreed, "But it comes from a place of love with Schooner and you know that, so there's a way to wrap your head around it." She paused, thinking, "Zac doesn't have that inherent goodness that Schooner does. He's arrogant, entitled, calculating, manipulative, rude, dismissive..."

She paused and Mia couldn't pass up the opportunity, "And those are just his good qualities." They both laughed.

"There's just something missing behind those beautiful blue eyes," Yoli finished.

"A heart?" Mia asked, seriously.

Yoli nodded. "And there's a very wide mean streak."

"I want to meet him, because I want things to be whole in Schooner's life again."

Yoli just shook her head, "Not going to happen, Mia. I mean, yes, at some point you will meet him. He'll be back east in the fall to go back to Exeter, but what you and Schooner have with Holly, you will never have with Zac. So, promise me this, you will not beat yourself up over it, because that leopard is never going to change his spots."

It was almost dusk as Charles carried a sleeping Paola in his arms and he and Gaby bid the rest of the party a goodnight.

Sitting out on the deck, under the stars, everyone in shorts and sweatshirts, Mia asked Seth, "Are you going to take everyone out to Cherry Grove dancing tonight?"

"But BBC, it's your birthday."

Mia smiled at him. "That is exactly why I think you, Kami, Yoli, Holly and Jared should go catch a water taxi to The Grove and dance until some ungodly hour. Just make sure you return Holly and Jared safely."

"Are you sure?" Seth triple checked.

"Don't make me hurt you," Mia threatened.

When the five finally left for a night of partying, Fire Island style, Mia turned to Schooner and wrapped her arms around his waist (they weren't wrapping around quite as far, now that her stomach was putting more distance between the two of them). He kissed the top of her head and they made their way out onto the deck off of their bedroom and she curled up in his lap on an Adirondack chair, his long legs stretched out with his feet perched up on the deck rail.

"This is the first time we've been alone all summer." He played with her curls that refused to stay straight in the sea air.

Mia smiled. "This—right here, right now—is my birthday present. Me. You. The beach. The stars. Alone. It does not get more perfect than this, Schooner."

He tightened his arms around her. "You are correct, Baby Girl."

They stayed like that for a long while, listening to the waves lick the shore. This was their calm before the storm and they both recognized that. The fall would bring the opening of L9/NYC and the winter would bring the baby. Both would churn their lives in ways they could only imagine. For now, it was just the two of them celebrating Mia's birthday, savoring their happiness.

"I have something for you," Schooner whispered.

Mia got up off of his lap and he went into the house. Schooner emerged a few minutes later, a large manila envelope in hand.

They sat down again and he handed her the envelope. "Happy Birthday, Baby Girl. I love you more than anything in this world."

Mia kissed him and opened the envelope. She pulled out a half inch of papers bound together with a large silver clip. She held them up in a stream of light from the house that was flooding the deck, so that she could read what they said. It was the deed to the beach house. Schooner had put the entire house in her name.

She looked at him and he was smiling. She kissed him softly. There was so much she wanted to say to him, this man who was so serious about taking care of what was his. This was his protection for her and their unborn baby. He was leaving nothing to chance this time.

She brought his hand to her mouth and kissed it, her eyes never leaving his. "I love you," she mouthed.

"Smoochal," he mouthed back.

Mia stood and extended a hand to Schooner, he took it and hand-in-hand they walked in from the deck to their bedroom.

Schooner took Mia's face in both his hands and kissed her passionately.

"Now can I have the rest of my birthday present?" Mia asked, devil grin on her face.

"Yeah, let's fuck like wild animals."

She laughed and grabbed his hand, pulling him to the bed, "Yeah, let's!"

Twenty-four years after she found it, on her forty-first birthday, Mia finally attained the full realization of her secret dream.

CHAPTER 27

Mia and Seth sat at the kitchen table in the beach house, windows open and a breeze blowing the white sheer curtains. On the table, Mia's laptop was open and they were Skyping with the gang in the city—Schooner, Yoli and Kami.

"I'm floored at the response on the guest list. Have you guys fed Charles the most updated version. I know he's going to want to rendezvous with some of these stars' personal security to make sure everyone is in sync. I think we should be giving his people twice a week updates at this point, and if anything or anyone big pops up in between, just make sure we let him or his organization know."

"I'll up my contact with his people to twice a week formal reviews." Kami wrote down the task.

"Kami, do we only have Isabelle running PR at this point?"

"Yes. Do you want to step it up?"

Mia nodded. "I want you to put both Lisa and Denise on this. Have we been working the Los Angeles press in addition to New York, health & wellness and fashion press?"

"No. We haven't gone near Los Angeles."

"Let's do it. Schooner, are you ok with that?"

"Why wouldn't I be? I think it's a great idea."

"From a business standpoint I totally agree. I just don't want to rock any boats, if you know what I mean." Mia's look conveyed her fear of causing more problems for Schooner with CJ and Zac.

"Mia, this is business and you're right, utilizing the LA press for even more buzz and possibly to alert members and press who will be in New York that week is just a good business idea, so I say we run with it."

"Okay, we're going to have three people on PR from now through the event. I told you I was willing to commit all my resources." She smiled her devil grin at him.

"That's why I like giving you the business." He was giving her a pure sex look via Skype.

"Stop it you two or I'm going to get hard!" Seth complained.

Schooner laughed, "Busted."

"Do you guys know when you'll be out yet?" Mia asked.

Being away from Schooner was becoming more and more difficult. She didn't sleep as well when he wasn't there. Mia found herself rolling over to his side of the bed and burying her face in his pillow trying just to get the scent of him. She wondered if it was just a hormonal aspect of the pregnancy that was making her feel so needy.

"We should be on the 8:10 on Friday night. I'm meeting with the building inspectors at 4:00, so we're definitely going to be sitting in traffic out to Bay Shore."

"Yuck. We'll be thinking about you," Seth smiled.

"We can do better than that," Mia laughed. "I'll have a Johnnie Walker Blue sitting on the table for you at Maguire's."

Schooner smiled. "Thanks, Baby Girl."

"You two are gross." Yoli rolled her eyes. "Are we done yet? I have work to do."

"Someone's going to need to dance off her nasty at-ee-tude in Cherry Grove this weekend," Seth snarked.

"Please get her laid while you're at it," Schooner begged.

"On that note, one that would send a Human Resources Director into a seizure, we'll sign off. Till tomorrow kiddie-winkles." And Mia hit end call on Skype.

"One big happy dysfunctional family," she laughed at Seth.

"They really fit in very well with us," Seth commented.

"Scary, but true," Mia agreed. "Beach time!" she announced with a big smile.

Saturday morning a sweaty Schooner, fresh off the courts and a walk back to the beach house, stripped off his tennis whites and crawled under the cool, crisp sheets next to his fiancé. Spooning up against Mia, he caressed her full breasts, "I love these," he whispered in her ear.

"They hurt," she complained.

"They were always gorgeous, but I really love them now. They are so round and your nipples are even more sensitive." He pinched and twisted the nipple on her right breast and she moaned.

He pulled her right leg back over his and positioned his hard cock at the entrance of her dripping pussy. "This is still a good position for us." He impaled her from behind with one hard stroke.

Mia gasped, "Very good position."

He held onto her leg and slowly drove into her. She squeezed his cock tight. "Oh yeah, you feel so damn good. I was slamming the ball on the court and thinking I couldn't wait to get home and be slamming into you."

Mia turned her head to look at him and grabbed his head down to her for a kiss. "Harder," she hissed into his mouth, as he drove up into her forcefully. "Oh God, your cock feels so fucking great." And she squeezed him tight. "I miss you so much during the week... oh yeah, just like that..." she gasped. "I love the way you fuck me."

He pulled out and dragged her to the edge of the bed and put her feet up on his shoulders and drove down into her. She gasped again and squeezed him tight.

"Mia, open your eyes. Look at me." She smiled up at him.

Smiling down at her, he rubbed her feet on his face, his teeth grazing her high arch. "Squeeze my cock, Baby Girl... oh yeah, just like that... oh God, that is good."

Mia's smile was huge.

"You are milking it out of me."

She tightened as hard as she could with each of his deep thrusts. "Pussy hug," she said, with a devil grin.

Schooner laughed and Mia bared down on him.

His eyes shot open wide. "What you do to me, Baby Girl."

He grabbed her feet tight to his face and she could tell that he was coming. His eyes were closed and he looked so young and sweet, his cheek pressed into the arch of her foot.

"Yes," he moaned, but Mia was already lost somewhere. The sweet look on his face with his cock driving deep into her had already thrown her over the edge and she was crashing and spinning like she'd caught a wave wrong.

Schooner fell on the bed next to her and looking across the pillow at his beautiful blue eyes, she reached out to stroke his face. Their sweet reverie was to be almost immediately cut short by the ringing of a cell phone.

Schooner growled and reached behind him and grabbed his phone off the night stand. "CJ," he mouthed, a look of faux horror on his face.

"Hello" ... "Fabulous." He reached out to play with Mia's hair. "Well, when does his semester start?"... "Isn't most of his stuff still in storage up in New Hampshire? We put it in there before Spain." ... "Well, he'll miss his first few days of classes, but I'm ok with that." ... "Yeah, am sure he is, too. I'll take him up after the opening." ... "You're right, I think it's best you're not there." ... "No, I'm not trying to be mean. Pulling off an opening event is stressful as it is and yes, you being there is a stress I don't want to deal with."..."You're right, I'm sure Mia doesn't want you there." ... "She doesn't need to say it." ... "CJ, I hate to break this to you, but you are not high on her radar screen and I suggest you keep it that way." ... "New York is my home, CJ." ... "Honestly, never again." ... "Is he there? Yeah, let me talk to him." ... "Hey Bud, I've missed you." ... "Yeah, I'd love to have you here for the opening and then I'll take you up to school. If you want to come out a little early, come hang out on the beach. Holly is here with us." ... "Yes, with me and Mia." ... "Zac, I understand it's going to take some adjusting, but this situation is not going to change. Let me be really frank with you, I will be with Mia for the rest of my life and both of us want you in our lives." ... "Why? Because you are my son and she knows how much I love you." ... "I only ask that you keep an open mind and that you treat her respectfully, because I will tell you this, I will not tolerate you disrespecting me or Mia. Are we clear on that?" ... "Look, I'm really happy we're going to get to spend some time together." ... "Ok, well email me your flight info, when you've got it." ... "Zac, I love you." ... "Talk to you soon."

Mia stroked Schooner's cheek and smiled at him. "See, it's all going to work out. It will."

He pulled her head down to his chest and kissed the top of her head.

CHAPTER 28

Mia, Seth and Holly stood at the center of L9's rotunda looking around in awe. Huge concave custom projection screens lined the rounded walls of the first floor and technicians were testing them with a mixture of iconic urban and bucolic landscape images. Another team was testing the lighting, soft ethereal jewel-tone spots flickered on and off.

Mia began to survey the perimeter where the caterer had begun to set up royal blue skirted tables and stations. She felt an arm sling over her shoulder and the soft, slightly accented voice of Claret Events owner and brilliant conceptualist, Elan Gerstler, whispering in her ear, "I want you to know that I left the Hamptons for this. Only for you, Meezie," he joked.

Mia looked up into Elan's big handsome brown eyes. "I understand, they made me leave Fire Island. I haven't worn shoes in two months."

Elan looked down at Mia's hot pink flip-flop clad feet and gasped.

Mia backhanded him in the arm. "Stop that. It's not like I'm wearing Birkenstocks."

Elan flagged down a worker nearby. "Let's see what that table looks like moved over there." And to Mia, "So, do you like?"

She nodded, smiling. "I love it. Clean, minimalist, chic."

Elan nodded. "Never more than three colors." Elan's designs were always steeped in classic with a modern edge that was so subtle it transported the attendee effortlessly to wherever Elan had chosen to send them.

"Meezie, thank you for this. I know you were wholly behind us getting to do this event for L9. We have been trying to work with them for years in LA and Brent Bolthouse has it totally locked up. This is our first time, so thank you."

"I told Schooner there is only one person I would let touch this opening." She rubbed his back.

"So, how do you know Schooner Moore?" Elan wanted the inside scoop.

Mia laughed and pointed to her belly. "Baby Daddy."

Elan's mouth and big brown eyes opened wide and Mia squeezed his arm, laughing.

"Isn't he married to a tall, blonde *shiksa* out in LA?"

Mia nodded, still smiling. "For the moment."

"You little tart, you." Elan stood back and looked at Mia. "He's very hot. How did you meet him?"

"He was my first boyfriend," Mia confided. "The evil *shiksa* broke us up. And it took a couple of decades, but karma is a bitch."

"Yeah, in the form of a short Jewish girl," they laughed. "I love this. I am definitely doing your wedding." Elan was looking intensely into Mia's eyes, clearly happy for her.

"Baby, you're doing the Bris, which might actually come before the wedding."

"My pleasure." He hugged Mia tightly (or as tightly as one could with her protruding stomach). "Now let me show you the rest of what we are doing here."

Elan walked Mia through the rest of the space, showing her the details that made the ethereal space magical. People were setting up banks of multiple sized white pillar candles along the railing edge of each of the mezzanines and on the marble staircase. Wide white raw silk ribbon with a thick silk braided cord of royal blue wrapped the banister.

Mia spied Schooner and Charles talking over near the offices. "Have you met Schooner yet?" she asked Elan.

"Never formally. Just members of his staff."

"Come, let's change that. He's about to head to the airport to pick up his son."

Schooner was listening intently to something Charles was telling him as Elan and Mia approached. He was looking down and nodding his head. Mia couldn't help but feel pride as they approached this tan, impossibly beautiful man.

Schooner looked up at Mia, as if he could sense her approach. His eyes crinkling at the corners with his smile, "Hey, Baby Girl." Wherever they were, it was only the two of them in the room.

"Schooner, I want to introduce you to the brilliance behind all of this beauty." Her arm swept the room. "This is Elan Gerstler, the President and Owner of Claret Designs."

Schooner put out his hand to Elan. "I've been wanting to meet you for a long time. This is beyond my expectations." He motioned to the rotunda.

"I'm thrilled to have been chosen for this project. Thank you very much."

"Mia and Charles both rave about you and I can understand why. I'm glad we have this opportunity to work together. I'm sure it won't be the last time." Schooner flashed his All-American boy smile at Elan, who was clearly a new fan.

Schooner looked at his watch. "I'd better go get the car." His hand stroked Mia's hair and he bent down to kiss her. "I'll see you out at the beach tonight, Baby Girl."

Mia clasped his hand and he gave hers a tight squeeze and a long look in her eyes saying, "It's going to be ok."

CHAPTER 29

Yoli and Seth were pounding down Bombay Sapphire and tonics while waiting with Mia at the beach house for Schooner and Holly to arrive with Zac.

"I wish you could drink, BBC." Seth gave Mia a sad face.

Mia was clearly nervous, pacing around the lower deck.

"Me too," she muttered, looking at the dusky sky over the ocean and tapping the deck railing with her foot.

"Me three, you're going to need it." Yoli was very tense.

"I'm glad you two are here. Hopefully that will alleviate some of the family dynamic thing."

Yoli shook her head. "Don't count on it. He's not going to give a shit who's here. Mia, I know this is going to be hard, but try to keep telling yourself that you're talking to CJ. You're going to think you're talking to a young Schooner, but you're really talking to CJ. Try not to forget that, please," Yoli was adamant.

"He really looks that much like him?" Seth asked Yoli.

"You know that waterfall picture in Mia's office? Haircut is different and Zac is not as tall as Schooner. I'd say he's maybe six feet tops and he's a slighter build than Schooner. But his face, it's that picture." She finished her drink. "With ice blue eyes."

She made an exaggerated shivering motion and Mia and Seth just looked at each other.

"Why am I so nervous about meeting a freaking teenager?" Mia looked at the two of them, palms in the air, shoulders shrugging.

"Because he's CJ's devil spawn." Yoli was on her next drink.

"You are not making me feel better," Mia laughed.

They heard the front door to the beach house and voices. Mia looked at Yoli and Seth, eyes wide, lips in a tight line and muttered, "Showtime" as they walked into the house.

He was exactly as Yoli had described and although she had been warned, Mia's face broke into a huge smile upon seeing Zac standing there.

In front of her was the boy on the path to Brewster Hall talking with her mom, the same one who knocked over a pitcher of water to save her from the evil sniffer, the guy who pulled her close to him on a mountaintop to warm her up after a snowball fight, and never left her side after her attack.

"Hi Zac," she greeted him with a bright smile and received an unreturned hug.

Stepping back, she looked at Schooner. "Wow, I know you said he looked like you, but wow. Flashback." Mia smiled brightly at Schooner, who bent down and gave her a quick kiss. Looking at Holly, it was clear she was not breathing and Mia gave her a smile and wide eyes saying, "Rut roh!"

"Well, let's get you settled, get your stuff put away." And she turned to Schooner and Holly. "We've got reservations at Maguire's."

"Yes," Holly fist pumped. "Lobster." Getting a laugh out of everyone but Zac, who still had not uttered his first word to Mia, Yoli or Seth.

Mia turned to Holly. "Would you show Zac where his room is?"

"Follow me, Cretin." Holly turned to Zac.

When they were upstairs and out of earshot, Mia walked over to Schooner and put her arms around his waist, he hugged her and kissed the top of her head. She looked up at him, trying to keep the tears out of her eyes. His eyes were tense and sad.

"It'll get better," she whispered, trying her hardest to be positive for him, knowing he was in the middle of two people he loved.

Wrapping his arms around her tighter, he gave her a hug, burying his face in her sea-air unruly curls. As soon as he heard Zac and Holly coming down the stairs, he let go of her, and although she knew he didn't want to exacerbate what was already a tense situation, hurt and disappointment slammed through her.

Yoli caught her eye and Mia could sense Yoli's anger about ready to flare at Schooner. Knowing the Bombay and Tonics might make her already loose lips even looser, Mia asked, "Yoli, would you help me grab our stuff from earlier off the deck?"

The two women walked outside and away from the view of the sliding glass door.

"Holy shit!" Mia turned to Yoli, her mouth hanging open.

"Rude, entitled little piece of shit," she began, "and I'm going to rip his father a new one. What the fuck was that about."

Mia grabbed her hand and squeezed it. "Trust me, I will take care of him... later. Sit next to me at dinner and we can kick each other under the table." Mia laughed at her own childish behavior.

"I need to be in kicking distance of Schooner."

Mia laughed, "Okay, that works for me, too."

They re-entered the house with empty glasses and half eaten bowls of munchies from earlier.

"Everyone ready to go?" Schooner asked, clearly forcing a happy mood.

Seth shot Mia a look silently begging her not to leave him alone with the Moores again. She rubbed his back and walked out of the house with him.

As they walked toward town, Mia said, "So Zac, what does your voice sound like? I haven't heard you speak yet."

Lines were being drawn and Mia was calling him out on his shit. Nice had not worked in the house.

He just looked at her, giving her an "are you kidding me look"
. . .

Mia laughed, "Gonna be a fun week, huh?"

He shrugged.

"Stop being such an ass." Holly smacked him in the arm.

"Ouch, Bitch," he snarled at his sister.

"Zac!" Schooner finally came alive.

About fucking time, Mia thought to herself.

"I owe you a scotch," Maguire's manager, Aiden McManus, greeted Schooner as they walked into the packed, loud restaurant.

He leaned down and greeted Mia with a warm hug and a kiss, before turning back to Schooner. "You ripped it last weekend on the courts! What is it going to take to be your doubles partner next summer?"

"Free lobsters nightly!" Holly piped in.

"Totally doable." He smiled at her, clearly happy to see the beautiful young woman. "This has got to be your son." He turned to Zac.

Zac graced him with an All-American Boy smile (not as beautiful as Schooner's, Mia noted). "Yeah, hi, I'm Zac. Wow, great bar scene you've got here," reaching out to shake his hand, charm turned up on high.

You little shit, Mia thought.

"Come in on Thursday, Karaoke night, you'll get to see your sister at her finest," Aiden laughed.

Mia looked at a blushing Holly. Without Jared there, Aiden was definitely making his interest known.

He showed them out to their table on the deck overlooking the bay. Mia and Yoli flanked Schooner on each side. The women smiled at one another as they sat.

Pots of steamers arrived at the table as an appetizer and everyone got busy dipping the sweet clams into broth to remove any excess sand and then into small ramekins of drawn butter.

"I used to clam on these beaches as a kid," Mia remarked. "We'd spend hours every day filling plastic buckets with clams."

"I can't wait to do that with the baby," Holly beamed at Mia.

"We are going to have such fun summers out here. I can't wait to teach him to body surf." Mia was smiling ear-to-ear. She reached for Schooner's hand under the table and gave it a squeeze. "So Zac, what was living in Zaragoza like?"

Zac shrugged, not looking up from cleaning his clam. "Like living anyplace else."

Yoli rolled her eyes at Mia. "C'mon Zac, you can do better than that," Yoli chided, sitting back and nursing her gin and tonic.

"What do you want me to say about it?" He leveled her a cold glare.

"Did you get laid?" She didn't break her stare right back at him. Mia could feel Schooner tensing next to her.

Zac smiled at Yoli, a smile that did not come close to reaching his eyes. "As a matter of fact, I did. A lot."

"Anyone meaningful?" Mia asked.

His "are you kidding me" look returned.

Mia ignored him and went on, "Actually Zaragoza is a place I would love to photograph," she looked at Yoli and Seth and said, "It was founded by Augustus Caesar and originally named Caesaraugusta. It had a huge thriving Jewish merchant and trade community from about 1000 AD into the 1400's."

"How do you know this?" Seth asked.

Mia laughed. "Okay, here's a random Mia fact that even you didn't know." She was smiling at him. "When I was a little girl, my mom used to take me all the time to The Met," she looked at Holly and Yoli and clarified, "The Metropolitan Museum of Art." She went on, "We would enter through the Greek and Roman antiquities and I was obsessed with this marble bust of Augustus. I would just stand in front of it and look at him. And this started when I was really little. I would literally stand there, staring at him until my mother dragged me out."

Seth laughed. "BBC! Marble stalking BBC. That's a new one."

They all laughed, except for Zac who regarded the table with practiced disinterest throughout the rest of dinner.

Walking home, Mia reached for Schooner's hand and slowed her pace to ensure some distance from the rest of the group.

"You were right," she began, moving her arm around his waist.

His arm did not go over her shoulder, tucking her in to him in the way it always had since the first time he pulled her close walking along The Quad, after the incident with Beast in the Dining Hall.

"This is not going to be easy and you really need to nip this in the bud," she was adamant.

Mia looked up at Schooner and he was looking straight ahead. "Put your fucking arm around me, Schooner." There was anger and hurt in Mia's voice. She stopped walking. "I'm going to give you some time to be alone with your son and daughter tonight. You may not be able to fix the situation with him quickly, but I suggest you fix the situation with us immediately."

His face gave up nothing. He nodded and draped his arm over her shoulder, pulling her into him as they walked in silence the rest of the way home.

Mia was reclining on pillows propped up against the headboard on the bed, knees bent, another pillow on top of her swollen belly and her laptop perched on her belly/desk. She was still Skyping with Kami when Schooner walked into the bedroom. She gave him a big smile and went back to her conversation. He sat down in a chair facing the bed, kicked off his Sperry Made in Maine boat shoes and put his feet up on the bed.

"Well what did Elan say about that?" Mia asked Kami, who was seriously going to need an amazing vacation after the event.

"He was not happy at all." Mia could tell by Kami's face that Elan was seriously displeased with one of his vendors.

"Don't sweat it," Mia advised, "if Elan was unhappy, it will be taken care of immediately. Were the membership brochures delivered to L9 today?"

"Yes, and they look good. I'll scan one and email it to you."

Mia nodded. "Yeah, I want to see one and I want to get it into Yoli's hands, so she can make sure the staff is properly trained." She turned to Schooner, "Membership desk at the event is going to be staffed with people from LA, right?"

He nodded and she turned her attention back to Kami. "It's all LA people staffing membership, so they'll be fine."

"Yeah, event night is not the night to make sure the NY team is properly trained on membership."

Mia made a face of fright. "Yeah, I agree. Okay, well get some sleep, you've been putting in sick hours. I think we should all come out here for a week after the opening and be beach bums. Oh wait, Seth and I have been beach bums all summer," they laughed and said goodnight.

Mia closed up her laptop and put it on the night table. She smiled at Schooner, "It's all falling into place."

He just nodded.

She extended a hand for him to come on the bed with her.

He didn't move and she could feel panic beginning to rise and her throat close.

"Talk to me, Schooner."

"I'm so stressed over this."

"I know." Mia nodded and moved to the end of the bed so that she could sit facing Schooner. She reached for his hand and took it between hers. "But the answer is not pulling away from me."

He didn't respond.

"You know that, don't you?" her voice was tight with tension.

He removed his hand from hers, got up from the chair abruptly and walked over to the sliding glass doors, looking out into the black night.

Mia's panic was descending on her like a thick fog. Oh my God, she said to me on the phone that he always goes back to her. She said that they were a family. He's going back to his family. He's going to leave me with a baby and a beach house. Oh God, the beach house was to assuage his guilt. He's going back to her. They are going to be a family again. He can't handle disappointing Zac.

Mia could feel her dinner starting to come up and got off of the bed as quickly as she could. Running around the end of the bed with her hand over her mouth, she made it as far as the bathroom, but not as far as the toilet before the heaving started, splashing around her feet all over the bathroom's beautiful terrazzo floor. She sunk to her knees crying and the retching continued.

Schooner came flying into the bathroom, "Are you okay?"

She nodded, but really wanted to say, "What the fuck do you care?" But instead said, "Can you please close the door? I'll clean this up."

He looked down at her, clearly confused. "I'll help you clean up."

"Schooner, please leave and close the door."

He backed out of the bathroom and closed the door. Mia reached up and locked it, the lock creating a deafeningly loud click. She then sat back down on the cold, terrazzo floor, put her head in her hands and cried.

CJ's words screamed in her head, *"He's my husband, Mia and just like he's done to you before, he's going to come back to me. You are just a little mid-life fling. We've built a family together."*

Zac would emotionally blackmail his father to ensure they remained a family.

Mia reached up on the wall behind her and pulled a towel from the towel rack on the wall and threw it down on the floor and started to clean. She unsuccessfully tried to stifle her sobs as she thought about the fact that she had not heard the words, "Baby Girl" since she was standing in L9, when he had no problem calling her that in front of business people. Yes, she told herself, I understand that we may need to dial it down a notch in front of Zac, but to act like there was no relationship at all, for Schooner not to show him how happy he was with her, Mia just did not understand that.

She wet a second towel and on her hands and knees washed the floor with hot water and hand soap. When she was done, she sat back and leaned against the wall and put her head in her arms. She was angry and disappointed in Schooner. Would this be another situation like after Interim, where he just couldn't do what he said he was going to do? That thought, hitting a raw nerve even after twenty-four years, set off a fresh round of body racking sobs.

He knocked softly on the door. "Come on, Mia. Unlock the door."

She didn't answer him. Instead, she pulled a bunch of towels out of the linen closet, laid them down on the floor and took a second stack of towels and linens for a makeshift pillow. Curling up on the towels, Mia cried herself to sleep.

It was only an hour later when she heard a scraping sound and the surprise of the light being flicked on woke her up. Schooner stood there with the door lock and a Phillips head screwdriver in hand. She covered her eyes to shield them from the light.

He came and sat down next to her. "What are you doing?" He was clearly annoyed.

"I was sleeping." She pulled a big beach towel tight around her shoulders.

"Why are you in here?"

She didn't answer him.

"Don't do this to me, Mia." Schooner was tired, stressed and his temper was quickly unraveling.

"I'm not doing anything to you, Schooner."

"You're acting like a brat."

Mia finally looked up at him, "I'm sorry that is how you see it."

"You're not sorry about anything." he sat back against the pale blue wall, sighing and shaking his head. "Please come to bed."

She noted that he still had not touched her.

She pushed herself into a sitting position. "Are you leaving me and Nathaniel?" A sob escaped.

Schooner looked like he had been hit in the solar plexus. "You think I'm leaving you?"

Mia nodded, "It's what CJ told me you would do. It's what Zac wants."

"And you think that is what I want?" He was clearly annoyed.

Mia nodded, "It's why you gave me the house, right?"

Schooner stared at Mia, "Do you know how much that hurts?" He raked his hand through his hair and shook his head.

She nodded, "I do," her expression defiant.

"Where is this coming from, Mia?"

She picked at a thread on one of the beach towels, when she looked up at him, her cheeks were tear stained. "You're separating from me, Schooner." She looked back down and put her face in her hands, sobbing.

Schooner stood and walked out of the bathroom. Mia laid back down, curling as fetal as she possibly could with her pregnant stomach and continued to cry. How could he be so cold, she wondered and the sobs grew deeper.

She heard his returning footsteps and opened her eyes.

He sat down next to her, "I'm not even going to begin to attempt to understand what is going on here. Lift your head."

Sliding a pillow underneath her face, he sat down and placed his pillow next to hers on the bathroom floor. Lying down, he covered them both with a blanket.

When he didn't reach for her to pull her on to his chest, that made her heart break even more. "Please don't be so cold," she whispered and moved over to put her head on his chest and her arm around him.

He didn't move for a moment and then wrapped his arms around her and kissed the top of her head.

"Nathaniel, huh?" he finally said.

"Nathaniel James."

"Nathaniel James," he tried out the name. "Nathaniel James Moore. I actually really like that. A lot."

She looked up at him. "You do?"

He smiled, "Mmm-hmm. I do."

"It's just what I've been thinking of him as. We don't have to name him that." She got up on an elbow to look at him.

"Do you really think I would ever leave you and Nathaniel? I have waited half my life for this, Mia." His eyes looked wounded. "And this house? This is not a consolation prize. This is to always ensure stability for the two of you. God forbid something happened to me, Mia, before the divorce was finalized. I did this to protect the two of you."

Mia could feel his sincerity and her heart ached.

"Schooner, I know we are all walking on eggshells around Zac, but you can't treat me like I don't matter to you because you don't want to rock the boat with him."

He was silent for a moment, just staring at the bathroom ceiling. "I'm sorry. You're right. He needs to deal with reality the way it is, not us changing reality to accommodate him."

Mia was silent for a moment, running her hand over Schooner's bare chest, "I'm really sorry that I doubted your love and hurt you." Her face and eyes expressed her overwhelming sadness.

Moving Mia off of his chest, he placed her head back on her pillow and looked down at her, staring into her eyes, a small, sad smile appearing on his face. "That was a very serious BBC moment there."

Gently, he pushed up her oversized tee-shirt, exposing her tan and shiny pregnant belly and lowered his lips to the rounded mound, planting a soft kiss. "Mommy got a little crazy tonight, Nathaniel, and Daddy definitely didn't help the situation, but do you think you can help me convince Mommy that sleeping in a bed would be a lot more comfortable than the bathroom floor." He put his ear to her belly and smiled, "Nathaniel's vote is for the bed."

He stood and then bent down to help Mia up off of the floor. They grabbed the pillows and the blanket and went out to the bedroom and crawled into bed. This time Schooner reached for Mia, pulling her to his chest. "Do you remember me telling you that I never stopped loving you and that I never would?"

She nodded, "Yes."

"I know I was a jerk tonight and not handling things well, but you have got to believe that I will never, ever stop loving you, Baby Girl, not for a second. Don't ever doubt it, ever. Okay?"

"Okay." She looked up into his eyes and nodded.

He brought his lips to hers, "I love our son's name. It's perfect," and grazed her lips softly before they both closed their eyes and fell into an exhausted sleep.

CHAPTER 30

Mia, Seth and Yoli were spread out in the kitchen and great room, all on their laptops, Skyping, emailing and working on multiple details of the opening. Holly had gone to the ferry terminal to wait for Jared's arrival, Schooner was on the courts and Zac was laying out on the beach attracting the attention of a throng of teenage girls interested in the new handsome blonde boy from California.

"Oh yes! Just heard back from MJP, she and CB will be there," Seth announced.

"I knew she wouldn't let us down." Mia looked up from her laptop.

"MJP?" Yoli asked, draining her third cup of coffee.

"Mallory Jessie Prince. She and Chris Brody live right in the West Village, so we know them from a lot of events," Seth explained. "This is the most killer A list I have ever seen in my life. This event is going to rock Fashion Week and L9 is going to be the hottest ticket in all of Manhattan."

"Have we heard from Heidi Berg? She's been a member of our Brentwood facility for years and one of Schooner's favorite clients." Heidi Berg was one of the most famous faces in modeling for over a decade

Seth checked the list. "Yes, Heidi plus one."

Yoli did a silent yes, with her fist pump.

A sweaty Schooner came through the front door, dripping from a workout on the courts. "Good to see you lazy people up and working."

Mia shot him the finger without looking up at him. "Oh, you'll pay for that, woman." He pulled off his L9 cap and bent down to rub his sweaty forehead all over her face.

She screeched, "Eww, you're gross!" pushing him away as he tried to pull her face under his sweaty arm pit.

"Actually, you're both gross." No one had noticed Zac come in from the deck. His face was screwed up with disdain.

Mia and Schooner were both laughing and said, "Yes we are!" in unison.

Mia looked up at Schooner smiling and he planted a loud wet kiss on her lips. She locked in on his eyes, silently telling him, "I love you."

"Zac, there are bagels and English muffins in the bread box, fruit, cheese and eggs in the fridge. Help yourself," Mia informed him, without taking her eyes off of Schooner's face.

"Your girlfriend Heidi's coming," Yoli updated Schooner.

"I knew my girl wouldn't let me down," he was beaming, as he grabbed a cold bottle of Fuji water from the fridge.

"Heidi's your girl, huh?" Mia looked at Schooner with a questioning look and he nodded his head vigorously. "Seth, show Schooner the updated list."

Schooner walked over to where Seth sat on the pale blue and white striped couch and peered over his shoulder at the laptop screen.

"This is mind boggling. This list looks like the Red Carpet at the Oscars."

Even Zac's curiosity was piqued and he began to peer over Seth's shoulder. "This is the guest list?" he asked.

"This is actually the confirmed attendee list," Seth explained.

"Holy crap!" Even Zac was impressed.

"We take care of our clients." Mia was now standing in front of the open SubZero refrigerator, staring at its contents, indecision marking her face.

"Glad I gave you the business." Schooner came up behind her, standing close.

She turned her head and smiled. "I'm glad you gave me the business, too." His proximity was making her horny.

He reached over her shoulder to grab a nectarine off the refrigerator shelf and whispered in her ear, "Come shower with me."

She leaned back against him, "I'll meet you in five." And he gave her neck a quick bite, then headed upstairs tossing his nectarine like he was getting ready for a serve.

"So all the Fire Island girls wanted to know who the new guy on the beach was, huh?" Mia smiled at Zac. It was still hard for her not to look at him and just see Schooner.

"Apparently," he smiled and then caught himself, the cold veil sweeping over his eyes like a curtain.

"Did you bring clothes for the opening or are you going to need to shop when we get back to the city?" Mia asked.

"I'm from LA, this is no big deal to us."

Mia laughed, "Clearly you have never attended an event in New York." She smiled brightly at him, but anyone who knew Mia would have known there was nothing friendly in that smile. It was a rarity for Mia, but that was not a real smile.

And on that put-down note, Mia turned from Zac and headed upstairs to join his father in the shower.

Steam was coming out of the bathroom when Mia got into the bedroom. She wanted so much to like Zac. He was Schooner's son and every time she looked at him, it was like looking at the beautiful boy who was the love of her life, but it was clear that forging a relationship with him was not going to be an easy path.

Schooner was standing under the streaming water of the rain head, his head tilted back, eyes closed. Mia just stood there staring at his long, muscular frame, his gorgeous chest that had always been the perfect home to her head, flat stomach, muscular thighs and his magnificent, thick cock. He was a sight to admire and she just stood there thinking about what she wanted to do to him.

Quietly, she slipped out of her sundress and into the shower through the open end of the glass enclosure. Her hands were on Schooner's balls before he opened his eyes, a rumbling growling sound coming from deep in his throat.

"Oh yeah." He looked down at her, smiling. "You are the cutest little pregnant thing."

"You think?" She smiled up at him and he just nodded his head.

"Oh that feels so good." She was stroking the length of him with both hands, one after the other, getting him rock hard. "Now look what you've done."

"Handiwork." Mia smiled up at him and then dipped her head down to take the crown of his cock into her mouth while letting the warm water stream through her lips. Rolling her tongue around the rim, she held him tightly in her hands, squeezing and stroking, before straightening up. "Too hard for me to bend anymore," she pouted, "I think you should fuck me."

"I think that is an excellent idea." He pulled her hair back, tilting her face up to him, his lips crushing down on hers in a deep rough kiss. He backed her up to the wall, never breaking their kiss.

"C'mere," he said, leading her to the corner of the shower and turning her around to face the wall. "This will give you 'belly room'," he whispered in her ear, taking her hands and raising them above her head and placing one on each wall, palms flat on the tiles, his hands covering hers.

His teeth grazed her shoulder and she moaned. "You like when I bite you," he commented.

"I love when you bite me, especially my neck." She tilted her head to the right to give him access as he slowly bit his way from her shoulder to her neck, softly grazing his teeth and sucking.

"Spread your legs," he demanded and she did, sticking her ass out toward him so that he'd have total access. Slowly, he ran his finger from her clit to her ass and back again, sinking his thumb into her ass, and his long forefinger and middle finger into her pussy.

Mia gasped and moaned.

"Feels damn good, doesn't it?" He worked his fingers in and out of each hole, bringing Mia to a frenzied point. She was muffling her sounds into the wall, not wanting everyone downstairs to hear her on the edge of ecstasy from Schooner's fingers vigorously working both her pussy and her ass.

Reaching over to the shelf, he grabbed a bottle of mango moisturizing lotion and flipped open the top. "Just like butter," he read from the label and made a "Heh" sound.

Schooner pulled Mia's face around to him and kissed her forcefully. She felt his breath on her ear and his teeth pulling at her earlobe.

"We have a house full of people downstairs and I think this morning I want to fuck your ass. Do you want your ass fucked, Baby Girl?"

Mia nodded, emphatically. Way past the point of speaking, she needed him inside of her—anywhere. Immediately.

"Say it, Mia. Tell me what you want. What you need."

She moaned.

"Come on, Baby Girl, tell me what you want me to do to you. Tell me," he hissed in her ear.

"I want you to fuck my ass," she whispered, harshly.

"I didn't hear you," he said into her neck, as he inserted two fingers covered with the buttery lotion into her tight, tight ass.

"I need you to fuck my ass," she gasped, as he worked his fingers in and out getting her ready to take him.

"Well that's a very good thing because I need to fuck your ass." He finished rubbing a thick layer of the mango cream on his rigid cock. "And that's what I'm going to do right now." He held her tight by her hipbones and pressed the head of his cock against her ass.

She moaned at the pressure.

"Feels good, huh? Well, it's about to feel a whole lot better," and he thrust deep into her ass.

Mia let out a loud moan.

"Fuck yeah, that feels good. You. Are. So. Damn. Tight." He thrust in and out of her unyielding ass.

Mia's head was back and she was whimpering sounds of pleasure. "Oh God, you feel so good," she panted. "I want it harder." And he complied.

"Play with your clit for me, Mia."

"No, this feels too good."

Schooner grabbed her by her hair, pulling her face back to him in the steam filled shower and kissed her roughly. "I said, play with yourself," and he gave her hair a tug.

She removed one hand from the wall and reached down between her legs to do what he said. After a moment she said, "It's too distracting. I just want to feel you," and put her hand back up on the wall to steady herself. She squeezed Schooner's cock tight with her ass muscles, knowing that would distract him and get his focus back 100% on his cock. Which is exactly where she wanted to focus.

"Oh God, what are you doing to me?" He moaned into her mouth as she continued squeezing and relaxing her muscles.

Wrapping both arms around her tightly, he laid his face in the crook of her neck as he thrust forcefully into her. The sounds coming out of him made her entire body quake with release.

"Oh Baby Girl," she heard him whimper as his body shook, then finally stilled. They stood there both shaking, Mia with her hands bracing her against the wall and Schooner with both arms wrapped tightly around her, still inside of her, both being hit with muscle spasming aftershocks.

"Oh God," she whispered, and he tightened his arms around her.

He slowly pulled out of her and she gasped loudly and whimpered. Schooner turned her toward him pulling her to his chest as he led them back underneath the large rain head shower disc. They stood under the hot stream of water wrapped around each other for a long while until their bodies calmed from the rush.

A little while later they descended the stairs hand-in-hand, both barefoot with wet hair, trying not to smile. Schooner gave Mia's hand a squeeze and she looked up at him, feeling like a shy sixteen-year-old with a secret crush. She hoped her tan hid the fact that she was blushing.

CHAPTER 31

They all stood in the center of the rotunda: L9's New York staff, L.A. staff working the opening and transition, Mia's entire team, Holly, Jared, Zac, and Yoli and her girlfriend, Debbie, who had flown in for the opening.

"As you all know, we've reserved several floors at The James Hotel in SoHo for tonight and also for tomorrow night after the opening. Tonight, we are taking over their rooftop pool and their roof bar, Jimmy, for a private party at 6:30," Schooner began.

A cheer went up from the staff, a crew that looked like a combination of models, movie stars and ultra-hip artists.

He continued, "I know this has been a long haul and tonight we just get to blow off a little steam—not too much though, because I need you all at 150% tomorrow. Tonight is our calm before the storm. When you check into the hotel, they'll give each of you your room assignments and a package with your itinerary and schedule. We're all meeting as a team for breakfast tomorrow morning and that meeting room will be noted in your itinerary. Also, in your packets will be your schedules and assignments for tomorrow and tomorrow night." He paused, "Tomorrow is a huge day—breakfast is at 9:30 and we are going to be balls to the wall for the next 18 hours. Tomorrow we take New York, folks. After tomorrow night, New York will not be the same. The biggest buzz in town will be L9/NYC. We've got an attendee list that rivals the Oscars and Mia and her team have the press in a frenzy over us."

Cheers and whistles went up from the team, who were getting pumped up.

"No man is an island, and what's been accomplished and what we are about to do, is because we have the best team on both coasts. The next twenty-four hours are going to be crazy, so let me take this opportunity now to say thank you to everyone. Trust me, everything you do does not go unnoticed or unappreciated. What everyone has done this summer to get us ready for tomorrow night is nothing short of a miracle, and I know I'm also speaking for Mia when I tell you that we both sincerely thank each and every one of you." Schooner gestured to the rotunda, "This is all of ours," he shot them his best All-American boy smile. "I'll see you on a rooftop at 6:30. Now get out of here!"

The staff responded with clapping and whistles.

Seth tapped on his iPad. "I've got everyone's formalwear being delivered to the hotel and I'll take care of making sure they get to the correct rooms. You, Holly, Kami, Yoli and Debbie have hair, makeup and nails starting at 11:00 tomorrow morning at Enzo B's salon, which is only two blocks from the hotel."

"Is Enzo doing my hair?" Mia asked.

Seth rolled his eyes. "Yes, BBC. Enzo is doing your hair."

"Don't take that tone with me, Princess. Enzo has curls and he understands curls, not everyone does. After all, CurlBlaster is his straightener. Are you coming with us?"

"Can I?" He brightened up.

"Of course. It's always more fun if you're there. You should do highlights or that ombre thing with your hair."

"I think I will. I'm so excited."

Mia pulled Seth aside and whispered, "What about Zac and clothes for tomorrow night?"

"Oh that one," he rolled his eyes, "crisis averted with Devil Spawn. I've got him in an Armani Collezioni tux jacket, white Armani shirt, skinny silk tie the color of his cold blue eyes, he's going to wear his own pair of faded jeans and I got him those Armani jean sneakers, they're kind of like a blue jean suede."

"Oh my God, the kid is going to walk out of here with a modeling contract. The little shit's going to look gorgeous."

Schooner came up behind them. "You ready, Baby Girl?"

She nodded.

He took a moment to look around and take stock. "I can't believe this is the same space we walked into in February. Freaking amazing."

"It's really stunning," she agreed.

Even with Elan's staff and vendors still laboring throughout the club, and electricians and carpenters furiously working to ensure all the details were executed precisely to Elan's plans, the space had already taken on a breathtaking and unique aura.

Schooner draped his arm over Mia's shoulder and pulled her into him, kissing the top of her head. She peeked up at him and reveled in seeing his look of satisfaction and pride as he gazed around his latest concept club. His expression elicited an enormous smile of her own.

"What are you smiling at?" he asked.

"You look happy."

He hugged her tighter into him. "I am very, very happy, Baby Girl." He looked down at her, "Truly happy." There was definite conviction in his words as he tilted her chin up to softly kiss her smiling lips.

Mia took one last look around, surveying the rotunda and side rooms. "You did it, Schooner."

He shook his head, "No, Baby Girl, we did it. Me and my team, you and your team. Our teams." His brows knit for a second and he corrected himself, "Our team."

Mia nodded, smiling to herself. He was right. What had begun in February as two separate people with two separate lives running two separate companies that were separated by the entire continental United States were now inseparable on every level, both personally and professionally. In six and a half months, Schooner and Mia had forged a union that encompassed all areas of their lives, allowing them to fully share and merge every aspect of their worlds. Together they had successfully built their tomorrow.

Mia felt her eyes begin to burn with tears. Every day had been focused on moving forward with their shared goal of the L9/NYC opening and making it the talk of the town, and now she was standing there watching Elan directing his team as they finalized the magnificent finishing touches. The enormity of what they had accomplished since she hit the "Friend Accept" button on that horrible Monday suddenly overwhelmed her.

"It's all real, isn't it?" she asked, unexpectedly astonished by the extent of all that had transpired since their reunion.

He hugged her to his chest and Nathaniel gave a hearty kick, sharply jabbing both Mia and Schooner. Mia looked up at Schooner eyes wide from the jolt and they both laughed, their eyes alight with the joy of feeling their son move and his timely surprise attack. "I guess that's my answer." Mia laughed.

"He's telling you, Mom, I'm very real and don't forget it or I'll kick you."

Mia tapped her belly, "Clearly a New Yorker in there."

Schooner laughed and tucked Mia under his arm as she snuggled into him. "Let's go check into the hotel and watch sunset from a rooftop."

As they left L9/NYC, Mia wondered how everything in her life had gotten so perfect and smiled to herself as she heard Seth yelling at her in her head, "Don't over think it, BBC!"

CHAPTER 32

The sun was hanging low in the hazy sky to the west over Jersey City as Mia and Schooner exited the elevator onto the roof deck. A burly shaved-headed security guard, one of Charles' staff, greeted them with a head nod.

They stood there for a moment, taking in the view, a soft breeze blowing Mia's short pale pink silk caftan. "Okay, let's go greet our guests." Schooner bent down and gave Mia a quick kiss and they headed off in opposite directions to work the roof.

Mia held out her hand in front of her in a vertical fist, raising it in increments.

"What is that you're doing?" Kami walked up to her, nursing a gin and tonic.

"Oh, that's a photography thing to gauge how long you have until sunset. Each fist is about fifteen minutes and the sun is about three fists up right now. Comes in handy when you're standing on a mountaintop in twelve degrees waiting to shoot sunset," she laughed.

Yoli elbowed Debbie, a vivacious blonde with a deep, hearty laugh, "Just like CJ, huh," referring to Mia.

Debbie practically spit out her drink. "I cannot believe how opposite ends of the spectrum they are."

Mia laughed and walked over to their table, "I am choosing to take that as a compliment!" She gave Debbie's shoulder a squeeze.

Yoli smiled, "You know it's got to be killing her that she won't be there tomorrow night, but I'm sure spy boy will give her the blow by blow."

They all turned to look at Zac in the pool who had several female L9 staff vying to be on his shoulders in a raucous game of Chicken Fight.

"Looks like he'll be pretty involved in his own blow-by-blows," Mia snarked.

"Love her!" Debbie turned to Yoli.

"Our boy got it right this time," Yoli concurred.

"Awww, give Baby Daddy some credit. He actually had it right the first time. I was the dummy that got played and left him."

"Well, the dummy's got the last laugh." Debbie raised a glass to Mia.

"You can't laugh when the dummy's yours!" and they all laughed.

"I'm never leaving New York." Yoli announced, watching the sun on its descent. The breathtaking view from the roof of the James Hotel provided a nearly 360° vista and made Manhattan feel like it was their own personal little island. "I can't believe I'm saying this, but I really love it here."

"You need to move here." Kami looked sad. She and Yoli had grown to be close friends. "Can't someone else run the California facilities?"

"You need to talk to your business partner," Mia urged, as she got up to go talk to other guests.

She made her way over to sit down at a table where Gaby, Holly and Jared were munching on Chef David Burke's Smoked Pastrami Salmon and Pretzel Crab Cakes.

"This could be my new addiction," Mia said to Holly, eating her third bite of the Pastrami Salmon.

Holly smiled, "This is so fabulous up here."

The sun was just beginning to kiss the Jersey City roof tops on the far side of the Hudson River.

"We're going to have a magnificent sunset once the sun drops below the horizon. That whole bank of clouds is going to light up." Mia pointed to clouds in the western and southern sky. "And we're going to get the whole show from the oranges into the pinks and reds tonight." She turned to Holly, "We had some great sunsets over the Great South Bay this summer, didn't we?"

"We had a great summer," Holly smiled at Mia. "This was one of my favorite summers ever."

"I really love that," Mia reached for Holly's hand and gave it a squeeze. "Lots more to come."

Holly leaned over and whispered in Mia's ear, "Dad told me the baby's name is Nathaniel James."

Mia gasped, "That man cannot keep a secret! Do you like it?"

"I love it. I just can't wait to see what he looks like. I still can't believe I'm going to have a baby brother."

They both looked over at the pool to see Zac making out with one of the LA staffers, a 20-something California blonde sporting brand new Double D's.

"I'm sorry he's such an ass to you, Mia." The pain and disappointment in her eyes was evident. More than anything she wanted her father to be happy and she knew Zac's behavior weighed heavily on Schooner.

"He's young. Hopefully, it won't always be this way."

"Well, I'm happy you and my dad are together. It's very evident how much you love each other and you make him so happy."

Mia smiled, "Thank you for saying that, you can't even imagine what that means to me. I am thrilled that you are a part of my life, Holly. You are the bonus."

Holly smiled and then shook her head, "Mia, you would've been heartbroken if you had seen him at his birthday party. He was so out of sorts. There was a restaurant full of people and he clearly didn't want to be a part of it. He was hanging out on a deck all by himself, it broke my heart and just look at him here. He is so at home and happy."

Sitting on the other side of the pool and laughing with Charles, Gaby and Seth, Schooner had his long legs stretched out, feet up on a chair, single malt scotch in one hand, cigar in the other. He was laughing heartily at something Seth had just said.

The sun had finally faded behind the buildings across the Hudson River and dipped below the horizon. The sky show was about to begin.

Mia walked over to where Schooner was sitting, "Excuse me while I borrow him for a few minutes." She held out a hand to Schooner and he took it.

They walked along the western side of the roof deck to a spot where they were alone. Mia turned to face the sunset. Schooner stood behind her, his arms wrapped over her shoulders. She leaned back into him and he kissed the top of her head. Silently, they stood and watched the cloud deck, a sky carpet, turn from gold to orange to pink to ruby, before the colors faded to gray and the lights of the city began their own show.

"I love you, Baby Girl," Schooner bent down and whispered in Mia's ear.

"It's smoochal." She turned her head back toward him and he bent down to complete the sunset with a kiss. "Okay, I'm going to go check on where the next food course is, there should be rib eye sandwiches, grilled prawns and asparagus and a few other goodies coming."

He kissed her again, "I'm going to check on my scotch."

She laughed and walked off toward the bar.

"Hey Mia," she heard Zac call her from the pool. Mia walked over to where Zac and the California blonde were. He looked happy tonight, not surly Zac, allowing him to really look like a young version of Schooner. Mia walked over, smiling. As she got near the edge of the pool, Zac and the blonde scooped up as much water as they could, splashing Mia from head to toe with a torrential wave.

Mia immediately tried to wipe the water from her eyes, but her soaking wet bangs were matted down in them, as if she'd been swimming. Her short pale pink silk caftan was plastered to her body like a second skin, hugging her breasts and her belly, the fabric now translucent.

Zac and the blonde laughed, viciously.

"Hey Zac," Mia said, returning his greeting, but with the added NY symbolism of rubbing her nose up and down with her middle finger.

"Classy bitch," Zac snarled at her.

The blonde laughed, "Real classy bitch."

Mia looked at the blonde with a 'you didn't just say that' look. "What was the third word you just used?"

The blonde didn't speak, so Mia went on, "Let me refresh your fleeting brain cells. It was bitch. You just called me a bitch."

The girl just looked at Mia with an attitude.

"What is your name?" Mia asked. The girl remained silent. "Okay, let's try this one more time. What. Is. Your. Name?" Mia spoke in a slow cadence.

The girl answered Mia in the same cadence, thinking that she was amusing, "My. Name. Is. Mandy."

Mia smiled at Mandy, her eyes narrowed into slits. "Well Mandy, unfortunately for you, cute *and* stupid does not have a long shelf life. You're fired."

"You can't fire me," Mandy retorted, breasts and chin thrust forward.

"I can and I did and it's in the past tense. You've been fired, Mandy. E.D.'ed means past tense, à fait accompli. As you are no longer an employee of L9, you need to get out of the pool and leave this party immediately. I'll have security accompany you to your room while you gather your belongings and leave the premises." Mia nodded her head at the big, bald security guy by the elevator who was watching a dripping wet Mia.

As he rapidly approached, Charles popped out of his chair at the far end of the deck and sprinted toward Mia. Schooner had his back to the situation and turned quickly to see what had gotten Charles to spring from his chair. He was immediately behind, racing up to a soaking wet, shivering Mia.

Mandy turned to Schooner enraged, breasts still thrust at full throttle. "She fired me. She can't fire me, can she?"

"Of course she can. You're fired," Schooner said coldly, with narrowed eyes, "Get her out of here."

"But Dad..." Zac began.

"Get out of the pool and follow me," Schooner hissed at him. He turned to Mia, running his hand down her wet head, "You okay?"

She nodded and he kissed her forehead before turning and grabbing Zac by the arm and hauling him off toward the roof deck's indoor seating area.

Charles wrapped a towel around Mia. "You sure you're okay?"

"Yeah, just cold, wet and pissed."

Charles gave her a hug and whispered in her ear, "Fucking little dick."

"You pegged that one."

"Come Meezie, let's get you into dry clothes." Gaby was at Mia's side, leading her to the elevator.

Mia was in a quasi-half-sleep state when Schooner slipped into bed next to her and spooned her, kissing her shoulder. She turned over in his arms to face him and softly ran her hand down his cheek, smoothing her thumb over his cheekbone. "How is everything?"

Schooner sighed, "That is one very angry young man."

"Angry at me and you?" Even in the dark, she could see the sadness in his beautiful eyes.

He nodded, "And Holly, too."

"It won't always be this way, Schooner. He's a petulant, beautiful boy, but at some point, with life experience, he'll realize this isn't a war."

"Mia Silver, you are the one with the beautiful heart. I'm not so sure that my son has one or ever will. I will tell you this though, I was very clear with him on what is acceptable behavior where it comes to you. I will not tolerate blatant disrespect."

"C'mere you." Mia pulled Schooner's head to her chest, kissing the top of his head in a gesture which he had patently comforted and expressed his love for her. Schooner nestled into Mia's soft breasts, getting himself comfortable and let out a soft "mmmm" sound. Mia wrapped her arms tightly around him and entwined her legs with his before drifting off into an uneasy sleep.

CHAPTER 33

"We'll see you over at L9. It's 'Showtime' folks," was Schooner's last words to the team before dismissing everyone.

Each person left the breakfast meeting pumped on adrenaline and excitement for the opening, clear on their assignments and ready to rock the New York social scene. The press for the event had already reached a frenzy and everyone was calling in favors trying to get an invite.

Charles was on hand to brief the staff on interacting with his team, as well as with celebrities and their private security. Mia and Kami gave precise instructions on dealing with the press and paparazzi. Yoli met with each of the teams and their team leaders to review roles and rotations throughout the night. There was some buzz about Mandy's departure, and if anyone was unsure of how Mia fit into the L9 organization, it was now clear that Schooner and Mia were partners in every sense of the word. Most of the staff were extremely savvy and professional and understood the ramifications of mouthing off to the boss. Calling your boss a bitch (unless you were Seth) was generally not a good career move.

"We're headed off to go beautify. I'll come over to the club when I'm done."

"Why don't you rest this afternoon, Baby Girl. You're going to be on your feet all night." Schooner reached down and brushed Mia's bangs from her eyes.

"I feel like there is some detail I'm going to miss if I don't do one last check." Mia looked up at Schooner, searching his face.

He shook his head. "Everything's under control. Between the two of us, Yoli, Seth, Kami, Elan and Charles, we've done as much as we can. I don't want you to push it."

"Are you trying to tell me I need to relax?"

Schooner laughed, "I would never..."

Mia swatted him in the arm, smiling up at him. "You know that is not in my DNA!"

"Baby Girl, do not make me sic Dr. Gary on you." His hands were in her hair, as he smiled down at her.

"Gary's coming tonight." She smiled back at him.

"Yes, I know, so don't make me rat you out to him." Schooner continued to play with her hair. "Go enjoy your girly stuff." He bent down to softly kiss her lips.

"Schooner-," she stopped.

"What, Baby Girl?"

"I love you." Mia's eyes were so earnest and every time she said the words to him, it was like she was saying it for the first time.

He leaned his forehead into hers and stayed like that for a moment before kissing her lips softly and saying, "It's smoochal" into them.

Mia, Kami, Holly, Yoli, Debbie and Seth walked the two blocks down Grand Street through SoHo to Enzo B's Salon. Turning left on Wooster Street, the blue Enzo B. Salon flag was gently blowing in the breeze.

"Oh my God, now it seems real, doesn't it? We're getting coiffed for tonight," Mia commented, as they walked into the salon. The entourage was met warmly, with Enzo whisking Mia off immediately.

He started to play with her hair as they talked, "You've always had thick hair, but pregnancy has turned it into a mane." He played some more. "I can see you have not been using my herb scrub on your scalp."

Mia looked guilty as she met Enzo's eyes in the mirror, "Busted."

"I'll go easy on you because I know you've got a lot on your plate, but you are not leaving here without an Herb Scrub Complete Pack. Now tell me about tonight, what you are wearing, your role, etc. This event is clearly the big ticket in town, everyone is talking about it."

"They are? You're hearing about it?"

Enzo nodded at Mia.

"Excellent, means we're doing a good job. Okay, so obviously we are the agency of record and we are handling all aspects, advertising, marketing, PR, events—all the details for this event."

"Have you worked with Level 9 on the West Coast? They are huge out there."

"No. Frankly, I had no clue who they were until February," Mia laughed. "Apparently, I was the only one."

"So, how did you connect with them?" Enzo was trying out different parts on Mia's hair, critically looking at her in the mirror as he pulled her hair up, put it back down, flared it on her shoulders, swept it to one side, then the other.

"Well, I have a relationship with the owner."

Enzo stopped playing and leveled a glance at Mia in the mirror, "With Schooner Moore."

Mia nodded.

"What kind of relationship?" Enzo was intrigued. Schooner was the new mystery man in town.

Mia laughed and rubbed her belly. "Knocked me up," she deadpanned.

Enzo led out a guffaw laugh. He laid his hand with the hairbrush on Mia's shoulder. "So, he is your significant other?"

Mia nodded.

"Mia, Mia, Mia. You have just made my day so much more interesting. Okay, so that makes you both the professional that has created the event as well as the hostess. Okay, let's get your hair washed and your scalp scrubbed."

Mia returned to Enzo's chair with her scalp feeling like it was glowing. "Tell me about your dress."

Mia looked at Enzo in the mirror and rolled her eyes. "Maternity evening wear is penance for something I did wrong in a past life," she pouted.

Laughing, "I'm sure you are wearing something very chic and flattering. Seth would not let you attend in something embarrassing."

"It's a midnight blue one-shouldered Grecian drape thing."

Sam was listening as he combed through Mia's hair. "Length?"

"Short, above the knee."

He stopped what he was doing, "Oh thank goodness, you are too small to carry long maternity."

Mia nodded, "That is what Seth said."

"Okay, so classic lines on your dress and since you are the hostess, I'm thinking old Hollywood for you tonight. Let's sweep these bangs over to the side. Think Rita Hayworth, Ava Gardner, Lauren Bacall. Soft waves for the rest. And I need to shape your hair, you are a mess from this summer."

"Do it!" Mia proclaimed with a smile. As she glanced to her left and her right, the rest of her party were in different phases of their makeovers.

When Enzo was done with Mia, she sat with her mouth open looking at her reflection. She checked out her left profile, then her right profile, tilted and cocked her head.

"You like?" Enzo looked very satisfied with his masterful handiwork.

"I love it."

As Mia headed toward make-up, she stopped behind Seth's chair.

He spied her in his mirror and gasped, "It's movie star BBC. I likee!"

CHAPTER 34

Mia stood in front of the bathroom mirror trying to maneuver her body into her dress properly. "This is some serious cleavage," she muttered at her changing body.

She heard the front door to the hotel penthouse loft slam.

"Hey, I'm back," Schooner yelled

"I'll be out in a few." Showtime, Mia thought and wished she'd had her shoes and jewelry on, so that Schooner could get the full effect of the silver screen image that Enzo had created for her.

Schooner had his back to her when she emerged from the bathroom. He was already in the pants of his Fendi Steel Mélange black suit and white Armani Collezioni dress shirt and was fumbling as he attempted to insert black stingray leather and silver cufflinks.

"Need help with those?"

Schooner slowly turned around, his eyes widening and a real smile spreading across his handsome face at the sight of Mia. "Hey, Gorgeous," his voice was little more than a growl.

"Hey, Gorgeous yourself." She took the cufflinks from his hands and inserted them into his French cuffs.

She looked up and he was smiling down at her, appreciatively.

"You look beautiful, Baby Girl."

"You think?" she asked over her shoulder with a devil smile as she headed to the closet. "Oh crap. Where are my shoes?" There was panic in Mia's voice.

"In the living room."

"In the living room, really?" Mia was confused and left the bedroom in search of her shoes. "What the…"

She turned around to see Schooner standing behind her with a shit-eating grin on his face. Mia cocked her head, questioningly. On the low coffee table in the living room were two matte black shoeboxes emblazoned with the silver *Jimmy Choo* logo.

Schooner took Mia by the hand and led her to the couch, where they sat down. She just smiled at him with a bemused look.

He took one of the boxes in his lap, "Christian Louboutin made you cry. So I bought you Jimmy Choo's." His eyes never leaving hers, he removed the box top and watched her gasp as the recessed lighting in the hotel loft caught the glint off of the shiny silver peep toe sling backs.

"Oh my God, Schooner." Mia was floored as Schooner took out the first of the "Clue" pumps.

"A sexy silver shoe. There just could not be a more perfect shoe for Mia Silver."

Mia lifted her foot for him and Schooner slipped the sexy and elegant silver shoe onto her left foot and then her right. She smiled at them in awe.

"They fit," Mia beamed at Schooner. "I love you so much." She leaned over and softly kissed his lips.

"Do you want to see what is in the other box?" He was the one giving her the devil smile now.

Mia nodded, but was clearly distracted by the beautiful sling backs gracing her shapely legs and high-arched, newly pedicured feet.

Schooner handed her the second box and she lifted the lid and gasped again.

"I figured your feet might not make it through the night in the first pair and you'll still need to look chic—or Seth will kill the both of us," he laughed.

In the second box, were a pair of Jimmy Choo flat silver thong sandals with a sexy ankle strap.

Mia wrapped her arms around Schooner's neck and pulled him in for a kiss. "You spoil me," she said against his lips.

He nodded, smiling. "And it's a rare treat when you actually let me."

She kissed his lips softly and said, "Wait here."

Coming from the bedroom, she sat down and handed him a long thin burnt orange box with black piping. The box was sashed with a thin black satin ribbon emblazoned in white with *Hermès-Paris*.

"I needed to complete your New York transformation."

Schooner opened the box and smiled at Mia. Nestled in soft tissue was an Hermes Faconnee H jacquard silk twill tie that matched Mia's midnight blue dress.

"Now that's class," he whispered, as he removed the hand folded tie from the box. It was Schooner's first Hermès.

He handed the tie to Mia, who draped it slowly and sensually around his neck and under his shirt collar, smiling at him and making a slow meal of it, before tying a perfect double Windsor knot and pulling him in by his tie for a kiss.

"You're killing me here," he groaned.

"Good," she kissed him again, devil smile reaching her eyes this time.

They finished dressing and Mia was standing in front of the full length mirror in the bedroom. Schooner came up behind her buttoning his suit jacket, looking at her petite and very feminine reflection, appreciatively. They both stood there silently drinking in the image in the mirror. Their image was not just one of beauty, but it also exuded happiness. Mia couldn't help but think there is nothing more than this.

Schooner and Mia did not just look like they belonged together. Schooner and Mia belonged together.

CHAPTER 35

Schooner and Mia reached the Sky Lobby on the hotel's third floor where the rest of their party awaited. "Wait until you see your daughter." Mia squeezed Schooner's hand, as they approached.

Dressed in an azalea red ruched Theia silk jacquard cocktail dress with her long blonde hair swept to one side, Holly looked as if she should be walking the runway. Schooner's face melted upon seeing his daughter and Mia gave his hand a final squeeze, before letting it go.

Schooner held Holly by her shoulders at arm's length looking at her. "You look..." he began to speak, but was overcome and shook his head, before pulling her in for a sweet hug.

Seth grabbed Mia's hand and gave it a squeeze as they smiled at the heartwarming scene unfolding in front of them.

It was then that Mia noticed Zac watching them from off to the side, where he stood leaning against a glass wall. Instinctively, she could not help herself from smiling at him standing there looking like a brooding Greek god. She knew who and what he was, yet could not control an underlying, and unwarranted, fondness— he was Schooner's.

"Zac, come over here. I want to take a picture of you, your dad and Holly." Mia motioned him over. It was the first interaction she'd had with him since the incident at the pool.

Zac stood there stone-faced, not moving.

Mia rolled her eyes at him and shook her head, "Just get your ass over there." Her tone was one that she would take with a friend, like Seth, saying "just cut the crap."

Not quite knowing how to take her, Zac complied and shuffled over. Refusing to smile for the picture, his scowl actually complimented both his looks and the eveningwear.

"Gorgeous," Mia said, showing Seth the picture. "You did an amazing job dressing him."

"I hate admitting how beautiful Devil Spawn is," he whispered at her through clenched teeth and Mia squeezed his arm.

Out of the corner of her eye, Mia saw Schooner nod his head at Zac and motion toward Mia. As Zac approached Mia, Seth gave her a look and backed away.

"Sorry about last night," he muttered, without conviction.

"Come walk with me." Mia took Zac by the upper arm.

They moved away from the rest of the party and rounded a corner before Mia stopped. She leveled a cold glance at him, her green eyes meeting his ice blue eyes head on. "Do you love your father?" she asked.

"Yes, I love my father." His eyes narrowed.

"Do you want him in your life?"

"What do you think?" Now out of sight of the rest of the party, he had no need for pretenses or civility.

"Trust me, you don't want to know what I think, and frankly, that is not the issue here. Do you want him in your life?" Mia asked for a second time.

"Yes, I want him in my life."

Mia said nothing more to him. She nodded her head, turned and walked away, leaving Zac standing there, confused.

"Mia?" He caught up with her at a quick pace and put a hand on her arm to stop her.

"Yes, Zac?"

"Was that it?" He wanted more, a conversation, a fight.

"Yes." Mia met him with indifference.

She could see his mind spinning with a million thoughts and before he went off in a direction she didn't want him to go, Mia decided to throw him off balance, "We have a really hot opening to get to and you look like a freaking model, so let's go." She slipped her arm through his and led him back to a surprised group and asked with the biggest, brightest smile she could paint on her face, "Everyone ready to hit the road?"

The limo pulled up in front of L9/NYC and there was already a crowd gathered out front comprised of guests arriving, security, paparazzi, and onlookers hoping to get a peek and photo of their favorite celebrity.

Mia saw Charles talking to seemingly no one, but knew he was giving staff orders through some type of hidden walkie-talkie device. A doorman opened the door to the limo and Yoli and Debbie exited first, followed by Kami and Seth, then Zac, who set off a flare of paparazzi flashes just by looking like a star or a model, the same with Holly and Jared.

Mia squeezed Schooner's hand, "This is it, Baby Girl."

From a walkway in front of Brewster Hall to the sidewalk in front of L9/NYC with paparazzi and press awaiting their arrival, Mia and Schooner were entering a new world, together.

Schooner stepped out of the car and reached a hand down for Mia, escorting her from the limo. Putting an arm around her shoulder as they began to walk, she looked up at him and they both smiled and simultaneously uttered, "Showtime"—breaking into huge smiles at their trademark synchronicity.

It was at that moment that the surrounding cameras began to flash, and the image that was captured of handsome California turned New York entrepreneur Schooner Moore, and his beautiful and very pregnant New York love Mia Silver, felt almost voyeuristic. Schooner and Mia were looking at one another with a love that made them oblivious to their surroundings, smiling as if they were clearly sharing a very private secret.

This picture would grace Women's Wear Daily, the social columns of the New York newspapers, fashion and fitness magazines, New York Magazine, The New Yorker, Paris Match and Vogue.

It would be this image that would forever remain in people's minds when they thought of Mia Silver and Schooner Moore.

CHAPTER 36

The offices were set up for press interviews and a steady stream of journalists and photographers were booked for their one-on-ones with Schooner. Kami and Schooner had prepped extensively for the interviews, conducting due diligence on each of the reporters. As Schooner was both well-seasoned and a natural—especially with women reporters (it just took a flash of his All-American boy smile), they didn't anticipate any surprises or situations he couldn't handle.

Mia had come in and was standing in the threshold of the office as Schooner was finishing up his last scheduled interview of the evening. He was sitting behind his desk, long legs crossed in his impeccable Fendi suit, very focused on the interviewer.

The reporter, a small, serious woman dressed in vintage Chanel, had bird-like features and a champagne blonde French twist. She quickly looked through her notes before looking back up at Schooner, "I have one last question, Mr. Moore. What is the significance of the name Level 9?"

Schooner cocked his head to the side and looked at the diminutive reporter with a small, appreciative smile. "Do you know, that you are the first member of the press to *ever* have asked me that question?"

The reporter looked surprised and pleased with herself.

"What does L9 mean?" Schooner smiled, repeating the question, an introspective smile on his handsome face.

He was silent for a moment, clearly inside his head, remembering something and formulating his response, "L9 or what has morphed into Level 9 is my personal inspiration for not only attaining the best that I can be, but also the best that I can do for others. It's a philosophy that I not only try to apply on a personal level, but also apply to any impact that I may have in a broader sense." He paused again, before looking directly into the reporter's eyes as he continued, "The summer after my freshman year in college," he began, his eyes flicked to Mia momentarily, and he gave her a small, sad smile, "I accompanied a group of doctors to the Southern Province of Zambia, to a village called Macha, where we helped set up a hospital. I went to lend an extra set of hands to the medical staff, or in my case, one hand, because my right hand was in a cast, at the time. Within the first few days after our arrival, I noticed that families were traveling long distances seeking medical attention and literally bringing their entire family on the journey. The children were waiting around all day with nothing to do while their parents were waiting to be seen by the doctors. So, after I had assisted with the initial set-up of the hospital, I asked myself, 'What can a one-handed jock do to really be useful to both the medical personnel and to the patients?' And there was only one answer to that, start a sports and soccer camp for the kids," he laughed, "and with the help of nine very dedicated children from the local village, I set up an exercise, soccer and wellness camp for both local and visiting children." Schooner paused, smiling at a memory, "We did everything from basic exercise to soccer matches to learning lifesaving techniques such as CPR and oral-rehydration therapy. At the end of the summer, we held a soccer tournament that turned into a huge event, where everyone in the village came out," he laughed, "basically a tailgate party, Zambian-style." Schooner was clearly enjoying the memory, "There was a village elder, named Levi Mambwe, who pulled me aside and had a very enlightening discussion with me on my last night there. He talked with me about gifts and passion and what I had done for the children of the village. His inspirational words touched me deeply, and I knew from that moment on, what my path in life would be. I also knew that the people of Macha had done much more for me than I had actually done for them. L9 is my way of paying homage to both Levi, and the nine children of Macha, who dedicated themselves to the sports camp. It has been my way of thanking them for what they taught me and the gift that they gave to me and that I have, in turn, been able to share with others. So, for me L9 is a level at which I aspire to live my life—a way of paying things both back and forward through inspiring people to maintain mind and body health. And that is the significance behind the name Level 9."

The reporter turned off her microphone and looked Schooner square in the eyes. "You are more than just a pretty face, Mr. Moore. I am honored that I will be the one to share that story. Welcome to New York."

Mia stood in the doorway smiling, as the reporter left. "Remember when I asked you if people knew who you really were?"

Schooner nodded.

"I think after this, everyone will have a really good idea."

With the interviews completed, Mia and Schooner went out to join the party. L9/NYC was packed, the champagne was flowing, waiters passed hors d'oeuvres on silver trays, live music pulsed from the center of the rotunda. Schooner grabbed a glass of champagne from a passing waiter.

They stood at the rail of the second floor mezzanine surveying the ethereal club. Elan had created a scene from a dream.

"I want a sip." Mia reached out for Schooner's champagne.

"You do?" he was surprised, as she had not had a single drink throughout the entire pregnancy.

"Mmm-hmm, just a sip. To celebrate." Schooner held the flute to Mia's lips and she took a small sip.

"Yum! I've missed that." She looked down at the throng of people in the rotunda below. "Look at this, Schooner."

She looked up at him and he was smiling, ear to ear. "Let's go work the room." She took his hand and they descended the marble stairs. At the bottom, she turned to him and gave him a quick kiss, "Go work your peeps and I'll go work mine," she gave his hand a squeeze, "till we meet again," and with a flash of her devil grin, they headed off in opposite directions.

Emma Stone, the Olsen Twins, Rachel Bilson, Bradley Cooper, Blake Lively & Ryan Reynolds, Kate Hudson, Liv Tyler, Selma Blair, Victoria & David Beckham, and of course, Katie Holmes. Mia thought, okay those are the ones that I can name, as she stopped to say hello and greet guests. There were so many faces she knew that she should know who they were, but couldn't put a name to the face. *Okay, they are on that CW vampire show*, she thought, as she greeted a couple with a huge smile and a "Hi there, isn't this space fabulous, are you having a good time, great to see you..."

After close to an hour of buzzing from conversation to conversation, Mia headed to the perimeter of the rotunda where there were a few tables set up. She had Elan keep the number of tables to a minimum, so that guests would have to mingle, but her feet were past the mingling point and her Jimmy Choo's were soon going to have a Christian Louboutin crying effect, if she didn't sit.

At a table situated near an alcove and slightly removed from the fray, Mia spotted Mallory Jessie Prince and Chris Brody sitting with a few people and there was an empty chair. *Salvation*, she thought, as she headed their way with a determined walk and a smile on her face. Her heart skipped a beat when she saw who was sitting next to the empty chair.

She came up behind him, placed her hands on his shoulders and whispered into his ear, "Just seeing you gives me a heart hard-on."

He turned to meet his whisperer, his huge trademark smile overtaking his face as well as a look of surprise, for he did not recognize the whisperer, who was quoting the words that he had tweeted out on Valentine's Day.

Mia met him with a huge devil grin and said, "I have the biggest crush on you! If I were a gay man, I'd stalk you."

His warm brown eyes widened at the bodacious introduction.

She went on, "Hi, I'm Mia Silver."

His mouth opened into a big surprised "O" before breaking into a smile, "*You're* Mia Silver? All night everyone has been saying to me, 'I can't believe you don't know, Mia' and 'You have to meet Mia'."

"Ta-Da." Mia put out her hands, "And now you have!" Before sitting down next to her secret crush, cable TV's Andy Epstein, Mia went around the table to greet Mallory Jessie and Chris.

"I can't believe you two have never met," MJP was surprised. "You look wonderful, Mia. How are you feeling?"

"Great, except for my feet tonight." She looked down at her beautiful shoes.

"Silver Jimmy Choo's—now that is perfect for you," Mallory Jessie laughed.

"I know! Schooner gave them to me. He thought the same thing."

"Schooner Moore?" Andy asked.

Mia nodded. "I had a meltdown in front of Christian Louboutin a few months ago thinking I was going to have big swollen platypus feet and that I was going to have to wear Birkenstock's, so Schooner thought that Jimmy Choo's would make me happy. And he was right," she laughed.

"I haven't met him yet," Andy began, taking a sip of his champagne, "which is amazing because he was quite the talk of all the *Real Housewives of Orange County*."

"I'll bet he was," Mia rolled her eyes. "I'll introduce you." She scanned the room, "There he is." Mia pointed across the rotunda where Schooner was talking with Heidi Berg, "The Brooks Brothers model talking to Heidi Berg."

Andy looked at Mia and laughed, "No wonder he was the talk of the Housewives. He's gorgeous!" Andy grabbed Mia's forearm.

"Inside and out," Mia smiled.

"So, you're his ad agency?" Andy asked, leaning in close for the scoop on Mr. Hotness.

"Amongst other things." Mia smiled and ever the journalist, Andy cocked his head to the side in a 'tell me more' gesture, "Baby Mama."

Mallory Jessie looked at Andy, "Get with the program, Epstein. That man is in New York because of Mia."

Andy leaned over and whispered in Mia's ear, "And the blonde OC *shiksa*?"

"A signature away from where she should have been twenty-four years ago when she hatched her evil plan to break us up. Gone. Goodbye."

Andy was staring into Mia's eyes shocked, when their attention was drawn away by a buxom bleached blonde shrieking his name, "Andy, it's been so long."

The smile was plastered on Andy's handsome face, but the look in his eyes said, "Who the fuck are you?"

Mia and Mallory Jessie exchanged smirks. She introduced herself and as fate would have it, she was a friend of a friend of one of the Housewives and had appeared briefly in the crowd at a party in one of the episodes, several years back.

"This is my cue to go upstairs and change into more comfortable shoes," Mia announced, standing to leave.

Before she could take a step, Mia heard her name being called as Katie Chisholm approached, "You look adorable! Schooner told me you two are expecting." Katie wrapped her in a warm hug, as if they were old friends.

"Katie," Mia smiled and hugged her back. "It's so good to see you. How do you like this space vs. the ones on the west coast?"

"This is amazing. I can't wait to start using the facilities. It is so unique. Just like Schooner though to create a fabulous concept."

Mia was smiling brightly at Katie's assessment.

Katie and Andy hugged and the Housewife wannabe was dying to get Katie's attention, but Katie and Mallory Jessie were already talking about school starting for their kids and Mia was left with Andy and the wannabe.

"Are you Mia Silver?" the wannabe asked.

Mia was concentrating hard on her face. It had no movement to it. Botox overload was Mia's assessment. "Yes, I am," Mia responded.

"I'm a friend of CJ Moore's. Schooner's wife." She leaned in toward Mia, with her tall, lean frame.

"Of course you are," Mia smiled. "Wonderful, then you'll be able to report back to her how fabulous *our* opening was. Now if you'll excuse me, Schooner had the foresight to buy me the cutest pair of silver Jimmy Choo flats to change into when these," she motioned to her gorgeous silver sling backs, "became too much."

She turned to Andy, "I'll introduce you and Schooner when I get back." And in a whisper, "Score one for the Jewish girl."

Andy's face broke into a huge smile, his eyes crinkling in the corners.

Mia made her way slowly through the crowd, stopping to say hello to guests as she migrated toward the main marble staircase. As she ascended the grand flight of stairs, she looked up and saw Zac standing at the top, a few feet from the steps.

He was leaning over the railing and looking at the crowd below. Mia couldn't help but smile at him, he looked so damn handsome. In his right hand was a champagne glass and Mia thought she was going to need to talk to the wait staff about cutting him off. Zac was still a minor.

She approached him with a smile. "Having fun?"

He shrugged his shoulders. "You know my mother should be the one here with him. Fifty percent of this *is* hers."

"Zac, I really do love how loyal you are to your mother." Mia was sincere as she looked into his glazed eyes. He'd clearly had quite a few glasses of champagne.

"Obviously not a trait I get from my father." He drained the remainder of his flute. "Since he's choosing a bitch and a bastard over me and my mother."

A waiter was passing by and he reached for a fresh glass of champagne.

"Zac, I think you've had enough to drink." Mia reached for his glass and he thrust his arm forward to push her hand away, knocking Mia backward, the champagne splashing down the front of her dress.

Mia felt the heels of her Jimmy Choo's slipping out from under her as she took a step backward to try and right her balance. The heel of her right shoe caught the edge of the top step, and as she began to fall backwards, she saw the complacent look on Zac's face.

The edge of the first step she hit slammed the lumbar section of her spine and she felt the pain searing through her body. "Protect Nathaniel" was the thought that flashed through her mind and she brought her flailing arms down to wrap around her stomach. She tumbled backwards over a few more steps feeling the stabbing pain in her shoulders as they slammed the cold marble, and then there was darkness, the pain gone as the back of Mia's head caught the very edge of a step and her limp body tumbled to the base of the stairs.

CHAPTER 37

Charles received the message in his ear that there had been an accident at the main staircase and that a woman was unconscious. Within seconds he arrived at the scene to see Mia splayed on the floor, blood already spreading from the back of her head. He gave orders to call 911 and have them arrive at the side entrance and have someone find both Schooner and Dr. Gary Cohen.

He kneeled down next to her to take her pulse and silently thanked God when he felt one.

"Meezie, we're getting you help. They're on their way. Just stay with us, Meezie."

Gary was now leaning on the other side of her, feeling the pulse at her neck. He had his cell phone to his ear making arrangements for what he needed in the emergency room.

Schooner arrived to see both Gary and Charles leaning over someone and as he got closer he saw Mia's shoes and pushed his way through the gathering crowd.

"Baby Girl," his choked voice barely audible as he dropped to his knees next to her. "Baby Girl," his panic was rising. Blood from Mia's head seeped into the pants legs of his suit.

"Is she going to be okay? What happened?" He looked from Gary to Charles and to the staircase Mia had just careened down. As his eyes traveled up the staircase, he saw Zac standing at the top, empty champagne glass in hand, a slightly amused, detached look on his face and in that moment Schooner knew all he needed to know.

Springing to his feet, his long legs taking the steps two at a time, Schooner charged up the staircase, a growl emanating from his chest. He rammed into his son head first, the force catapulting Zac fifteen feet backwards into the wall with the second sickening thud of the evening, knocking the wind out of him.

Schooner grabbed Zac by the neck and slammed him into the wall for a second time. "What did you do?" he hissed.

"I didn't do it on purpose. She was grabbing my drink. I was trying to get her off of me." Zac met his father's eyes with venom.

Schooner had Zac pinned to the wall. Although only two inches taller, Schooner was dwarfing Zac with his aggressive stance. "If anything happens to her or the baby..."

Zac cut him off with an indignant, "Yeah, I know the bitch and the bastard are more important to you than me and mom, you've made that perfectly clear."

Schooner drew back his right arm, hand fisted, driving forcefully toward Zac's face. Inches before its intended target, Schooner's arm was jolted back, stopped in mid-air and a very calm voice whispered in his ear, "Meezie needs you with her in the emergency room, not in a jail cell."

Schooner closed his eyes and let out a long slow breath. He nodded his head and in a low voice, "Get him out of here. I want him on a plane back to LA tonight. If you can't get him on a commercial flight, charter a plane. I'm not kidding. I want him out of here tonight."

"But Dad, Exeter..." Zac began.

"Exeter is done. I don't want to be within 3,000 miles of you. Get him out of here tonight," Schooner repeated.

Two of Charles' men were now flanking Zac.

Schooner raced down the stairs to where the EMT were arriving for Mia.

Charles put a hand on Schooner's back, "For what it's worth," Charles said to his friend, "I would've done the exact same thing."

Schooner knew he was referring to attacking Zac.

Mia was still not responding as the EMT's began to immobilize her, bracing her neck and head and gently log rolling her onto a stretcher.

Schooner stayed alongside of her, "It's okay, Baby Girl, they're going to get you to the hospital. Gary's already there, waiting for you. Everything's going to be okay. You're going to be okay. The baby's going to be okay."

The ambulance was waiting outside the side entrance of the club. Three EMT's slid Mia's gurney into the ambulance. Schooner began to climb into the ambulance when one of the EMT's put a hand on his shoulder, stopping him and said, "Sir, what is your relationship to the patient?"

Schooner looked at him with an incredulous look, "I'm… I'm her fiancé," he stuttered.

"I'm sorry, Sir. I can't let you ride with her. You're not family."

"Not family?" Schooner's voice was raised, "She's my fiancée. That's my baby." Schooner moved toward the ambulance.

"Sir, please stop." Two EMTs were now between him and Mia. "Sir, the longer you detain us, the more risk there is for the patient. Please let us leave."

They climbed into the back of the ambulance, the doors closing with a loud clank. Schooner winced at the sound.

Paralyzed, he stood there on the curb watching the vehicle recede into the night, the flashing red lights growing smaller as the ambulance moved farther away.

He heard a noise behind him and then Zac's voice, "Dad."

Schooner turned around as two of Charles' team were escorting Zac into an SUV. Their eyes met. Schooner felt nothing. Looking at Zac was no different than passing a stranger on the street. Schooner was numb.

He turned back around to see where Mia's ambulance was, but it was gone. No sign of the flashing red lights remained on the avenue. He heard the engine of the SUV as it pulled away, but it didn't really register.

Stepping to the curb, Schooner raised his right arm to hail a cab. Within a few moments, a yellow cab pulled up in front of him. He reached for the door handle and as he went to pull it open, he realized that he had no idea where they had taken Mia. He did not know where Mia was or to what hospital to direct the cab driver. The realization slammed him with a wave of nausea.

He waved the cabbie on and stepped back from the curb.

As he stood staring up the avenue in the direction the ambulance had gone, Schooner had a sinking feeling in his stomach, a feeling of utter hopelessness that he had felt only once before, many years ago, in a dorm hallway. Mia's last words to him earlier in the evening were ricocheting around in his brain like an out of control pinball, "till we meet again," she had said.

He closed his eyes and in a silent prayer begged, "Please don't leave me, Baby Girl. Please don't leave me again."

END OF PART ONE

AUTHOR'S NOTE:

s that it? Did she just leave us hanging there? I know, pretty evil of me, huh? But I promise I'll make it up to you.

Book Two, *Moore to Lose* and Book Three, *Moore than Forever* are both currently available, so there is no wait required to finish the series.

Thank you for reading Searching for Moore and I hope that you enjoyed reading it as much as I loved writing it.

Till we meet again...
~JAR

ABOUT THE AUTHOR

Author Julie A. Richman is a native New Yorker living deep in the heart of Texas. A creative writing major in college, reading and writing fiction has always been a passion. Julie began her corporate career in publishing in NYC and writing played a major role throughout her career as she created and wrote marketing, advertising, direct mail and fundraising materials for Fortune 500 corporations, advertising agencies and non-profit organizations. She is an award winning nature photographer plagued with insatiable wanderlust. Julie and her husband have one son and a white German Shepherd named Juneau.

CONTACT JULIE

Twitter @JulieARichman
or
Website www.juliearichman.com
or
Facebook www.facebook.com/AuthorJulieARichman

54533654R00226

Made in the USA
Charleston, SC
07 April 2016